PLATINUM

PLATINUM

k.a. linde

Platinum, All That Glitters, Book Three

By K.A. Linde

Copyright © 2016 by K.A. Linde

All rights reserved.

Cover Designer: Sarah Hansen, Okay Creations, www.okaycreations.com

Editor and Interior Designer: Jovana Shirley, Unforeseen Editing, www.unforeseenediting.com

This book is a work of fiction. Names, characters, places, and incidents either are products of the author's imagination or are used fictitiously. Any resemblance to actual persons, living or dead, events, or locales is entirely coincidental.

Visit my website at www.kalinde.com

ISBN-13: 9781682308714

To every girl who needed to learn to trust again and each guy who proved her worth.

ONE

THIS WAS A VERY BAD IDEA.

Trihnity Hamilton sighed heavily as she stared at the name on the screen of her phone and avoided the knowing looks from her best friends, Bryna Turner and Stacia Palmer.

"Just don't invite him," Bryna said irritably.

"I'm not inviting him," Trihn snapped back.

Trihn had been dating her boyfriend, Neal, for over a year and a half. They had met and fallen for each other over their mutual love for artistic endeavors. He was a graphic design major while she studied fashion design with a focus in art. Unfortunately, the artsy lifestyle didn't exactly fit with Trihn's love for partying.

Or so Neal had said.

Frankly, Bryna flat-out hated him, and at this point, Stacia barely tolerated him. The disconnect between the two most important things in her life—her friends and her boyfriend—was causing some…unnecessary strain.

"I'm just going to answer this, and then we can go," Trihn said.

She turned away from her friends before they could say anything to change her mind. And she knew Bryna would try.

"I just don't think it's a good idea," Bryna said to Stacia behind Trihn's back.

"Leave it be, Bri," Stacia said.

Trihn took a breath and answered the phone with forced enthusiasm, "Hey!"

"Hey, what are you up to tonight?" Neal asked.

Trihn twirled her long brown-to-blonde ombré hair around her finger and tried to calm herself down. She was *not* going to argue with Neal tonight, not about going to the club for a girls' night. He'd understand.

He will.

She would just keep telling herself that.

Her stomach knotted anyway, twisting and turning against her will, as fear crept up her spine. No matter how much she tried to tamp it down, it'd just slither its way back up.

She took a deep breath. "I was just about to head out with Bri and Stacia. We're going to this club that's having some kind of crazy dance party."

"Let me guess," he said dryly. "Bryna's suggestion?"

"Maya actually!" she said, trying to keep pep in her voice. "She's meeting us there later after she gets off work."

Maya was their favorite bartender at the local club they frequented, Posse. It was located just off the Las Vegas State campus where Trihn was starting the second semester of her sophomore year.

"I see. Well, never mind then."

"I would *totally* invite you," Trihn insisted.

Bryna coughed noisily behind her. Trihn swiveled around and glared at her and Stacia.

"But...it's a girls' night. I'm so sorry. I didn't know you would be getting back early. I should have checked with you about your schedule."

Stacia snorted and shook her head. Bryna looked like she was ready to rip the phone out of Trihn's hand and tell Neal exactly what he could do with his schedule.

"It's fine, Trihn. I was going to see if I could come over since I just got back from San Francisco."

"I know," she whispered.

Over winter break, Neal had had a graphic design internship in San Francisco where his parents lived. It had been a continuation of his work from last summer. She had only seen him for a couple of days when her parents had flown him out to New York City for New Year's.

He had gotten back to Las Vegas two days early. She had thought he wouldn't be in town until the Sunday before school started, but his parents had decided otherwise. She felt bad that she already had plans. She would have run over there in a heartbeat, but Maya never got out of work to hang out with them. Trihn couldn't pass up the opportunity. She figured she would just see Neal tomorrow, and all would be fine.

"So…" she said softly.

The silence stretched between them as she waited for him to say something. She bit her lip and fought against the growing awkwardness in their relationship. When he had visited her only a couple of weeks ago, things had been strange. He'd been more interested in getting to know her sister, Lydia, than spending time with Trihn. She and Lydia still had a strained relationship after what had happened post–high school graduation, and it didn't help that Trihn had *another* boyfriend who seemed to be enamored by Lydia.

"I'll just talk to you later or something," Neal said after a few silent seconds. "I'll probably go to The Kiln since you don't want to see me."

Trihn cringed. She actually hated The Kiln. It was an artistic dream in theory—a bar with live music and slam poetry under the same roof as a pottery studio. But, in reality, everyone would sit around and bemoan the state of

3

the art movement, or the lack thereof, in America while getting high as fuck, and then they'd make art with their bodies with whoever was around. It wasn't uncommon for the place to turn into an orgy.

"It's not that I don't want to see you," she insisted. "I really do, but we've had this planned for a while."

"Okay."

"But…do you have to go to The Kiln?" she managed to get out.

He *knew* she hated that place. It was a breeding ground for bad behavior. All the while, he'd claim that the clubs she went to were bad.

"You're going out to some club to get wasted with your friends and basically have sex on the dance floor, and you're asking *me* not to go out?" he asked in a tone that brooked no argument.

"I'm not going to have *sex* on the dance floor," she argued anyway. "But I know that people do at The Kiln. It's just…gross."

"Trihn, don't lecture me about what I can and can't do."

"I wasn't," she whimpered. "I just—"

"Look, I'm going to go. If you decide to stop fucking around and want to take us seriously, then come to The Kiln, and we can talk."

"I—"

The line went dead in her hand, and she nearly screamed. *How dare he insinuate that I'm going out to fuck around and that I don't take out relationship seriously!*

She was the one putting all the effort into their relationship. Half the time, he would be pissed off about what she was doing and who she was hanging out with. It was blatantly clear that he didn't trust her. She didn't get it because she had never done anything to make him think otherwise. She was the most loyal person alive.

After the fiasco with Preston, she couldn't even imagine fooling around behind someone's back. Just the idea of cheating pissed her off.

She tried to rein in her emotions. The last thing she wanted was to be in a bad mood when she went out with the girls. Things with Neal would work out. They always did. He would get mad and lash out, but when they got back together, everything would be fine. He was just frustrated.

"All right," she said, dropping the phone to her side, "are you guys ready to party?"

Bryna and Stacia exchanged equally sympathetic looks. They knew things between Trihn and Neal were rocky even if they had only heard half of the conversation.

"Is everything okay?" Stacia asked hesitantly.

"I really don't want to talk about it," Trihn said stiffly. "Let's just go have a good time."

She hoped that would still be possible.

TWO

"THERE YOU ARE!" Trihn shrieked. She threw herself into Maya, standing just off of the packed dance floor.

Maya gave her a hug and laughed. "Are you drunk already?"

"Nah! But Bri and Stacia have been trying to feed me shots like candy," she confessed.

"Oh, dear." Maya turned to face Bryna and Stacia. "You've been getting my girl drunk?"

Bryna and Stacia innocently shrugged their shoulders, but nothing else about them proclaimed innocence. Bryna was a total blonde bombshell in sky-high Louboutin heels and a skimpy red dress that showed off her killer figure. Stacia had her own short blonde hair piled into a sexy messy bun at the nape of her neck. She was decked out in a royal-blue top that plunged to her navel and shorts so tiny that half of her ass hung out. Both girls were cheerleaders at Las Vegas State and enjoyed playing the part.

"I'm not drunk," Trihn insisted.

They hadn't been at the club long enough, and she had been dancing so much that the alcohol wasn't hitting her that hard.

"See? She's not drunk," Bryna said.

"As if I'd trust you," Maya said. She twisted her luscious African American caramel-toned body toward Trihn and gave her the same look she would give drunks at the bar when they insisted they were sober. Maya was tall enough to stare down at Trihn, which was a rarity for someone who used to model.

"Who cares anyway?" Trihn cried. "We're here to have fun. You never come out with us. You're not on bar duty. You don't have to take care of anyone. Let's just go dance."

Laughing, she grabbed Maya's hand and dragged her onto the dance floor. A part of her wished that she had switched out her Gucci heels for her combat boots. They were more comfortable, but she loved being dolled up, sporting her designer grunge, as Bryna called it. She had opted for black leather shorts, a lacy racerback bralette, and a glammed up jean vest that she had reconstructed herself.

"I'm going to need a drink if you want me to dance," Maya said. She laughed at Trihn and released her. "Here, dance with the Cheer Slut in the meantime."

She pushed Trihn into Stacia, who started shaking her ass against Trihn.

Maya raised her eyebrows at Bryna. "And what about you? Has Eric settled you down?"

Bryna responded with a defiant look that only she could pull off. Trihn was happy that her friend had found someone who made her happy. She'd had a wild couple of years.

In some ways, Trihn envied the way her best friend could say and do whatever the fuck she wanted without caring what anyone thought about her. Trihn had never been like that. She wore her heart on her sleeve and always wanted everyone to like her. But she pitied Bryna as well. Her life wasn't as easy as it looked from the outside. Trihn couldn't even imagine going through the shit Bryna had gone through last year, and Trihn was just glad that Bryna and Eric Wilkins were finally a couple.

"I'll take that as a yes," Maya said with a giggle. "Go dance. I'll be back."

Trihn fell easily into the practiced movements from years of dance training mingled with endless nights of clubbing with her friends. Dancing was her happy place. It was one of the reasons she loved to party. Expectations would disappear, and she could live through the pulse of the music, the bright lights, and the rhythm of the people around her. She didn't need anyone or anything in that moment. She could just be herself while dancing completely alone in the middle of a crowded room.

The moment she lost herself, she found herself.

A current ran through her body, and she soared as free as a bird high above the clouds. She turned and whirled and let loose. Half of the time, she'd freestyle to the hip-hop beats the DJ was blaring through the speakers. Sometimes, she'd perform remembered choreography from when she had been a part of the New York City Dance House in high school. She had a strong ballet background, but she had found a passion in underground pole dancing with her friend, Cassidy, after-hours at a burlesque club in New York City. Then, Trihn had followed Cassidy out to Las Vegas and never looked back.

"Whoa!" Stacia cried. "Did you see that?"

Trihn stopped moving. "What?"

"That." Stacia pointed to a group of guys who were dancing a few feet away from them. "Some guy did a back flip!"

Trihn had a good half a foot on Stacia and Bryna, so she craned her neck to figure out what was going on. "It looks like people are showing off."

"Let's get in there!" Stacia cheered.

"Where do you think we are, S?" Bryna asked. "We didn't just walk into *Save the Last Dance*."

"Actually," Trihn said, straining to to get a clear picture, "it doesn't look that different than the movie. Come on."

Without a second thought, Trihn threaded through the crowd and forced her way to the front of the circle. Stacia and Bryna came up behind her. As Stacia watched the people dancing, she bounced from foot to foot in excitement. Bryna looked a little bored, as if she would rather be the center of attention than let other people take the spotlight. But Trihn felt an inexplicable giddiness rising up in her stomach.

Three main guys kept moving in and out of the circle while a handful of girls were jumping in and shaking their asses to loud cheers. She wasn't interested in the girls' performances. They looked all right, she supposed, but the guys were way better.

One was a tall black guy with black hair under his navy blue hat with NY stitched on in white. He was throwing some pretty impressive break-dancing skills. The second guy was shorter with light hair. He was smirking at some other girls nearby. He had some fancy footwork, but he kept nudging the guy next to him, as if waiting for his approval.

That guy wasn't even paying attention. He was teeming with energy. He was tall with short dark hair and wearing all black clothing. He was rolling his hat back and forth between his fingers while waiting for his turn to go out there, but his hips were moving, and he clearly knew what he was doing.

Trihn couldn't tear her eyes away from him.

He was so damn good.

As if sensing her staring, his eyes found hers. She sucked in her breath as he just watched at her, his gaze resembling a challenge. But if he thought she was going to walk into that circle, he was out of his mind.

She was sure muscle memory would help her throw a few tricks of her own if she went out there—not that she had any intention of doing so, but it would be funny to show him that girls could do more than shake their booties.

Despite the fact that she loved performing, she couldn't imagine doing it now. Performances had always been scheduled in her life with lots of notice and prepared choreography. She wasn't drunk enough if she was worrying about what people might think about her dancing out there. Her stomach was twisting into knots while she considered it.

The first guy finished his break-dancing move, and suddenly, the last guy stepped into the space. With the circle all to himself, he moved his body, as if he owned the place. He didn't have one single self-conscious bone in his body.

"He's hot," Stacia murmured next to her. "Not my type, you know, because he *obviously* doesn't play football, but he's still hot."

Trihn nodded. "Definitely."

"I think I know him from somewhere," Bryna said curiously.

Bryna knew everyone, so that wouldn't surprise Trihn, but she was pretty sure she would have remembered him if she had seen him before.

Maya pushed through the crowd to get to them in that moment. "Jesus Christ! Just abandon me, why don't you?"

"Sorry," Trihn said without taking her eyes off the guy dancing.

"Well, I see why you did," Maya said.

Maya nudged her forward a little, and Trihn nearly fell across the invisible threshold. That drew the guy's heated gaze, and he gave her that same knowing look. He smirked at her stumble, and she felt her heartbeat skyrocket. She wanted to believe it was from embarrassment and not the hot guy in front of her.

"Maya! God!" Trihn cried.

She pressed back into the throng of people once more. She didn't want to be noticed.

"Seriously, how do I know him?" Bryna cried. "This is going to bug me. I'm need to talk to him. Stacia, go shake your ass or something."

"With pleasure," Stacia said.

Trihn grabbed her hand. "Don't go out there. You'd just be perpetuating the stereotype that the only girls who can dance are girls who shake their asses."

"And?" Stacia said in confusion.

"Well, you'd be feeding into the patriarchy."

Bryna busted out laughing. "*That* is how she'd be feeding into the patriarchy?"

"She has a point, Trihni," Maya said. "Admit that you just don't want Stacia dancing with the hot guy looking at you like he wants you for dessert."

"You guys are unreal." Trihn glanced back over at the guy.

Some girl had just entered the circle before Stacia could and was trying to dance up on him. He moved his hips around a couple of times before gliding his feet across the floor, as if he were floating and moving away from her. He relinquished the dance floor to the girl. When his head popped back up, he was looking at Trihn.

"He's staring at you," Maya said.

"No, he's not."

But he was.

THREE

"GIVE IT UP FOR MY MAIN MAN, Damon, killing it on the dance floor!" the DJ called over the speakers. "Damon will be back in the DJ booth, bringing you all your favorite mixes, after this break."

"Oh my God!" Bryna shrieked. "That's how I know him!"

"How?" Trihn asked.

Maya laughed. "This should be good."

"Not like that actually," Bryna said.

She turned her fierce gaze on Maya, but Maya just rolled her eyes. She could deflect Bryna like no other.

"Would it have really surprised anyone though?" Stacia asked.

"I suppose, he isn't her type. She liked them older and filthy rich," Maya said. She laughed and tipped back her drink.

Bryna shrugged her shoulders, unperturbed. "He was the DJ at my party last year when I moved into the mansion. I just couldn't remember his name, but that's definitely him."

Trihn looked up at Damon again. He had this air about him, like nothing could change his good time. He was so carefree and utterly intoxicating to watch. He wasn't even the best dancer that Trihn had seen before, but he'd moved with such confidence that everyone in the place cheered for him.

"Are you sure it's the same guy?" Trihn asked. She found it hard to believe that she wouldn't have noticed someone like that at one of Bryna's parties.

"I'm positive that he is the same guy," she said.

"Hmm..." Trihn shrugged and backed out of the circle as it started to close in on itself.

Damon caught her eye in a way that said he knew all her secrets.

She shied away from his gaze. It wasn't like she wanted to jump into the middle of the circle and take over. Her best friends were more likely to do that than she was. It'd be better to forget all about Damon and just walk away.

So, she did.

The girls followed her back to the bar where Maya promptly ordered them all drinks. Trihn sipped on her gin and tonic and pushed her hair off the back of her neck. It was boiling hot inside. The dancing certainly hadn't helped to cool her down.

Some guy started talking to Stacia, and then she promptly disappeared onto the dance floor, dragging Bryna with her. Ever since Stacia and Pace Larson— Bryna's stepbrother and the backup quarterback for the LV State football team—had broken up, Stacia had been all over the map. Sometimes, she'd mess around with other people. Other times, she'd slip off to try to make amends with Pace even though she had been the one to break it off, only to come home and cry herself to sleep over the loss of her quarterback because she'd decided it would be best for them not to work it out. Trihn suspected she hadn't seen the end of them while Bryna thought it was all done with.

As Trihn danced with Maya near the bar, she kept the girls in her line of vision. She finished off her drink and dropped it off on the counter. She was getting ready to drag Maya out on the floor when someone sidled up next to her.

"Hey," he said. His voice was rich and deep with a posh British accent that sent shivers down her spine.

She slowly turned around, already knowing who she was going to see. When she got a full look at him, she had to pull back a step because they were basically on top of each other. She hadn't realized how close he was.

"Um...hey," she said with a smile.

"I was waiting for you."

She laughed softly. "Waiting?" she asked, thinking she had heard him wrong.

"Yeah, out on the dance floor."

Her eyes widened in surprise. She knew that he had been staring at her out there, but he hadn't made it seem like he was waiting for her. He had just looked...inviting.

God! She needed to stop thinking about him like that. *Who cares if he looks inviting?* She was dating someone, and this was exactly what she had been worried about with Neal going to The Kiln. Well, she had been more concerned that an orgy would break out in the club, and he'd somehow be a part of it, but a hot British guy talking to her wasn't that far off.

"Well, you didn't gesture," she said offhand. She looked away from his eyes and the welcoming tilt of his head.

He had his hat back on, but it was effortlessly tipped up. She didn't know what to make of him.

"I'm gesturing now," he said. He swept his arm back and motioned for her to take the floor with him.

When Trihn glanced over at Maya for support, her eyes were as big as saucers.

"What's it going to hurt?" Maya asked.

Trihn couldn't answer that because he was really hot. And the way her stomach was fluttering at his bold statements wasn't helping anything.

She shrugged her shoulders and looked back at Damon. "You looked good out there," she deflected.

"I know," he said.

Her jaw nearly dropped to the floor at that statement, but laughter bubbled up before she could show her surprise. "Cheeky."

"But you're good, too," he said easily.

His gaze locked with hers, and she tried not to beam at his compliment.

"I know you are. I was watching you from up there." He pointed at the DJ booth. "You don't just know how to move. You dance, right?"

She nodded. "Yeah, I do."

"I could tell."

"Thanks."

Maya nudged her, but Trihn didn't dare look at her. Trihn knew that Maya was going to try to get her to say more, to encourage her to do things she knew she shouldn't.

"Show me," he told her.

"I don't even know who you are," she shot back.

"Does it matter?"

"I…"

No, it didn't.

Who cares who this guy is? It was just dancing, something she had done her entire life. She'd come from a renowned dance studio in New York City. Dancing at a club for some guy she'd just met shouldn't even matter.

"I don't have space," she told him.

He shot her a devil-may-care grin and then started backing up with his hands spread wide to either side. "I'll make space."

The look he was giving her said, *Bring it.*

How can I back down from the challenge?

She could dimly hear Maya's exclamations behind her, but the knowledge of what she was about to do deafened her to everything else going on around her.

Damon kept backing up until he had formed a circle big enough for her to dance in.

She stared in awe for a minute. *How is this happening to me?*

Then, her mind whirred to life. *Ball change, prepare, double pirouette, floor drop, roll, tilt kick, prepare...*

And on it went.

Choreography filled her vision like a fight in a *Sherlock Holmes* movie. It was euphoric. Adrenaline kicked into overdrive. All that existed was the here and now and the drive to not make a fool of herself in front of a large group of people...in front of *him.*

Damon stopped moving, crossed his arms, and just looked at her. That was her cue.

Taking a deep breath, she moved into the space with as much grace as she could muster from her years of training. Then, the dance took over. She executed the choreography in her head with her eyes glued on Damon's face. Her friends back home would have called it sex eyes—picking one person out in the audience and making love to them with your eyes while you were onstage. She hadn't believed it would enhance her dancing...until that moment.

She dropped to the ground to crazy screams from the surrounding crowd. Then, she rolled forward and got up in Damon's face. The challenge was there. She might as well act on it. At this point, it was too late to back down.

He gave her a heart-stopping broad smile. He was nodding his head as he slowly clapped his hands. "That's right," he murmured. "That's what I thought."

She twirled in place, avoiding that sexy gaze. It felt good to be acknowledged for something she loved. He'd picked her out in the middle of a crowded club—not for her looks or anything else, but for her own ability. It was refreshing.

One of his friends had moved to the center of the circle, and the attention deviated from her as he started showing off his breaker moves again. Her body was still moving though. She was too energized now not to keep going. Her heart was pounding, and her head felt light. It was as if she had sparks under her skin, igniting her flesh and keeping her in motion.

Damon was near her, and he reached out for her hips, guiding her against him. She let the dance take them away with her body pressed to his chest and their hips moving in time. She raised her hands above her head and laughed with pure joy at the freedom in the dance.

He didn't just stand there either. She was right. He definitely knew what he was doing. He grabbed her hand and twirled her until she was facing him. Then, their hips rocked seductively back and forth. Her breathing was quick, her chest rising and falling in time with the music.

"God, you can move," he breathed into the small space between them.

Her head snapped up to look at him. They were so close, so achingly close together. His hands were like fire, one against the small of her back and the other gripping her hip. For some reason, she couldn't stop looking at his lips. He had these lips. *Oh God, those lips.* They were perfect lips—full and sexy and utterly kissable…and something she most definitely should not be looking at.

She forced her gaze back up to his eyes, and it was as if he knew every thought in her head. He knew she had been staring at his lips. He knew exactly where her treacherous mind had been going.

And she froze.

Paralysis hit her like nothing ever had before.

Her hips stopped, and she dropped her hands from around his neck.

It was no big deal. It was just dancing. But her thoughts were another thing—a very bad thing.

"I'm sorry," she muttered.

"For what?"

"Leaving." She turned and started walking away. Her heart was beating so fast, and she just needed to find Bryna.

Bryna would calm Trihn down and know what to do. Bryna took control of situations, and Trihn needed her to take control of this one because having thoughts about kissing some other guy was absolutely *not* okay.

She nearly made it across the room before Maya caught up to her. "Hey. What the hell happened back there?"

"Nothing."

But something had happened.

She felt ridiculous. Damon and she had been having a good time. It was just dancing, nothing out of the ordinary. Then, she had thought about kissing him, and she couldn't believe herself. She wasn't upset with Damon but with herself. That was *not* the person she was. It wasn't the person she ever wanted to be. She would never put anyone in the position she had been in herself.

"That sure as hell didn't look like nothing."

"Well, it's nothing. I just want to go," she said softly. She wasn't even sure if Maya had heard her.

When she looked back up, she saw Damon running after her.

"Hey," he called.

"Oh God…"

Maya looked between them and then shook her head. "You're right. We should just go." She put her hand on Damon's chest before he could get any closer and gave him the best don't-fuck-with-the-bartender look. "Back off, buddy!"

He looked at her quizzically. "I didn't mean to upset your friend. I don't even know why she left."

"She's not interested, so just back off," Maya spat.

"Maya!" Trihn was freaking out, but Maya didn't need to lie. Trihn was interested. That was the problem.

"Sorry. I just…" He pulled his hat off and started self-consciously flipping it between his fingers. "I don't even know your name."

Trihn pushed past Maya and smiled hesitantly. "I'm Trihn, but I have a boyfriend so…" She trailed off. *What more do I need to say?*

"Oh." He nodded his head and took a step back. Already, his eyes were searching elsewhere. All of that confidence that had been in his dancing fled him at the first sign of her rejection. "I'll see you around then," he said. He took one last look at her and then left the floor.

She hated the way her stomach plummeted in his absence and the way doing something right felt so wrong.

"What the hell?" Maya demanded, swiveling to face Trihn. "He was totally into you!"

"Yeah, that's the problem," Trihn said. She chewed on her lip and averted her gaze from where Damon had just disappeared. "Thanks for having my back though."

"I only did it because you had given me that terrified look. I immediately went into bartender mode, but maybe I shouldn't have." Maya placed her hands on her hips. She leveled Trihn with a knowing look. "I think you were into him, too."

Trihn shrugged. "He's cute."

"He's cute? That's all you have?"

"Really cute?"

"Hot. Smoking hot. And he can *move*."

"And I still have a boyfriend," Trihn said.

It really didn't matter how hot Damon was or how he could move because she was taken. If she had learned anything from the bullshit with Preston, it was that dating two people at once was *never* a viable option.

"I'm not Bryna or Stacia. I'm not going to tell you to break up with Neal or that he's an asshole. I know the things they say about him."

"Thanks."

"But," Maya said, "I want you to know, we're all just looking out for you. We want you to be happy."

"I am happy," Trihn said. "I just want to go home to my boyfriend. That's all."

"Okay." Maya held her hands up, but she looked sad. "Are you sure you want to leave already? We haven't been out that long, and I don't get many nights off."

"I just haven't seen Neal in a while, and I miss him," Trihn told her. "There will be plenty of other nights like this."

Maya frowned but nodded. "All right. Well, catch a cab, and be safe. I'll tell the girls that you headed out."

Trihn pulled Maya into a hug. "Thank you for being such a good friend."

"You know I'd do anything for you, Trihni. Call me if you need anything."

"I will," Trihn said. Then, she turned and walked out of the crowded club.

Her head was fuzzy, and for some reason that she couldn't quite pinpoint, she felt disoriented.

Walking away was the right choice. Finding a guy attractive was one thing. Fantasizing about kissing him was an entirely different matter.

Maybe Neal was right after all, and she shouldn't have come out to the club tonight. She had thought The Kiln was bad, but she had been in a world of temptation all on her own.

Trihn flagged down a cab, and on the way to her place, she pulled her phone out and dialed Neal's number. It rang four times before going to his voice mail.

She sighed but waited for the beep. "Hey. I'm leaving the club now. You were right. I probably should have just stayed in with you tonight. I miss you. I'd love for you to stay the night with me. Call me back. Love you. Bye."

She slumped back in the seat and stared out the window as the Las Vegas Strip disappeared behind them. She lived in an apartment with Bryna and Stacia. It was just off the LV State campus, which was only a couple of miles from the Strip.

The cab dropped her off outside her building, and to clear her head, she trudged up the steps to the top floor instead of taking the elevator to clear her head.

Her phone dinged just as she got into the apartment.

Too loud to hear your voice mail.

Trihn stared down at the message and grated her teeth before replying to Neal's message.

> *Left the club early. You were right.*
> *Stay with me tonight?*

I know I'm right.

Trihn rolled her eyes at the return message. She was jotting out a response when she got another text from him.

> *I'm going to be out all night. I'll just stay at my place.*

Should I come over in the morning?

Trihn waited and waited for a response.

"Fuck that," she groaned with a shake of her head.

She tossed her phone onto her bed and changed into something more comfortable. She didn't know what the hell she was doing. She could go to The Kiln to see Neal, but she honestly hated that place. And he wasn't responding to her message. The last thing she wanted was to get there and start an argument. She was tired of arguing. Lately, every conversation had been ending up in an argument, and it was getting to be exhausting.

Rubbing her temples, she pulled out her sketchbook and flipped it open to her latest work. She was lucky to be in the Teena Hart School of Design as a fashion design major. After discovering that her boyfriend, Preston, had been secretly dating her sister, Lydia, behind her back, Trihn had dropped out of NYU to come to LV State two weeks before school started her freshman year.

When the whole thing had blown up in Trihn's face, her sister had chosen Preston over Trihn, and rather than be around them, Trihn had chosen to leave New York City for good. She still couldn't believe that Preston and Lydia were still together a year and a half later. Preston was a manipulative cheating scumbag, and Lydia had never held a boyfriend for longer than a couple of weeks. They were a match made in hell.

Thankfully, Trihn had ended up loving Las Vegas, and the design school was a dream come true. Teena Hart herself—a world-renowned fashion designer with her own line and a boutique in Caesars Palace—would personally work with the students. Trihn had been taking art classes to fulfill major requirements, and she completed her first round of intro design classes last semester. This semester she would be into more advanced program work. If everything went as planned, she might even get to help with the senior fashion show in the spring. The winner would go on to New York City in the summer.

In her spare time, she would work on her own clothes. It seemed to calm her down when her anxiety took over.

Like right now.

Trihn worked on her artwork until she heard Bryna and Stacia coming home. Not wanting a confrontation with them, she quickly switched off her light and got into bed. They knocked on her door as they passed, but Trihn ignored it and pretended to be asleep. She just lay in her bed and stared at the ceiling until she finally fell asleep late that night.

FOUR

Trihn woke up bleary-eyed at the crack of dawn. She had slept horribly with a serious case of nightmares that she had been haunted with since she had found out about that bullshit with Preston a year and a half ago.

Trying to shake off the lingering feeling of unease, she dialed Neal's number. Even though it was early, he was usually up long before she was, no matter how late he'd stayed out the previous night. When it went straight to voice mail, she frowned. He was probably just getting in a few extra hours of sleep or something. She figured she might as well help him with that.

She hopped into a quick shower. When she got out, she threw her wet hair up into a perfect ballet bun and then hurried into a pair of destroyed skinny jeans, a black tank, and her leather jacket—her favorite wardrobe staple.

She skipped out of the house hours before Bryna or Stacia would surface and drove her red hybrid to Neal's house. Even almost two years after leaving New York, it was still strange to have to drive so much. She had gotten her license in the city only to prove that she actually could. Truth be told, it had taken her three times to get it, too. But with all the driving she had done in Vegas, she had gotten exponentially better.

Trihn pulled up in front of the house that Neal rented with a few of his art friends. When no one answered, she knocked on the door and tried the knob, but it was locked. She had a key, but her purse was stuffed with so much shit that she knew it would take forever to find.

She pounded on the door again and then started digging around in her bag for the key. She found an extra pair of workout shorts, two pairs of socks, a mini sketchbook, a to-do-list journal, and half a dozen tubes of lipstick, but no key.

Just when she was about to give up on her quest and try Neal's cell again, the door opened to reveal a mussed Neal.

"Trihn?" he croaked, as if he had just rolled out of bed. And he looked like it, too. His dark hair was a hot mess, his shorts and T-shirt were rumpled, and he had bags under his eyes.

"Hey. I tried to call you, but you must have been sleeping," she said, mustering an enthusiastic smile.

"No, I wasn't," he said. He crossed his arms over his chest.

"Oh. Okay. Were you ignoring me?"

"I was going to call later but might as well get it over with now. I think we should break up."

Trihn's heart plummeted to her stomach. She gasped in disbelief. Her mouth hung open. There was ringing in her ears, and she could feel her pulse all the way through her fingers and toes.

"What?" she asked.

"This has been coming for a long time, Trihn. We're not compatible. You're a different person than who I thought I was dating. I'm over it."

"We've been dating for a year and a half," she sputtered. "How are we suddenly not compatible?"

"It's not sudden. I've just been ignoring it for a long time. Last night was the end for me."

"What happened last night?" she asked shakily.

How could this be happening? He couldn't just leave. After all they had been through together, she didn't want this to be over. She wanted to fight for this. She *needed* to fight for this. She had done everything right in this relationship. He couldn't call it quits.

"Nothing in particular. I just didn't miss you, and I didn't miss you when I was home in San Francisco either."

It was a knife to the heart.

Trihn stumbled back a step, her hand going to her mouth. He hadn't missed her. She had missed him every day that she was stuck in New York without him. She had spent a lot of her time in her room or with her friends from home—Renée and Ian—but mostly she avoided her sister, Lydia.

She just didn't understand. She felt like her body was being crushed. Everything ached and hurt.

"Is there someone else?" she managed to get out. She was surprised her voice was even functioning.

Neal looked down at the floor and then off into the distance, as if this were the last place he wanted to be right now.

He must have cheated on her. It was the only logical explanation.

Preston had cheated on her and left her to pick up the pieces of her heart off the floor and try to sew them back together. After that, she had been extremely careful about giving her heart out again. Neal had seemed like the perfect guy at the time. She had made sure he was for real about their relationship before introducing him to any of her friends. Things had been perfect from then on. They'd had their ups and downs, like any other relationship, but as a whole, she'd thought they had a good thing.

Now, her heart was shattering all over again, as if the last year and a half meant nothing at all to him.

"Tell me!" she yelled into his face. "Don't just stare at the floor. Do you have someone with you right now?"

Trihn tried to force her way into the house, but Neal put his hand out, barring her from entering.

"Just give it up. It's over."

She raised her eyebrows and tried not to cry. She held on to the anger that welled up in her.

"I need an explanation. Do you have some whore in your bed right now? Is all that frustration you've been taking out on me actually just bullshit *guilt* for cheating on me?" she asked.

"Just believe whatever the fuck you want to believe, Trihn," Neal said, pushing her backward, out of the doorway. "It's fucking over, so it doesn't even matter. I just don't want to be with you."

Neal slammed the door in her face, leaving her standing there in shock.

She banged on the door and shrieked, "It matters to me!"

When it was clear that Neal wasn't going to answer the door or Trihn's question, she screamed in frustration and turned away from the house. As she walked back to her car, her hands were shaking. She dropped the car keys twice before she got them the door unlocked.

Once she finally got inside, she sank into the driver's side. Tears washed down her cheeks like rain. Hiccupping deep breaths racked her body.

She hadn't cried like this in a long time. Sure, she and Neal had argued. Tears had been involved, but they had always worked it out. He wanted her to be just the artsy type, and she wanted to have fun and party with her girlfriends. No harm had come from it.

The only time she had ever thought about hooking up with someone else had been last night, and she had felt so guilty about it that she left the club entirely. Maybe Neal knew about that somehow. Maybe that was what this was about.

Maybe she wasn't good enough for him.

"Fuck!" She banged her hands against the steering wheel.

How can a guy make me feel this stupid?

She was all for feminist ideals—until this shit happened to her. Then, she'd curl into a ball and let the man win all over again.

She hated thinking that she wasn't good enough for anyone. She was strong and beautiful and smart. Maybe one day, she would even be a brilliant designer going somewhere—rather than a designer who had turned down NYU because of a guy, rather than a girl who had tucked tail and run instead of facing her issues, rather than a girlfriend who had let her boyfriend walk all over her instead of facing the facts.

The drive back to her apartment was seen through a veil of tears. She wasn't even entirely sure how she'd made it there. It was a blur.

Did I stop at that stop sign?

She truly couldn't remember. Autopilot had gotten her home in one piece, up the elevator, and back into her apartment.

She stripped out of her jacket and jeans and trudged down the hallway to Bryna's room. She opened the door and peeked inside. Half the time, Bryna's boyfriend, Eric, would stay the night, or she'd crash at his place. But since it had been a girls' night last night, she was all alone.

Trihn sniffed and then crawled under Bryna's silky sheets.

Bryna shifted in her sleep and then jumped up. "Fuck, Trihn!" she cried. Her hand flew to her chest. "You scared the shit out of me."

"Neal broke up with me," she whispered.

Bryna frowned and sighed. "Oh, Trihn, come here." She wrapped her arms around Trihn and pulled her close. "What happened?"

Trihn wiped her eyes with the back of her hand. "At least I didn't waste my mascara on him," she said to avoid the question.

"That's good because that shit is expensive."

"Really fucking expensive."

Trihn burst into tears again. She rolled onto her side and cried into Bryna's pillow.

Everything hurt, and her mind was moving a million miles a minute. She didn't know if there was a way that she could have avoided this or fixed it. *If I had stayed in with him last night, would it all have been okay? Had he been planning this all along?* Every possible scenario ran through her mind, but she couldn't find one situation where she could have made this right.

Bryna ran her fingers through Trihn's long black-to-blonde hair and waited until her tears subsided before speaking, "Tell me what happened."

"He said we weren't compatible and that it was over. He said that he didn't miss me when we weren't together," she groaned. Another sob escaped her. "Then, I asked him if there was someone else...if he had a girl with him right now, but he refused to answer me."

"Bastard!" Bryna cried. "Do you think he was really cheating on you?"

Trihn looked up into Bryna's blue eyes and felt like crying all over again. "I don't know. Maybe."

"Ugh! I'm sorry, Trihn."

"He said that it didn't matter whether I thought he was with someone else because he didn't want to be with me. How could he say those things, Bri? We'd been together for so long. We were so good together."

"Well, I think it matters whether or not he cheated," Bryna said.

"I know. That's what I tried to yell at him, but he slammed the door in my face."

Bryna clenched her jaw. "You're making it really hard for me not to call Eric and have him send half of the football team over to Neal's house to beat the shit out of him."

Trihn's laugh turned into a moan of despair. "Don't do that. I still love him."

"I won't send them, but you know Eric has your back. The whole team would go to the ends of the earth for any of us."

"I know."

"You'll get through this. You're strong and beautiful and smart. I'm biased because you're my best friend, but you're not a cold, heartless bitch, like me. When you let people in, you give it all, a hundred and fifty percent. I know you don't want to hear this, but you can do *so* much better than Neal."

Trihn laid her head back and stared up at the ceiling. "I'm surprised that wasn't the first thing you said to me. You hate Neal."

"I don't *hate* Neal. I hate the way he treated you, and I hate that he made you feel like less than the incredible person you are. You know the shit I've gone through in my past," Bryna said with a sigh. "Jude made me feel amazing, but bit by bit, he stripped my confidence from me and morphed me into something I wasn't. I hadn't even seen it until I got away from it. I think you'll see that soon, too."

"You think I changed because of Neal?" Trihn asked.

"I think Neal wanted you to change, and it's hard to ignore that forever."

Trihn just lay there. Bryna had good points, but all Trihn wanted was for Neal to take back everything that had just happened.

"I just want him back," she whispered.

"I love you, Trihn, but I honestly don't know why you want to be with him. He abandoned you last year at my party. You ran out of that party in tears, and that was nearly a year ago. He canceled plans to see you after you were apart last summer. He sabotaged Halloween and avoided you all last semester. Don't even get me started on the emotional abuse of wanting you to only be an artist and have no other life outside of him." Bryna sat up in bed and stared down at Trihn. "Everyone else saw this but you. You made excuse after excuse for him, but I didn't think his behavior deserved to be excused. You're better off."

Trihn groaned. "I know. I know you're right. I just wanted this to work out so bad."

"You shouldn't have to force it. Like this Damon guy," Bryna said with a twinkle in her eye. "Maya told me he was hitting on you, and you were into him."

"Ugh! She did not."

"I have one word for you, Trihnity Hamilton," Bryna said dramatically. She hopped out of bed, and in the tiny blue slip she had worn to sleep, she walked over to her closet.

"Do I even want to know?" Trihn called out to her.

A minute later, she returned with a slinky little black dress. Trihn had seen that dress on Bryna, who was a solid seven inches shorter than Trihn, and it barely grazed her mid thigh. On Trihn, she would be lucky if it covered her nonexistent ass.

"What is that for?" Trihn asked.

Bryna smirked, and Trihn knew what that meant— trouble.

"Rebound."

FIVE

"REMIND ME WHY I'M HERE AGAIN?" Trihn asked.

She was standing with Bryna and Stacia at Posse, their local hotspot, where Maya worked as a bartender. Bryna had forced Trihn into the tiny black dress, and it looked pretty amazing, but the amount of makeup that she'd had to use to cover her puffy eyes, not so much.

Eric had dropped them off earlier and returned with some football player friends. Stacia was currently hitting on Marshall Matthews, the star quarterback for the LV State football team. Her dream in life was to marry an NFL quarterback. She had been going from one quarterback to the next in the hopes that she would snag her guy.

That was not Trihn's objective, and the assortment of men that Eric had provided for a rebound weren't exactly her type. She wasn't even sure what her type was, but douchey hot college guys who liked to promise her the world and break her heart were not it.

"You are having fun and not thinking about that asshole," Maya called from behind the bar. With raised eyebrows, she pushed a shot toward Trihn.

"I don't want to get drunk," Trihn said.

Maya shrugged. "You're not paying. You're not driving. Take the drink. It'll heal the wound for a bit."

"So, you're really on board with Bri's rebound plan?"

Trihn took the shot in her hand and stared down at the clear liquid. Maya pushed a lime and a salt shaker toward her. With a determined glare, Trihn licked between her thumb and index finger and shook salt onto the area. She raised the tequila to Maya in a cheers motion, licked the salt off her hand, and then tipped the glass back. The alcohol burned all the way down, and she quickly sucked on the lime to try to mitigate the painful aftereffect.

"Completely," Maya said, pouring them each a shot. She raised her glass to Trihn, and they threw it back. "Go fuck someone else, and you'll feel much better."

"That doesn't sound like you."

"Oh, yeah?" Maya asked, as if it were a challenge. She looked around at Eric's friends and then picked out a guy in the group. "Excuse me," she said to him.

The guy turned around. Trihn was sure she had seen him before, but she couldn't remember his name. He was one of the many football players who hung around their group of friends.

"Yes?" he asked, confused but appreciatively looking at Maya.

Everyone did. She was a bombshell.

"What's your name?"

"Drayton, but my friends call me Dray."

"Well, Dray, I get off at three thirty," she said with a wink.

He raised his eyebrows and nodded. "Maybe I can buy you a drink."

"Maybe I'll let you do more than that." Then, Maya looked at Trihn and smirked. "See? Easy enough."

Trihn shook her head. "You're all insane."

"Hey," Bryna said, running into Trihn, with Stacia at her side. "We have a surprise for you."

Stacia bounced up and down. "It's a good one."

"Oh no," Trihn groaned. "I don't want any of the football players."

Stacia rolled her eyes. "We're so generous, and you hate our gifts."

"I think you're having enough fun with Marshall all by yourself."

"He is delicious, isn't he?" Stacia asked. Her eyes roamed back over to his muscular six-foot-four build, and she smiled. "He'll make Pace so jealous."

"Oh, fuck, Stacia," Bryna groaned. "Just stop!"

Pace was Bryna's stepbrother, and they had a horrible relationship. He had sabotaged her one too many times and seriously needed to grow up. It didn't matter how hot he was—and he was pretty hot, not that she would ever tell Bryna that. She'd freak when anyone mentioned it. Also, he could play ball. Football wasn't Trihn's thing, but she knew he was better than Marshall. Unfortunately, Pace had to bide his time to get the starting position—just like he was biding his time until he got back into Stacia's good graces. Trihn had a feeling the latter would be more difficult than the former.

"Anyway," Stacia said with her bubbly personality, "we caught you a smoking hot guy. Don't worry. He's not a football player!"

"Lucky for me. That guarantees one of you hasn't slept with him," Trihn quipped.

Maya snorted and then went back to pouring drinks.

"Hilarious," Bryna deadpanned.

"But she's right," Stacia said with a shrug.

"Just earn your nickname, Cheer Slut," Trihn said with a half smile.

"It's Damon," Bryna said.

"No."

"What? Why not?" Bryna asked.

"No way."

"Look, he's hot, and he's into you. He's perfect. Did I mention how hot he is?"

"He is hot," Stacia agreed. "Perfect rebound material."

"I've never seen him at Posse before, so I don't think that's going to happen."

Bryna pointed upward. "He's right there."

"In the ceiling?"

"DJ booth!" Bryna said with a shake of her head.

"Oh my God, just imagine the hot sex inside the booth!" Stacia cried.

"I'm not having sex with him in the DJ booth."

"But somewhere else?" Bryna asked with a wink.

Trihn sighed heavily. "I'm going to have to talk to him, aren't I? There's no way you're going to leave me alone otherwise?"

Both her friends shook their heads. Trihn wasn't surprised. She didn't even know why she had agreed to try a rebound at all. She wasn't the type of girl who rebounded. She usually wallowed hopelessly in her own personal hell pit of depression until she felt like she could crawl back into the light.

But it wasn't as if that had made any difference in the past. She had just ended up in the same place as the last time. And there was no guarantee that, by having an easy rebound, she wouldn't end up here all over again.

"I don't want a relationship of any sort."

They nodded their heads, as if they understood. They were all serial relationship people, hopping beds and hearts without the scars that seemed to hit her so much harder than everyone else. She wished it were as easy for her to move on.

"If I do this, it's just physical."

"I believe the term you're looking for is a one-night stand," Bryna offered.

"That sounds so slimy."

"It's fun," Stacia said with a smile. "Just try to have fun."

Trihn rolled her eyes. She couldn't believe she was even considering this.

Bryna pushed Trihn in the direction of the stairs that led to the DJ booth, and she steeled her nerves for what was about to happen. Right now, she was thanking Maya for those two shots of tequila. She probably should have taken a few more.

She made it up to the booth, but she was disappointed to find a bouncer in front of the door. She hadn't planned for that.

"Excuse me. You're not allowed to be up here," the man said. He crossed his beefy arms over his chest and stared down at her, not even blinking an eye. His dark hair was pulled back into a man bun, and he was wearing a black blazer over a black T-shirt with black pants.

"Hey! Sorry to bother you." She chewed on her bottom lip. "I was just coming up to see the DJ."

"He's not seeing anyone. He's working."

"I totally understand. I just wanted to talk to him for—"

"No," he said plainly.

"But he's expecting me."

"No," he repeated. He stood his ground and gestured for her to walk back the way she'd come.

"But—"

"What is going on down here?" a man asked, walking toward them.

When Trihn got a good look at him, her eyes bulged. He was super hot with short honey-blond hair, to-die-for lips, and a bulky muscular physique clad in a cut black suit.

"Sorry, boss," the guy said. He respectfully nodded at the man. "I was just telling this girl to leave. She wanted to speak with the DJ."

"You're here a lot, aren't you?" the guy asked casually.

Trihn narrowed her eyes. "And how would you know that?"

"I work in security. I make it my business to know who is in the club. You know Maya, right?"

"Yeah. She's a good friend of mine."

"And how do you know the DJ?"

"Damon deejayed a party for a friend of mine, and we hung out last night at a different club," Trihn explained. "I was just going to say hi."

The man critically looked down at her. He had the greenest eyes she had ever seen. They were even greener than her own, and that was saying something. Modeling agencies had coveted her eyes when she was in the industry. She wondered if he modeled. He was probably in his late twenties or early thirties, but she thought he could model if he wanted.

Actually, when she looked closer, she noticed why his suit fit him so damn well. Armani.

Damn! How can a security guard afford an Armani suit?

"All right. Let her inside for five minutes. It's Damon's break soon anyway," he said to the door guy. He looked back at her. "If you bother him though, I'll have to ask you to leave," he told her.

"Thank you so much," she said, the anxiety leaving her body. She had no idea what she was doing, and she had a hard time believing that she had just passed an interrogation from a bouncer and a security guard to see Damon.

"Just don't rip out his heart," the guy said with a wry smile.

She looked at him, taken aback. "I don't think anyone has ever had to worry about that from me."

"I highly doubt that," he said with a smile before nodding at the bouncer and walking away.

She shook off the words of warning and turned back to the door. "Well?"

"Five minutes," the guy said. Then, he opened the door and stuck his head inside. "Hey, Damon. You have a visitor."

Trihn walked through the open door just as Damon swiveled in the chair he was seated in. The new Chloe Avana song, "Heartbreaker," blasted through the booth with a cool remixed backbeat. It made Trihn feel alive and unafraid instead of how she had been feeling in that hallway. The way Damon looked at her when she strode into his booth definitely helped.

"Hey, Damon," she said. She let the hot new beat wash over her. She was sexy and seductive, and she could do this.

"Trihn, I wasn't expecting you," he said with his amazing English accent before turning back to face the spread of equipment in front of him. He didn't exactly sound enthusiastic.

She figured she couldn't blame him after the way last night had ended. It wasn't exactly encouraging to go from sexy to dancing to "I have a boyfriend" in the span of a couple of minutes. Maya probably hadn't helped anything by laying into him either.

"I know. I didn't expect to find you at Posse."

"Yeah, I've deejayed here a couple of times. The manager gave me my first real gig, and when their regular guy backs out, I cover for them," he said, purely business.

Trihn walked across the small booth and looked out through the one-way window. The entire club was spread out below. She could see Bryna dancing with Eric and Stacia all up on Marshall. Maya was talking to that Drayton guy while she poured drinks. So, Damon must have seen that she was here tonight.

"This is a great view."

Damon sighed and closed his eyes. When he opened them, he glanced back up at her with a disgruntled look on his face. "I'm working here. Do you mind?"

She took a step back and held up her hands. "Sorry. I like this Chloe song. I've never heard this version of 'Heartbreaker.' They don't play it on the radio."

"That's because it's not a radio edit. It's my mix."

She could hear the pride in his voice.

"You're serious?" she said, surprised. "It's amazing. You should post it on YouTube or something, so other people can hear it!"

He shrugged. "I guess."

When he didn't say anything else or look back up at her again, she took a deep breath and dived in. "My boyfriend broke up with me."

His head shot up. His expression showed a mixture of relief and concern. "I'm sorry to hear that. Are you okay?"

She lost the smile on her face for a split second and then quickly plastered it back into place. She could not lose it right here in front of Damon. She was definitely not okay with what had happened with Neal, but she needed to get over it, and this was step one.

She nodded. Speaking wasn't possible.

He narrowed his eyes and looked like he was going to say something else, but Trihn silenced him by straddling his body. His hands came up almost defensively, as if he didn't know what she was doing. Then, she sat down on his lap and rested her hands on his chest.

He had on a black T-shirt and jeans. His signature ball cap was tipped back, so she could see his face. *God, he's sexy.*

"What are you doing?" he asked.

"Well, I'm single, and you're single. Last night, you were into me," she said boldly. She could channel her inner vixen and act as forward as her friends. "And…I'm into you."

Damon stood quickly, and she stumbled to her feet. Her cheeks heated at his departure.

"Look, Trihn, I don't want to be some rebound."

Her mouth dropped open, and then she quickly recovered. That was exactly why she had come up here— for him to be her rebound. That was what she wanted. She wanted someone to help her forget the shit she had just gone through. She was pretty sure Damon could do that.

"And I don't want a relationship," she told him.

"Maybe that's what I want."

She scoffed. "You don't even know me."

"I don't have to know you to know that I want a relationship. I've seen you in the club. I see the kind of person you are. When you look down at people every weekend, you can generally see who the good ones are."

"And I'm a good one?" she asked skeptically.

"You're real and genuine."

Trihn shook her head. "You can tell that from looking at me in a nightclub. I think that's ridiculous."

He shrugged. "Didn't ask for your opinion. I know it for a fact."

"So, you don't want to have sex with me then?"

He clenched his fists together and looked back down at his equipment. "Don't make this hard on me."

Trihn took a step forward, emboldened since he hadn't said no. "I want you to fuck me, and you're not interested?"

"Of course I'm interested," he said. He pulled his hat off his head and twirled it between his fingers. "And maybe a couple of months ago, I would have done just that but not tonight."

Trihn's stomach sank as she heard the finality in his voice. Her cheeks heated, and the confidence that had gotten her through this conversation deteriorated. She was just a girl feeling the sharp sting of rejection.

"Okay, fine," she said.

She hurried away from him, heading toward the door. All she needed was to be out of his booth where she had just humiliated herself in front of a guy who she had thought was interested in her. *Why had I thought it would be okay to ask him to have sex with me? Fuck!*

These kinds of conversations worked for her friends, but she just sounded and felt ridiculous, trying to put herself out there. Everything always blew up in her face. She shouldn't even be surprised that this hadn't been any different.

"Trihn!" Damon called after her.

"No, I get it. Forget I said anything."

Then, she was out the door, rushing past the bouncer, and heading down the stairs that led back to her friends.

She leaned against the wall and took a few deep healing breaths. She wasn't going to cry. She promised herself that. Her heart ached because of her breakup, but the slap in the face that Damon had delivered with his refusal hadn't helped anything.

Trihn's rebound mission was officially over.

SIX

"YOUR IDEA SUCKED," Trihn said when she calmed down enough to return to her friends.

Bryna had been dancing with Eric but had stopped her movements at Trihn's approach. She cocked her head to the side. "What do you mean?"

"He turned me down. I offered to let him fuck me, and he said no."

Trihn wasn't sure who looked more surprised—Bryna or Eric.

"Is he gay?" Eric started laughing.

Bryna jabbed him in the ribs. "That is *not* funny!"

If Trihn weren't so embarrassed after what had happened with Damon, she would have found the joke funny. For more than a year after Bryna had first met Eric, she had thought he was gay because of some offhanded comment her ex-boyfriend had said to keep her away from Eric. Then, she had discovered the truth that he was one hundred percent not gay and one hundred and fifty percent in love with her. He was also the best thing that had ever happened to Bryna.

"No, he is decidedly not gay. He said he wanted to fuck me, but he wouldn't fuck me."

Bryna opened her mouth and then closed it twice before speaking, "That's…wow. I've never had that happen before."

"We all know that, Bri," Trihn said.

"Hey!" Eric cried.

Trihn smiled genuinely up at Eric. She really liked Eric and had been rooting for him and Bryna from the start. He was easy on the eyes and quick to make Bryna smile.

"I know it's just you now, but we all know how she was."

"I'm not Stacia!" Bryna said. "Anyway, that has nothing to do with the fact that Damon obviously has some mental problem. Who would turn you down?"

"Clearly, every single guy I've ever been interested in," Trihn said, throwing her hands up in the air.

"I could hook you up with one of my friends," Eric suggested. He pointed out a guy standing by the bar. "That's Patrick. He's a redshirt junior on special teams right now. I'm working with him to plug him in as a defensive back. Probably will get some good play time next year."

Trihn looked over at the guy and then shook her head. "I'm not sure anything you just said was even English. No offense, but the last thing I want to do is date a football player."

Eric laughed. "Fair enough."

"Fuck, I need a drink," she said before heading to the bar. She elbowed her way through the crowd and walked straight into someone. "Ugh! Watch where you're going!"

The guy stepped back and held his hands up. "Trihn, your New Yorker is showing," Pace said.

Pace was the person she hadn't wanted to run into. Stacia would have a fit if she knew that he was at Posse tonight. Their on-again, off-again thing clearly wasn't working for anyone and made Pace even more irritable than usual.

"Whatever, Pace," she said. "I'm really not in the mood."

"Well, have you seen my girlfriend?"

"I have seen my friend, who you are currently not dating. I recommend you just walk right back out of here because you tend to make a fool of yourself when it comes to Stacia."

"I'll take that under consideration, but I know the real reason you're trying to keep us apart," Pace said with a wink. His blue eyes twinkled.

"Oh God, I don't think I even want to know."

"I heard that you and Neal broke up, and you're dying for a good rebound."

Trihn rolled her eyes. "It's good to see you, too, Pace."

She pushed past him without another word and hoped for the best for Stacia. She knew Stacia could take care of herself. She just prayed that, when Pace found Stacia, she wasn't having sex with Marshall somewhere. Trihn could only deal with so much drama in one night.

"Gin and tonic," Maya said, pushing a glass full of clear liquid toward her.

"Just keep them coming."

"It didn't go so well?"

"By *not so well*, if you mean, it was horrific and humiliating, then yeah, I'd agree with that."

Maya frowned. "I seriously never would have guessed that."

"You know, everyone keeps saying that, but it doesn't really help."

"You're right. Well, forget Damon, and let's focus on you. Have another drink, and go dance the night away.

You don't need a man to make you feel amazing. Show him what he's missing," Maya said with a wink.

Trihn nodded and raised her chin. Maya was right. The world was beating her down, and running away would mean it'd won. Neal had broken up with her and left her in pieces. Damon had refused her and humiliated her. She didn't need either of them.

Or at least that was what she told herself as she made her way out onto the dance floor.

Dance was always her outlet, and she hadn't been doing as much of it as she would have liked. She used to take Cassidy's pole class in her spare time, but last semester, she had been swamped with work, and then she had been gone for break. Ballet was a close second. After her time at the New York City Dance House, she had enrolled in a ballet class at LV State, but that had only lasted a semester. Those classes hadn't really fit into her schedule.

But she still had this.

She raised her hands over her head and started dancing seductively in the middle of the crowded room. Her body moved perfectly in sync to the music blaring through the speakers, and she let adrenaline fuel her forward. This was power and passion, lust and love, all rolled into one incredible package. And it was free for her to claim at all times.

Her eyes landed on the Patrick guy who Eric had pointed out to her. She had no interest in being with a football player and knew that she wouldn't stoop to Stacia's level, but he would do for dancing. He was hot enough.

She crooked her finger at him, and he lumbered over to her with a smirk on his face. He tried to engage her in conversation, but she ignored his attempts and danced up on him. She pressed her back to his chest and let her head drop backward.

He was all right but nothing compared to Damon. She figured it didn't matter if she was just trying not to think anyway.

Trihn had downed her drink and was halfway through another one that Patrick had bought for her when someone interrupted her dance with Patrick.

"Mind if I cut in?" he asked in his posh British accent.

Her head snapped to the side, and her mouth dropped open.

"Fuck off," Patrick said.

He eased his arm around Trihn's waist and tried to pull her away, but she was rooted in one place.

"What do you want, Damon?" Trihn asked.

"A dance," Damon said.

He had his hat in his hand and was twirling it between his fingers. She didn't know if that was a show of confidence or nerves.

"I thought you made your position clear."

"You know you'd rather be dancing with me."

Patrick flexed like he was going to butt in, but Trihn just pushed him away.

"Save a dance for me later," she said to Patrick.

"Man, whatever," Patrick said. He glared at Damon before stomping off like a kid throwing a tantrum.

Damon tipped his hat back onto his head and smiled. "You're way too good for him, you know?"

"We were just dancing. Last I checked, people could do that without having a relationship."

He nodded and then pulled her close. Their hips effortlessly moved together. There was no thought to the motion. It was just a seamless perfection.

But it didn't explain why he was down here or why he was dancing with her or why he was talking to her at all.

"What are you doing down here, Damon?"

"It's my break."

"I went up there and made a fool of myself. Now, you're here, dancing with me?"

"You're a good dancer."

Trihn stilled and stared up at him. "What do you want?"

"Well, I wanted to dance with you," he said, "but I also wanted to talk to you."

"I think we've talked enough."

"Later. After I get off work, wait for me."

His hands landed on her hips again. It was so simple with him. Despite the embarrassment she still felt in his presence, dancing made total sense and made all the other emotions vanish. It was her favorite thing about dancing. Damon just made it that much easier because he was so good.

"Why should I?" she asked.

"Just wait for me, okay?"

He sealed their hips together, and they rolled in heart-stopping circles that pushed her body so tightly against his that she barely had room to breathe. She could feel the hard contours of his washboard abs under the dark T-shirt he wore. Her dress was so short that when he pressed a knee between her legs as they danced, her ass nearly hung out the back. If they wanted to, they could probably have sex right there on the dance floor. Their movements were so in tune together that it was basically foreplay. And when he finally pulled away at the end of his break, Trihn was breathing heavily, and his pupils were dilated.

"You'll wait?" he asked.

"Against my better judgment," she whispered hoarsely.

"Good."

Then, he disappeared into the crowd to return to the DJ booth, leaving her more confused than ever.

"You sure you don't want to ride home with us?" Eric asked.

He was holding up an extremely drunk Bryna, who was vacillating between giggles and rants.

When Bryna got drunk, she only had two modes—crazy and psychotic. It all depended on how happy Bryna was. Luckily, psychotic hadn't been out in a while, but Trihn had seen her blow her fuse a few too many times not to always be a little wary of a drunk Bryna.

"Yeah. I'll catch a ride with Maya if I have to," Trihn reassured him.

When her friends finally cleared out of the bar, Trihn sat down on a barstool that was normally covered with people, and with jitters in her stomach, she looked up at Maya.

"I'm surprised you made it this long," Maya said, wiping down the counter.

"I can't believe I'm sitting here, waiting for a guy who rejected me when I offered him sex."

Maya guffawed and then tossed her towel down. "You could have had sex with any guy in the place tonight, but you want him now because he said no."

"I do not!"

"Yeah, you do."

"Ugh! That's not true. That makes it sound like I have issues."

Maya leveled her with an accusatory stare.

"I don't have issues. You all cooked up this idea together, so I'd forget about Neal."

"And it's working! Plus, you were into Damon last night," Maya said with a wink. "But come on, tell me, you aren't the least bit intrigued as to why he wants to talk to you after turning you down?"

Trihn rolled her eyes. "Of course I'm curious."

"Well, good because here he comes. Fill me in on the details when you find out." She fluttered her fingers at Trihn and then walked away.

Trihn sure hoped Maya wasn't leaving her behind because, if things didn't work out, she was going to need someone to take her home.

"You waited," Damon said.

Trihn hopped off the barstool and teetered in her high heels. "You said you wanted to talk."

"Yeah. I wanted to apologize for earlier," he said, tipping his hat off his head.

His dark hair was mussed in all the right ways, and it made her want to run her fingers through it.

"I wasn't expecting you or…your proposition, and I think I came off as a jerk," he said.

Trihn shrugged and looked at the ground. "Not any more than how awful I came off."

"If you just went through a breakup, your head probably isn't even on straight. So, how about we just…I don't know…start over?" he suggested hopefully.

"Yeah, sure," she agreed easily. The last thing she wanted was to be reminded of what had happened in the DJ booth.

"Hey. I'm Damon Stone. Pleasure to make your acquaintance," he said formally, sticking his hand out.

She took it in hers and shook firmly. "Trihnity Hamilton, but my friends call me Trihn."

"Well, Trihn, can I offer you a lift home?"

She nodded with a smile. "Yeah, I'd like that."

They walked out to the back parking lot and stopped in front of a silver Civic.

"I know it's not much, but she's gotten me through a lot of hard times," he told her.

"It's cute."

"Oh no, the dreaded cute," he said as he opened the passenger door for her.

She laughed and took a seat. He shut the door and ran around to the driver's side. He got into the car, revved the engine, and he immediately fiddled with the heat.

"God, it's freezing," he said.

Damon blew on his hands to try to warm them up as the car thawed.

Trihn huddled in her leather jacket. "My high school self would be laughing at me for going outside without a winter jacket and tights this time of year."

"Oh, yeah?" he asked. "Where are you from?"

"Brooklyn," she said into her hands. "I would have been freezing in this dress back home. Still, I can't believe it's thirty-seven here."

"Back home in London, it would technically be about the same temperature, but it's so much colder there with the rain, snow, and wind rather than the desert."

"Exactly. So, you're from London?"

"My dad's from there. I attended primary school in London with my mum and dad, but he ditched us, and we moved here because my mum got a teaching job," he explained casually, as if he weren't telling his life story to a perfect stranger.

"Oh. I'm sorry."

Damon smiled at her as he backed out of the parking spot. "Don't be. I'm not. He and my mum were always fighting. We're all better off."

"Does your mom still live here?" Trihn asked curiously.

He'd sounded really excited when he mentioned her.

"Yeah, she still lives in the house I grew up in. She's a theater professor at LV State now and probably cooler than I am," he told her with a genuine smile.

"It sounds like you two have a great relationship." She wished that her relationship with her family were as cut-and-dried as it had been before Lydia and Preston. At least she was still close with her father, who had put in all the effort to move her out to Las Vegas, to get her into school at the last minute, and to set her up with an apartment.

"We're really close," he agreed. He glanced over at her when he realized he had been driving without thinking about it. "Uh…where is your place? I went on autopilot."

"The opposite direction actually," she admitted. "But I like talking to you. Maybe we could just go to your place and do more of this." She gestured between them.

He narrowed his eyes, as if he wanted to say something. She could see that he wanted her to come back with him and talk because the conversation was good. But he had made his point earlier about wanting a relationship and not being just some rebound guy.

He was debating with himself, but he finally nodded. "I'd like that."

SEVEN

DAMON PULLED UP in front of an apartment building and cut the engine. "This way."

They hurried out of the car and up the first flight of stairs. He carefully unlocked the door and then ushered her inside the apartment. It was a small studio with typical bachelor furniture—black sofa, oversized television, PlayStation, Xbox, and an assortment of cups and dishes.

"Sorry about the mess," he apologized immediately. He grabbed everything in sight and then rushed it into the kitchen. "Wasn't expecting company."

"It's fine," Trihn said. She stripped out of her leather jacket and slung it on the back of the couch.

"Do you want a drink or something?" he asked.

"Sure. Whatever you have is fine."

Damon came back a minute later with a beer in each hand. He handed one to Trihn and took a long swig of his.

"I don't drink on the job," he told her, "so it's nice to come home and unwind."

She tipped the bottle up and took a sip. She was still buzzing a bit from the bar. Maya had been pouring her drinks with a heavy hand tonight—on purpose, she was sure.

"Do you live here alone?" she asked.

"Yeah. It's a one bedroom."

"That's nice. I live with my friends, Bryna and Stacia."

Damon smirked. "I know who they are."

"Oh, I'm sure. Everyone knows who they are."

"Everyone knows you, too."

She raised her eyebrow. "I really don't think so."

"Trust me. You're hard to miss." He flipped off his baseball hat and set it down on the table before taking the seat next to her. "I noticed you a long time ago. Yesterday was just the first time I got up the nerve to talk to you."

"What took you so long?" she joked before taking another drink.

"Well, I thought you had a boyfriend, so I tried to steer clear. Then, when you were alone with your friends, I thought that might have changed."

Trihn glanced up and met his dark eyes. "It did."

His eyes dropped down to her lips and then back up. "Yeah. What happened with that?" he asked.

She shrugged. "I don't really want to talk about it. It happened. It's over. And I'd rather just be here with you tonight."

"He must have been a total arse," Damon said.

Trihn took another big gulp. "You have no idea." She set the empty beer down on the coffee table and leaned forward toward Damon.

He raised his eyebrows at the finished drink. "That was fast."

"Why did you come downstairs after turning me down?" she asked.

"The truth?"

She nodded her head.

"It drove me nuts, watching you dance with that other guy."

She smiled wide. "That so?"

Damon took another swig of his beer and then placed it down on the table next to hers. "You know it did."

"Actually, all I could think about was you turning me down," she said with a shrug.

Maya had told her to show him what he was missing, but that hadn't been her motivation.

"Yeah, well, I was watching," he admitted. "Where do you dance?"

"I used to dance at the New York City Dance House back home. Mostly ballet, but some contemporary."

He nodded with a smile. "I'm not surprised you're technically trained. It shows in your movements."

"And you?"

"I learned here and there. My mum put me in dance and gymnastics when I was young, but I got bored quickly. I had a knack for the piano, and she pushed me toward that instead."

"You play piano?" she asked.

"A couple of instruments actually. I just graduated a semester early in December with a music degree. All the good it's doing me."

"Oh, wow. What are you going to do with that? Why aren't you in L.A. or something, trying to become famous?"

Almost sheepishly, he looked down at his hands. "Is it crazy to say that I don't like the spotlight?"

Trihn laughed. "A little, but I know what you mean. I modeled in high school, and it was sometimes overwhelming."

He raised his eyebrows. "You modeled? A ballerina, model, and club dancer. What kind of idiot would break up with you?"

"The kind who wanted me to just be an artistic fashion designer and nothing else," she admitted.

Her shoulders drooped. That had been the problem with Neal. Only half a day from the breakup, and already, she had more clarity to her thoughts than she'd had in months. It ached, knowing that he'd clouded her mind in the worst possible way.

"Hey," Damon said, reaching out and touching her bare knee. "I didn't mean to take you down a bad road. Just trying to figure you out."

"No, it's okay. Don't worry about it."

"So...fashion designer?" he asked. "Is there anything you're not good at?"

"Relationships?"

Damon gave her a serious look before closing the distance between them. His hip pressed into her side, and her stomach fluttered at his nearness. His hand came up to brush her dark hair off her face. His thumb lingered on her cheek, and she lost herself in the endless depths of his eyes. Her breathing hitched. When he looked at her like that, it was as if time stood still.

"That remains to be seen," he told her.

Then, his lips landed on hers, soft and undeniably tempting. Something awakened within her. It wasn't just the alcohol coursing through her system. It was the desire that came with a perfect kiss. Their lips moved together, and then his tongue ran across her bottom lip, opening her up to him. As he delved into her mouth, she groaned softly. Their tongues met in harmony, exploring a new frontier.

Her hands breached the small space between them, and she dug her fingers into the soft material of his T-shirt. Suddenly, the room shifted. Everything moved with her need to have him closer.

Damon's arm swept around her body, crushing her against him. She spread her legs and straddled him on the couch, like she had done only a few hours earlier in the DJ booth. But this time, he wasn't standing up and walking away. Instead, he was dragging her harder against him and running his hands up her exposed legs.

Trihn threaded her fingers up into his hair. Ever since she had seen it out of that baseball cap, she had wanted to grab ahold of it. The noises he was making when she tugged on it only fueled her forward.

He broke the intense kiss to come up for a breath, and then he started leaving kisses across her cheek and down her bare neck. She tilted her head back, letting her hair fall loose behind her, allowing him better access to her body. His lips were pressed over her collarbone and back to her neck where he nibbled gently until she was squirming on top of him.

"Fuck," he groaned. "If you keep moving your hips like that, I'm not going to be able to stop this."

"What, like this?" she asked, circling her hips in a figure eight.

"Exactly like that."

He clamped his hands down on her hips, as if he wanted to still her. But she just moved his hands backward to cup her ass, most of which was exposed at this point.

"Why would you want to stop? You already know we move well together."

"Yes, we do."

"But…if you want to stop, we can," she said with a smile.

She started to stand up, but before she could even get her feet on the ground, Damon picked her up and tossed her back on the couch.

"I don't want to stop anything," he said.

Then, he covered her mouth with his, and she was lost all over again. His body lowered onto hers. He held himself up on his forearms, but their lower halves were pressed firmly together. He ground his hips against her. If she had thought dancing with him was sexual, that was nothing compared to this. He could do things with his hips that made her body hum.

Her heart pounded in her chest, and her breathing was ragged. They hadn't even done anything yet, and already, she was fucking aroused. She dragged her legs up to either side of his hips and thrust upward to meet his movement.

He bit out a moan and then pulled back to look down at her. His dark eyes were practically black in the dim lighting. "You totally fuck me up," he admitted.

She ran her hand down his pants and then over his dick. It was stiff and pulsing. She stroked it twice and watched his eyes roll into the back of his head.

Damon kissed her one more time and then slid down her front to land between her legs.

"What are you doing?" she asked.

He didn't answer, he just slipped his fingers under the mesh of her dark green thong and ran a digit over the slick folds. "Jesus."

"Yeah," she groaned.

Then, he pressed his finger into her. A second joined the first, and he started up an easy movement within her. She felt her body building with desire as he worked her in and out. His tongue shot out and flicked her clit. Her hips bucked beneath him, and she swore that she saw him smirk.

Damon yanked her thong off and pressed her legs open in front of him without another word, and then he dropped his head to lavish her pussy. His fingers stroked her while he licked, sucked, and nibbled on her clit until she was shaking and couldn't move. She practically ached with exertion as he drew more and more from her.

Then, just when she thought she couldn't hold out any longer, he started moving in deliberate slow strokes inside her. She shivered as her orgasm hovered just out of range. It was so close and so far away. She was quivering. Her walls sucked on his fingers as he held her in place, as if he knew exactly how to work her body.

"Fuck," she cried.

He licked her clit, causing a long shudder to run through her. "Don't worry. I'll let you come soon."

"Let me?" she gasped.

At her question, he pumped his fingers into her faster. "Yeah. I want you to feel every ounce of pleasure I'm giving you, and I want you to remember exactly who gave it to you."

"Damon," she purred.

"That's right."

While still moving his fingers within her, he sucked on her clit, and everything seemed to explode within her. She came apart in waves and saw spots in her vision during a climax that she might have never reached before.

She lay back on the couch, taking in deep healing breaths while letting her body ride out the release.

Damon sat back on his heels and stripped out of his shirt. Her eyes widened when she got a look at him. She had known he was built. She had felt that from dancing and the way he was riding her earlier, but seeing it in person was different. He had a killer body, not too big and bulky but not skinny either. He had a perfect rock-star body.

He undid his pants and left them lying on the ground. He stood before her in nothing but a fit pair of black boxer briefs that hardly concealed the bulging erection within.

He held his hand out. "Come here."

Trihn stood on shaky legs and took his hand. She ditched her heels. After her orgasm, there wasn't a chance in hell that she was going to be able to walk anywhere in them. She followed him back to his bedroom, which had a simple wooden bedroom set with a queen-size bed with a dark blue comforter. He walked her backward to the foot of the bed and then lifted her black dress over her head.

Bryna's rebound dress had officially done the trick.

"Don't need that," he said as he tossed it to the ground.

He went to work, unclasping her matching green mesh bra and letting it drop to the floor, revealing her model-thin frame to him. She fought the urge to cover herself up. She didn't have the same body issues she'd had in high school, but it was easy to think that she was either too thin or too fat or too anything but perfect. Damon's eyes traveled her figure with appreciation, lingering on her small breasts, flat stomach, her hip bones that naturally protruded forward, and then down to her thigh-gap legs. They were all things she would kill to change, but when Damon looked at her, that all disappeared.

"You're so gorgeous," he whispered.

She laughed nervously, not used to the attention. She couldn't remember the last time Neal had said something like that to her. And the only person she had been with before that had been Preston and a random guy she'd met on a modeling job. Those had turned out to be all bad decisions in the end.

All of a sudden, Damon seemed to notice her nervousness, and he took her hands in his. "You *are* gorgeous. No doubt about that."

"Thank you," she said automatically.

He brought his lips down on hers again, and her nervousness melted away. The way he touched her and talked to her and acted around her made her feel totally safe. For all intents and purposes, her trust issues should be rearing its ugly head, but when he kissed her, she felt calm. Maybe it was because it was just physical. That was what she had promised herself. The girl who wore her heart on her sleeve was giving up relationships and just filling her void with a rebound, no matter how much her heart might manage to get in the way while she tried it out.

Damon easily picked her up and set her back on the bed. The tension in the room skyrocketed as he stripped out of his boxer briefs and climbed onto the bed after her.

She couldn't believe this was actually happening after he had turned her down, but she didn't want to question it. He clearly wanted to do this, and she had made her intention clear from the start.

Trihn wrapped her arms around Damon's neck and kissed him deeply, reveling in the feel of his body pressed against hers. He moved his hips in a sexy circular motion, waking her up all over again. Whatever had happened out on the dance floor only fueled what was going on in the bedroom.

Doubt clouded her mind when he pulled back to reach across the bed and remove a condom from his side table. Looking up at him as he tore open the condom and rolled it on himself, she reminded herself that this was just a one-night stand. It didn't have to be more than that. It didn't have to have feelings or emotions attached that weren't purely physical. Damon made her feel good, and she needed to feel good tonight.

Damon's eyes searched hers in the dark. "Hey, are you okay?"

"Yeah."

"We can stop if you don't want to do this," he offered softly.

She reached out and touched his hand. "I want to."

He leaned forward and pressed his lips to hers, positioning himself before her. "I want this, too, but we can wait. I'm not going anywhere."

"Damon," she growled. She had made up her mind. She wasn't stopping now. "Stop trying to talk me out of this. I want you to fuck me."

He laughed a guttural deep laugh that revealed how much he was controlling himself in that moment. Then, after another kiss, he eased deep inside her.

"Oh God," she moaned when he filled her.

Yeah, I made the right decision.

Trihn wrapped her legs around Damon's hips and met each of his measured thrusts.

Fuck, is it supposed to feel this good? She had always thought that a one-night stand would be like a bad book—quick, boring, and completely not worth the hype.

But she was already ramping up for another release as they moved together, like they had been doing this for a long time. She wasn't sure what caused it, but whatever it was, she was glad that she had gone through with it. This was exactly what she needed.

"Fuck, I love your body," he said, sliding his hands down her sides and then up to cup her breasts.

She laughed and reached up to kiss him hard. Their lip-lock intensified the force with which he drove inside her. Her fingers clawed his back, and she couldn't hold out any longer. She threw her head back and cried out as her climax hit her. Damon leaned his head onto her forehead as he released just after her. For a minute, they both lay there, panting, and then Damon slid out of her and headed to the bathroom.

He returned a minute later and leaned against the door, in the buff. Her eyes traveled down his body, and she sighed, completely sated.

"That was a happy noise," he said.

She nodded. "Mmhmm."

Trihn rolled off the bed and wandered into his bathroom. She returned a few minutes later, feeling refreshed and also exhausted. She crawled back into bed and waited for some sort of embarrassment or awkwardness to settle between them, but it never came.

He just pulled her into his arms and held her close.

Then, after several minutes of companionable silence, he bent down and kissed her on the mouth.

"How about round two?" he suggested with a wicked grin.

EIGHT

TRIHN SLIPPED BACK into the too small dress and then grabbed her heels, purse, and leather jacket. As quietly as she could, she tiptoed toward the front door of Damon's apartment. She had the handle turned all the way when she heard footsteps behind her.

"Going somewhere?" Damon asked with a yawn.

She turned to face him with a sheepish grin. "Um...yeah."

He looked too good for this early in the morning. He was only in a pair of boxers, and she could count every defined ab. Plus, his hair...it only looked that way because she had been pulling it all night.

Christ! Focus!

"My ride is here," she told him.

"I could have given you a lift home."

"Yeah. But, well…" Trihn shrugged. She didn't have a response to that. She'd had a great time last night—an unbelievably amazing, jaw-dropping, unfathomably incredible good time last night—but when it came down to it, this still had been a one-night stand, just some really good sex. From the beginning, she had said that she didn't want anything more. Neal had broken up with her less than twenty-four hours ago. She couldn't even consider putting herself out there again already.

"This isn't a one-night stand, Trihn."

"Well, I'm not ready for a relationship."

"I'm not letting you go this easy."

She shook her head. "You should. I'm a wreck."

"Yet I want you."

"Damon, can we not do this?" she asked. "I just got out of a relationship. You're an amazing guy who deserves a really great girl. I'm…not that girl right now."

"I'm going to change your mind," he told her without a trace of doubt in his voice.

In that one moment, she hoped that he was right. But then she frowned and looked away. "I'm sorry. I really don't think so. This didn't mean anything to me."

Then, she pulled open the door to his apartment and hurried outside.

It was early morning, and her bare feet on the cold concrete didn't help anything. She slouched into her leather jacket and raced down the stairs, shaking all the while. Her eyes darted around the full parking, but she didn't see Bryna's telltale Aston Martin.

Someone honked off to her right, and her head whipped to the side to see a Jeep parked a few spots over. Eric waved from the front seat, and she shook her head. *Of course Bryna had sent Eric to get me in the morning.* She couldn't be bothered to get up from her beauty sleep.

"Hey," Trihn said, popping open the passenger door and sliding into the seat. She pushed her hands against the vents with a sigh. "Thank God, it's so warm in here."

"Morning, Trihn," he said with a smirk on his face as he pulled out of the parking lot before heading toward her apartment. "Have a good night?"

"The best," she said.

"Not so good of a morning if you're rushing out the door."

"Neal broke up with me yesterday. Pretty sure that getting cozy with someone the same night is not a good idea."

"For who?" Eric asked. "Neal was a loser who fucked with your life. Seems like a good thing for you to move on."

Trihn shrugged. "I just think it'd be better for me to find myself again rather than jump right into something else. Last night was fun, E, but it was just fun."

"So, you're madly in love with him?"

"Oh my God, no! I'm not in love with him. I just met him!"

"So defensive."

"Eric Wilkins, you're insufferable. Bryna needs to keep you on a shorter leash or else I'll have to kick your ass," she said with a smile on her face.

"I'm not on a leash!"

"Puh-lease. You're so whipped."

Eric drove into the apartment complex with a broad smile on his face. "For Bryna, I'll be anything."

"Stop! You two are disgusting."

Eric parked the car. They hopped out and and took the elevator up to the top floor.

"Don't worry about a relationship right now, Trihn. If you think you need to work on you, then work on you. It took Bri and me over a year to finally get together. I wish we'd had all that extra time together, but I'm going to be with her for the rest of my life, so it's all worth it in the end. That guy will find you at the right time."

Trihn followed Eric into the apartment. "Thanks, E."

"Maybe he already has," he said with a laugh.

She nodded with an eye roll. "Maybe."

The next morning, Trihn was up at the break of dawn, jittery with excitement over the first day of school.

Bryna and Stacia hadn't yet surfaced, but she didn't think they had morning classes. They certainly weren't morning people. She wasn't really either, but her first big fashion design class was this morning, and she was anxious to get started.

Her mother never let her live it down that she'd left NYU, one of the best fashion programs in the country, to go to LV State. The program was top-notch after Teena Hart had taken it over, but it still didn't compare NYU. Not to mention, being that close to the US fashion mecca came with benefits and networking opportunities that just weren't available in Las Vegas.

As Trihn was about to get her things together to leave for class, the doorbell rang. She hurried over to answer the door, worried that it might wake up her roommates. The doorbell rang again, and she cursed aloud. It was too early for all of that.

"Coming!" she called. She yanked the door open to find a delivery man standing there. "Can I help you?"

"I have a package. Sign here, please." The man held out an electronic signature pad.

Trihn scribbled on the pad and then took a vase of red, pink, yellow, and white tulips along with a small box from the man.

"Um…thanks," she said before tocing the door closed behind her. "Bryna! Eric is spoiling you again!"

Bryna ambled out of her bedroom in nothing but a tiny black baby-doll and yawned loudly. "This'd better be good for waking me up."

"Looks like Eric sent you flowers." Trihn placed the flowers and the box down on the table and slid them toward Bryna. "What's in the box? Some kinky sex toy for later?"

Bryna's eyes lit up. "We can only hope." She grabbed the box and started to unwrap the paper but then stopped. "Um...Trihn, this isn't for me."

"What?"

Bryna held it out to her. "It has your name on it."

"It does not! Who would send me anything?" Trihn asked.

"Open it, and find out."

Trihn tore the paper off the box and opened it up. Inside was an envelope and exactly one Hershey's Kiss. She held it up for Bryna to see, and she shrugged.

Trihn opened the envelope and retrieved the note within.

TRIHN,

IT MEANT SOMETHING TO ME.

DAMON

Trihn just stared at the message until it became blurry before her eyes.

"Well?" Bryna demanded. She grabbed it out of Trihn's hands and then immediately started laughing.

"What's going on out here?" Stacia asked. "You guys are so fucking loud."

"Trihn got flowers from Damon."

Stacia's eyes popped. "Really? How romantic."

"And a Hershey's Kiss," Bryna added.

"I guess that counts as chocolate?" Stacia asked.

"It doesn't mean anything," Trihn said with a shake of her head.

Truthfully, she had no idea what any of it meant. Of course Damon was contradicting the last statement she had made to him before leaving his place the day before. She had just figured that would have been the end of it.

How could a guy who had just met her want to push so hard for her? He hardly knew her. They'd barely talked. Sure, they'd had amazing sex—more than once. She just hadn't believed him when he said that he was going to try to change her mind. Guys didn't fight for her. They usually fought with her.

"I'm pretty sure flowers and…chocolate mean something," Stacia said.

"Plus, the card says it means something," Bryna reasoned.

Trihn snatched the card out of Bryna's hand and stuffed it into the box. "Well, it doesn't mean anything to me. I have to go to class."

"Forget class. Call this guy, and blow him," Stacia said. "Guys do not put in effort like this in the real world, Trihn."

"As ever, Stacia, your logic is impeccably sound." Trihn shook her head at her friend and then hurried to the door.

"Hey, don't forget your Kiss!" Stacia called.

Trihn held her hand out, and Stacia plopped the Hershey's Kiss into her palm. She popped it into her mouth with a tight smile, flipped her two roommates off, and then left for class.

NINE

TRIHN'S FASHION DESIGN CLASS reignited her passion for her work. All the art and textile classes she had taken were really helping out with her new classes. A lot of it was basic, but she knew that they would move into more difficult and complicated techniques as the semester went on.

The most exciting part was that all the design majors would get to help with the annual Teena Hart Fashion Show. Advanced design students would put together a selection of their best pieces and would get to feature them on an actual runway. The winner of the fashion show would take their designs to New York City in the summer to compete against the top programs from all over the country. The grand prize was that the line would be picked up by a large market. Last year, it was Macy's!

Trihn had been selected to help with the models throughout the entire process. She wasn't all that surprised, given her background in modeling. She just wished she'd have more hands-on experience in working with the actual designs, but her day would come.

The best part about being so busy was that it didn't leave her as much time to sit around and obsess. Part of her really missed Neal. She knew how much her roommates hated him and that he had been a jerk to her, but she still missed him. And she didn't know if that was just because she didn't like to be alone, especially while Bryna and Eric were so happy together and Stacia was always content with the various men in her life.

Not to mention, there was Damon. Nearly a week had passed, and he hadn't reached out to Trihn since he had sent the flowers. She tried not to be disappointed. She had pushed him away after all, and it was too early to be interested in someone else.

Her thoughts were clouded with their one-night stand when she made it home on Friday afternoon.

"Get dressed, bitch. We're going out," Bryna said when Trihn opened the door.

"God," Trihn said, jumping backward. "Don't you and Stacia have cheer practice or something?"

"Nope. Canceled for tonight since the football season is over. We're getting ready for competition, but haven't really geared up yet."

"What about basketball season?"

Bryna gave her a blank stare. "Does anyone care about that?"

Trihn laughed. "I hear some people do."

"Well, we have a B squad for basketball because they suck, and no one here gives a shit. Now, get changed. We're going out," she repeated.

Twenty minutes later, Bryna, Stacia, and Trihn piled into Bryna's Aston Martin and drove to the Strip. The girls generally avoided the madness of the tourist trap, but some necessities could only be found in The Forum Shops at Caesars Palace.

They passed Tiffany & Co., and Bryna shot it a wistful look.

"You really don't need anything else from there," Trihn said, grabbing her arm and tugging her away.

"I met Hugh there," she said with a sad smile.

"Didn't you just see on the news that he's dating some movie producer? He's fine."

"It was fun while it lasted though," Stacia said with a giggle. "How about that mansion?"

"Feels like a lifetime ago," Bryna said.

"Well, I'm speaking for everyone when I say, I prefer you with Eric than as a gold-digging bitch," Trihn told her.

Bryna shrugged. "He is pretty great."

"He's, like, godlike status," Stacia chimed in.

"Ah!" Bryna said. "We're here!"

Trihn looked at the entrance to La Perla, and it made her miss home where upscale boutiques were lined up on Fifth and Madison. Nowhere really compared to New York City in her eyes.

"What's the occasion?" Trihn asked as they stepped inside.

"I don't need an occasion to get sexy lingerie. I pretty much live in it, but *you* need to get fucked tonight. So, we're going to work on that," Bryna said. She breezed by Trihn with a confident strut in her step.

"Whoa! Rewind. I am not having sex tonight."

"You're going to see Damon at Posse tonight and repeat last weekend until you feel better again."

"I'm fine!"

Even Stacia's look was withering. "You're so far from fine."

"We had two options—ask ask you to talk about it, which we knew you wouldn't, or take you lingerie shopping for the hot sex you're going to have this weekend." Bryna exchanged a look with Stacia. "We obviously chose the latter."

A sales clerk approached them with wide eyes, clearly having just heard their conversation. "Can I help you, ladies?"

"Yes. I need a new lingerie set, and my friend here needs something to get fucked in."

The woman smiled shyly but hardly batted an eye at Bryna's language. Trihn wasn't surprised. Bryna smelled like money. The clerk had probably seen it when she walked through the door.

Her father was a famous movie director, and her mother was an actress. They'd met at LV State, which was why she had come to the school. She was a legacy.

Trihn's parents were on the opposite of that spectrum. Her father had skipped college to pursue photography and became a professional fashion photographer. He'd met her mom at *Glitz* where she was currently a senior executive for the fashion magazine. Her sister, Lydia, had followed in their dad's footsteps while Trihn had ended up on the more artsy side of fashion rather than the business end.

That was why, despite the fact that she had no intention of sleeping with anyone this weekend, she tried on all of the La Perla lingerie the girls had thrown at her and left with a bagful of goodies that could totally get her laid.

"Damon's not here."

Trihn raised her eyebrows. "Hi. It's nice to see you, too, Maya."

"Oh, yeah. Hi. Here's a gin and tonic. Damon's not here," Maya said, pushing a drink her way.

"Well, I didn't come here for him tonight. I come here every weekend."

"You so want to get fucked tonight. I mean, you're wearing a corset top."

"Nothing to do with Damon!" Trihn cried. She snatched her drink up and took a long swig. It burned on the way down, leaving behind a floral aftertaste. *Good stuff.*

"I do love that fucking skirt though," Maya said, leaning over the bar to examine it. "Where did you get that?"

Trihn beamed. "I made it!"

"Look at you, Miss Fashion Designer. Well, I'll take one of those when you have a chance."

"Sure. I'll get to it in my spare time," Trihn said.

"Good."

"So, wait," Trihn said before Maya could go pour someone else a drink, "he's really not here?"

Maya flashed her a bright smile. She looked Trihn up and down, as if taking her measure. "I knew you were here to get some ass."

"Oh my God, honestly?"

"Honestly, he's not here."

Trihn nodded and tried not to think about that. She didn't even know what had compelled her to ask Maya about Damon. She wasn't interested. It had been a one-night stand. That was that.

A couple of drinks later, "Heartbreaker," her favorite new Chloe Avana song, came on. She grabbed Bryna and Stacia and forced them out onto the dance floor. Their bodies grinding against each other were every guy's wet dream.

Trihn let the freedom of the dance take over. It was practically hypnotic, the way the mixture of the alcohol, music, and movements could relax her like nothing else— except for sex. And since it was pretty clear she wasn't going to be having any of that…

"I love this version!" Stacia cried.

Bryna shrugged. "Chloe is…okay."

Trihn knew that Bryna had some issue with Chloe, who had been in a movie with Bryna's ex-boyfriend Gates Hartman, but she really didn't know what it was. Bryna was a buzzkill for Chloe's music though.

"This version should be on the radio," Stacia said.

Trihn realized where she had heard this before. Her eyes traveled up to the DJ booth. This was the mix that Damon had said he created when she went to see him in the booth last weekend.

Damon was here.

She was one hundred percent sure of that now.

Trihn spent the next hour wondering if and when Damon was going to come down from the DJ booth to see her. She was sure Maya had lied and said that he wasn't there to keep her from obsessing about it.

She had just gotten another drink from Maya when she saw a circle forming on the other side of the club. Stacia was occupied with Marshall, who seemed to be giving into her antics. She guessed it was an off-again time for Stacia and Pace. Bryna was glued to Eric against the bar, making a sickeningly cute display for everyone to see.

Trihn pushed her shoulders back and decided to go figure it out for herself. She was pretty sure she knew what she was going to find.

It wasn't Damon.

But it was his two friends from the other club they had gone to before school had started. The African American guy was warming up his break moves while the other guy kept glancing around the circle, as if waiting for something. *Or someone*, Trihn reasoned.

He caught her eye across the circle and started weaving around the crowd to her. "Hey, I'm Jimmy," he said with a head nod.

"Trihn."

"Yeah, I know who you are."

Trihn raised her eyebrows for an explanation, but he didn't give her one. He was about eye-level with her and kept his head tilted back, an imitation of Damon. She wondered if they were friends or if Jimmy just idolized him.

"You know Damon?"

"Grew up together."

"Ah."

"Don't jerk him around, you know? He's a great guy, and he doesn't deserve that, even from someone as hot as you."

Trihn shook her head with a sigh. Jimmy was just being a good friend. She would do the same thing for any of her friends if it were needed. But she wasn't jerking Damon around. She thought she had been clear that she didn't want a relationship, and if the flowers were any indication, he thought he'd made his point clear, too.

"Got it," she said.

"Good. You seem nice. I'm just looking out for him."

Trihn looked directly into his little puppy-dog eyes. "You really don't know anything about me. Maybe I'm not nice."

"Damon likes you, and he has good taste. He sees the good in people, even when they don't see it in themselves." Jimmy sounded like he had been on the other end of that speech before.

Also, she was pretty sure idolization was higher on the list than friendship.

A hand clamped down on Jimmy's shoulder, and Trihn's gaze moved upward to find Damon staring at her.

"What's going on here?" he asked Jimmy.

"Uh…nothing," Jimmy squeaked.

"Yeah. It'd better be nothing," Damon growled.

He actually seemed irritated with his friend. *Or is that fear clouding his eyes? Is he worried about what Jimmy had said to me?*

"Go do that move I taught you last week. Xavier probably needs a break."

Jimmy saluted him with two fingers and then glided into the center of the circle to the cheers of the onlookers.

Trihn and Damon stood there together with a sexual tension that she couldn't deny. His eyes drank her in, as if he'd been dying of thirst during the week apart. She could feel need rolling off of him, and she wanted to lean into him. It made her want to forget all the rules she had constructed for herself about the one-night stand and rethink those walls she had just rebuilt around her heart. But she needed those for protection. A hot guy with a few charming words was more destructive than a nuclear bomb to the heart.

"Maya said you weren't here," Trihn said when she couldn't stand the silence any longer.

"I thought it would be easier for you if you didn't know that I was here."

"And then you played that Chloe song."

He grinned. "It was requested."

"It was a dead giveaway."

"Maybe I couldn't stand up there in obscurity any longer while the one thing I wanted tempted me from afar."

"Damon," she said, turning away from him.

Her cheeks heated at his words. He made something so minor sound so meaningful that it was hard to ignore him.

"Did you get the flowers?"

"Yes."

"And the Kiss?"

She turned to face him with a sigh. "Yes."

"You know why I sent it, right?"

"As a joke?" she guessed.

"Because I plan to earn back the right to your kisses. In the meantime, I'll just send you chocolate ones to remind you of me."

Damon held out his hand and passed her a Hershey's Kiss.

She tried to refuse. "Stop saying those kinds of things to me."

"What kinds of things?" he asked. He tucked his hands behind his back so that she had to keep it.

Defeated, she kept it in her palm. "Sweet things."

"Not if you think they're sweet," he said with a grin.

And that British accent wasn't helping her resolve any.

This was a bad idea, a horribly bad idea. He was hot and charming and sweet and trying to get her to open up to him, but the last thing she wanted was to attach feelings to another human being. It'd ended with Preston choosing Lydia over her and Neal likely cheating on her and deciding they were incompatible after a year and a half of dating. Mostly, it'd just ended in heartbreak.

"I should go," Trihn said, backing away.

"Trihn"—Damon reached out for her and took her hand—"don't go."

Her phone buzzed in her purse, keeping her from having to respond him. *Saved by the bell.* "Sorry. I have to take this."

She dug into her bag and pulled out her phone. She nearly groaned when she saw who was calling. If she had known it was Lydia, she might have braved the conversation with Damon.

She and Lydia used to be best friends, but after the stuff with Preston, botching all of her and Lydia's plans to live and go to NYU together, and Trihn leaving the city, their relationship had never really repaired itself. Lydia acted like it wasn't as big of a deal as it was to Trihn, but that was her hippie sister. Plus, she had won.

"Lydia, I'm in a club. Give me a minute to get somewhere quiet," Trihn said into the receiver.

She mouthed, *Sorry,* to Damon, but he just held on to her hand.

"I have to be back in the booth soon. I'll wait for the end of your call."

She nearly groaned but just nodded. He followed her as she sought out a place to talk to Lydia. She was not looking forward to having these two conversations all in one place.

Trihn finally made it to the back patio. During the warmer months, it was an outdoor pool area, and Sunday afternoons, they would have crazy parties that attracted all the hottest crowds in Las Vegas. But tonight, it was cold and empty. Trihn was glad she had worn a blazer over her corset top.

"Sorry, Ly. What's up?"

"Oh my God, Trihn! I'm so glad I got ahold of you." Her voice was shaky, and she sounded like she was in tears.

A part of Trihn was excited for Lydia's discomfort, and then she silently smacked herself and got back into sister mode.

"Lydia, are you okay?"

Lydia sniffed twice. "I'm just so emotional."

"It's the middle of the night in New York right now, Ly! What's going on?" Trihn asked.

"Preston proposed! We're getting married, Trihn!"

TEN

"I'M SORRY. COME AGAIN?" Trihn said.

Whatever Lydia had just said couldn't possibly be real life.

"Preston proposed, and I said yes!" Lydia cried.

Trihn pitched forward. Someone reached out for her before she fell down, and she dimly realized that it was Damon.

She couldn't form coherent thoughts. There was nothing coherent about the statements that Lydia had just made.

"Preston...proposed..."

"Yes! We were out late, walking through Washington Square Park, and he just got down on one knee right there. It was so romantic."

Trihn took a seat on one of the stray lounge chairs and tried to remember to breathe. This couldn't be happening. She needed to get it together—at least while she was on the phone with Lydia. She could freak out after she got off the phone.

"Wow," she said with fake enthusiasm. "That's great, Ly."

"Thanks. You could try to sound excited for me."

"I just didn't realize you guys were that serious. It hasn't been that long."

"Almost two years. Well, two years in May, but whatever."

Trihn felt the knife stab through her chest and twist.

Trihn had met Preston two years ago in June. He and Lydia had been dating for a few weeks prior to that, but Lydia had claimed they weren't official until August, right before Trihn had left.

Trihn hadn't realized that they acted like those months hadn't existed with Trihn in them.

"Oh," Trihn said.

"But we wanted you to be one of the first to know. I have to call Mom and Dad next, but I had to talk to you to ask you to be my maid of honor!"

Trihn leaned forward and put her head between her knees. She thought she was going to be sick. "Really?"

"Yes! It will be so amazing. We don't have a date yet, but we'll let you know as soon as we do. I'll talk to you later, Trihn." When Trihn didn't respond to her comment, Lydia hung up the phone.

Two years. Married. Maid of honor.

Her head was spinning. She was definitely going to be sick. She slipped the phone back into her purse and blankly stared forward at the brick wall.

Trihn had never in a million years thought that Lydia and Preston would make it to this moment. She had been shocked when they made it past six weeks. The thought of them being together for almost two years and getting married was unthinkable.

How could two people who made absolutely zero sense together get married? Lydia was a free-loving hippie. Preston was a philandering asshole. One or the other was going to end up cheating, if they weren't already in that boat. Trihn had her money on Preston. He'd set a precedent.

Who am I kidding? This whole thing was going to be a fucking disaster, and she would have to stand by and watch the train wreck happen.

"Trihn?" Damon asked uncertainly. "Is everything okay?"

She glanced up at him and took a deep breath. "My sister is getting married."

His face lit up. "That's great! Congratulations!" When he noticed her frown, he held back on his enthusiasm and looked puzzled. "Is it not great?"

"I'd rather not talk about it," she said, standing up and trying to regain her composure.

"You looked pretty upset when you were on the phone."

"And, now, I just want you to fuck me," she told him.

His eyes widened in surprise. "What? How could you go from upset to sex that quickly?"

"Have you never had angry sex? Hate sex?"

He frowned. "I have, but I don't think that's what you need right now."

Trihn placed her hands on his chest and leaned into him. "I really think that I should be the person to determine what I need. Right now, I need you to find a private place for us to fuck."

Damon put his hands around her wrists. "I'm not really sure what's going on with you, but maybe we should just talk about it rather than hiding it with sex."

"Why am I the only girl in the world who begs a guy to fuck her and he refuses?" she asked. She pulled her arms back from him and waited for his response.

"Trihn, I thought I made myself clear last weekend. I don't want to be just a one-night stand, and I don't want to be your fuck buddy either. I wouldn't mind you taking your emotions out on my cock," he said coarsely, moving closer to her again. He dragged her body against him and leaned forward, as if he were going to kiss her. His voice was deep and husky with that smooth British accent that made her knees weak. "In fact, I would love nothing more than to be inside you again, but I want to know that you're not running from every step we take forward."

"And what if I do?"

"Then, I'll leave you alone. I don't want that, but I don't want to be used either. A couple of months ago, I would have been all for this, but I've changed since then. I can't go back to the person I was." Damon looked away from her and sighed. "I have to get back in the booth or else I'm going to get in trouble at work. But will you stay until I get off work?"

"For a repeat of last weekend?" she asked hopefully. It would be great to forget about Preston and Lydia for a night.

He gave her a sad smile. "I just thought you could use someone to talk to."

"I don't really want to talk. I'd like to do other things to get my mind off of everything."

"Just wait for me, okay?" He almost sounded resigned to her request, even after just telling her that he didn't want to make this a friends-with-benefits situation.

"Okay," she told him.

He leaned forward and kissed her hard on the mouth. It had been a short but powerful kiss. As soon as she got into it, he was already backing away. Then, he headed toward the DJ booth.

When the door closed behind him, Trihn's bravado disintegrated. She tried to be so strong for everyone else, but she was dying on the inside.

How could Preston and Lydia be getting married? A sob escaped her, and she smacked her hand over her mouth to stifle it. She could not break down about this—not in public and definitely not at Posse with all her friends here.

Trihn snatched up her purse and hurried back into the club. She beelined for the door. She knew that she had promised Damon that she would wait for him to get off work, but she couldn't stay trapped in the club all night, feeling horrible.

Trihn didn't see Bryna or Stacia, so she flagged down Maya. "Hey, if you see the girls, will you tell them that I took a cab home?"

"Sure. Why are you leaving already?" Maya asked.

"I just don't feel like partying."

"I saw you with Damon. Are things not going well with that?"

Trihn shook her head. "No, they're not. I'm still beat up about my breakup, and I just want to sleep." Her voice broke on the last word, and she worried that, by talking about this, she was going to start crying. She took a deep breath and dug her fingers into the bar to try to stop herself from reacting to everything that was piling on top of her head.

"Okay. I'll tell them, but I wish you would stay."

Trihn swallowed hard. "Can't. Love you."

"Text me when you get home!"

Trihn waved at Maya and then rushed out the front doors of Posse. She inhaled the wintry desert air and flagged down a cab. It took her across town, and after she paid, she hurried up the elevator.

Dropping her purse and jacket in the living room, she stripped out of her corset top and skirt and buried herself in her comforter in the sexy lingerie that she had gotten earlier that afternoon. She could have gotten laid in the lingerie, but instead, she was curled up in the fetal position, trying not to cry. She had shed so many tears two summers ago because of Preston, and now after all of that, Lydia was going to marry him.

Without even meaning to, tears leaked from her eyes. She felt like a ton of bricks were resting on her chest. She didn't want to feel like this.

"Fuck," she whispered into the silence.

Her efforts were for naught. Deep sobs escaped her body, and she swiped uselessly at the tears on her cheeks. She felt like screaming and yelling and throwing a tantrum. She wanted to go back to that moment when she had first met Preston and erase his existence from the universe. *How could one man cause so much heartbreak?*

Her first love.

Her first boyfriend.

Her first everything.

And then he had thrown it all back in her face, as if everything she had given him meant nothing.

And that was what she meant to him.

Nothing.

And that was what she felt like.

Nothing.

And that was what she would be.

Nothing.

ELEVEN

BLACK SMEARS MARRED HER PILLOWCASE.

Trihn didn't even want to know what her face looked like if her pillow seemed to have come out on the wrong end of a war zone.

After staying up, crying for hours, she had finally fallen into a fitful slumber. Her chest ached, but thankfully, her eyes were dry. She reached for her phone on the nightstand. She cursed when she saw that she had let it die. She plugged it in and trudged to the bathroom to shower off last night's crippling depression.

She pulled her wet hair up into a ballet bun and then changed into some lounge clothes. She checked her now charged phone and saw that she had a bunch of missed calls and texts. Her head ached from just looking at all the people who had tried to reach out to her. She was the most introverted extrovert out there, and today was a day to shut the phone off, crawl back into bed, and start over.

The only message she would check was the voice mail from a number she didn't know. It might be important. People didn't leave voice mails unless it was important, and then she could text them back.

She pressed the message and then lay back in bed and closed her eyes.

"Hey, Trihn. It's Damon."

Trihn popped up in surprise. *What the hell?*

"I got your number from Maya. She seemed worried about you before you left, and you never texted her to let her know you made it home. So, now, I'm worried about you, too. Well, now, I'm more worried. I thought you were going to wait for me. Anyway, I just hope you're okay. Call me back to let me know if you're okay or if you need anything."

The voice mail ended, and Trihn rolled over and buried her face in her pillow. She'd forgotten to text Maya. She jotted out a quick text to let Maya know she was alive, but she couldn't handle Damon right now.

She needed to talk to someone who understood what she was going through. She hadn't told Bryna or Stacia or anyone else why she had decided to come to LV State.

Instead of responding to the rest of her mountain of text messages, she dialed her friend Renée's number. Growing up, they had danced at the New York City Dance House, and then Renée had accepted a full ride to Juilliard, going on to pursue her dream of becoming a professional ballerina. It was impressive for anyone, but Renée hadn't had the best upbringing, as an African American female in the Bronx.

"Well, this is a pleasant surprise," Renée said when she answered the phone. "What can I do for you, hooker?"

"Is that any way to talk to your best friend?"

"The only way, as far as I'm concerned. How is it, being back in fabulous Las Vegas?" she trilled.

"Meh," Trihn said softly. "My boyfriend broke up with me. I had a one-night stand with a guy who wants to date me, but I'm too emotionally fucked up to commit to anything, except crying myself to sleep. Oh, and did I mention that Preston and Lydia got *engaged* last night?"

"Shut the fuck up!" Renée cried.

"Yep."

"I sympathize with you about the first two things, but Lydia and Preston! Tell me you told her to go fuck herself when she said they were getting married."

"Not exactly."

"Trihn! This guy ruined your life. You can't just let him win."

"He already won!" Trihn cried. "He won back at the stupid fucking Hamptons, Renée! Now, they're getting married. And she asked me to be the maid of honor."

Renée snorted. "That's fucking rich. Lydia never ceases to amaze me. It's like she rewrote her own version of history, just forgetting everything that had happened that drove you to Las Vegas in the first place."

"History is told by the winners," Trihn murmured.

A part of her desperately wanted to be back in New York right now, so she and Renée could have this talk in person. They could go to the studio afterward and take class until her muscles were too sore to continue. But she had chosen Vegas, and she loved her life and friends here. Just hearing Renée's voice though made Trihn miss home.

"You absolutely cannot go to that wedding, and you definitely can't be her maid of honor," Renée told her.

"She's my sister."

"Seriously?"

Trihn heard another voice on the other end of the line, and then Renée muffled the phone.

"You talk some sense into her," Trihn heard Renée say to someone else.

"Hello?" Ian said into the phone a few seconds later.

Trihn's and Ian's parents would vacation together throughout the year. Since she was a kid, she had spent nearly every summer, spring, and winter break with him and his family. He was at Columbia, studying computer science, and since she had been out of town, his crush on her had disappeared, and he had a blossoming relationship with Renée. Trihn thought it was adorable.

"Hey, Ian."

"Renée said that Lydia and Preston got engaged?"

"Yeah, they did. Last night."

"You're not thinking of going, are you?"

"She's my sister, Ian," she whispered. It felt like that should mean something.

"And a horrible one."

"Ian—"

"She chose a guy over you, her own sister. I was there. I remember how you were that day. Renée and I both do. Just think about it. She wouldn't do this if the roles were reversed."

Trihn buried her head in her pillow and reconsidered this wanting-to-be-in-New York thing. Her friends knew her a bit too well.

"Shouldn't I be the bigger person?" she mumbled into the phone.

"If you want to be miserable," he said.

There was another scuffle on the other line, and then Renée was talking again, "You do not want or need to be the bigger person. Lydia never apologized to you, and she's still dating the douche bag. He's probably cheated on her and given her some kind of disease by now. She'd deserve it."

"I don't know. I just found out. I need more time to process."

"Yeah, well, if you come back to New York for this shit, I'm going to beat your scrawny ass. That's a promise."

Trihn laughed a real laugh for the first time in what felt like weeks. "I miss you."

"We miss you, too, beautiful. But we have to get to class. City never sleeps, hooker."

"Love you guys. Bye."

When Trihn hung up, she felt an eensy bit better. It was enough to send Damon a text that said she was alive and had made it home in one piece. But it was not enough to get out of bed.

In fact, she spent the next three weeks either lounging around or hiding out in the studio at school.

All design students were given after-hours access to the studio. Most of the time would be spent putting extra hours into the techniques they had been learning in class or working on various fashion show projects. The senior students in the fashion show would work overtime all week, tweaking designs and patterns into beautiful creations. The show wasn't for another two months, but everyone had seemed to be in a constant fever.

The studio was the only place Trihn could find inspiration anymore. And even though she was supposed to be helping the models for the show, she found herself sketching her own clothes and working in the studio to see her designs come to life. Since she was a kid, she had done some of sewn her own clothes at home, but it was always a hobby, just something she did for fun. It was easy to fall back into it when she needed to take her mind off of everything.

Trihn was sewing the final touches on a skirt that she was going to give to Maya to wear at work when she felt a presence over her shoulder.

"Can I help you?" Trihn asked, stopping the sewing machine. She glanced up at the person standing behind her. She had never seen the woman before. She was probably one of the senior students who Trihn didn't know.

"Whose design are you helping with?" she asked. The woman was in a fashionable black skirt suit that looked as if it had been made for her with a bright purple silk blouse that tied around her neck. Her red hair was pinned back off her face, but it clearly had its own natural bounce.

Trihn raised an eyebrow. "Mine."

"Really?"

"Yes, really." Trihn couldn't help sounding snappish. Normally, she could work in here all alone without anyone even noticing her, let alone bothering her. It pulled her out of her Zen.

"And this dress?" the woman asked.

She fingered the black dress Trihn had nearly finished this afternoon. The design had been stuck in her head for days, and she had it almost perfect. It was an all black number that crisscrossed across the collarbones with cutouts at the sides and hugged every inch of her body. She wanted to wear it out the next time she had enough energy to go to Posse, but it wasn't quite ready yet. And neither was she.

"Mine, too." Trihn went back to sewing the skirt.

"Hmm…"

Trihn sighed heavily. "What?"

"I love the lines, but if you pull in this hem right here and hand-sew darts here," she said, pointing out the very problem that had been staring Trihn in the face all day, "I think it would be spectacular."

Trihn snatched up the dress and assessed what the woman had said. "Wow. Yeah. I hadn't thought about that. Thank you."

"I assume I'll be seeing this piece in the fashion show later this semester."

"Yeah, right," Trihn said with a laugh. "Not unless someone steals it."

"What does that mean exactly?" the woman asked. "You are one of the senior fashion majors, are you not?"

"No, I'm a sophomore. I just came to do this for fun." Trihn shrugged. "But one day."

The woman shook her head and then glanced between the skirt and dress. "Do you have any more pieces in the work or sketches I could look at?"

"Um…yeah. Sure," Trihn said. "Hold on." She pulled out a notebook from her bag and handed it over to the woman. She looked through it for several minutes while Trihn worked on the skirt, humming to herself all along.

"Well, it seems that your day has arrived."

Trihn looked at her with wide eyes. "What do you mean?"

"I don't believe we've been formally introduced. I normally attend the courses for juniors and seniors. I'm Teena Hart."

She held her hand out, and Trihn numbly took it.

Teena Hart.

The Teena Hart.

Trihn couldn't believe this was happening.

"And you are?"

"Sorry. Trihnity Hamilton, but my friends just call me Trihn."

"That name sounds familiar. How do I know you?"

"I transferred in late last year from NYU. My mother is Linh Hamilton...with *Glitz* magazine," she added.

"Oh! Linh! Of course I know her. She's wonderful. I was aware that you were coming here, but I didn't realize..." She trailed off. "Your talent is amazing for a second-year student. I know talent when I see it, and I'm moving you into the fashion show this year. You'll need all the practice you can get."

"Wait...what?" Trihn asked, dumbfounded.

"Your designs will be featured in the fashion show."

"But I'm a sophomore," she stammered out.

"There is no age or class requirement. I can tell you have talent. So, you'd better get to work. You're a couple of weeks behind the other students." Teena smiled at her. "It was nice meeting you, Trihn."

In shock, Trihn just stared at her retreating back. *What had just happened?*

Teena Hart had appreciated her designs. She'd liked them enough to feature Trihn in the fashion show that was typically reserved for senior students.

A smile broke onto her face, and she did a twirl.

This was exactly what she needed. She would have a million things to do to get ready, but she could do it. She would have to get all the requirements from her design teacher tomorrow, so she could get started.

She carefully folded her work away and darted out of the studio. She sent off texts to Bryna, Stacia, and Maya, letting them know she had good news and that they needed to go to Posse tonight to celebrate. She wished that the new dress was ready, but she couldn't risk wearing it now that it was going to be in the fashion show.

Trihn returned home to an empty house and started digging around in her sketchbook box for the book that she would need for her next project. She knew it was around here somewhere. If she was going to do this fashion show, she would need something with a bang, and she had the perfect idea, a design she'd done a few weeks before Christmas. She distinctly remembered drawing the dress.

Her heart sank.

"Fuck," she whispered.

She remembered the last time she'd had it. She had been drawing in it at Neal's house and didn't remember ever bringing it home.

Trihn had been adamant about leaving everything at Neal's place for him to toss out or whatever he wanted to do with her things. But not that sketchbook. She needed that one.

Taking a deep breath, she fished out her phone. She had responses from her friends, saying that they were going to meet her at the house to go out and were happy to hear that she was happy. But that enthusiasm was falling away as she sent a message to Neal that she'd never wanted to send.

Hey. I think I left something at your place. Can I come over and get it?

Is this some pathetic attempt to get back together with me?

I just need my sketchbook.

Come on over. I'm sure you've missed me.

Trihn cursed under her breath and then quickly changed. She would just meet the girls at Posse after she went to get her notebook from Neal. She didn't want an audience for this. She doubted it was going to be pretty.

TWELVE

FIVE HUNDRED CARS LITTERED THE STREET in front of Neal's place.

"What the actual fuck?" Trihn's eyes scanned the row of cars. She had never seen this many people parked outside of his place.

She had to drive practically a mile away from the house to find a parking spot. She trudged the distance back to his place and cursed herself for the sexy Louboutins that graced her feet. She could dance in them for hours, but one normal walk pissed her off to no end.

Or maybe it was just the anticipation of seeing Neal.

She hadn't heard one peep from him since he'd slammed that door in her face. Now, her stomach was in knots as she was about to come face-to-face with him all over again.

Trihn took a deep breath and walked up the driveway. He was the one who had dumped her. She didn't have anything else to say to him. She just needed her sketchbook, and then she would get out of there. She had done enough dwelling in the past lately.

She could hear music through the door and was surprised there hadn't already been a noise complaint. She tentatively knocked, unsure of what she would find inside.

Neal had always hated the fact that she loved to party. He had his tight-knit group of friends that he liked to go out with, but he'd claimed it was nothing like her hanging out with Bryna and Stacia. She had believed him until the moment a chick opened the door in a skimpy skirt and bralette top. She had electric-blue hair shaved on one side and thick dark eyeliner.

The girl gave Trihn a once-over and then laughed. "Wrong house," she said before starting to slam the door in Trihn's face.

Trihn's hand shot out. "I'm here to see Neal."

"Really?" she asked. She seemed a little drunk or high or something. Her eyes were glazed, and she looked out of it.

"Yeah. So, if you'll just excuse me." Trihn walked past the girl without another word.

The house was a wreck. Everywhere, people were holding red Solo cups brimming with beer, and the smell of pot clogged her lungs the instant she stepped inside. She coughed twice and pressed through the throng of people.

"How do you know Neal? You're a little out of place," the girl said, still behind Trihn.

"It really doesn't matter. I just need to see Neal, and then I have somewhere else to be."

"He's probably in the kitchen with the keg."

Trihn startled. "Keg?"

Maybe she was at the wrong house. Neal had never been to a kegger in his life that she hadn't forced him to attend. There was no way that he had a keg in his house.

Trihn pushed her way into the kitchen, and there he was, exactly as she remembered him...except not.

There was definitely a keg in his kitchen. He had a red Solo cup in his hand, and beer pong was set up on a table. She blinked to try to clear the image, but it didn't go away.

Neal finally noticed her standing there, and a slow smile spread on his face. He held his arms wide and laughed. "Well, look who we have here."

"I just came for my sketchbook. Didn't realize this would be a bad time," she said softly. She was having a hard time mixing the Neal she had known with this reality before her.

"It's not a bad time. This is a perfect time. Come have a drink, Trihn. This is right up your alley," Neal teased, gesturing to the keg.

"*You're* Trihn?" the girl with blue hair asked from behind her.

Oh, great. My reputation preceded me. "Neal, the sketchbook?"

"Too good for our party?" Neal asked.

He strolled over to her, and she knew that walk. He was wasted. And when Neal got drunk, he either got arrogant or mean. It was worse when he was both. Tonight was not her lucky night.

"You broke up with me. I just want to get my stuff and get out of your life. So, can we hurry this up?" she asked.

She tried to keep her voice even and level, but by the way he was looking at her, she knew that she had failed.

"Is that what you really want?"

Neal ran his knuckles down her cheek, and she flinched away from him.

"Stop. Why are you doing this?" she whispered.

He had ended things. He had stomped on her heart. He was the one who was supposed to be cold and distant. She didn't want him to touch her...yet her heart betrayed her. His touch was comforting and easy. She had stayed with him all that time because everything about him was familiar. But she couldn't do this tug-of-war.

"What do you think? That I want you back?" he asked, taking a hit to his ego with her rejection.

She knew it tipped him over the edge from arrogant into mean.

"Kicking you to the curb was the best day of my life."

"Fine," she said. She would not cry. Her heart was pitter-pattering around in her chest, and she had to breathe in and out through her mouth to control it. But she would not leak one tear. "Can I have my fucking sketchbook now?"

"Yeah, let's get it."

The girl grabbed his arm as he passed and said something into his ear.

"Just stay here, Blu," Neal said, brushing her off.

Blu's eyes found Trihn, and she knew somehow that they were together. It pinched her insides that he had moved on this quickly. And it piqued the deep, dark curiosity within her that wanted to know if Blu had been at his house the day of their breakup, if she was the reason this had all come crashing down.

Trihn passed Blu and couldn't help looking her over, wondering what Blu had that she didn't. When their eyes locked, it was like looking into a mirror, and Trihn realized that this girl was probably wondering the same thing. It made Trihn even sadder about the situation.

She hurried back through the house and to Neal's bedroom. He opened the door, and a couple was making out on his bed.

"Get the fuck out," he said.

The two looked at them in a haze of lust before realizing who it was, and then they disappeared. Neal let her enter first. He closed the door behind her, drowning out some of the music. Trihn tried not to look around. There were too many memories here, and she didn't want to spiral out of control.

Neal entered his closet and came back out a second later with the sketchbook in his hand. He extended it to her, but when she reached for it, he yanked it back really quick.

"Real funny," she said, holding her hand out.

"What are you going to give me for it?"

"What do you mean?" she asked warily. "It's my notebook. I just want it back."

"Come on, Trihn. You and I both know that you're just using this as an excuse to get back with me."

Her eyebrows rose. "Um…no. It's really not. As far as I'm concerned, you cheated on me and then kicked me to the curb. I thought you made your point pretty clear." When he didn't deny it, she rolled her eyes and felt her heart harden. "So, that's how it was then? Blu, I'm assuming?"

Neal shrugged, nonchalant, and changed the subject. "What do you need another sketchbook for? You have a million at your house. You only need this to try to get with me. Well, I'm here. Have your way with me," he said.

He laughed and cocked his head to the side, as if in invitation. But she saw through his bravado. He was drunk and rambling. Some thought you could hear the truth when people were intoxicated, but she sure hoped this wasn't the truth out of his mouth.

"I need that notebook because it has a dress in it I'm designing for school. That's it. No ulterior motive."

"I know you must miss me."

Trihn breathed out heavily. "You know, I really don't."

Neal's nostrils flared at her dismissal. "You're probably dying for sex."

"Yeah, I am," she admitted.

He smirked and leaned toward her.

She grabbed the notebook from him. "But just not from you."

Trihn yanked open the door to his room and dashed down the hall. She didn't care that Neal was drunk and high. The way he'd acted was completely uncalled for. *Had he always been like this, and I'd just ignored it?*

She pushed her way through the crowd in the living room and out the door. Once she was back out in the clean air, she took shuddering deep breaths.

Neal might have broken up with her, but he had just given her the keys to move on. She had thought that seeing him would cause all the old emotions to flood back in her. She'd worried that she really would miss him since he had been out of her life.

But she didn't.

It had just reinforced the fact that she was better off without him. She felt like a weight had been lifted off her shoulders.

And she knew exactly what she needed to do.

"Hello?" Damon said uneasily into the phone.

"Hey. This is Trihn."

"Yeah, I know. What's up? Everything okay?"

"Are you working tonight?" she asked.

"Nah. Tonight is my day off. Why?"

"Can we meet up somewhere?" She took a deep breath and waited for his response. She knew that he had said he would change her mind, but she hoped she hadn't ruined it by ignoring him the past couple of weeks.

"Uh, yeah." She could hear him shuffling around in the background. "Did you want to meet at Posse?"

"Not really. Just somewhere we can talk."

"The radio station on campus?" he suggested. "I still have a key, and no one should be there right now."

She was glad he hadn't suggested his place. She didn't trust herself not to jump him if a bed were nearby, and she wanted to get everything out in the open before going down that route again. She owed him that much.

"Sure. Sounds good. Meet you there in twenty. Is that good with you?"

"Yeah. Yeah, that works."

"Cool."

"And, Trihn?" he said before she could say anything else. "It's really great to hear from you—unexpected but still really good."

She smiled bright and nodded even though he couldn't see her. "I'm glad. See you in a few."

Trihn hung up and started her drive back toward campus. Her sketchbook was sitting pretty in the passenger seat, reminding her that she was making the right decision. Her heart was torn—not on Damon. She liked Damon even though she had been ignoring that. It was just torn over whether getting into a relationship would be a good idea. Anything that had the potential to trample her heart made her wary.

As Trihn neared the campus radio station, a message came in from Bryna.

Where are you?

"Shit," she murmured. She pulled into the radio station parking lot and replied.

Have to cancel. Got into it with Neal, and now, I'm meeting Damon. Sorry!

Yay! Go off and have a scandalously sexy Brit bang fest, and tell me all the juicy details later!

Trihn laughed and shook her head. *Leave it to Bryna.*

Only a minute after she'd arrived, his car parked next to hers. They both stepped out and he smiled when he saw her.

"Hey." He walked around her car and pulled her into an embrace.

She wrapped her arms around his neck. "Hey yourself."

When he released her, he nodded his head toward the door, and they walked to the building together. He used his phone to illuminate the door and then produced a well-worn key from his pocket. The lock turned easily. Twisting the door handle, Damon let her enter the dark space first.

"Wow. It's a little creepy in here," she whispered.

"Yeah, sorry," he said. "Give me a minute." He fiddled with a box and then flipped on a series of switches. The hallway lit up before them. "Here we go. This way."

Trihn followed him into the studio. It was a relatively small room, all things considered. A bunch of computer monitors sat before a keyboard and a pretty impressive-looking soundboard. A speaker hung suspended from the ceiling. A few seats for interviews with musicians were placed in front of the soundboard. Trihn had heard local artists come on campus radio to try to gain exposure with the college crowd.

Damon sank into the seat behind the soundboard and habitually fiddled with a few of the controls.

Trihn walked around to his side. She leaned against the desk. "I'm sorry," she finally said.

His eyes shot to her. "For what?"

"I haven't been myself the last couple of weeks, and that was the girl you got to know. My breakup really messed me up. Then, you had to see me when I found out about my sister's wedding." Trihn choked up when she mentioned the wedding. That part still burned with a fiery passion. "Her fiancé is an asshole, and I was shocked when I found out the other night. Basically, you and I have gotten off to the wrong start."

"I kind of liked our start."

She let loose a breath. "You liked the sex, but you wanted more."

"Look, I'm sorry, too. I wanted more. I *want* more with you, but that doesn't mean I have to force you into it."

"I don't feel forced. I just feel like I have major trust issues. And it's hard, letting in someone new."

He nodded in understanding, but she knew he could never really understand.

She moved forward and sat down in his lap. Her hands snaked up around his neck. "But I'll try for you."

His arms circled her waist, and he smiled the most brilliant smile. "I like the sound of that," he said before kissing her.

THIRTEEN

Wear white. Something you don't mind getting ruined.

TRIHN RAISED HER EYEBROWS at the text she had just received from Damon.

All white and something I could get ruined. Is he planning to tear it off of me? Now, that would be fun.

They'd spent a couple of hours in the radio station, talking. Damon had picked up a few instruments around the location and played for her. It had been a nice, chill evening, something she hadn't realized that she needed.

Now, they were going to go on their first official date, and after that bizarre request, she really had no clue what to expect.

An hour later, Damon knocked on the door, dressed in jeans and a plain white T-shirt. He had a bouquet of tulips in his hand. "For you."

"Thank you," she said, taking them from him. She found the vase she had put the last bouquet in and placed the flowers inside.

He came up behind her and kissed her shoulder. Then, he slipped something in her hand.

"What's this?" she asked. She turned to face him and opened her palm to reveal a Hershey's Kiss. She laughed. She could get used to this.

She opened the wrapper and popped the chocolate into her mouth. It melted almost instantly, and Damon leaned forward, capturing her lips in a searing kiss. The taste of the chocolate lingered between them.

"Oh, I like the kiss," he said.

"Which one?"

"Both."

He kissed her again and then had to drag himself back. "Come on. This isn't an event you'll want to be late to."

"Where are we going?" Trihn asked, following him out of her apartment.

They hurried out of the building and into Damon's car before he answered, "So, we're going to see this DJ."

"Cool. Like you?"

"Sort of." He revved the engine and started to drive them out of the city. "We started doing shows around the same time, but now, he's kind of a big deal. He got a record deal, and his shows are pretty packed."

"All for a DJ?" she asked curiously.

"Well, yeah. I mean, Calvin Harris is recording with huge celebrities, and Skrillex has his own gig. They're huge in the music industry. If you make it, you make it. And Poet is on his way."

"Poet?" Trihn asked. She tried to hold back her laugh. "He just goes by Poet?"

"Yeah. His last name is Poe, and the label thought he'd be more recognizable with a stage name." Damon shrugged. "Poet was his nickname in high school because he was always scribbling lyrics into his notebook."

"Did you go to school with this Poe…Poet guy?"

"No, but I have a friend who did."

"You seem to know a lot of people."

"That's the industry," he said with a smile.

"What's his real name?"

Damon glanced at her. "James Poe. Not exactly the sexy stage name they were looking for."

"And what about Damon Stone? Would they make you change that?" she asked curiously.

"I wouldn't let bigwig asshole music producers who were paying me thousands of dollars to do what I loved change anything." He looked over at her with a smirk on his face.

"Well, for the record, I think Damon Stone stays. You don't want them to call you something like Stoned or Stoner."

"I heard that enough in high school," he said. He brushed a hand back through his unruly dark hair, and the strands fell back into place almost instantly. "And what about you?"

"Me?"

"You're going to be in that fashion show. What's your line going to be called?"

Trihn chewed on her bottom lip. "You know…I never thought about that. Maybe just Trihnity."

"That's not you. Go with just Trihn."

"You think?"

"Yeah. Then, when I'm on the red carpet, people can ask me who I'm wearing, and I can say Trihn."

She burst out laughing. "You are insanely way ahead of yourself…but I like it."

His eyes lit up at her enthusiasm. "Good. I like it, too."

A few minutes later, Damon pulled into a parking lot. He had a tag that let them pass the crazy line of cars waiting to get into a general admission section. But even their passes kept them pretty far from the venue. She was glad that she had chosen to wear boots tonight with her white jeans and shirt. The jeans weren't exactly something she wanted to ruin, but he'd said white, and she couldn't help herself when it came to dressing fashionable for an event, especially a first date.

Damon handed over two passes to a guy, and he nodded his head for them to take the line to the right. Someone checked her small purse and gave them each a handful of glow sticks, and then they were through.

They entered what more or less looked like a closed-in mosh pit. There was a stage at the far end of the football field–sized area. Damon took her hand and seamlessly threaded his way through the crowd, getting as close to the stage as they could get.

In confusion, Trihn held out her glow sticks to Damon.

"You're going to need those," he said.

After breaking them in half, she pushed the ends together and created a necklace as well as a few bracelets. Damon had a long chain up his arm. The sky darkened, and soon, the entire audience was glowing. Black lights flickered to life around them, illuminating their white clothing, and then the music started.

"Welcome to Poet's Paint War. Rock on."

The music grew with intensity as DJ Poet got into the groove. The crowd immediately started dancing all around Trihn, but she was focused on one word that had come out of Poet's mouth.

"Paint?" Trihn asked.

Then, she felt it. A giant glob of neon green paint landed in the middle of her white T-shirt. Damon laughed at her reaction just as more paint rained down on them.

"Where the hell did you bring me?" she asked.

His hands landed on her hips, and their bodies moved together, as if they were made for each other. "A rave."

"This isn't any old rave."

"It's like those color runs everyone goes on about but with dancing and good music. And you."

Paint covered their bodies. Her skin was already plastered with neon green, orange, pink, and yellow. It was on her clothes and skin and in her hair.

Everyone threw their hands up in the air and danced with their glow sticks over head.

Losing her inhibitions, Trihn threw her arms around Damon's neck and leaned against his body. She teasingly circled her hips as the techno backbeat picked up the tempo. The crowd around them started jumping, but Trihn leaned forward and pressed her mouth to Damon's.

Their heated bodies slammed against each other, and paint-slick wet hands grasped onto bare skin. Desire flared in her stomach. Lust mixed with hope and the promise of something real. She had feelings she had sworn off for undeniably good reasons. But his kisses tasted like chocolate. His skin was a canvas she wanted to turn into a masterpiece. His seductive movements hypnotized her. Cognizant thought fled, leaving behind something she hadn't felt in a long time—abandon.

Damon brought out the old Trihn, the one who had danced on rooftops in Milan, flirted with strangers in London, and lived her life without fear.

But fear had a way of eating you up from the inside out.

Slowly, over time, fear had done its job and mingled with his bastard cousins—doubt, regret, and depression—leaving a hollowed out corpse of a person.

Damon crept into those empty spaces and infused them with light. His mere presence seemed to rid her of the dark despair that had fallen on her shoulders like a familiar blanket.

This could be real. This could work out. She at least owed it to herself to give it a real shot. If she opened herself up one more time and found heartbreak waiting around the corner, then it would really be the end. She couldn't survive it a third time.

And Damon's soft kisses over the pulse of the music honestly made her believe it was possible.

The DJ played well into the night, but Damon pulled Trihn from the crowd when he got to the point where he couldn't seem to take his hands off of her. They sped back into the city, and without a word, Damon drove them to his place.

He parked, rushed around to the other side of the car, and held the door open for her. She sympathetically looked back at his painted cover interior.

"Don't worry about it. It all washes out," Damon said before drawing her in for another kiss.

He couldn't seem to get enough of her. At the show, they'd been all over each other—not that anyone else had noticed or had been lucid enough to care.

They took the stairs to his studio. Trihn kicked off her shoes at the entrance. Damon took her hand, and she was careful not to touch anything as they walked through his suite.

When they got to the bathroom, he closed the door behind them and turned the shower on full blast. He peeled her destroyed white shirt over her head and tossed it to the floor. He kissed across her collarbone and then down her stomach before sinking to his knees before her.

Her heart stuttered as she watched him worshipping her body. His fingers deftly unsnapped the button on her jeans and dragged the zipper to the base. Then, he took his time inching her once white jeans off her legs and threw them into a pile with her shirt. His hands crawled up her legs, admiring every bare inch of her skin.

He moved to her face and smudged away some paint on her cheek. "There. Better."

"One smudge, and that was all it took?"

"You're my pièce de résistance."

Their lips met again, bridging the distance between them. He snapped her bra free with one hand. She felt exposed with him in so much clothing, so she worked her way up his shirt. He pulled away long enough for her to remove it. His jeans followed, but she wasn't as patient as he was. Her fingers tugged at the material, stripping him out of everything as quickly as she could. He made no protest as his boxers fell to the floor next, showing just what their stripping had done to him.

Her body quivered at the thought of being with him again. She hadn't forgotten for one second how good he was in bed or the pleasure he brought forth from her body. She had shoved that knowledge in the dark recesses of her mind when she was too afraid to move forward— but no longer.

She stepped out of her last article of clothing, and they both walked under the steaming hot spray. The shower floor was soon the same neon wash that had coated their bodies.

Damon poured soap into his hands and massaged it into her back. Her muscles released any remaining tension at the touch. His hands slid down her back, around her stomach, over her shoulders, and then her neck, removing any trace of the paint. Then, they dipped down to cover her breasts. He kneaded them in his hands, pinching the nipples, causing her to arch backward into his body.

Then, with a clean hand, he trailed lower, caressing her clit before delving into her aching core. She could feel his stiff cock pressing against her lower back, but he made no move to take her. He just worked her body until she was trembling beneath the hot water, coming on his fingers.

As she came down from her high, Trihn rested her hand on the wall to steady herself. When she turned to face him, lust hung heavy between them. He grabbed her by the back of the neck and crushed their lips together.

"Fuck, I've missed you," he growled into her mouth.

"Me, too," she admitted.

She had no idea how she'd ever thought this could have been a one-night stand. Her body was dying for him—his touch, his lips, his cock. The built-up sexual tension between them was a chasm that was cracking wide open.

She couldn't even wait to get out of the shower, and Damon clearly had the same idea. He turned her around to face the opposite wall. Seeing what he was thinking, she bent in half at the waist and put her hands on the shower bench.

His dick slid against her slick body, and she shuddered. Her body reflexively backed up toward him, pulsing and ready to take him. He guided himself to her opening with one hand while holding her hips in place with the other. Then, he shoved forward, and her body shook as he forced himself all the way in to the hilt.

"Oh God," she cried. "Wow."

"Yeah," he said, short of breath.

He started pumping into her, and even though she was warmed up, this position hit so deep that her body rocked forward with each thrust. He leaned his wet body against hers, holding her in place, as water streamed down onto them. Their bodies smacked together over the sound of the shower.

Wet hair still matted with paint hung forward in front of her. Her slick hands clutched on to the acrylic lining of the shower seat. It had been a while since they had last been together, and she was craving another release.

Damon grunted behind her, and she could tell he was there with her.

"Fuck, Trihn," he groaned. "Oh, fuck. This is the best fucking view."

"God, you feel so good."

"Yes. Oh, fuck. I'm going to come."

"Please. Oh God, yes!" she screamed just as her own climax hit. "Oh yes…yes…yes. Fuck…fuck."

His grip on her hips was painful as he jackhammered into her before coming and repeating her words almost verbatim.

Damon pulled out of her, and Trihn fell forward onto her knees as her equilibrium disappeared.

"Hey. Are you okay?" he asked, reaching for her.

"You're kidding, right?" she said breathlessly. "I've never felt this good in my life."

He helped her to her feet and pressed another kiss to her lips. "That makes two of us, love."

FOURTEEN

"SO MUCH FOR TAKING IT SLOW," Trihn said.

Damon rolled over in bed and pulled her naked body toward him. He nuzzled into her neck and kissed her shoulder. "I didn't say I wanted to take things slow. I said I wanted you to be mine."

"That's not exactly how I remember it, but it's sweet." Trihn twisted around and wrapped her arms around his neck.

"I'm just glad you're here now."

"Speaking of that," she said, unwinding from his body, "I have to get to class."

Damon groaned. "Are you sure?"

"I get the full instructions for the fashion show from my design professor today. So, yeah, kind of important."

He reached out for her, but she slithered off the bed and into a pair of his shorts and oversized T-shirt. Her ruined clothes weren't going to be useful.

"I can keep this, right?" she asked with a wink.

"Fuck, you look good in my clothes. Granted, you look good in everything."

"Model," she said with a dismissive shrug.

"Well, will my beautiful model be coming back over later today?"

"If you're lucky," she quipped.

"Clearly, I am."

Trihn laughed and shook her head. "It depends on how long I have to be at the design studio tonight or how much I'm panicking about the work I have to do to make this fashion show a reality come the end of April."

"You'll get it done."

"Not if I don't get out of here." Trihn bent down and kissed him once more before pushing herself to hurry out of his apartment.

She needed to get out of there before she forgot everything and lay in his bed all day and night. He made it easy to ignore the rest of the world.

Trihn saw Eric's Jeep idling in a parking space. She jogged to him and hopped inside.

"We have to quit meeting like this," Eric said with an easy smile.

"Next time, I'll make sure I drive to here first. I hate inconveniencing you."

"Trihn, I'm joking. I don't care. It's just good to see you with a smile on your face again."

"Yeah, well, I'm sure it's too good to be true."

He gave her one of his signature looks. "Give it a chance before you sink the ship."

"Yeah, yeah," she said, glancing out the window.

"Also, what the hell did you do last night?"

"What do you mean?" she asked.

He fingered a lock of her dark hair. "You have paint all in your hair. I thought Neal was the artist."

She rolled her eyes. "Ugh. Let's not mention that cheating douche bag. Damon and I went to a paint rave last night."

"Cool. That doesn't sound as fun as what I was thinking."

"I'm sure I don't even want to know."

He smirked at her. "I think I'm going to try it when we get back to your place."

Trihn shook her head in exasperation.

But she didn't ask questions when Eric disappeared into Bryna's room once they'd gotten to the apartment.

She quickly showered out the rest of the paint from her hair, changed, and dashed to her first class. She made it with only a few minutes left to spare. Despite the late start, she felt like she was walking on a cloud. Even though she worried that what she had with Damon was some kind of ticking time bomb, the elation she felt from a new relationship propelled her through the rest of the day.

Soon, she was walking out of her final design class and straight toward her professor.

"Excuse me, Professor Brown. I'm just here for the fashion show paperwork," Trihn said.

"Ah, Trihn. I'm so excited that you're going to be participating." The professor shuffled things around on the desk and then produced a packet. She handed it over. "Here you go. You'll need to submit preliminary sketches of your designs by the beginning of next week. Samples of the clothing material should be in the week after that. We can work on full designs and models in March, so try not to stress. Please let me know if there's anything I can help you with."

"Thank you so much," Trihn said.

Just hearing the list of things she needed to do left her overwhelmed. It was a challenge she wanted to take on, but she knew it was going to be a lot of work. The seniors used the show as their final portfolio, and she was just doing it for the experience. It was a lot of pressure.

She was leafing through the packet on the way out of the classroom when her phone started buzzing noisily in her purse. Her heart stuttered. She hoped it was Damon, but when she glanced down at the phone, she frowned. For a minute, she contemplated letting it go to voice mail so that she wouldn't have to deal with Lydia, but in the end, she pressed the Answer button.

"Hello?"

"Trihn, hey!"

"What's up, Ly?"

"We picked a date!" she practically shrieked into the phone.

Trihn's heart sank. She had known this was coming. Lydia had said they were getting married, so picking a wedding date had, of course, shortly followed. But Damon had successfully taken her mind off the weight of her issues, and she hadn't been prepared for it.

"You did?" Trihn managed to ask when Lydia hadn't said anything more.

"Yes! We're getting married the first Saturday of August."

"So soon?" she whispered.

"Yeah. We didn't think there was any reason to wait."

"Did you already pick out a venue?" Trihn asked. She hated that she was being the supporting sister. All she really wanted to say was, *I don't give a fuck about your wedding. I think you marrying Preston is the worst mistake of your life*, and then hang up.

But she knew Lydia would have been dismissive. She'd never cared what Trihn thought about Preston.

"We're going to get married on the beach at the house in the Hamptons."

Trihn couldn't hold back at that. "Are you fucking joking?"

Her world had fallen apart in the Hamptons. It was the place she had found out that Preston had been cheating on her. It was all bad memories. She couldn't believe Lydia would want that.

"God, Trihn, do we have to do this?"

"You're marrying him, Lydia. After the shit he pulled, you're still going through with it. Fine. I think it's dumb, but if you think you love him and think that he's faithful, then go through with it," Trihn grumbled. "But the beach house?"

"That's where we first really started dating."

"I can't do it, Lydia. I can't pretend to be happy for you and go stand up as a witness to your marriage on that beach."

"Trihn—"

"No," Trihn said. "The answer is no. You're my sister. I love you. But I can't be your maid of honor. I can't act like I support you marrying Preston when I never even supported you dating Preston."

"Is this all because you're still in love with him?" Lydia demanded.

Clearly, Trihn had pissed her off, and Lydia was striking back with the only ammunition she had.

Trihn had given up on loving Preston when she left for Las Vegas. He was her first love, and it hurt, knowing that he'd not only been dating her sister but now intended on marrying her. Trihn felt disoriented by that, but she didn't love him.

Actually, she quite hated him. Just the thought of him made her blood boil. But her hatred for him wasn't jealousy. It was anger for him wrecking their family, for driving her away from New York, and for poisoning her sister.

"No. And the fact that you think that, let alone have the nerve to ask me that, just solidifies my position," Trihn said, her voice like ice. "Just leave me out of this, Lydia."

"Trihn—"

Trihn hung up before she could hear whatever Lydia was about to say. Her hands were shaking when she tossed her phone back into her purse. She walked over to a campus park bench and took a seat. It was still pretty chilly out, but she didn't even notice the conditions. She was processing what had happened.

Standing up to Lydia hadn't been easy. Trihn wanted to be happy for her. With any other groom, she would have been, but with Preston, she just couldn't be.

Her phone started ringing almost immediately. Trihn checked the screen and saw her mother was calling. She silenced the phone, letting it go straight to voice mail. She was sure she'd have a long message from her mother yelling at her for upsetting Lydia. After all, Lydia was the favorite.

But her mother didn't know what had happened that summer. She might be singing a different tune if she did.

When the voice mail notification lit up the screen, Trihn clicked off of it. She didn't need to even listen to it to know what her mother had said.

Instead, with shaky fingers, she dialed Damon's number and waited for him to answer.

"Hey, love. How were your classes?" he asked.

"You wouldn't happen to be in a position to pick me up, take me back to your place, and help me forget the last fifteen minutes, would you?"

"What happened? Are you okay?"

"I just got into a fight with my sister, and my mother called to yell at me. The last thing I want to do is sit around and think about all that."

"I would love to pick you up," he said, "but I'm actually going over to my mum's. You could come if you want...if that isn't weird."

"Hmm...maybe a little weird," she admitted. They'd only been on one actual date, but she felt like she knew him so much better than that after the weeks building up to that date. "But it also sounds nice."

"You sure?" Damon asked.

"Yes."

"All right. I'll see you in a minute."

Trihn sent him a text with where to pick her up on campus, and he arrived a few minutes later. They drove across town and into the nicer suburbs away from campus. She stared out the passenger window, lost in thought. She knew that she had done the right thing with Lydia, but it still hurt that it had come to that, and she couldn't stop obsessing over it.

"Do you want to talk about it?" Damon asked as they pulled off the highway.

"I told my sister I wouldn't be her maid of honor and stand up for her at her wedding," she told him. Saying it aloud sounded so official.

"Wow. That's big. All because the guy's an asshole?"

"He's cheated on her."

"Shit," Damon said under his breath. "You're sure?"

"Yes—at least once though I'm sure there are others," Trihn said. "Cheating is my hard limit. I don't understand how she can overlook it. It breaks people and friends and families. It ruins lives. It forces people to do things they'd never do otherwise. I can't go to that wedding and pretend it's okay."

"I don't have siblings, so I don't think I can weigh in on that. But I couldn't imagine finding out someone had cheated on you and then staying with that person. I'm assuming she knows?"

Trihn snorted. "Yeah, she does."

"Well, I know it must be hard. You feel like you're turning your back on your sister?"

Trihn nodded.

"Kind of sounds like she turned her back on herself."

"Yeah, a long time ago."

Damon pulled into the driveway of his mom's house, effectively ending their conversation. As Trihn got out of the car, she straightened her outfit and fidgeted with her hair. She wished she'd had more warning before meeting

Damon's mom. She might have worn something a little nicer.

"You look great," he said, taking her hand and kissing it. "You ready?"

Trihn took a deep breath and nodded. "Sure."

FIFTEEN

TRIHN HADN'T ENVISIONED meeting Damon's mom on the second date. In fact, maybe she had never thought about meeting his mom—not because she didn't want to. It was something she hadn't ever thought about. She had never met Neal's parents even though they had dated for a year and a half, and he'd come home with her to New York twice. So, meeting Damon's mom just hadn't crossed her mind.

But now that she was thinking about it, her stomach flopped.

Will his mother like me? Does this set the tone of our relationship? Why did I think this would be a good idea?

She hated being nervous. She wanted to be cool and confident, but essentially, she was panicking.

Damon opened the front door, and Trihn followed him into the one-story house.

"Mum! I brought you a surprise," Damon called.

A disjointed song being played on a piano could be heard down the hallway. Damon winced as whoever was playing had missed a few keys.

"In the music room," she called back.

The house was cozy. Pictures lined all the walls. Photographs of Damon at every age looked back at her. Random theater props took up a large portion of the space. As they walked down a hallway, they passed several musical instruments. The space was the perfect testament of the love a mother had for her son and her more creative passions. Trihn already felt at home.

They entered a massive den that had been converted into a music room. A boy no older than ten sat in front of a grand piano positioned in the corner. It completely dwarfed him as he mashed at the keys. Next to the boy sat a middle-aged woman with her hair held back into a bun by a pair of pens.

Damon cleared his throat. "Mum?"

The woman swiveled around on the seat, and the boy stopped playing.

"Damon! Perfect timing." She turned back to the boy. "No, don't stop playing, Joseph. Keep going."

The boy sighed heavily and started up on the piano again. Damon's mom hopped up from her seat.

"Mum, this is the girl I've been telling you about," Damon said.

"Hi. So nice to meet you," Trihn said, extending her hand.

"Don't mind me. I'm more of a hugger," his mom said. She pulled Trihn into a quick embrace. "Trihn, right?"

"Yes, that's right," Trihn said.

She was surprised that Damon had spoken about her. She wasn't that close to her family, and with them so far away, she hadn't discussed anything like her dating life with them. They didn't even know she and Neal had broken up.

"I'm Melanie, but feel free to call me Mel. Everyone does."

"You have a beautiful home, Mel."

Mel snorted. "It's a disaster." She tugged at a loose lock of dark hair. "Don't judge me for it. It's the curse of a creative type. Projects everywhere!"

Trihn laughed. "I like it. Feels very homey."

"Probably for the better. If I haven't changed by now, I'm not changing anytime soon," she said with a smile. "Now, Damon, come take over my lesson with Joseph."

"Mum! Do you only invite me over, so I will teach your lessons for you?" he asked, his British accent thickening around his family.

"Free labor, kid," she said with a wink.

Damon huffed but sat down at the piano. Joseph looked up at him with hero worship. They must have done this before. Damon started helping Joseph with the piece he had been botching.

"My son, the prodigy musician, wasting his talents on a soundboard in nightclubs," Mel said, shaking her head.

"Not wasted," Damon called over his shoulder.

With a smile, Trihn admired the easy flow of him playing the piano as he and his mom teased each other. There was a quality to his music here that resembled his DJ work. It wasn't so much that he just mixed music, but he made masterpieces from existing songs.

"He's so good at that, too," Trihn said.

"She doesn't think it's wasted talent either," Damon said.

"He's right. I wouldn't have spent years in small productions in London if I didn't love it. I know he'll do what he loves, too."

"I think he already is," Trihn mused.

Mel nodded. "Play your girlfriend something cheerful."

Trihn opened her mouth to protest that she wasn't in fact his girlfriend but quickly shut it when Damon hadn't said anything. Instead, he started playing an upbeat tempo.

"Good," Mel said. "Now, while he's distracted, let's slip out. I need to start making dinner."

Trihn laughed as Mel pulled her toward the exit. Damon must have heard their retreat because he switched from his cheery song to Darth Vader's theme song "The Imperial March."

Trihn followed Mel into the kitchen, and her nerves set in all over again. Mel seemed nice and chill, but that didn't mean that Trihn wanted to be alone with her.

What if Mel wanted to get me alone so that she could ask me a bunch of questions about myself?

Trihn had a good family background, excluding the fact that her stupid sister was engaged to her ex-boyfriend.

"So," Mel said, "what do you think we should make?"

"Um...I'm not sure."

"Anything in particular you like? Any allergies?"

Trihn shook her head. "Nope. I'm allergic to penicillin, but I don't think that counts."

"I'll keep that in mind if you get strep throat," Mel said with a smile. "I'm thinking roasted chicken and potatoes with corn on the cob."

"Sounds amazing."

"Great!" Mel pulled a wine-colored apron over her head with lettering in white that said, *I cook with wine. Sometimes, I even add it to the food.*

She started pulling pots and pans out of the cupboards when Trihn's phone began buzzing. Trihn grabbed it out of her bag and silenced it. She winced when she saw that she had already missed two additional texts from her mom.

"Do you need to get that?" Mel asked.

"No," Trihn answered immediately. "It's not important."

She sulked over to Mel, the weight of her mother's phone call resting on her shoulders. She needed to forget about it.

"So, you're a fashion designer, is that right?" Mel asked as she reached into the refrigerator and started removing ingredients.

"Yes. Well, a design major."

"I love that. Fashion designers are artists, like musicians, actors, painters, sculptors. You assess what best drapes the human form. It's fitting since you look like you could be a model."

"I was," Trihn admitted. "While in high school, I modeled some."

Mel raised her eyebrows. "Oh, wow. That's incredible. Fashion design and modeling. Damon mentioned you're a dancer as well."

Trihn nodded. "I was in a ballet company in New York."

"Such a talented person for so young," Mel said. She glanced at Trihn with a smile. "Sounds just like Damon. I see why he likes you."

"He's really great. We just started dating, but I feel like I already know him well. He's so easy to talk to."

"Gets that from his father," Mel said. "Here."

She handed Trihn a potato peeler, and they moved into A rhythm around the kitchen. Trihn's mother was an exceptional cook, and the familiarity in something so basic made her ache with homesickness.

It wasn't that she regretted coming to Las Vegas. She loved her school. Her friends were here. She wouldn't have met Damon. But things would have been a lot different in the city.

"Trihn, I know I don't know you all that well, but is everything all right?" Mel asked.

Trihn blinked up at her through a teary blur. *Shit. Am I crying? How had that happened?* She didn't even have onions to blame it on.

"Yes. Sorry." She wiped at her eyes and looked away, embarrassed.

"Call them mum instincts, but you seem very down for a woman with so much going for her." Mel gave her a concerned smile. "It might be awkward for you, but if you want, you can talk to me. I'm a good listener."

Trihn blew out her breath and wiped at her eyes again. "I'm not normally this much of a mess, but I just got into an argument with my sister. So, my mom has been calling me nonstop, and I know she's just going to yell at me about it."

"What started the argument?"

"My sister is getting married."

Mel tilted her head. "Not a good thing?"

"No, he's a jerk. But my mom and sister are really close, and my mom would never understand why I refused to be there for my sister."

"I bet your mother is more intuitive than you give her credit for. She wants you to be as happy as your sister is, and I doubt she wants to see her daughters fighting. Damon is an only child, but I hated him having arguments with anyone. I couldn't imagine if it were with another sibling."

"Yeah. It's just complicated."

Mel nodded. "It always is. Maybe you should just hear her out, and if you don't like what she has to say, I have a bottle of wine we can open. It's five o'clock somewhere." She pulled out a bottle of wine and set it down in front of Trihn.

Trihn laughed. "Can we open the wine anyway?"

"Way ahead of you." Mel reached for a corkscrew in a drawer and held it in front of her face for Trihn to see. She poured each of them a glass of a pinot grigio.

Trihn took a sip for good luck and then stepped out of the room to call her mom back. She didn't even bother listening to the messages. She would rather go into this blind.

"Trihnity," her mother, Linh, said in a huff.

Trihn glanced over her shoulder and took a few more steps down the hallway, away from the kitchen.

"I've been calling you for an hour. Where have you been?"

"Hey, Mom. I'm great. Doing just fine myself. How have you been?"

"Take this seriously."

Trihn rolled her eyes and moved further out of earshot into an empty room. "For your information, I'm out with this new guy that I'm dating."

"A new guy? What happened to Neal? I really liked him," her mother said, forgetting for a moment why she had called.

"He broke up with me a month ago."

"You didn't tell me," Linh said. She sounded sad.

"Yeah, well, sorry. I've been busy," she said lamely. "Did you want to talk about why you called?"

"I spoke with Lydia."

"I'm sure you did." Trihn ran her hand back through her hair and closed her eyes, waiting for the blowup to happen.

"Do you want to tell me why you're upsetting your sister about this entire thing? She won't tell me anything, except that you won't come to New York for the wedding and that you won't be your sister's maid of honor."

Trihn took a deep breath. *Here goes nothing.* "I can't support Lydia and Preston because he's cheated on her."

"That's absurd."

"And that's the reason I haven't told you."

"Okay," Linh said. "If he did cheat on her—and I'm not certain he did—then Lydia must not know."

"Not exactly," Trihn whispered.

Lydia knew that, while she was dating Preston, Trihn had slept with him. She was pretty sure that he had done it after he and Lydia had become official.

"And you have proof?"

"Sort of."

Her mother sighed. "Maybe both of you just need to cool off. I can't force you to be at your sister's wedding, and if you really have this big of an issue with Preston, then perhaps you should actually work it out with Lydia."

"I think we're past that point."

They had been past that point for a long time.

"I hate to see you two fighting. I'd love to fly you home for a weekend. We could all talk this out, and hopefully, by the end of it, we could go wedding dress shopping in the boutiques. I know you'd love that."

Wedding dress shopping for Lydia sounded amazing—if it wasn't for the fact that she was marrying Preston.

"I don't know, Mom. I just...need time to process all of this."

"Okay. I understand. I'm only a phone call away if you need me. You know that, right?"

"Of course," Trihn said, softening at her mother's words.

"I love you."

"Love you, too." Trihn hung up the phone.

That had gone better than anticipated. It wasn't great, but it wasn't like her conversation with Lydia. Her mom wasn't on Trihn's side about this thing with Preston, but she didn't want to tell her mother the truth. That would make things difficult.

Plus, she couldn't prove that Preston had cheated on Lydia after they had become exclusive. She just had her knowledge of Preston and the fact that he had fucked her at the beach house while there on vacation with Lydia.

"Hey," Damon said behind her.

Trihn quickly turned around. She hadn't even heard the music stop. She had been so wrapped up in her own thoughts. "Hey. Sorry. I didn't realize you were done."

"Yeah, all finished. Are you okay?"

She nodded. "Just talked to my mom. Wasn't as bad as I'd thought it would be. Your mom gave me the courage to give it a try."

"Did that courage come in the form of wine?" he asked, gesturing to her glass.

Trihn took another sip and smiled. "Nothing wrong with wine."

"Well, I'm glad it went well—or at least better than you'd planned. You still up for staying for dinner? I think my mom is freaking out because I brought a girl home."

"Yeah, about that..." Trihn said. She glanced up into his big brown eyes and smiled. "Girlfriend?"

"Fuck. I knew you were going to bring that up."

Trihn shrugged. "Kind of hard to miss."

"I know it's too early. I don't want to rush you." He stepped toward her and brushed her hair behind her ear. "But I like the idea of moving forward."

"It is kind of early. I'm glad that I'm out of my last relationship, but it's really only been a month since it ended."

"I get it."

"But I like you," she told him. "And I like this."

She leaned forward and dropped her lips onto his. He pulled her flush against his body. He licked his tongue against the seam of her lips, and then she opened herself to him. His kiss was electric and enticing, reminding her of all the reasons that she was giving in to him.

"Well, well, well..." Mel loudly cleared her throat in the doorway.

Trihn and Damon abruptly stepped apart. Her cheeks heated. That was not what she'd wanted Damon's mom to see the first time she was meeting her.

"Sorry, Mel. It won't happen again," Trihn said quickly.

"Oh, who cares? We're all adults here. I just needed someone to finish peeling the potatoes. So, when you two lovebirds are done, I could use some help in the kitchen."

131

Damon laughed when his mom walked away. "Sorry about that."

"Are you kidding? She's so cool."

"Well, I'm glad you like her."

"She's clearly the reason you're so wonderful," she said.

"Wonderful, huh?" He planted one more kiss on her lips.

"Yep."

His hands started roaming her body again, and she stepped in closer.

"We should probably go help out or else we're going to miss dinner," he said.

"Oh, I like the sound of that."

He groaned. "Later. I promise you, later."

It was with great effort that he pulled away, but she liked it so much more later when he followed through on his promise.

SIXTEEN

"I'M KIDNAPPING YOU."

Trihn looked up at Bryna standing there in mile-high black Louboutins and a skimpy red dress.

"What?" Trihn asked.

"You heard me, bitch. You have exactly one hour to get dressed and ready, and then we have plans."

"Um…Bri, I'd love to, but I already have plans with Damon tonight."

Bryna sank into her hip and gave her a perfect I-don't-give-a-shit look. "You always have plans with Damon."

"And you pushed me to him," Trihn said. She dropped the pencil she had been using to work on her designs. Final proofs were due next week, and she was almost finished with what she hoped were fashion show—worthy designs.

"Yes. That's all great, but he can't have all your time. I haven't even seen you the past couple of weeks."

It was true. Since Trihn had met Damon's mom, she and Damon had been spending all their time together. It was as if the term *girlfriend* had flipped the switch between them. Trihn knew that she should be cautious, waiting for the other shoe to drop or for someone to pull the rug out from under her. Damon was the rebound one-night stand guy after all. Yet she couldn't help from jumping feetfirst into this scary endeavor all over again. Her heart was on the line, but when she was with Damon, her worries would disappear. And it felt good to just be with him.

"I've still been around," Trihn argued. "Plus, you practically live at E's house."

"Whatever. Just get dressed. Stacia and Maya are coming, too."

"Maya is coming?" Trihn asked in disbelief. "She got out of work?"

"I think she had a date with some football player. Drayton?"

Trihn laughed. Of course Maya would actually follow through on dating the guy she'd randomly picked up at the bar at the start of school. "Really? So, she has the night off for a date, and she's meeting us afterward?"

"No, she's canceling. This is an opportunity she couldn't pass up, and you can't either. So, go get dressed!"

"Are you at least going to tell me what we're doing?" Trihn asked.

"Something that shows I obviously love you."

Trihn raised her eyebrows and waited. She wasn't about to give up her own date with Damon for nothing.

Bryna seemed to realize that Trihn wasn't budging. She sighed dramatically and then pulled out a set of tickets from her purse. She flashed them in front of Trihn, who bounded out of her seat and snatched them up.

"Oh my God, oh my God, oh my God! You do love me! Chloe Avana tickets? First row!" she squealed.

"Yeah. Keep it down."

"But you hate Chloe!"

134

"But you love Chloe."

"And you love me," Trihn said, wrapping her arms around Bryna. "How did you get these? I thought they were sold out."

Bryna shook her head. "Do you know who I am?"

"Bryna Turner. Did you call your hotshot director dad or your big-time movie-star ex-boyfriend? I'm still swooning over Gates, you know? Gates Hartman!"

"Yes, I know. Gates is...whatever. He wouldn't have gotten them for me. He and Chloe don't talk anymore. I just have connections. No woman ever tells all her secrets. You've just been spending so much time with the new boyfriend, and I wanted some girl time."

"Wait, wait, wait," Trihn said. "We're not boyfriend and girlfriend. We're taking it slow."

"Slow fucking sucks," Bryna deadpanned.

"Well...not *that* slow."

"So, you're fucking," she said with a grin.

"You're so crude, Bri."

Bryna shrugged, as if that was the most obvious thing anyone had ever said.

"But, yes, we're sleeping together."

"Good. Everyone needs a good fuck. Who knew rebound dude would turn into fuck buddy slash boyfriend material?"

Trihn shook her head and handed the tickets back to Bryna. "You're ridiculous. You thought your boyfriend was gay the entire time you knew him, and now, you guys are together. If we want to talk about weird things, let's start with E."

"Or not."

Trihn grinned. "I'm going to change. Can't wait."

An hour later, all four girls were dressed to kill and on their way to the Chloe Avana concert at the MGM Grand Garden Arena. Bryna had rented a limo, and as soon as they were seated in the back, Maya popped open a bottle of champagne. Bubbly was passed around, and they toasted to the epic girls' night to follow.

Trihn had called Damon earlier to cancel when she found out about the tickets. He hadn't minded, especially since she'd sounded so excited. He'd said that he'd been called into Posse, but since they'd planned a date, he'd turned it down. Hopefully, he would be able to still work tonight now that he was free. He'd told her not to worry about it, and with first-row tickets to her favorite artist's concert about to happen with her best friends, she was definitely heeding his advice.

Their limo pulled up to the front of the MGM Grand, and the girls walked through the lobby and into the packed arena. Nearly seventeen-thousand people were seated within the venue, already screaming their heads off for Chloe's sold-out show.

Trihn was dazzled by the immense crowd. She had been to sold-out shows at Madison Square Garden at home, and this venue had the same vibe—exhilarating, heart-pounding, and hypnotic. It was a shot of adrenaline straight through the system. Nothing was better than thousands of people all endorphin-doping on the same music high.

When they made it past the last barrier to their front-row seats, Maya grabbed Trihn's hand. She was practically bouncing up and down. "I can't believe this is real life."

"Every day in the life of Bryna Turner," Trihn said, flipping her hair.

Maya laughed. "She's the best."

"Definitely."

"Can you guys believe these seats?" Stacia screamed. She threw her hands in the air and danced in a circle.

"I don't care who you had to blow to get these seats. I totally approve."

"So, do you think she'll open or close with 'Heartbreaker'?" Maya asked.

"That's my *favorite*!" Stacia squealed.

"End," Bryna deadpanned. She plopped down in her seat, less than enthused.

"You're killing me, Bri," Maya said. "We all know you hate Chloe. Why did you get the tickets if you were going to mope?"

"I'm not moping," she said. "I did it because I love you guys, and I know you all love her music. That's it."

"But really...why *do* you hate her?" Trihn asked. She could never get a straight answer out of Bryna about this.

"I don't hate her."

"But you don't like her either."

Bryna shrugged. As the lights started to dim for the opening act, a girl screamed in her ear. Bryna turned around to face the girl and said a few choice words that probably shouldn't have been directed at high school students. Stacia just cackled and sat down in her seat, ready for the hot up-and-coming musician, Matt Thompson, to play his set.

Trihn sank into a seat next to Bryna and leaned over. "Are you ever going to tell me?"

"No," she said immediately. "It's ancient history, and I'd like for it to stay that way."

"You hold a grudge like no one else."

Bryna's blue eyes bore into hers. "For this, you would, too." Trihn opened her mouth to ask more, but Bryna narrowed her eyes. "Just drop it, okay?"

Trihn held her hands up and leaned back. "All right. Sorry. Thank you for the tickets even though she's not your fave."

"Anything for my squad," she said as the lights winked out.

The crowd roared for Matt. He was a new act, but his music was already on the radio, thanks to his association with Chloe. Trihn liked his stuff and was glad that she would get to hear more of it now that he was opening for such a big star.

Chloe came on next, and just as Bryna had predicted, she waited until the final encore to sing "Heartbreaker." The girls were all breathless and humming with energy by the end of the show. Even Bryna had gotten into it. It seemed that, if she forgot who was singing the songs, she could enjoy the music. Chloe was a great performer, and it was crazy for Trihn to think that they were the same age. While she was slaving away in college, Chloe was touring the world, playing sold-out shows and making unforgettable movies. *What a life!*

"Thank you. Thank you. Thank you!" Trihn cried, throwing her arms around Bryna. "This was incredible."

"Seriously, Bri, you outdid yourself," Maya said. "It was worth a canceled date."

Stacia nodded. "Totally."

"I had fun, too," Bryna said. "So much fun that I'm glad I got these, too." She pulled out shiny blue passes with Chloe's face on them. Each ticket read *Backstage Pass* in shiny white letters.

Trihn's eyes bulged in shock. "You've been holding on to backstage passes this whole time and didn't tell us?"

"Ah!" Stacia screamed. She jumped up and down and did a twirl. "Backstage passes! Bryna is queen."

"I wasn't going to go backstage if the show sucked," Bryna said with a nonchalant shrug.

"You're insane," Maya said. "Now, gimme one of those, and let's go meet her!"

Bryna handed out the passes and then directed them to the backstage entrance. A hot bouncer stood at the door and checked their tickets before letting them pass. They had to pull Stacia away from his large muscled biceps before she did something totally Stacia-esque, like finding the nearest restroom for a quickie.

The bouncer pointed them toward a small lounge where a line had already formed for people with passes.

Bryna wrinkled her nose at the line. "I don't do lines."

Trihn shook her head. "It's not like you want to meet her. You already know her."

"Oh my God!" a girl in front of them cried. "You *know* Chloe Avana?"

Bryna shrugged. "Whatever." Then, she turned back to the girls. "I'm going to need a drink to get through this." She wandered off without a backward glance.

Trihn had no idea where she was going to find a drink. There wasn't a bar in sight.

The only time Trihn had been backstage where she wasn't dancing was at a ballet that Preston had taken her to. They'd used his press passes from the magazine he was interning for and fucked backstage. She frowned at the memory. Sometimes, she wondered how she had been so young and reckless and utterly blind to him.

The screams pulled her out of her negative thoughts, and she huddled together with Maya and Stacia at the back of the line. She didn't care what Bryna thought about lines. She was not going to miss the opportunity to meet Chloe.

"Can you believe this is happening?" Maya asked.

Trihn shook her head, and Stacia looped arms with them. She was more than a head shorter than both girls and looked ridiculous, but she clutched on, bouncing around in her high heels with excitement.

"This is going to be killer. Bri has the best surprises," Stacia said. "This was worth giving up fuck-buddy privileges with Marshall for the night."

"So, what about Pace?" Maya asked. "I see you with him at Posse sometimes."

Stacia narrowed her eyes at Maya. "Pace Larson is the last person I want to think or talk about right now."

"So, you're off again?" Trihn said.

"Off forever. That asshole is sleeping with another cheerleader," she snapped.

"Aren't you sleeping with another football player? The starting quarterback?" Maya pointed out.

"So?"

Maya's eyes widened, and she laughed. It was clear that Stacia either didn't see or didn't care about the hypocrisy in her words.

"Nothing," Maya finally said. "You just still seem into him."

"I'm not," Stacia said defensively.

Trihn laughed and turned her attention back to the line. It had dwindled down to just a few people in front of them. The screams had ended, and there was Chloe.

In her four-inch platform thigh-high boots, Chloe was at eye-level with Stacia and wearing a slick, straight black dress. Her dark hair was pulled up into a high ponytail at the top of her head, and her characteristic big brown eyes were rimmed in charcoal and highlighted with fake lashes. Her makeup was stage heavy with luscious cherry-red lips and contouring that could have only been achieved by a professional.

Trihn was speechless. She had modeled and dealt with all manner of celebrities, but Chloe Avana turned her into a fourteen-year-old fangirl.

"Great show!" Stacia cried. "It was stellar."

"Really amazing," Maya agreed.

"Thank you all so much for coming," Chloe said. Her thick ponytail bounced as she moved closer to them. "It's really a pleasure to get to meet you."

Her smile was bright and genuine. It made Trihn wonder why the hell Bryna didn't like her. Chloe seemed so nice and friendly. She had just performed onstage for two hours, and she was happy to speak with her fans.

"I love your music," Trihn blurted out.

"Thank you!" Chloe said. "Would you like a picture?"

The girls all scrambled together, and one of Chloe's PR reps snapped a shot of the four of them together.

"What a nice candid," Bryna said, walking back over to them.

Chloe whipped around at the sound of Bryna's voice. Chloe's mouth dropped open, and her cheeks turned rosy red. *Shock* was not even the best word to describe the look on her face. She was mortified. Somehow, Bryna had knocked the confidence right out of her.

"Bri," she whispered as small as a mouse.

"Hi, Chloe."

The tension was thick. Trihn glanced between the confrontation and Stacia and Maya. They looked equally as confused as she was.

"It's so good to see you. It's been so long, like…two years."

"Mmm…yeah," Bryna said.

"I had no idea you were going to be at the show."

"My friends like your music." She gestured to them as they stood together, wondering what the hell was happening.

"Wow. That's just…so great," Chloe said. She noticed that people were staring at her, and she seemed to shift back into her other persona. "Well, it's great to see you and to meet your friends. We should go out tonight!"

"Oh my God!" Stacia cried. "That'd be awesome."

"How fun!" Maya said.

Trihn was staring at Bryna. She looked like the last thing she wanted to do was hang out with Chloe.

But Bryna gritted her teeth and nodded to placate them. "Sure, Chloe. Whatever you want."

SEVENTEEN

"WE'RE GOING OUT WITH CHLOE AVANA tonight," Trihn whispered to Stacia and Maya.

They were hanging out backstage, waiting for Chloe to finish up. She was playing back-to-back shows at MGM, which was the only reason she wasn't leaving the venue to hop on a plane for her next show in a different city.

"It's insane," Maya whispered back. "I can't believe Bryna knows her that well."

"That's so Bri—to just hold back her movie-star connections like that. I mean, we didn't even meet Gates until last semester," Stacia said. "Though I guess she and Chloe aren't close or anything."

"No, they definitely are not close," Trihn agreed. "Chloe seemed to be a little terrified of Bri."

"Isn't everyone?" Maya only half-joked.

"True."

Bryna had finished her vodka tonic and had run off to get another one while they waited. She reappeared a second later without a drink. When Stacia asked about it, she just shrugged. "Finished it already. Chloe is taking forever. I hate waiting. Maybe we should just bail."

Trihn looked at her best friend as if she had sprouted antlers from the top of her head. Stacia and Maya mirrored her expression.

"It's Chloe Avana," Trihn said.

"And I'm Bryna Turner."

"Come on, Bri. It's one night," Trihn pleaded.

Bryna sighed heavily and sank down onto the couch.

A few minutes later, Chloe sauntered back into the lounge area with a fake smile plastered on her face. "Sorry about that! I'm all cleared to go!"

"Great!" Trihn said. "Where to?"

"Wherever you guys normally hang out. I just want to blend in with you, get the real college experience and all that," she said.

Maya laughed. "After all this, and we're going to end up back at Posse on my night off."

Bryna stood stiffly. "Great. Now that that's settled, let's go get a fucking drink. And with you not working, Maya, someone better know how to make my martinis right."

"Oh, you're a bartender?" Chloe asked.

"I am. I make the best drinks in town."

"This is just going to be the best night," Chloe said with a giant smile. All pretenses of discomfort left her face. She seemed genuinely excited to leave and hang out with some girls who were her own age.

"The best," Trihn agreed, sidling up to her.

Chloe gestured for them to follow her out the back entrance where a Hummer limo was waiting for them. She had a security detail with her, but she promised them that she would only have one bodyguard with her at the nightclub. Her staff were pretty chill about her going out, but she'd apparently had some incident in London that had forced them to tighten her strings. The way she talked about it made her life sound very lonely.

"Yeah. It's just Matt and me on the tour. He's great, but the studio keeps him in a separate bus when we travel to nearby cities, and we're hardly together on planes. They want to stem the possibility of rumors getting out about us seeing each other or something else that would be tabloid fodder," Chloe explained. She was so candid for someone with such tight security measures. "The only other people I'm around are my publicist, music executives, bodyguards, makeup artists, and…you know, business people—not many girls my age and even *less* guys who aren't just crazy fans."

"Sounds like a hard life," Bryna deadpanned. She flipped her blonde hair and stared out the darkened window as they zoomed off the Strip and headed toward campus.

"You've been in the spotlight before though, Bri. You know it's not all it's cracked up to be," Chloe said. She fidgeted with her hands every time she spoke to Bryna.

"But you're doing everything that you love," Maya said. She stretched out her long, lean black legs and kicked back. "I'd kill to have a job where I could sit around all day and read, but no one is paying me for that."

Chloe laughed. "True. I wouldn't want to be doing anything else. I'm very grateful."

"Everyone has a different path," Trihn piped in. "Chloe's a famous singer and movie star. Maya is going to be a publishing editor. Stacia will be an NFL quarterback's wife. And Bryna will be directing some incredible movies. We're all pretty lucky."

"What about you?" Chloe asked.

"Trihn is a fashion designer. She's wearing her own clothes tonight," Bryna said with a wicked glint in her eye. "You'd be lucky to wear a Trihn original."

Chloe covetously eyed Trihn's black dress. "Is that right?"

Trihn blushed. "She's exaggerating."

"Own it," Bryna said. "She's going to showcase her designs at a fashion show in New York City over the summer."

"Congratulations!"

Trihn's eyes rounded, and she shook her head at Bryna. That was so far from the truth. She would have to win the fashion show at school before that would ever happen, but that didn't seem to matter to Bryna. It was just an obstacle that she was certain Trihn would hurdle with ease. Chloe seemed to be interested at least, and if Chloe Avana wore one of her designs, Trihn wouldn't need a fashion show.

"Thank you," Trihn said.

This was a surreal life—hanging out with her best friends and Chloe Avana in the back of a Hummer limo, talking about her designs. She was pretty certain things could not get better than this.

A few minutes later, they pulled up to the front of Posse, and Chloe's bodyguard, Mateo, followed them into the busy nightclub. Mateo covered Chloe, who had pulled out sunglasses and an oversized hat to walk through the room. Trihn thought it was conspicuous, but what did she know?

They went straight up to the VIP section without any trouble and took over a booth with bottle service. Once Chloe took a seat, she tossed the hat and glasses down next to her and immediately demanded tequila.

"I love this place!" Chloe cried over the music. "Great vibe."

"It's the best spot," Trihn said.

"Yeah. Trihn's boyfriend is the DJ," Maya said, waggling her eyebrows as she expertly poured the shots.

"He's not my boyfriend," she objected.

"Oh! Boyfriend! Exciting!" Chloe said. "Do all of you have boyfriends? Is it so great and totally normal?"

"Bryna is the only one with a boyfriend," Trihn said with a shake of her head. She liked Damon and already knew they were moving in that direction, but she wasn't ready for that word yet.

"You're dating someone?" Chloe asked Bryna.

"Yeah. Eric Wilkins. He's one of the coaches of LV State's football team and used to play here," Bryna told her, looking her dead in the eyes.

"Oh, cool. That's great for you. I haven't seen you in the tabloids or anything, so I wasn't sure about…you know."

"No," Bryna said hastily.

"Right. That makes sense."

Trihn looked between them in confusion. None of what they had just said made sense.

Shaking off the strangeness of their non-conversation, Trihn accepted the shot that Maya had handed her. All of the girls clinked their shot glasses together and then downed the alcohol in one quick motion. She hastily reached out for a lime and shook her head as the tequila burned down her throat.

"I'm going to need a few more of those," Chloe said, energized from the shot.

Maya poured out another, and after they downed that, Trihn knew she was going to need a break or else she'd get plastered even though she was pretty good at holding her liquor.

"I'll be back in a minute. Damon is working tonight, and I want to say hi," Trihn said, standing.

"Say hi to the BF for me," Bryna said with a wink.

"You're a bitch."

"The one and only."

Trihn hopped out of her seat and left the VIP section. She was on her way down the stairs when she ran into Eric.

"Hey, Trihn!" he said, enveloping her in a hug.

"Hey. You going to see Bri?"

He nodded. "She seemed out of it when she texted me."

Trihn leaned forward to talk to him even though she doubted anyone could overhear her. "She's up there with Chloe Avana. I don't know their history, but Bryna is in a horrible mood and drinking heavily. You and I both know where that leads with her."

He furrowed his brow and nodded. "Hopefully, I won't have to throw her ass into the pool again."

Trihn laughed. "I hope it doesn't get that out of control. She's better when she's with you."

"Thanks." Eric beamed.

"All right. I'm going to go see Damon now, so take care of her until I get back."

"Is that the guy who lives at the place I have to keep picking you up from?" Eric asked.

Trihn nodded. "That's the one."

"Y'all together now?"

"We're dating, but it's not serious."

Eric smirked, and Trihn could see why Bryna had fallen for him. He totally saw through Trihn.

"It's always serious with you, Trihn."

"Don't remind me," she said warily.

People had been saying that about Trihn her entire life. She took everything too seriously—dance, modeling, fashion, and relationships. Compared to Lydia, the hippie flower child who preached free love to anyone who would listen, Trihn was the polar opposite. And she had hated that until she had moved to Las Vegas and realized that being serious about her work was a good thing. Even being serious about her relationship with Neal had seemed like a good thing.

But at the same time, she knew something was blooming between herself and Damon, and she couldn't ignore it. Her head told her to be careful. Damon could break her into pieces all over again. But her heart said to throw caution to the wind and just be with this truly incredible guy.

"You'll make the right choice for you. You always do," Eric said. "Now, I'm going to go rescue my crazy girlfriend."

With a sigh, Trihn watched Eric leave. If Bryna could find Eric Wilkins, then surely someone was out there for Trihn.

She moved over to the stairs leading to the DJ booth and climbed them with her mind clouded. The same bouncer who had been there the first night was standing guard.

He recognized her and nodded. "Hey, Trihn."

She startled. She didn't think that he'd know her name. "Hey. Can I go in to see Damon?"

"Sure thing." The bouncer opened the door and stepped back to let her pass.

"Thanks." She practically skipped forward into the room. With how amazing her night had been going, she was ecstatic to see Damon. "Damon, guess what?" she cried.

Then, she stopped dead in her tracks.

Damon wasn't alone.

A busty blonde in a tight-fitting corset top with her breasts nearly falling out of it and a micro miniskirt with black pleather heeled boots was sitting next to him. She was facing Damon with her arm draped across his thigh, and her ear was plastered to one side of the headphones he was wearing.

Damon jerked around at her voice. "Trihn?"

EIGHTEEN

TRIHN STOOD, FROZEN, IN DISBELIEF. She wanted to bolt. Every fiber of her being screamed at her to kick it into high gear and get the fuck away from this moment. She had been here before. Between Preston and Neal, she'd had her fair share of cheating boyfriends. With a girl like that hanging on Damon so casually, it couldn't possibly be innocent. This was the exact reason she had been taking things slow. Nice guys didn't exist.

"What's this?" she demanded, her voice rising an octave.

Her breath was uneven, and her hands were shaking. She felt tears welling up and tried to stop them from spilling by taking a shuddering deep breath.

Even if she and Damon weren't officially together, she hadn't expected this. They had been moving in the right direction, and it had suddenly come to a screeching halt.

"Trihn," he said again, standing abruptly and tossing the headphones down on top of the soundboard.

The girl leaned back in her seat and crossed her legs. She looked smug, as far as Trihn was concerned.

"This is not what it looks like," Damon said.

"And what does it look like?" she managed to get out.

"Nothing. It looks like nothing because it's nothing."

She shook her head. "It looks like something. Clearly, I am a total idiot."

"Trihn, come on."

"No." She shook her head. "I told you that Neal cheated on me and that I have trust issues. You should have…I don't know…just fucking known better. This"—she gestured between them—"must mean nothing to you. Fuck!" She spun on her heel and wrenched the door back open.

She couldn't stand there and let him spout bullshit to her. He was with someone else, some stupid fucking blonde bimbo who had to flaunt her enormous breasts for attention. It was no wonder he was interested in someone else if that was what he was into. Trihn was pretty much the opposite of that girl—physically, mentally, and emotionally by the looks of her.

Ugh! She wanted to scream. She hated that she was being a bitch and judging that girl.

It was Damon's fault in the first place. He shouldn't have been anywhere near another girl, no matter what she fucking looked like or what she was fucking wearing. Blaming the girl for her clothing felt contrary to Trihn's core belief system, but anger kept pushing rational thought out of her head.

With her head up in the clouds, she was halfway down the stairs to head out onto the dance floor. She doubted Damon would follow her. Guys didn't fight for her. Preston hadn't. Neal hadn't. She wasn't worth enough for them to do that, and she was fucking tired of it. She didn't even have the energy to go back up to the VIP section to hang out with Chloe. She just needed to be alone to process. This had officially ruined her night.

"Trihn!"

She whipped around in confusion, not recognizing the voice. Standing in front of her was Damon's friend, Jimmy.

"I'm really not in the mood right now."

His face fell. "I was just seeing if you had talked to Damon. I was glad to hear that you guys had worked things out."

"Yeah—until he had some chick up in the DJ booth with him." She rolled her eyes and started to walk away.

"Wait, what?" Jimmy asked, following her.

"You heard me."

"There's no possible way that he had a girl up there. He's extremely professional. The only girl I've heard of him having in his booth since shit went down a couple of months ago is you."

"Well, that doesn't seem to be true anymore because I was just up there, and some blonde chick was hanging all over him. What happened a couple of months ago anyway?" she demanded.

Jimmy shook his head. "That's a question for him, but I've known him a long time, and there's no way."

"Whatever," she said, brushing him off.

"Hey, hey, hey," Damon called, hurtling through the crowd.

Trihn's eyes widened as Damon approached her and Jimmy. She turned to keep walking away from him, but he latched on to her arm.

"Please don't leave," Damon pleaded.

Jimmy melted into the background, but in solidarity with his friend, he didn't go too far.

Trihn just shook her head at the both of them. "I can't do this, Damon."

"Don't leave. I'm not doing anything with Cadence. I swear to you," he said. He grabbed her hands in his own.

His eyes were wide and terrified. "I promise with everything that I am, nothing is going on with me and Cady."

"Then, what the fuck was she doing up there?" Trihn asked.

She wanted to believe him. He looked so earnest. *But didn't that fool me in the past?*

"She's another DJ."

"Really?" Trihn rolled her eyes. "She really *looked* like another DJ, sitting practically on top of you."

"I know that must have looked bad to you, but she's just another DJ. I've seen her around at other venues. I'd already turned down the gig tonight before you canceled to go to the concert, but they said I could come back in anyway. Cadence was the DJ who had come in to fill the spot. We were both here, so we were just working together."

"Working together," Trihn said. "I've heard that one before."

He heavily blew out his breath and flipped off his baseball hat. His hair was a wild mess. His eyes looked crazed. "I'm not into her. In fact, she felt so bad about what happened that she's holding down the fort in the booth until I get back, and then she's bailing. You can talk to her yourself."

Trihn held up her hand. "Really not necessary."

"I get that you're upset because you think something was going on. That happened with your last boyfriend, but I'm not him. At some point, you're going to have to see that I'm not like the guy who messed you up."

"How could I see that after what I walked in on? I've been made a fool of in the past. Twice! Fool me once, shame on you. Fool me twice, shame on me. I won't be fooled a third time, Damon. I'd rather be alone than have someone stomp on my heart and leave me in a fucking mess all over again!"

"I won't do that. I couldn't do that to you!"

He reached out for her, but she took a step back away from him. She wasn't ready for him to be consoling.

"What happened a couple of months ago?" she asked.

"What?"

"When I came on to you that first night, you said you would have done it a couple of months ago but not now. And then Jimmy just mentioned it again. What happened a couple of months ago?" Trihn crossed her arms and waited for an answer.

Damon winced. "You remember that, huh?"

"Yes," she said flatly.

He blew out a long breath. "A few months ago, I was working at a club. It looked like a solid gig to pull me out of the house-party rabbit hole I'd been stuck in. I got really hard into the scene—music, dancing, booze…girls. Lots of girls," he admitted.

Trihn winced.

"The club owner warned me to stay professional, but I felt invincible, doing what I loved and getting attention for it. Things got out of hand one night, and I made a mistake. It wasn't anything life-altering, except that I lost my job. Since then, I've wanted to stay in control of my life, and I take music seriously. So, I turned you down that night because I didn't want you to be just another girl in my life."

"But I was."

"No, you weren't. *You* treated it like a one-night stand. I never did. I've always wanted more with you, Trihn, and I always will."

He took a step closer, and when Trihn didn't back away, he dropped something in her hand. She looked down to see a Hershey's Kiss. She cracked a smile at the small gesture. That seemed to be all he needed. He tugged her against him, his hands circling her waist. She didn't relax just yet. She just let him hold her there.

"God, I was so scared," he admitted.

"Scared?" she asked, confused.

"The look on your face—I never, ever want to see it again." He breathed out a heavy sigh. "I'm so sorry I made you doubt me."

"She's really just a DJ?" Trihn asked hopefully.

"Yes, she's really just a DJ. Nothing more."

Fuck, she wanted to believe him. She would rather be the girl who overreacted over every little thing than the girl who got cheated on even though she felt like she deserved not to have to deal with either scenario.

But she couldn't shut her brain off. She couldn't disconnect. If that girl was hanging on Damon, she was into him, which automatically equated to them fucking on the side. Maybe she was irreparably damaged. One too many hits to her heart had left the jigsaw puzzle pieces unable to fit together.

Trihn ran her hand back through her hair and nodded her head. "I want to believe you. I have just had a lot of issues in this department. It's not easy for me."

"I wish it were," he told her. "I wish that no one had hurt you so much that you didn't think you were enough. You're more than enough, Trihn. I don't want anyone else in my life. I know we've only been dating for a short time, but you have shifted my world. You can't pull back now."

She looked up at him and tried to find the truth in his words. "Why?"

"Because I'm falling for you."

"You are?"

"Unequivocally."

He took her hands in his. His lips tenderly landed on hers, expressing every emotion in that one moment of pure bliss. Trihn closed her eyes and let the feeling wash over her.

Every other time, she had pushed for the relationship and met a brick wall. She had always professed her intentions and her love first. She had always put her heart on the line.

Now, here was Damon, fearlessly putting himself out there for her.

"I told you I'd fight for you and that it meant something to me. You do, and I won't stop. That's a promise."

Trihn felt safe in his arms.

She tried to let herself go—just be there with him and forget her past. Damon wasn't like those other guys. There was a logical reason for him knowing that Cadence girl. She wasn't Lydia or Blu. This hadn't been on purpose. It had just been the wrong place at the wrong time. That was all.

She took a deep breath and decided to let it go. "Okay. I believe you." She took a step back from him. "I guess I kind of overreacted."

"Hey, it's okay. You didn't overreact. You're just cautious. If I'd seen you alone with some other guy, I probably would have lost it, too."

"Yeah," Trihn said, "that wouldn't happen."

"I hope not."

"No, really. The only other guy I even talk to is Bryna's boyfriend, Eric. Fashion design isn't exactly crawling with guys, and I have no interest in anyone else. I wasn't even looking for a relationship when this happened." She gestured between them.

"And are we in a relationship?" he prodded.

She looked up into his dark eyes. "I would say we're in some sort of relationship. I don't think I'd freak out over just anyone."

He smiled down at her, bringing butterflies to life in her stomach. "So, are you my girlfriend then?"

"I…" She closed her mouth and glanced down at the ground.

That was a step forward. *Didn't I just push us forward with my freak-out? Weren't we moving in that exact direction whether I claimed to want it or not?*

"It's okay if you're not ready," he said, backpedaling.

"No, you're right." She moved her fingers up his shirt and then wrapped her arms around his neck. "My friends are already calling you that. I care about you. We're not just dating because I just made it abundantly clear that I want to be exclusive. So, yeah, I guess I am your girlfriend."

He let out a happy sigh and then sweetly kissed her on the lips. "That's what I like to hear."

Trihn felt like she had just made one huge step forward. A chip that she had tried to harden fell away from her heart. When she fell, she fell hard. And she had been trying to avoid letting herself get to that point, but Damon seemed determined to be the guy for her.

"I'm going to go tell Cadence that she can head out. You can come with me if you want," he offered.

"You know, while she's up there," Trihn said, an idea forming in her mind, "why don't you come up to VIP with me?"

"I still have to work."

"I know, but I want you to meet someone."

"Yeah? Color me intrigued."

NINETEEN

TRIHN GESTURED FOR DAMON AND JIMMY to follow her up the steps to the VIP section.

Compared to when she and the girls had first gotten here, it was packed. Trihn didn't know if it was a result of the news getting out that Chloe was here or what, but it was a fight just to get through the crowd.

She felt the reassuring pressure from Damon's hand in hers and slowed down. She was excited to introduce him, but she didn't need to throw down with someone to get through. Plus, this introduction was with her boyfriend. She swallowed hard at the realization that she was going through this all over again. It was scary, terrifying really, but still exhilarating. Damon wasn't like anyone else, and she prayed to God that it would stay as the truth.

The bottle of tequila was empty when they made it to the corner booth. Chloe was standing on their table, dancing with Bryna, who looked like she had drunk her fair share of the bottle. Eric and Maya were supervising. Stacia was nowhere to be seen, which likely meant she was with a guy. Whether it was Pace, Marshall, or someone else entirely, Trihn had no clue.

"Is that—" Damon whispered next to her.

"Holy fuck, that's Chloe Avana," Jimmy said.

Chloe, hearing her name, swiveled around on the table and nearly lost her footing. She grabbed on to Bryna and cracked up laughing. Before they could tumble to the ground, Eric was there, supporting them both.

"Trihn!" Chloe cried. "Come dance with us."

"When you said you were introducing me to someone, I thought that I was going to finally get the official introduction to your friends," Damon said, his eyes wide. "Not that you'd brought a celebrity with you to Posse."

"Well, yeah, I wanted you to meet my friend. But, also, this is Chloe Avana," she said.

Chloe hopped off the table and strolled over to them. "Oh my God, you must be Trihn's boyfriend!"

"That I am."

"Good choice," Chloe said with a wink. She turned to Jimmy. "And who are you?"

"Uh…" he murmured, seemingly losing his voice.

"This is Jimmy, Damon's friend," Trihn introduced them.

"Cute. We need another bottle, and it's on the way. You guys should join us for shots." Chloe sauntered back over to Bryna and nearly fell into her lap.

"She was not this drunk when I left her," Trihn told Damon.

"Well, I don't think we can turn that invite down."

Trihn took the seat next to Chloe, and Damon and Jimmy filled in the rest of the booth.

Bryna leaned over Chloe and looked right at Damon. "So, you're the hot piece of ass she's been fucking?"

Trihn dropped her head into her hands. Drunk Bryna was always a little bit of a hot mess.

"Good to see you again, Bryna. Always a pleasure." He glanced over at Trihn and laughed. "And, um...yeah, I guess that would be me."

Eric pulled Bryna back with a shake of his head. "What she means is, *Hey, how's it going? Thank you for being a great DJ at all party. It's good to see you again and to officially get to meet you as the guy Trihn has been talking about.*"

"No, that's definitely not what I meant," Bryna said.

"Now, this is the Bryna Turner I've always heard about—cheerleader, gold digger, riotous drunk," Damon said with a smirk. That British accent made Trihn swoon all over again.

"Everything you've heard is true," Bryna said.

Trihn laughed. "And worse."

"Gold digger?" Chloe asked, wide-eyed. "But you're fucking rich."

"Everyone has their vices," Bryna said with a nonchalant shrug.

A bartender came over and placed another bottle of tequila and a bottle of vodka down on the table with some more mixers. Maya thanked the girl and started pouring out drinks for everyone.

"No, thank you," Damon said when Maya offered him a drink. "I have to get back upstairs soon. This was cool."

"You're leaving already?" Chloe asked.

"Yeah, I'm kind of on the clock."

"Thanks for humoring us, Chloe. I just thought it would be cool to introduce him to you," Trihn said, unable to believe this was real life. "He has this remix of 'Heartbreaker,' and it's my favorite of the tracks he's put together."

"Really?" she asked, reaching for the drink that Maya was handing her.

"It's actually really good," Bryna chimed in. "Quality. He knows what he's doing."

Chloe seemed to reassess Damon. She probably had people who wanted to make it in the music industry try to get close to her all the time. She'd seemed to tune out as soon as the conversation had shifted to her career. But Bryna's words held a lot of weight.

Trihn hadn't even thought that saying something about the mix would turn Chloe off. That wasn't Trihn's intention at all. She had just wanted to thank Chloe for the great music.

Chloe shrugged and took a sip of her drink. "Well, if Bryna approves, then I want to hear it."

"You do?" Damon and Trihn said at the same time.

"Yeah. Can I hear it now? Is that possible?" she asked.

"I could cue it up for you in the booth," Damon offered.

"Then, let's go to the booth," she said, standing and taking the lead even though she had no clue where she was going. "Come on, Mateo," Chloe barked.

Mateo plopped a hat down on her head and forced the sunglasses back on her before departing. Trihn, Damon, and Jimmy followed close behind her. Damon looked at Trihn in astonishment, and she was sure that her face mirrored his, both unable to believe this.

She had just put Damon on the spot in front of a big name in the music industry, and now, he was going to showcase what he was good at in front of this celebrity. She hoped this would turn out to be a good thing.

As they walked through the crowd, it was clear the news about her appearance here had definitely spread. Damon and Trihn crowded in around Chloe as they made their way through the throng of people who was excited to find her in their midst.

When they finally made it up the stairs to the DJ booth, Chloe leaned back against the wall and was breathing heavily. She was counting under her breath, and Trihn could see her hands were shaking.

"Are you okay?" Trihn asked.

Mateo took a step between them. "Give her a minute."

After a few deep breaths, Chloe took her hat off and seemed to regain her composure. "Sorry about that. After London, crowds freak me out. Last year, I had a panic attack while walking to my car after leaving the AMAs with all the people in the parking lot. Oh, shit," she said, looking at Mateo with fear in her eyes. She glanced back at Damon, Trihn, and Jimmy fearfully. "Please don't tell the press that."

"It's okay," Trihn said. She took Chloe's hand in hers. It was heartbreaking to see the other side of the confident girl from the stage. "We won't say anything. Promise."

"Thanks," she said hopefully. "Let's, uh…just go hear the song."

Damon nodded his head at the bouncer. Seeing Chloe with her bodyguard, the bouncer widened his eyes as he swung the door open to the booth for them. Damon and the bouncer clasped hands before their group entered the booth and Jimmy shut the door behind them.

Cadence swiveled around at the commotion. She had her headphones on and seemed to have been jamming to the techno music in the background. "Hey, Damon. Super sorry about earlier. I'm all set to leave whenever you're— shit! Is that Chloe Avana? If not, you're a total doppelgänger."

"Nope. It's me. Hi." Chloe waved at the girl.

"Whoa. Can we get a selfie?"

Chloe laughed, as if the panic attack in the hallway hadn't just occurred because of psycho fans. "Sure."

Cadence jumped up and pulled out her enormous cell phone. She clicked a picture with Chloe. "This is awesome. So great to meet you."

"You, too."

"Cady, we're going to cue up my remix of 'Heartbreaker,'" Damon told her. "You're free to go, or you can stay if you want to hear it."

"I'd love to hear it, as long as that's okay with your girlfriend," she said, hesitantly looking at Trihn.

"It's fine," Trihn said automatically. "I'm Trihn."

"Cadence."

They shook hands, and Trihn promised herself that she would be the bigger person in this situation. Damon was falling for her, and they were exclusive. This was nothing. Just a blip on the radar.

Damon fiddled with the controls, and Chloe leaned against the table, staring at the computer he was syncing up. Trihn was so excited that this was happening. She would get to watch Damon work, and it was cool that Chloe would hear his talent.

"All right. Here is just a sample. I'm pulling it up to play in the club, but I'm going to let Cady's track finish out."

He flicked a few more buttons, and then "Heartbreaker" started playing in the sound booth. Chloe tapped her foot as she listened to her lyrics come through the speakers. Trihn could see the instant the beat really hit her.

She stood up straighter and intently looked at the screen. "Huh," she whispered.

Damon frowned. "What?"

"You added something. It's not just the remix, like most DJs do. The vocals are different."

"Oh, yeah, that," he said, silencing the music. "Sorry. I just added in a harmony to you on the chorus, and I recorded a piano and guitar to go with the bass line. Then, I remixed the song from there."

"Don't be sorry," Chloe said, shaking her head. "Can you key this up to play without the lyrics?"

"Um…yeah, sure. Give me a second," Damon said. He went back to work on his computer. A few minutes later, he was playing the song again. "This what you want?"

She listened and then nodded. "Yes, perfect. Play that version, and mike me."

"What?" Damon asked. He stilled on the computer and looked at her in confusion.

"Everyone down there already knows that I'm here. What better way to give a show than for me to sing the song while miked to your sound system?"

"Chloe," Mateo said stiffly from the corner.

"It'll be fine," she insisted.

"You'll have to leave right after," he told her. "I'm going to call the limo."

"Ruining all my fun."

"I'll need the full detail to escort you out of here."

"Fine," she snapped. "Cue it up," she said to Damon.

"Okay, yeah," Damon said, energized. "Just give me a second."

Chloe was excited. She was bouncing up and down while softly singing scales to herself. Despite how much she'd had to drink earlier, she was still warming up her vocal cords like a pro.

Trihn couldn't believe this was happening. When Chloe had said she wanted to hear Damon's version, Trihn had thought they'd listen to the song, and that would be that. She hadn't thought Chloe would want to sing to Damon's music.

"Your boyfriend is mega talented," Chloe said to Trihn. "That mix? Ah, love!"

"He is, isn't he?" Trihn said with a smile, watching her boyfriend work.

"Uh, yeah! And hot! And that accent! You're so lucky!"

Trihn laughed. "I guess I am."

"All right," Damon said. "You're good to go."

"Announce me."

Damon didn't even hesitate. He'd worked at the radio station long enough to know how to introduce an artist even if he'd never had anyone on the show as big as Chloe Avana.

"Posse! Have I got a surprise for you," Damon said into the microphone as the end of the last song changed into a synthesized instrumental. "We're about to take down the house, and I've got someone here all ready to bring it down with me. This is 'Heartbreaker,' and here with me tonight is none other than the international superstar Chloe Avana."

The crowd below them roared with approval.

Damon and Chloe smiled the same smile. They were both in their element.

"Heartbreaker" started on cue. Damon worked his magic on the board, getting into the music and letting loose. Then, Chloe's vocals came in, and she sang her heart out. To Trihn's surprise, Damon silenced the backup vocals he had recorded and sang into his microphone. He dropped the sound on it so that it came out in the background, but it was perfect with Chloe's high notes. It was hands down the best performance of the song Trihn had ever heard. It was even better than the one Chloe had sung at her concert that night for the final encore in front of seventeen-thousand people.

The song came to a close on a heartbreakingly mellow note, and Damon quickly mixed it into another song, letting the track take over.

He sank back into his chair and looked up at Chloe. "That was killer."

She smiled. "That's my life, baby."

"You guys were great together," Cadence said.

Trihn had completely forgotten that she was there. "Yeah, it was perfect," Trihn said.

Anxiety gnawed at her stomach. She wanted to be happy and just live in this moment with her boyfriend. But all she felt was fear, a mingling deep fear, because they had, in fact, sounded incredible together.

Damon stood from his seat and walked right past Chloe, as if she weren't even there. When he kissed Trihn, it obliterated every bad thought she'd ever had. There was nothing between him and Chloe. Trihn had been overreacting all over again.

"Thank you," he whispered against her lips.

She laughed, a little light-headed from that kiss. "You're welcome."

"And thank you, Chloe. That was a lot of fun."

"It was," Chloe said, her cheeks pink. "Now that I've announced my presence to everyone, I guess I have to go, but this was a great time. I hope I come back to Las Vegas soon, so I can hang out with you all again. Tell Bryna good-bye for me, okay?"

Trihn nodded. "I will."

Chloe gave Trihn, Damon, and Jimmy each a quick hug and then followed Mateo from the premises.

Cadence had a huge smile on her face. "Sorry again about earlier. I'm going to head out." She nodded at both of them before following Chloe.

As soon as the door shut, Damon started walking Trihn backward toward the soundboard. His hands roamed up the sides of her tight black dress. When her butt hit the table, Damon pushed his computer out of the way and hoisted her up so that she was sitting on the edge, facing him.

"That was crazy," he said. His lips hungrily landed on hers. A heated desire rose off of him from his adrenaline rush.

"I know. You were amazing."

"You know what's amazing? The way you look in this dress."

Trihn laughed huskily. His hands ran down her sides to her exposed thighs and hiked her legs up around his waist.

"I thought you were trying to stay professional at work," she murmured.

"I was thinking I could go back to that after I fucked you."

The lights were dim, and from a distance below, they had to be just silhouettes. Up until she had started dating a DJ of her own, she had never really looked up at the man behind the music.

Now, she couldn't stop staring.

Damon was gorgeous and dominating and sensual.

He flipped his baseball cap off his head, and she ran her hands through his messy dark hair as he leaned forward to kiss her. He was greedy and amped up from the performance, making him more aggressive.

She nibbled on his bottom lip. He groaned, capturing her lips in a searing kiss. Their lips melded together, and passion took ahold of them, leaving behind the dark club, the chaotic, boisterous crowd below, and even the music until it was just them.

"God, I'm so fucking glad you're here right now," he said, pressing her back into the booth.

She lay flat, backward, and raised her arms, giving him the perfect view of her body.

"And how do you want me?" she teased.

He firmly grabbed her thighs in his hands and yanked her body down toward him until her ass was just teetering on the edge. Her dress had ridden all the way up to her hips. He traced the outline of her underwear, and she writhed, eager for his touch.

"Right here, right now"—he tugged her underwear down her body and discarded it onto the floor—"where the sound of the club will drown out your screams."

His hands ran back up her legs before his fingers circled her opening, coating them with her wetness. She tried to hold steady, but the feel of him made her shudder beneath him.

"God, you're so ready," he said, plunging two fingers deep into her pussy.

"Oh, fuck," she cried.

"You did something for me tonight, and I have every intention of returning the favor."

"It was nothing," she said. "I enjoyed watching you with your music."

He smirked and flipped his hair out of his eyes. He looked ready to devour her alive.

"Oh, I'm going to enjoy watching you, too."

Damon leaned forward and claimed her mouth once more. His tongue lashed out, and they took their desires out on one another.

It was feral and intoxicating, power-hungry and demanding. The force of a million blasted supernovas shattering into the solar system collided into this one moment. It was heaven and hell and eternity. It was the hope that humanity needed to survive a continually heartbreaking existence. It was the reason that love conquered all. This one kiss meant *everything*.

And they both gave in to it. Letting the moment sweep them away, they forgot their pasts and any consequences of their actions because where they were right now was all that mattered.

Trihn sat back up a little to grab at his pants. She unbuckled his jeans and pulled the zipper down to the base. Damon was still wrestling with her lips while his hands tangled in her hair when she yanked his pants to the ground.

He looked at her with hunger in his eyes. She met his gaze. He pushed his boxers to the ground next, freeing his cock. Her eyes darted down to it, and a smile crossed her lips.

"See something you like?" he joked before laying her back flat against the empty booth.

"Mmhmm."

Then, without warning, he slammed into her. She rocketed forward with the momentum, but he didn't stop. He just grasped her hips and worked back and forth into her. He grabbed one of her legs and put it up onto his shoulder, stiletto high heel and all. The change in angle forced him deeper, and she cried out as he thrust into her.

Her world was spinning. Everything was teetering on the precipice of this moment, waiting for her to fall over the edge into oblivion.

"All I wanted was this—just me and you together."

He leaned his elbow on the table, and she was glad that she still had her dancer's flexibility. Then, he used the added leverage to steadily drive into her until she was crying out into the abyss.

Their voices carried out into the crowd beyond and were lost to the noise of the pulsing nightclub. Heat radiated off their skin, and sweat slicked their foreheads.

Her breathing was labored as she fought to hold back the waves crashing down all around her. She was going to lose it.

Trihn grasped for his hand and pulled him back down to her, letting her leg drop to the side. She voraciously kissed him, knowing that she was about to split apart.

"I can feel you holding back," Damon growled against her lips. "Let go. Come for me."

"Fuck," she murmured. "Come with me."

Then, they both let go and the tidal wave crashed down over them as they succumbed to the release.

TWENTY

TRIHN ROLLED OVER IN BED and snuggled against her boyfriend. A sigh escaped her lips at that thought—her boyfriend...her talented, wonderful, gorgeous boyfriend, who she had spent the entire night with at his apartment.

She let loose another soft noise, and her hand ran down his toned chest to the six-pack abs hiding beneath the baby-blue sheet.

"Mmm," he murmured. "You keep purring like that, and I'm going to have to give you a reason to purr."

"I wasn't purring," she said, trailing her fingers along every defined ridge down to the waistband of his boxers. She popped the material between her fingers, causing him to squirm beneath her.

He flipped over on top of her, going from just waking up to fully awake in a split second. She pushed back into the bed and smirked up at him.

"You most definitely were," he whispered.

His kisses weren't rushed. They were gentle and tender, laced with the strength from last night.

They had both worn themselves out at Posse and then back at his apartment afterward. The adrenaline had finally worn off during the early hours of the morning, and they had slept straight through to the afternoon.

Trihn knew she needed to get up and put in some hours on her designs. Samples were due this week, and she had so much work left to do. But when Damon started kissing down her front, removing her panties as he went, she reveled in the early-morning lust that clouded her vision.

She let him take the lead as he slipped back inside her sore body. His hand cradled her head as he started moving. She stared up into his dark eyes and saw nothing but warmth and love mirrored back at her. It was staggering to walk into this realm so quickly. But she had promised to let herself fall for him, despite her past relationships, and right now, she was head over heels.

They finished together at their own pace and then lay there on the bed, panting from exhaustion.

Damon leaned over and kissed her forehead. "You should take a relaxing shower. I'm going to make us breakfast. How do you take your coffee?"

Trihn sighed. "Coffee sounds amazing. Where did you come from?"

"I've always been here. I was just waiting for you, I guess."

"Good answer. I'll take cream and sugar. Don't drown it."

He laughed. "Got it."

Trihn hopped off the bed and jumped into the shower. It was steaming hot as the water cascaded down her back. She washed off last night's sexcapades until she was squeaky clean. Then, she turned off the water, dried off, and wrapped the towel tight around her body. She located a pair of boxers and a T-shirt from Damon's drawer and slipped into them. Then, she tied her hair up into a bun at the top of her head and trotted out into the kitchen.

"Oh my God, it smells good," she said. She came around the island and circled her hands around his middle.

Damon had put on basketball shorts, but he was still shirtless, and it was a sight to behold.

"I hope you like French toast."

"My favorite."

"Your coffee is on the counter."

She reached for it and took a careful sip. It was still piping hot but delicious. "Hazelnut?" she guessed.

"Yeah. You like it?"

"It's great. You have some high-tech coffee stuff over here," she observed.

There were an assortment of different grinders, brewers, and various beans. It smelled like heaven.

"I'm kind of a coffee snob. I like to grind and brew my own coffee. I live off of the stuff."

"Well, you have excellent taste, it seems."

"Mmm, I would agree with that."

He slid two pieces of French toast onto a plate, and she loaded them up with butter and syrup. She sat down at a barstool at the island and ate while he cooked for himself.

"Did Mel teach you how to cook?" she asked between mouthfuls.

"Yeah. My mum is talented, as you could tell. She said you could come over again for dinner, if you wanted. I think she likes you."

Trihn blew out a breath of relief. "That's good."

"She seems worried about you and your family though."

"Oh, that," Trihn said. "I haven't spoken to anyone in her family since speaking to my mom that day. She wanted me to come home to look at wedding dresses"

"What do you think about that?" he asked. He dropped another piece of French toast onto her plate and then turned off the stove.

"I can't go back home right now. I'm swamped with work for the fashion show. I still have to decide on a few more pieces. I need to get models. I have to work the designs into runway material. I have so much to do."

"I know. But how do you feel about the wedding?" Damon took the seat next to her.

Trihn looked down at her plate. This was the moment of truth. She hated breaking this spell that they were under, post-coital bliss and all that. But if she was going to give one hundred percent to this relationship, then she needed to be honest with him about what was bothering her.

"So, you know how I said that Preston cheated on Lydia?"

Damon nodded.

"Well, it was with me."

Damon nearly spit out the food he had just put into his mouth. He coughed and slammed his fist on his chest to try to clear his throat. "What?" he gasped out.

"It was a long time ago. We met right after I graduated high school. I thought he was single. He was my first real boyfriend, the first boy I ever loved. I invited him to go away with me and my family to the Hamptons at the end of the summer, but he said he couldn't go because he had to work. It turned out, he was going away with Lydia to the Hamptons, and he just thought that they were going alone."

Damon's jaw was practically on the ground. "He had been with your sister the whole time?"

"Yes. When I told Lydia, she seemed like she understood. She was going to end it, and I would stay in New York and go to NYU."

"Really? NYU?"

"Yeah. I had been accepted there and had plans to go until all of this went down. But Preston manipulated Lydia into believing that he hadn't been serious with either of us and that he actually just wanted to be with Lydia."

"And she bought that bullshit?" he asked.

"Hook, line, and sinker."

"Wow."

"But he had no intention of breaking up with me, and he would have continued with the lie, if neither Lydia or I had found out. We actually…had sex in the Hamptons that week after I knew he was with Lydia."

"Fuck. No wonder you hate him and are terrified of relationships."

"I'm not terrified of relationships. I'm terrified of getting my heart ripped out all over again. I find it hard to trust people after what Preston and then Neal did to me."

"But you trust me?"

She nodded slowly. "I really want to."

"I really want you to, too." He linked their fingers together and pulled her in for a slow kiss.

"What about you? Any past girlfriends?" Trihn asked, trying to take the spotlight off of her for a minute.

"Sure. A couple. None really worth mentioning."

"That usually means something bad in my book."

He chuckled and took another bite of his French toast before drowning it in coffee. "I guess I had a serious girlfriend in high school, but we went to different colleges, and long-distance worked for all of two weeks before she wanted to see other people. There were a few short-term girls in college. Just didn't work out."

"I'm surprised by that."

"Why?"

"Because you're so…perfect," she finished.

Damon laughed disbelievingly. "I've cleaned up my act a bit since then. Decided I wanted to be someone other than the life of the party."

"So, you partied a lot?"

"Comes with the territory. DJs usually end up at parties. You get to know a lot of people—frat boys, jocks, stoners. When you mingle with them all, you start to find yourself drifting in that direction," Damon admitted. He frowned and looked down, as if he were remembering something particularly troubling. "I kept my cool, but I saw a lot of people who didn't."

"I bet you did. What was the worst thing you saw?" she asked.

Damon shrugged. "That's all relative, of course. But one memory kind of sticks out."

She questioningly raised her eyebrows.

"I was at this insane party last March. This crazy blonde cheerleader was throwing it because some sugar daddy had bought her a fucking mansion."

Trihn laughed. "Bryna's party?"

"Yeah. This *gorgeous* girl was at that party. Hands down the most beautiful woman I had ever seen."

"Oh," Trihn said, wondering why the hell this was important.

"But she was there with another guy."

"How unfortunate for you."

"Yeah. All I wanted to do was go over and introduce myself. But she was way too far out of my league. She had these beautiful friends who would do anything for her and a boyfriend who she seemed to care way too much about. The guy was a total dick and made it his personal mission to be as horrible of a boyfriend as possible to this girl."

Trihn narrowed her eyes. "Me?"

"You." He nodded. "He chose to come to the party. Then, he moped the whole time and got pissed at you for being there. He made you cry, and then you ran out after him."

"I did," she whispered. "You remember that?"

"I remember because I swore if I ever got a girl as amazing as you, I wouldn't do the same things that douche bag did."

Trihn sighed in satisfaction. "Where did you come from again?"

"Born and raised in London, love." He tucked a stray strand of hair behind her ear and leaned forward to give her a kiss.

"If all Londoners are like you, then I fear for the hearts of the women in England."

"I only fear for my own heart because of my drop-dead gorgeous girlfriend." Damon laughed and pulled her in for another kiss. "You taste like cinnamon."

"I like when you say that."

"Mmm...delicious cinnamon."

She shook her head and playfully slapped him on the shoulder. "No, calling me your girlfriend."

"You're my girlfriend," he repeated before kissing her nose. "You're my girlfriend." Then, he kissed her lips. "You're my girlfriend." Then, he kissed down her neck.

"I'm never getting any work done ever again," she said.

"Is that a complaint?"

"Absolutely not."

Damon picked her up and carried her back into the bedroom. He dropped her on his bed. She laughed and lounged back.

Something lit up on the nightstand that drew both of their attention for a split second.

He narrowed his eyes at the phone. "Weird."

"What is it?" she asked, sitting up on her elbows.

He reached for his phone and looked at the screen. "I have four missed calls from Jimmy."

"Do you think he's okay?"

He looked worried. "We're about to find out." He dialed the number. "Hey, Jimmy. You all right, man?" He leaned the phone between his shoulder and ear and then sat down on the bed next to Trihn. "Whoa, slow down. What are you talking about?"

Damon's face drained of color, and Trihn's stomach sank.

What the hell happened?

"Is he okay?" she whispered.

He pulled the phone back and pressed the speaker feature. "Hey, Jimmy, slow down, and say all of that one more time."

"Fuck, Damon. Just listen to me already. Cadence posted a video of you on YouTube. It's of you performing with Chloe last night at Posse. It's all over the Internet. Get online right now. You're fucking trending on Facebook and Twitter."

Trihn's mouth dropped open. "Oh my God!"

"I have to see this," Damon said.

She opened the Facebook app on her phone, and sure enough, there was the headline.

CHLOE AVANA, GRAMMY-NOMINATED ACTRESS,
PERFORMS WITH DJ AT NIGHTCLUB

She clicked on the link, and the video started playing automatically.

Trihn couldn't believe it. Cadence had gotten a great shot of Damon and Chloe singing, and the vocals were perfect. Even though the booth was dark, it was clear who was singing. It even looked like it was just the two of them with no one else there.

"Damon! Fuck, are you still there? Everyone is asking who you are and where you came from. Your name is starting to show up online. I saw an article with it in there. Hold on. Let me send it."

A second later, Damon's phone dinged, and he opened up the link to reveal a picture of himself with Chloe beneath another headline.

CHLOE AVANA PERFORMS A REMIX OF
"HEARTBREAKER" WITH UP-AND-COMING
DJ DAMON STONE

"Up-and-coming," Damon whispered.

"You've hit the jackpot!" Jimmy cried. "Can I get your autograph?"

"Fuck off, Jimmy. It's nothing. This is about Chloe. It'll blow over."

"I fucking hope not!"

"It will, but thanks, man. I'll talk to you later."

"Congrats. Later."

Damon hung up, and Trihn and Damon silently sat there as the rest of "Heartbreaker" played on Trihn's phone. When the song finally ended, she closed out of the video and then refreshed the page. Her eyes bulged when she checked the stats on the video.

"One point two million views, and it's only been up for a few hours," Trihn said.

"This is Chloe's life."

"But you're in it," she said.

She started scrolling through the comments. Every fifth one mentioned Damon in some capacity. It was variable on whether it was favorable or not, but he was as much a part of this as Chloe was.

Trihn didn't think Damon even realized it until his phone started ringing again.

"It's a blocked number," he said.

She shrugged. "Just answer it."

"Hello?"

Damon straightened immediately and stood up. "Uh, hey, Chloe."

He took a few steps into the other room and chatted on the phone. He even laughed a few times at whatever she was saying.

Trihn pulled her knees up to her chest. Her stomach was in knots. She wanted to know what Chloe was saying on the other line, but some part of her didn't want to know. At some point, she knew that whatever Chloe said had something to do with the 1.2 million views on their now viral video.

It wasn't often that a person could point to one specific moment in time and say, *This changed everything.* But here, right now, was Damon's moment. And it was about to change everything.

He walked back into the room as he hung up the phone and turned to face Trihn with clear shock and exhilaration on his face. "I'm performing 'Heartbreaker' tonight at Chloe's concert at the MGM."

TWENTY-ONE

"LADIES AND GENTLEMEN, the moment you have all
been waiting for," the announcer called out into the
stadium. "Chloe Avana."

The crowd erupted with deafening applause.

From backstage, Trihn watched as Chloe rose from an
underground platform onto the stage. It was insane to
think that, just last night, she'd had front-row seats to this
show with her best friends, and now, she was watching it
live with her boyfriend, who would be performing the final
number with Chloe.

Her life had flipped upside down in the span of
one day.

Damon laced their fingers together and rubbed his
thumb up and down her hand. "Breathe," he told her.

She turned away from Chloe's show and stared at him,
taking in his chiseled strong jawline, sharp cheekbones,
long dark lashes framing even darker eyes, and perfect

kissable lips. His messy hair was tucked up under his signature flat-brim baseball cap, and he'd gone with an all black ensemble. Chloe's people had said they would dress him if he wanted, but he'd wanted to be comfortable and confident out there. Trihn was biased, but she thought he was strikingly handsome tonight.

"Why are you comforting me? You're the one about to go out in front of seventeen-thousand people."

"And you're the one who looks like you're going to hyperventilate."

"I do not," she said. She took a few even breaths and reminded herself to calm down. She was supposed to be here for moral support, not freaking out herself.

"I did a sound check already. Chloe and I practiced the song a dozen times today. It's going to be fine." His fingers grazed her chin. His dark orbs bore into hers, and it was as if he could see right through her. "We're going to be fine, too, love." He raised their laced fingers to his lips and pressed a kiss there.

They watched the remainder of the show from the sidelines. Near the end, a guy came over to collect Damon for his role in the closing number.

"I'll see you after the show," he said.

"Have fun."

"I will."

And then Damon was gone.

A few minutes later, Chloe had made another full costume change, the last of some ten outfits she'd worn during the two-hour show. It was a black front-zipper high-waist miniskirt and a jeweled black bra top with spiked high heels that Trihn would die for.

Chloe had a rhinestone microphone and spoke into it, "Hello, fabulous Las Vegas!"

The crowd cheered for her.

"I have one last song for you tonight before I go. You might have seen my new single 'Heartbreaker' online today. Did everyone watch it?"

The stadium practically shook with cheers from her dedicated followers.

"Well, my good friend is here tonight to sing *that* version of 'Heartbreaker' for you. Everyone, DJ Damon Stone!"

Damon walked onstage with confidence in every single fiber of his being. The crowd cheered just as loud for him as they had for Chloe, and he soaked it up. What would terrify most people was a straight shot of adrenaline to his system. He was purely in the zone when he stepped up to the booth.

The drummer kicked in. The guitar melody thrummed to life. The bassist started up the backbeat. And then Damon mixed it all together with his soundboard until it sounded as amazing live as it did every single time he had played it in Posse.

Chloe was cued up for her intro, and then she went full swing into her number one hit. Damon picked up the backup vocals with ease, and soon, they were singing together. Their voices mingled, hers shining above his, and the harmony was perfect. Near the end of the song, when her big vocals came into play, she turned to face Damon, and with their eyes locked, they sang the final words to each other.

Trihn's heart stuttered.

The crowd cheered for the finale. Chloe turned away from Damon and took a bow, and then she ran back and grabbed his hand, forcing him to bow with her.

"Thank you," Chloe said breathlessly. She waved at her audience and then strutted offstage, still holding Damon's hand. Once they were offstage, Chloe threw herself into Damon's arms. "That was incredible!"

He hugged her briefly and then put her back down on the ground. He hastily removed himself from her, but he was smiling wide from their performance. "That crowd! You have the best fans."

Trihn just stood there and watched with a sinking pit of worry in her stomach. She was happy for him. The show had been incredible. He had the world at his feet. She didn't want to think about anything else—not the fear clawing away at her or the knowledge of what fame could do to people and definitely not the look Chloe had on her face when she looked at Damon.

In that instant, he turned to Trihn, as if knowing she was watching. His smile lit up, and he called her over. She walked to him, and he pulled her to his side.

"Hey, Damon, stick around. I'll be right back," Chloe said.

Mateo was already hurrying her away to her dressing room.

"See you in a bit." Damon turned his attention back to Trihn. "What did you think?"

"You were great out there," she honestly told him. "Truly amazing. You were meant to do this."

"Thanks." He pulled his hat off his head and then ran a hand back through it before plopping it back down. "It's easy to do with you watching me."

"You're silly. It's easy to do because you're incredibly talented." She ran her hands up his chest and pulled him in for a kiss. "And *very* sexy."

"Oh, I like where this is heading."

He grabbed her real tight and started slow dancing with her right there in the middle of the backstage area, as if no one else was around.

"What are you doing?" she asked with a giggle.

"Dancing with my girlfriend."

"Right now?"

He twirled her around in place and then dipped her without warning. She giggled again, but he looked completely serious and in his element. His lips touched hers, and she melted into him.

"Sorry to interrupt," Chloe said from behind them. Someone had blown out her hair and retouched her makeup. She looked fabulous.

Damon immediately righted Trihn and then turned back around. "What's up?"

"I just have some autographs to sign and then a meeting with my manager." Chloe glanced over at Trihn. "You don't mind if I steal him for a minute, do you?"

"No," Trihn croaked. She cleared her throat and shook her head. "No, of course not." She turned to Damon. "Go. I'll wait here."

Damon kissed her again. "I'll see you in a minute."

She watched him walk away with Chloe and sighed. She didn't know how to handle this. She knew the lifestyle well enough from having modeled back in high school, but being an international musical superstar was a totally different story. She needed to talk to someone who had been through this.

Trihn pulled her phone out and texted Bryna. When Bryna had dated Gates Hartman, he'd been an up-and-coming movie star. Now, for his age range, he was the *it* male actor in Hollywood. Bryna had been raised in Hollywood. She would know how to deal with this.

And my boyfriend is now a music god.

It went that well?

Yeah. He's signing autographs and speaking with management right now with Chloe. It's great.

You sound so enthused. #rollseyes

I am happy for him.

Yeah, but you're not happy about it.

I'm worried. You dated a movie star. You must know what it's like. Obviously, Damon's not at that level right now, but what if that happens, Bri?

Fame is different. If anyone knows that, it's me. But nothing bad has happened yet, so don't wish it into existence. The more you freak out over it, the more you're going to put that out into the world. Damon likes you. He's been chasing you since you two met. He wouldn't do anything stupid to jeopardize that.

Yeah. You're right.

Damn straight I'm right. And just remember, you're a rock star already, and he knows it. Plus, I'd send E and Pace and the rest of the football team to beat his ass if he stepped out of line.

Trihn laughed and shook her head. *Of course she would.*

Thanks, B.

What felt like hours later, Damon and Chloe finally came back to where Trihn had been standing restlessly. They both looked completely energized from the events that had unfolded. Trihn crossed and uncrossed her arms as they approached, laughing like old friends.

Trihn forced a smile onto her face. "Hey! How did it go?"

"Great!" Chloe said. "So, so amazing!"

Damon nodded. "Pretty awesome. I've been on the Internet with Chloe for a day, and people already know who I am."

"As they should," Trihn told him.

"I'm so glad that both of you could be here tonight," Chloe said. "This was so much fun for me. It was even better than a regular show."

"Anytime," Damon said. "Where are you headed to next?"

"Phoenix, I think. Then, Dallas and Austin, and then we're ending this leg of the tour in New Orleans. And I'm finishing up the new record. Once it releases, I'll have so much more music for the summer tour."

"Busy," Trihn said.

"Yeah, well, that's the music industry—produce, promote, and tour." Chloe shrugged. "After this next tour though, I want to do another movie. The studio's not going to like hearing that, but I miss acting."

"Sounds like a rough life," Trihn joked.

"Harder than it looks."

"But with crowds like that, totally worth it," Damon said.

Chloe nodded. "Completely. Well, I'll let you two head out. You have my number, right?"

"Yeah, I got it," Damon said.

"Cool. I'll be in touch if I hear anything."

"Sounds good."

Chloe hugged them both before strolling off to her dressing room.

"In touch about what?" Trihn asked as they walked through the back exit to Damon's car.

"I spoke with her manager and some other music people who were there for the show. Nothing is set in stone, but they want some samples of my music."

"Really?" she gasped. "Are they going to sign you?"

"It kind of sounded like they were interested in at least hearing what else I've done. A record deal would be...out of this world. Chloe thinks it could happen. She kept telling them to sign me on the spot," he admitted.

"Wow. That was...nice of her. She believes in you that much?"

"Enough to pull me onstage for her own concert, so I'd say yeah," Damon said. He unlocked the car, and they both sank into the seats. "It would be epic, but I'm not getting my hopes up. Either way, it was incredible to play live on that stage. A dream come true."

"I'm glad I could see it."

"If I had it my way," he said, speeding out of the parking lot and away from the Strip, "I'd have your beautiful face at every one of my shows."

Trihn lit up at his comment. "So, what are you going to do now?"

Damon shrugged. "Wait."

TWENTY-TWO

"YOU HAVE GOOD CLEAN LINES," Teena Hart said, examining the clothing samples that Trihn had put together.

"Thank you." Trihn wrung her hands in front of herself as Teena swept through the various designs. They weren't all finished. They were just the shells of what she was going to have as final pieces to fit to her models.

"What is your inspiration for the line?"

"My inspiration?"

"Yes," Teena said. "There seems to be a theme among your work. If you don't have a speech on what inspires you, then you're already lost."

Trihn pulled herself together. With all the stuff that had been happening with Damon, she had been so out of it with her own work. Focusing on her art was the thing that had gotten her through a lot of ups and downs. She needed to continue to focus on it if she wanted to win that fashion show—even though she thought it was highly unlikely.

"My inspiration for the line comes from my diverse background in New York City and the nightlife around the world. I wanted to make a fluid line that went from everyday wear and straight to the club. These are clothes that can be worn on a runway or the Strip or in Central Park."

"I see what you're saying, but I recommend you find a specific story for your line. The judges will need something to latch on to. Don't be afraid to get personal."

"Right. Thank you for your insight," Trihn said. She made notes in the notebook she was carrying. She had a long list of things she needed to do before she would be ready for the runway. As far as she was concerned, getting personal was the least of her concerns.

"And do you have your models yet?"

"Not yet."

Teena carefully eyed her. "I don't have to lecture you on the importance of having the right models for your line."

"No, you don't."

"Gucci, right?"

Trihn nodded. She was surprised that Teena knew that she had modeled at all, let alone who she had modeled for.

"I'm going to have a model call in the next week or two. I have some people in mind, but I'd like a variety."

"Excellent. I do hope this is all cleaned up before the fashion show," Teena said, blindly gesturing to a few of Trihn's designs.

She froze, wondering what the hell Teena was talking about. After that comment, Trihn would have to go over every single stitch and extensively work on them. Preparing for this fashion show was taking up so much time on top of her already busy class schedule. She hoped it would all be worth it.

"Thank you," Trihn said.

Teena signed off on the paperwork for Trihn's samples and jotted out the suggestions she had made. "Keep up the good work. Next time I see you, you'll be directing your models down the runway."

Trihn sighed and plopped down onto a barstool by her station. That had gone better than expected, but she still had a mountain of work to do. Just looking at it was giving her a headache. She needed to take a break, yet she had no intention of leaving the studio until she had some of this under control. Not to mention, she now had to get a model call together.

She buried her face in her hands and took a few healing deep breaths. She could do this. It was possible.

She could finish her classes for the semester and rock this fashion show. She could push back her apprehension about Damon's newfound success. She could resist the all too-present fear about the future and her relationships.

For so long, she had been cautious about relationships. Time and again, she'd had her heart shattered to the wind. Now, she could feel she was falling for Damon. He was stealing her heart away, and this time, if something happened, she didn't think she would be able to rescue it.

Damon was different from everyone else. He was so *sincere*. She hadn't realized the difference in Preston and Neal because there was none. But Damon wasn't like either of them.

She so desperately wanted it to be the truth and to never change that she worried she was strangling it, strangling herself. Her own insecurities were real and raw. He knew about them, of course. She'd told him about all of her issues. But that didn't mean it would change anything in the end.

She shook her head, frustrated with her dark thoughts. Fishing out her phone, she dialed his number, desperate for a friendly voice. It went straight to voice mail, and in shock, she glared at her phone. Her breath started coming out quickly. She had to close her eyes to try to push back the threat of hyperventilation.

"Fuck," she whispered. She needed to get this under control.

What the hell was happening to her?

When had she turned into this shell of a woman?

She gasped and looked upward. Her frustration was replaced with anger—anger at herself for letting this get to her. She needed to put this into her art, not obsess over a phone call.

Damon would call her back. He would.

Hours later, Trihn's phone lit up.

She looked up, bleary-eyed, at the display. She had been staring at her designs all night. She had made some headway on a few, but overall, she felt like she was too close to the clothes to really see how she needed to move forward.

She reached for the phone and answered it, "Hey."

"Trihn, fuck, I'm so sorry. I meant to call you back hours ago," Damon said.

"Oh, that's okay," she lied. "I've just been at the studio. What have you been up to?"

"Chloe's manager called me. I was on the phone with him when you called me, and then when I got off the phone, Chloe called right away."

"Really?" she asked.

"Yeah. So weird that Chloe Avana called me. What is my life?" He laughed huskily. "We talked for a while. She was on her way to New Orleans for the last stop on her tour."

"Great." She lacked all emotion in her voice.

"Are you okay?"

"Yep." *No.*

"Okay," he said softly. "Well, they listened to the other stuff I'd sent over, and they liked it. They're going to take it to the studio heads to see what happens. Still no guarantees, but Chloe thought that meant I should hear soon what they want to do."

"Did she think that?" Trihn knew she sounded catty, but she couldn't help it. She had been trying so hard to be happy about all of this. Her near panic attack earlier was making her bitchier than normal. Not to mention, she couldn't remember the last time she had eaten.

"Okay…you seem upset. What's wrong?"

"Nothing," she snapped.

"It doesn't sound like nothing."

"I'm just tired and hungry. I need to get out of the studio and get some sleep or something."

"Why don't you come over here? I can make you something, and we can talk about this."

"I really don't want to talk right now."

He sighed heavily. "I don't want you to go to sleep angry."

"I'm not angry," she practically shouted. She took a deep breath and closed her eyes. Fuck, she needed to calm down.

"Trihn, just come over. I can tell you're upset. I want talk to you in person about what's going on in that head of yours. I don't want this to simmer between us."

Trihn grumbled and started packing up all her stuff. "Fine. I'll be there in fifteen minutes."

She gathered up the last of her supplies, locked her designs up in her assigned locker, and then carried her sketchbook with her out of the studio. She hurried across the quad and down a long pathway until she reached the parking lot ten minutes later.

Her nerves were shot by the time she pulled up in front of Damon's apartment. The drive had cleared her thoughts. Too long in the studio coupled with her issues with relationships and Damon's newfound success hadn't done well for her psyche.

She felt pretty stupid that she'd let everything get to her and that she had snapped at Damon when he was just excited about his blossoming opportunities in the music industry.

As she took the stairs to his apartment, she started humming the melody to her anthem, "My Own Worst Enemy" by Lit. She knocked twice and then waited.

Damon pulled the door open. He was on the phone but gestured for her to come inside. Her guard automatically went up. It had only taken her fifteen minutes to get over to his place, and already, he was on the phone with someone else again.

"Hey, I've got to go," Damon said, closing the door behind her. "Yeah. It was good to talk to you, too. Sure. I'll let her know. Night. Love you."

Trihn recoiled into herself and hurried over to the living room. She dropped her bag down on the coffee table before turning back to Damon. She anticipated the blow that was sure to follow.

"Hey," he said with a bright smile. "My mum says to tell you that she hopes you can come by this week for dinner. She said she'd make whatever you wanted."

"That was Mel?" Trihn asked hesitantly.

Damon cocked his head to the side. "Yeah. Who did you think it was?"

She shrugged. "I don't know. I just…"

"Think I throw *I love you*s around pretty casually?" he asked with a gleam in his eye.

"I…well, I don't know what I thought."

"Well, I don't. Just to my mum."

"That's good," she admitted. She didn't want to tell him what she'd thought was going on.

"So, do you want to tell me what's wrong?"

She shook her head. "Nothing. I'm just under a lot of stress, and it's making me irritable."

Damon took a seat on the arm of the couch and looked up at her with those all-knowing eyes. He looked so good in a plaid button-up with the sleeves rolled up to his elbows and dark jeans. He'd done his hair for once instead of the mess it was usually in from his hat. But she still wanted to run her fingers through it. Looking at him made her realize how crazy she had sounded earlier. It was much easier to feel safe when she was with him.

"I know you're under stress, but it's more than that. I called to tell you the good news about talking to the manager, and you nearly bit my head off. I just wanted you to be happy for me."

"I *am* happy for you."

Damon questioningly raised his eyebrows.

She sank down onto the coffee table and faced him. "I *want* to be happy for you."

"But…"

"But I'm also terrified," she whispered. She hated how vulnerable she felt with that admission.

"You're terrified? Why?"

"This whole thing is terrifying. We just started dating. I'm putting myself out on the line. And then, the first time things shake up, you ignore my call."

"I didn't ignore you," he said immediately. "I was just talking business."

"I know. I get it. I do. But when Preston didn't return my calls, it was because he was with Lydia."

"Trihn, I'm not Preston," he said with a heavy sigh. "I'm not sure what I have to do to convince you of that."

"I know you're not."

"Do you?"

Trihn closed her eyes and tried to calm down again. "If I thought you were like him, we wouldn't even be having this conversation."

"Okay." Damon held his hands up. "I didn't mean for it to come out like that. I know you're struggling with trust issues. You told me that, but please don't hide what you're feeling from me. I need to know, so I can be there for you."

"I'm not used to talking about my issues, and I feel incredibly stupid about having any issues when your dreams are coming true."

Damon reached out and took her hand. He looked her dead in the eyes. "You're my dream come true."

Trihn gave him a half-smile and a look filled with disbelief. "You can't say those kinds of things when I've been a total bitch."

He laughed and drew her into him, tucking her up on his lap.

"You're not a bitch. You're worried and letting it get to you. And I can say those kinds of things because they're true."

"I just…don't want to put effort into this, only to eventually lose you," she whispered her biggest worry. "Your music is taking off. You're going to get busy and have crazy fans and Chloe and…everything. I don't know how I fit into any of that."

"Look, none of what you're worrying about is set in stone. It's all completely up in the air. We can't stress about it before it has even happened. They could come back to me and say that the executives thought I sucked. No record deal. The end. You know?" he asked. He squeezed her a little tighter and pressed a kiss on her shoulder. "But either way, you're not going to lose me."

"You're not worried at all?" she asked self-consciously.

Damon laughed lightly and ran a hand back through his hair. He seemed to have forgotten that he'd actually done it. "Of course, on some level, I'm worried. All I want to do is live in this moment with you, get to know you, and have a normal, easy relationship. I'm lucky to have this opportunity with you and with the music. Without you, I wouldn't have any of this. So, I just want you to see that, no matter what happens in the future, I want to be with you. Just let me."

Trihn snuggled into his chest and kissed his neck. "Okay. I'm sorry. I'll try to be more open. I don't want you to think you're the only one invested in this relationship. I worry about the future because I don't want to lose you."

"I know." He tilted her head up and kissed her lips.

She broke the contact with a smile. "Can you play that song for me, the one you turned in to her manager?"

"Which one?" he asked.

"You know, the one about the girl at the party. I'd never heard that before you showed it to me for the manager."

"'We Never Met,'" he said with a laugh. "You like that one?"

"Yeah. It's catchy. Plus, who doesn't like a good love story?"

Damon shook his head. He looked like he wanted to say something more, but he just stood and carried her into the bedroom. He effortlessly set her down on the bed, and then he took a seat across from her and tuned his guitar.

"Oh, acoustic," she said with a smile.

He glanced up at her, and then he started singing. He was good with a soft, breathy tone to his voice that worked well with the pop and hip-hop beats. But this was raw and real.

"Walked into the club.
Music up, crowds pumped.
With one smile you flipped my world.
Heaven knows you draw me in.
And only hell knows what I'd do
for just one chance.

I'd give it all up for the girl at the party.
Ready. Set. Go. Light me up.
It's time. No saying sorry.
And one day I'll find the courage to say:

That I know you're the one.
Even though we never met.
Yeah I know that you're the one.
Even though we never met."

Damon went through the second verse and then repeated the chorus twice before strumming the last chord. He smiled up at her, and she realized her heart was racing. With the backbeat, all the other instruments, and his amazing mixing skills, the words would get lost in the music. She had never really grasped exactly what he was singing about. It had just been another catchy song that would probably kill it on the radio and in nightclubs.

But this was different.

Because she was pretty sure that song was about her.

"When did you write that?" she whispered.

He smiled. "A couple of months ago."

"Before we met?"

"If you're asking if the song is about you, then yes, it is. All musicians have a muse."

"You didn't even know me!" she said with a laugh. She stood and walked over to him.

He placed the guitar down, and she straddled him.

"That's the point of the song. You were the girl I'd give it all up for."

"You're something else, you know that?"

He brushed her hair back. "I take that as a compliment."

Then, he was hungrily kissing her, as if all the pent-up frustration had finally broken. He hoisted her up and they fell into bed together, stripping each other's clothes with ferocity. Their bodies melded together. They took their time, savoring the feel of one another.

They knew that everything might change, but today, they had each other. And that was what was important.

When they finished, Trihn curled up in his bed. Damon retrieved his phone from the other room and placed it on the nightstand. Then, he jumped into the shower. She wanted to join him, but she was just so tired. She yawned and felt like she could succumb to sleep at any minute. Her eyes closed, and she burrowed into the pillow.

A loud buzzing jolted her out of the half-sleep she had fallen into. She glanced over at Damon's phone. Her eyes fell on the lit up screen. It read *Chloe* in bright letters.

"Damon!" She snatched it up and hurried into the bathroom.

"Hey, you decided to shower. Get your cute ass in here."

"Chloe is calling."

"Shit!" He switched the water off and stepped out of the shower, with water dripping down his abs.

She got completely sidetracked by every glorious muscle that was slick and taut. He hastily draped a towel around his lower half, breaking her out of the spell, and she handed him the phone.

"Chloe?" he asked eagerly into the phone.

"I'll just…" Trihn pointed at the door and walked back into the bedroom. She put on sleeping clothes, crawled back into bed, and waited to hear why Chloe was calling him in the middle of the night.

She could pick out a few of the words coming from the other room but nothing substantial. She was jittery with nerves for him.

After their talk, she'd felt so much better about them going forward. Now, all she felt was excitement for what was to happen in their future. Sure, there would always be factors that could change their relationship, but that would be a possibility with or without the music. So, she at least wanted him to be happy.

When the conversation ended, Damon walked back into the room. He tossed the phone down onto the nightstand, sighed heavily, and frowned.

"What happened?" she asked softly. She sat up on her elbow. A whole new world of fear hit her.

Then, a smile lit up his face. "I'm in!" He jumped onto the bed and wrapped her up in his arms.

"Oh my God! You're still soaking wet!" she yelled.

He laughed and kissed her hard on the mouth, not releasing her. "They want me to record a song with Chloe for her upcoming album."

"That's incredible."

"I leave for Los Angeles next week."

"Oh, wow. So soon?"

"Yeah. They said that she only has a few more songs to record, and this will be the last session that they do. I'll be there for a couple of days, and then the album will release over the summer."

"That's insanely fast-paced."

"I know. Everything is kind of happening out of nowhere. One night, I'm deejaying at Posse, and the next, I'll be recording with Chloe Avana in LA." He kissed her again, as if he couldn't seem to stop doing it in the midst of his excitement. "You and I have nothing to worry about, okay? This doesn't change us."

"I know," she said. "We'll do it together."

"Yes, we will."

TWENTY-THREE

"I SHOULD BE BACK by the end of the week," Damon said a week after getting the recording schedule.

"I know. I'll just miss you."

"I'll miss you, too. But maybe it will be even less time," he said optimistically. "Chloe is a pro at this stuff, and everything should run smoothly."

"I wish I could be there with you."

He laughed and softly kissed her. "I would love that, but I think you'd be bored. It's, like, eight-to-ten-hour days. The studio is putting me up in a swank hotel, but I have a feeling that I'm going to be so exhausted that I'll just crash every night."

"No, you won't. You're a night owl."

"True. Then, I just won't be productive in the mornings."

Trihn wrapped her arms around his waist and hugged him. "You're going to be great."

"I'll be back before you even know I'm gone."

"Doubtful."

"Well, at least you have your model call this week to keep you busy. The fashion show is only a month away. It'll probably be good to have the extra time to work on your designs."

"I know you're trying to be helpful," she said with a smile, "but nothing is as good as having you here."

He squeezed her tight and picked her up off the ground, bringing his mouth to her lips. "Man, I'm going to miss you."

"You should go before I decide not to let you leave at all."

He planted another kiss on her lips. They lingered there like that for a minute. It was a moment mingled with sadness and happiness. They were both excited for Damon's future and sad that it was going to take them apart.

Then, he quickly released her and got into his car. She had wanted to go with him to the airport, but he didn't want her to miss any school and thought that might make it even harder to say good-bye. They had basically been inseparable, and it was going to be hard enough with him going away for those few days.

Trihn sighed and got into her own car. She headed back to her apartment and entered into silence. She hadn't spent a night here in over a week. She felt bad that she hadn't seen her friends as much, but she knew they understood and were happy that she'd found a stable relationship.

Trihn slammed the door shut behind her and trudged to her room where she changed for class. As she was walking out of her room, Stacia entered the apartment.

"Hey, stranger!" Stacia said cheerfully.

"Hey yourself. Where have you been all night?"

"As if you've been here."

"Nah, I was with Damon. He left for LA today."

"That's so awesome!" Stacia skipped over to where Trihn was and took a seat on the couch. "I can't believe everything that's happening for him."

"Me either. It's pretty unreal."

"Definitely. I mean, who knew that going to that concert with Bri would change your life?"

"Change Damon's life."

"Well," Stacia said thoughtfully, "yours, too. Now, he's going to be gone a lot. And if all goes well—and it's Chloe Avana, so duh—he'll be recording albums, going out on tour, and doing promotions all year round!"

Trihn frowned. "Yeah."

She swallowed hard and tried to remind herself of all the things that Damon had said to her. They would be okay. They could make it.

"That'll be amazing for him. At least I'll be around the apartment more," she said.

"No one blamed you for being gone. Anyway, the apartment has pretty much been empty. Bri has been at Eric's, and I've been with Marshall." Stacia giggled at the end of her statement.

"So, does that mean that you and Marshall are together now?" Trihn asked. She knew it was always a tough call with Stacia. Her relationship status usually changed from one day to the next.

Stacia shrugged. "I'll get him there. Right now, he's in it for the sex."

"And you?"

"I'm in it for the money." Stacia winked.

"No, you're not!" Trihn said, laughing at her friend. She had finally gotten Bryna to see the insanity behind her gold-digging ways. She was bound and determined to get Stacia to see it, too.

"Well, he doesn't have any money yet, but when he gets drafted next year, he will. And then I'll join the NFL quarterbacks' wives club!"

"Is that a real thing?"

"Duh!" Stacia flipped her short blonde hair and relaxed backward on the couch.

"Such high goals you've set for yourself."

"I would take that as a compliment, but I know you're being sarcastic," Stacia said. "You're dating a soon-to-be mega-successful music star. It's really not any different than a star quarterback."

Trihn sputtered in disbelief. "Damon was a nobody when we met and started dating!"

"And so is Marshall."

"A college quarterback at a major university is hardly a nobody."

"Details, Trihn!"

"Okay," she said, holding up her hands.

She couldn't argue Stacia's logic with her. Stacia had no intention of listening to a word Trihn said.

But Trihn did know one line of conversation that would get Stacia to break out of this bubbly character. "Have you heard from Pace?"

Stacia stiffly sat up and seemed to retreat in on herself. "He's been around," she said softly.

"Around like, you've been sleeping together? Or around like, he wants to get back together?"

"Just around. I don't know," she said, looking down at her hands. "I miss him sometimes, you know?"

Trihn knew where she was coming from. Pace might have been a total asshat, and Stacia might be a dumb blonde cheerleader, but together, they had seemed to work. It hadn't made sense, but it'd worked for them.

"Does he know that you miss him?"

She scoffed. "As if I'd tell him. He's so arrogant. He would use that to his advantage, and I can't be with him the way he is now. Plus, I have Marshall…and that's what matters."

"I just think that Marshall seems like a tactical choice, and Pace seems like one that comes from your heart."

"Pace is a quarterback, too, Trihn," Stacia reminded her. Her eyes were wide, as if she didn't want to consider that she actually cared for Pace.

"I know, but he's not the starter. You don't even know if he's going to the NFL."

"I don't want to talk about Pace," Stacia said quickly. "We broke up. We're...whatever...on and off again whenever he feels like it and isn't fucking someone else. I'd rather talk about Damon and him working with Chloe and your model call! I'm really excited for that."

"Me, too. Are you and Bri still coming to the studio to help out this afternoon?"

Trihn had booked out the studio for her model call. She'd emailed some of her friends who she'd modeled with in the past. She hadn't heard back from anyone, not that she had really expected to. The university didn't pay for models, and unless she wanted to pay out of her own pocket, she would have to get a bunch of models with little to no experience. Offering free headshots and runway experience wasn't exactly the same as hiring models for a magazine shoot. Having gone through this process herself, she knew it was going to be an ordeal. She had a feeling she was going to be there all night, even with Bryna's and Stacia's help.

"Yep! We'll be there. Hopefully, it's only one day though because, from here on out, we'll have four to six hours of practice every day to get ready for the NCA national competition in Orlando."

"Think you guys will bring home first prize this year?"

Stacia nodded vigorously. "Getting fifth last year was an embarrassment. We can do better, and we will!"

"I believe it." Trihn grabbed her purse. "I have to get to class. So much work to do on top of this fashion show. It's going to keep me plenty busy. I'll see you guys at three."

"See you then!"

Trihn left the house, and the weight of all the work she had to do before the end of the semester crashed over her. It was well and good that she was wrapped up in her boyfriend, but she couldn't let everything else slip.

By the time the afternoon rolled around, she was already mentally exhausted and had three new papers to work on for next week.

Bryna and Stacia showed up ten minutes after her, and the visual arts major she'd gotten to photograph the models appeared right behind them.

"Hey, thanks so much for showing up," she said, shaking his hand. "I'm Trihn."

"Jasper." He swept his longish mop of hair out of his eyes and itched for the ponytail holder at his wrist. He was lugging a giant camera bag, a tripod, and some other equipment, including one that looked like a boom.

She wasn't entirely sure how he was carrying it all around.

"You can set up in there. We'll send models in to you after their interviews and measurements," Trihn told him.

"Cool." He nodded and then disappeared.

He'd had experience working with the fashion design school in the past, so she was sure that he would get the shots she wanted. It would be different when they did the photo shoot with her designs. She'd want to be there to see what was going on. But, right now, he could handle it on his own.

"Where did you pick him up?" Bryna asked, sitting down on the desk and raising an eyebrow.

"He's working for free."

"You get what you pay for," she said.

Trihn rolled her eyes. "And that's why millionaires pay for your time."

"Because I'm worth it, of course."

"Okay. Girls should be showing up soon. I'm going to sit out in the waiting room with the girls, so I can observe them without them knowing who I am yet. I'll need one of you checking people in. Stacia, probably you since you're friendly."

Stacia skipped over to Trihn and took the clipboard. "Got it."

Bryna rolled her eyes. "I'm friendly…when I want to be."

"Right. Let us know when that time comes around this year," Trihn said.

Bryna flipped her off.

"Once everyone has shown up, I'll work with you on interviews, and Stacia will direct people into the room."

"Sounds like a plan. I'll just sit here and wait then," Bryna said.

Stacia went out to the front room as girls came in to audition for the model call. Trihn came in shortly afterward and pretended to sign in with Stacia.

Trihn observed the girls and even made friends with one gorgeous redhead. Trihn had gone to dozens of model calls before being selected to model for Gucci. She could pick out the bitchy girls, the divas, and the high-maintenance girls who wouldn't listen to anyone's critiques. It was cut-and-dry and made her life so much easier once they got into the interviews.

The looks on the girls' faces when they saw that Trihn was interviewing with Bryna were priceless. Modeling was so competitive that everyone should be on their best behavior at all times.

By the time they had gone through most of the girls, Trihn and Bryna were both in pissy moods. These girls just were not up to the caliber she had been hoping for.

The redhead was the last girl to come through. Trihn had high hopes for her, and even though she didn't ace the interview like Trihn had hoped, she sent the girl through to the photo shoot anyway.

Jasper returned after the final model had finished and laid out all the images in front of Trihn. After selecting the girls to move on to round two, she realized it wasn't that many. She would need at least twenty girls for her line, and of the nearly hundred who had come today, she had sent through only twenty-three to the next round.

"Shit," she murmured.

"Yeah," Bryna agreed.

"Guess you'll have to use us after all!" Stacia cheered.

"Excuse me. Is your open call over?" a woman with a thick South African accent said from behind them.

Trihn hadn't even heard anyone come into the room.

"Yes, sorry, we're done. We finished promptly at eight," she said without looking up.

"Well, what a pity."

"Trihn," Bryna said, nudging her, "I think we should open the call back up."

"What? Why would we—" The words died on her lips as she turned around to see the woman standing before her. "Francesca!"

Trihn ran across the room and pulled her friend into her arms. She and Francesca had modeled for Gucci the summer after her junior year of high school. They'd worked together on a few more campaigns before Trihn had decided to quit the work to go to college.

"What are you doing here?" Trihn asked.

"Well, you messaged me, and I'm in between jobs. We wrapped up the new line earlier this week. I thought I would come help out a friend." She flipped her stick-straight blonde hair to one side. "And I brought in some reinforcements."

Standing in the entrance to the design studio were nine other gorgeous models, all girls who Trihn had worked with at some point in her time as a model.

"Thank you so much for coming. I can't pay you though."

Bryna cleared her throat. "That's not exactly true."

"You cannot pay for this!"

Bryna shrugged. "I can do what I want."

"Well, that's not necessary," Francesca said. "We're doing this for fun. I just wish I could have gotten a few more people together for you."

"No, this is perfect. I just have to pick another ten then," Trihn said in wonder and bewilderment.

"Oh, let me take a look," Francesca said. She leaned over the images they had been sorting through before she'd shown up. "Hmm…"

With ease, she went through them and picked out nine. After a minute, she selected the redhead as their last model.

"That's who I would go with. They seem to fit the Trihn I know. And we can work with them in the meantime," Francesca said. "It'll be like a three-week mini vacation."

"This is going to be amazing," Trihn said, feeling more excitement than ever for this project. For the first time, she really thought that she could do this.

Trihn reached for her phone that she hadn't looked at in hours with all the interviews they had done. She had missed a few texts and a video message from Damon. She clicked on the message and was transported to LA where he was standing in what looked like the midst of a recording studio.

"Hey, love. I just got into the recording studio. Chloe wanted to show me around. Here's Chloe. Say hi, Chloe."

The camera veered over to Chloe with her dark hair piled up into a ponytail on the top of her head. She was in dark jeans and an oversized sweatshirt. She waved at the camera. "Hey, Trihn!"

Damon flipped his phone back to face him. "We have to work bright and early tomorrow morning at eight a.m. I have no clue what I'm going to do with myself that early in the morning. All I know is that I'm missing you like crazy, and I hope that your model call went well. Call me back when you get this message."

The message ended, and before she could even sigh or smile, Francesca leaned over and looked at her with wide eyes. "Was that Chloe Avana?"

Trihn laughed. "Yeah."

"And Damon Stone?"

"You mean, her hot rock-star boyfriend?" Bryna said with a wink.

"Girl, we have a lot to catch up on," Francesca said.

"I guess we do," Trihn said.

TWENTY-FOUR

As much fun as it was to have all her model friends around Vegas for the days that Damon was gone, it was also exhausting with all the work Trihn had to do. She had stayed up late into the night and gotten up early every morning just to try to finish her papers while working on this project.

It hadn't hurt that Damon called every morning and every night before she went to bed to fill her in on what was happening. It'd sounded like a long, tedious process, but he'd said, other than one hiccup, everything had been running smoothly, as planned.

He was supposed to come home in the morning, and she was all jittery ready to see him. She knew he finished in the studio around ten at night on a late day, so she was sitting around the house working on one of her papers and waiting for his call.

Bryna and Stacia were wandering around the house in short cut dresses and dancing to a playlist Stacia had put together on Spotify.

"Trihn," Stacia cried, "come on! Dance party!"

Trihn looked up at them over the top of her MacBook. "As much as I'd love to, I have work to do."

"All work and no play makes you as bitchy as Bryna," Stacia said.

"Hey, I'm queen bitch. Trihn is just a moody, angsty, serious bitch. There's a big difference. I was born this fabulous," Bryna said.

"I'm not bitchy. I'm just the only person in this house who cares about my education."

Stacia laughed. "We all care…sort of."

Bryna cracked up. "Come on. It's Friday. Let's go to Posse and have a drink. Maya is working, and you could probably stand to get out of the house."

"I'd love to, but I'm going to pass."

"You can't just sit around and wait for Damon to call," Bryna said. She crossed her arms over her chest and fixed her quintessential stare on Trihn. "And don't try to deny that's what you're doing."

"Fine. That's what I'm doing. I'm *that* girl. But he'll be coming home tomorrow, and then I won't be freaking out anymore."

"Or you could just trust him," Bryna said.

Trihn closed her eyes and counted to ten. "I do trust him. I just miss him."

"We both know you well enough to know that you're worried," Stacia said, taking the seat next to Trihn.

"And we think it's in your best interests to get out of the house. Damon isn't Neal," Bryna said. "There's really no reason for you to be so stressed."

"I don't think he's like Neal," she said. "In fact, maybe he's the opposite of Neal. I just want Damon to be home."

"Well, he won't be home until the morning. So, a party it is," Stacia said. "Plus, everyone is going out tonight—the whole football team and all the cheerleaders. We only have a week until nationals, and the guys are playing their spring game the weekend we get back."

"So, you want me to go and hang out with your boyfriends—"

"Whoa! I don't have a boyfriend," Stacia said automatically.

"And, well, Eric is worried about you moping around here," Bryna added.

"No," Trihn said. "Maybe I'll go out after Damon's call, but I have to pick him up early in the morning, so I wouldn't want to be out late anyway."

Bryna sighed. "Fine. He'd better call soon then."

They walked back to their rooms to finish getting ready.

Trihn whispered under her breath, "Yeah, he'd better."

It was one o'clock in the morning when Trihn's phone rang.

She had given up on even the semblance of getting work done. Her computer was sitting half-open with Facebook winking up at her. Her design notebook was flipped to a blank page. Her imagination had run away with her but not toward her creative endeavors.

All she had thought about was the time she had waited up all day and night for Preston to call her back and how she had so easily swallowed his bullshit the next day. He'd been at work. He'd been so busy. He'd fallen asleep at his desk.

Yeah, right.

She should have seen it then. He'd been with someone else. The devastating part, of course, was that the someone else had been Lydia, but it would have been just as hard if it were anyone else.

As she reached for her phone, she had a horrible sinking feeling of déjà vu.

"Hello?" Trihn said.

"Trihn!" Damon called into the phone.

She yanked the phone back from her ear. It was insanely loud on the other end of the phone. Music slammed into her ear, and Damon was practically yelling to be heard over the noise.

"Where are you?" she asked.

"Fuck, I'm so sorry, love. I'm out at a nightclub with Chloe and some of the production crew. They wanted to celebrate finishing up the album. I was going to call you when I got back to the hotel, but then time just ran away from me."

"It's almost one in the morning," she said.

"I know. I looked down at my phone, saw the time, and freaked out. I hope you weren't worried."

Trihn took a deep breath. Of course she had been worried. "Well, I was. Kind of. I mean, you normally call right when you get out of production."

"Damon, come on!" Trihn heard someone yell in the phone. "I want you to meet someone."

"Chloe, just give me a minute," Damon said. The phone was muffled, like he'd put his hand over it, as he talked to Chloe. "Sorry about that. Chloe has been introducing me to a lot of people. She's been really supportive."

I bet she has.

Trihn tried to clear the ugly thoughts from her head. Chloe had been nothing but awesome for Damon. And she had been incredibly nice to Trihn. She had spoken to Chloe a couple of times since Damon had been gone. Their relationship seemed entirely professional, and there was no reason to think it was otherwise. That wasn't the kind of person either of them were.

"That's good, Damon. I just didn't think that you'd be out so late when you're coming back on an early flight tomorrow."

"About that," he said so quietly that she barely heard him.

Her stomach sank.

"Chloe set up a few interviews and meetings with people around the city for the upcoming album release. She thought that it'd be good for me to be there to meet people in the business. It's such a good opportunity that I don't think I can turn it down."

"Wow. You're promoting the album already?"

"Yeah. It'll come out at the beginning of the summer. Preorders are up everywhere, and the full track listing will go up once they release the title track."

"That's fast-moving," she said. She took a deep breath. "How long are you going to be gone?"

"I think just a day or two. I had to sign a lot of paperwork to record this song, and I need to get my own talent agent and manager while I'm out here. Don't want to get screwed over or anything."

"Oh, okay."

"Hey, I wouldn't do it if I didn't have to. I'm still missing you like crazy. Can't wait to get back to you."

"I know. I can't wait either."

"Damon!" Chloe called again.

He sighed heavily. "Hey, I've got to go, but I'll call you tomorrow."

"All right. I'll talk to you then. I miss you."

"Bye, Trihn."

The line died in her hand, and she stared at her phone.

This was a good thing for Damon. This was what he had been working toward. He needed to be there for his career. But it didn't stop the first edge of panic from taking over her body.

She repeated to herself all the things Damon had said to her before he left. They were all that mattered. He cared for her. They could make it. They were a team. It pushed the panic back a little, but knowing she had been sitting around all night waiting just irritated her.

All night, she had been freaking out about him instead of just trusting him and having fun with her friends. That was what she should have been doing—not sitting around her apartment, all alone, and getting worked up.

Trihn changed into one of her signature outfits—black leather miniskirt and black rhinestone bra top with her leather jacket and knee-high leather boots. She blew out her dark hair until it was stick straight and then added dark makeup with cherry-red lips.

She called a cab, and ten minutes later, she was breezing through Posse's crowded entranceway with nothing more than a flutter of her fingers to the bouncer as she bypassed the fifty people waiting in line. The nightclub was jam-packed. It was usually busy, but since Chloe's appearance, Posse had been unstoppable with lines out the door, a full dance floor, and flowing drinks. Even the VIP section was crowded.

Luckily, Trihn knew everyone who worked there. She found Maya under a mountain of drink orders.

"Trihni!" Maya cried when she saw her. "You don't happen to want to pour drinks tonight? I'm swamped."

"I'd be useless. You should ask E."

"If I wanted margaritas, I would." Maya passed over a round of shots, two beers, and a few mixed drinks to the people in front of the bar. They were quickly replaced by another group desperate for drinks. Maya handed Trihn a drink. "Gin and tonic, right?"

"Thanks. I'll take a Peppermint Posse martini, too, when you get a chance."

Maya stopped what she was doing and looked at Trihn. "You want to get fucked up tonight?"

Trihn shrugged. "Basically."

Maya shook her head but started making her the drink. She handed the potent mix over to Trihn. "I don't even want to know what lover boy did, do I?"

"I'll give you one guess."

"Chloe Avana?" Maya asked.

"Bingo." Trihn downed the gin and tonic and handed the glass back to Maya.

"You made it!" Stacia cried, barreling into her from the dance floor.

Bryna was hot on her heels with Eric and Marshall following close behind. "A Peppermint Posse martini?" she asked. "I didn't know we were getting belligerent tonight. Make that two, Maya."

"Oh! Three!" Stacia said.

Maya shook her head but started working on the drinks.

"What happened?" Bryna asked intuitively.

"Nothing. Damon is staying in LA for a few more days to help Chloe with promotion and to get an agent and manager."

"Those are important things," Bryna rationalized.

"Yep. I'm just going to sit here and drink until it really feels like that's the reason he's there."

"That boy is crazy about you," Maya said.

"And you're crazy about him," Stacia added.

"I don't get why you're stressing. I mean, Chloe is a bitch, but Damon digs you. I'm not entirely sure where this is all coming from." Bryna searched Trihn's eyes. "You act as if he's already cheated on you when he's only going to be there for a few more days. Neal was an asshole, but you didn't even really love him. I don't get the extent of your fears. What am I missing?"

Trihn grabbed her martini from the bar and started drinking. Of course they didn't get it. They didn't know her whole history. She had always compartmentalized her life. Maybe it was time for her to open up.

"You know Preston, my sister's fiancé?"

"Yeah," Bryna said, clearly wondering about the abrupt shift in the conversation. "You said he was a douche."

"Yeah, that's because he was my first real boyfriend. I fell in love with him, and then it turned out that he'd been with my sister the entire time. They didn't even break up when the truth came out the summer after graduation. I'd been planning to go to NYU, but two weeks before classes were going to start, I dropped everything to come here. It was all because of him, all because he ruined my life."

All of her friends were staring at her with their mouths hanging open. Even Maya had stopped pouring drinks to look at Trihn in shock.

"So there...trust issues on full display. And, yes, Damon knows all about this. And he's still in LA and he still didn't call right away and he still is with another girl at a club. And in case anyone has a shoddy memory, a club is where we met. So, don't mind me if I decide to drink heavily tonight."

Eric put his hands on Bryna and Stacia. "Maybe we should give her some space, y'all."

"All right, Cowboy," Bryna said, taking a step back. "We were just trying to help."

He kissed the top of her head. "You did what you could, Hollywood."

Trihn closed her eyes against the image of how freaking cute they were.

Stacia reached out and rubbed her shoulder. When Trihn opened her eyes, she was staring directly into Stacia's baby blues.

"I know I'm not normally the serious one of the bunch, but just for the record, I don't think Damon is cheating on you. I think he's very much in love with you, and you have nothing to worry about." Her voice dipped lower. "If I had something like that, I wouldn't let it go, no matter what, Trihn. You're really lucky."

"I don't feel particularly lucky tonight," Trihn admitted. It was really strange to see Stacia be visibly vulnerable.

"Just have fun with us tonight, okay? It'll be better in the morning with fresh eyes."

Stacia held her hand out, and with a deep breath, Trihn put her hand in Stacia's.

Maybe Stacia was right. Maybe things would be better in the morning.

TWENTY-FIVE

DAMON HAD ALREADY STAYED a week longer than he'd expected. It was a lot more work than he'd thought it would be, and Chloe had been introducing him to a lot more people. But he had been prompt in calling Trihn every single day, which lessened her stress.

Stacia was right. After Trihn's breakdown at Posse, she'd seen it with clearer eyes the next morning. She was letting her past relationships cloud this perfectly good one, and if she didn't stop, she was going to lose Damon over her own foolishness.

Damon would get back when he got back. It was about time for his call again anyway. Trihn had her phone near her, but she was working diligently on some last-minute changes to one of her skirts. Everything had to be turned in for final approval on Monday, and then she could have her photo shoot and work on getting the models ready for the runway. Thankfully, Francesca had agreed to help.

When the phone rang, Trihn smiled brightly. "Hey you," she answered.

"Oh, man, I have missed that voice."

She laughed. "I miss you, too. How were your meetings today?"

"Long and tedious. If I have to make small talk with one more person, I'm going to stab myself in the eyes."

"Don't do that," she said. "You'll mess up your pretty face."

"Yeah, well, Los Angeles is its own beast. Not sure how I'd feel if I had to be there all the time."

"You grew up in London and Las Vegas. Shouldn't you be used to big cities?"

"Sure. But LA has its own flare. It makes me want to eat a cheeseburger," he admitted with a chuckle.

"Cheeseburgers sound good."

There was a knock at her door, and she sighed, wondering who was here so late at night.

Bryna and Stacia were gone for the NCA nationals, and Trihn had the apartment to herself. It was nice for the peace and quiet but not so much for strangers knocking on the door.

"Hey, hold on. Someone is at the door," she said, cradling the phone between her face and shoulder.

"Oh, okay. Sure."

She peered through the peephole, but no one was there. Then, she pulled the door open and nearly dropped the phone.

"Oh my God!" she shrieked. "What are you doing back already?"

Damon laughed and pulled her into his arms. "I wanted to surprise you!"

She jumped, wrapping her legs around his torso and kissing him hard on the mouth. He carried her through the front door and kicked it shut behind them. Without a word, he walked her through the house and into her bedroom.

She dropped to her feet in front of her bed, a huge smile plastered on her face. "God, I've missed you."

"Good surprise?"

"The best."

"Fuck, it is so good to see your beautiful face." He cupped her face in his hands and tenderly kissed her, as if she were the very air he breathed and that kiss sustained him.

And then the tide broke.

He released her face and started tearing at her clothes. Her shirt and bra fell into a heap at the foot of the bed, and then he dropped to his knees, hungrily kissing his way down her front. He unbuttoned her jeans and dragged them down her legs. She stepped out of them, and his hands searched up her legs to her exposed inner thighs before spreading her legs further apart.

He buried his face against her lace thong and blew until she was squirming.

"Do you like that?" he growled, his voice deep and husky, his British accent rolling over every single word like a heated caress.

And just at his touch, she was on fire. Her body tightened, and when he slid her panties aside and pressed his fingers up inside her, she arched backward.

"Fuck," she murmured. She was wet from just having him close. Her body responded to his demands.

"That is exactly what I intend on doing."

He moved his fingers in and out of her, and then he slicked his thumb down her folds before pressing it to her clit. She moaned loudly, not realizing how much she had missed his touch until just that moment. She hadn't been prepared for this, and now, her body was hyperaware of every move he made.

He circled his thumb against her clit until she felt her legs turn to Jell-O. She nearly collapsed forward onto him with the force of her orgasm.

Damon left a soft kiss on her thigh before removing her underwear completely. He lifted her, as if she were weightless, and set her down on the bed. She lay back flat, the remnant of her release still flowing through her body.

She watched him pull his black T-shirt over his head, revealing his six-pack abs beneath. His hands went to his belt buckle, yanking it free from his jeans. He folded his belt in half and snapped it together, making a loud thwack each time the sides met, and then he flicked her leg with it just hard enough to leave a biting sting on her thigh.

"Ow," she said, her eyes wide.

He chuckled softly. "Careful now, or you're going to deserve a lot more than that."

Her mouth fell open in surprise. *Who is this gorgeous man in front of me?*

He laughed at her expression and tossed the belt to the side.

"Guess you have some of that bad boy left in you, huh?"

Damon raised his eyebrows. "You bring it out of me, lover."

He flicked the button on his jeans and then dragged them to the ground. His boxers followed until his dick was in full view before her.

"Come here," he said, beckoning her over.

She crawled across the bed to him. He sat down and pulled her over on top of him. She straddled his body. His hands crawled up from her hips to her breasts. He brought his mouth down onto her nipple, and she felt the ache in her core start up all over again. He flicked his tongue across the erect ridge, circling and sucking. Then, he moved to the other one, and all the while, she felt heat pooling in her center.

Trihn twisted until she felt the tip of his dick pressing against her. She was all for the foreplay, but her body was demanding his attention. She circled her hips in an intricate dance, trying to get him inside of her. But he held her in place, only giving her an inch to try to get herself off.

"Fuck me. God, I need you," she cried as he spent extra special attention on the other breast.

Damon looked up at her with a wicked, devious grin and then forced her down all the way onto his cock.

"*Oh*," she breathed. She tilted her head back, letting her eyes close.

He bounced her up and down, thrusting up into her when their bodies met. "I've wanted to do this every day I've been gone."

"Maybe you should be gone more often," she joked.

"If you wanted it rough and dirty, all you had to do was ask."

Her pussy clenched around him at the words, and it was his turn to groan. He slammed her back down on top of him, and then he seemed to lose all semblance of control. They moved together perfectly in sync. The days apart had made their desire that much more heightened.

"You take the reins," he said, leaning back on the bed to watch her fuck him.

She pulled her hair over one shoulder and started bouncing up and down on his dick with force, her breasts moving with her. She could feel herself coming to the height of her climax once more. She rested her hand on his hard chest and rolled her hips.

"Oh, fuck," he said. "Fuck. You are the most beautiful thing I have ever fucking seen in my life."

She quirked a smile between heavy breaths. Then, he took her hips in his hands and rocked her down onto him harder and harder. She hit her release with a scream just as he came inside her. Her inner walls squeezed him tight until she collapsed forward on top of him.

He kissed her temple as they both lay there, panting.

"Wow," she whispered. "I really missed you."

"I missed you, too."

"I changed my mind. I don't think you should leave again."

He chuckled and lightly kissed her lips. "Hey."

She glanced up at him through hooded eyes. "Hey."

"I love you."

Her heart stopped beating in her chest. "What?"

"I love you so much," he repeated. He pushed her loose hair off her face and brought his lips to hers once more. "I've wanted to tell you every day, but I didn't want to scare you. Trihn, I love you."

"I love you, too," she whispered.

His smile lit up the world. "That's the best thing I've ever heard."

In the past, Trihn had been the first to say those words, and they had been her downfall. She knew then that part of her worry had been centered around those three words. Deep down, she had known that she felt that way about Damon, but she hadn't wanted to fully commit to that if she were just going to get her heart broken.

But now, here they were, and she couldn't take it back. She would never want to take those words back because they were the unequivocal truth.

She loved Damon Stone.

TWENTY-SIX

"OH MY GOD, I am never leaving you two alone ever again," Trihn said to Damon and Eric.

They were currently *directing* the models around for her photo shoot.

Her designs had been approved earlier in the week, and she had gotten all the models together for the real deal now. Soon, she would have hundreds of pictures of her designs on gorgeous models. It was almost too hard to believe. But then she looked around the studio where all of her models were just arriving and realized it was very much her reality.

Since Bryna and Stacia were out of town, she had corralled Damon and Eric to help in their places. Unfortunately, that meant a whole lot of goofing off and not all that much actual work.

"You two are killing me," she said.

"We're just following orders," Eric said.

"Yeah, Trihn. It'll all happen just how you want it to," Damon agreed.

"Plus, this one's phone keeps going off every five minutes," Eric said. "Makes it hard to pay attention and not goof off."

Trihn raised her eyebrows.

Damon punched Eric. "Thanks for telling on me."

Eric laughed and walked away to get more work done. Damon stepped up to Trihn with a sheepish grin on his face.

"I thought you were going to take this seriously."

"Love, I am taking your work seriously. This is all fucking incredible. I'm so proud of you."

She beamed. "Thanks. I can't believe how great it's all turning out."

Damon's phone dinged again, and he groaned, checking the display, before shoving it back into his pocket.

"Your phone never stops going off now."

"I know," he grumbled.

"So popular."

"It was easier dealing with all of this in LA, but I wouldn't trade being here with you for the world. I want to see your success as much as mine." His phone pinged three times consecutively. "Fucking hell."

"Maybe you should just silence it," she suggested.

He looked down at his phone and apologetically back at her. "I'm waiting on a call from my agent. Chloe said that something was in the works and to wait to hear about it."

"Just for a couple of hours?" she pleaded. "One hour?"

"You're right," he said automatically. He turned the ringer off and pushed the phone out of sight, unanswered. He pulled her forward by her belt loops and planted a kiss on her lips. "I want to be here for you, not halfway to LA."

She leaned into him and sighed. Ever since he had gotten back from LA, they had been in this happy lovey-dovey honeymoon stage that she wouldn't trade for anything.

"I wish we could stay in this moment forever," she admitted.

He dropped his head so that he could whisper into her ear, "Well, I could think of a few other things we could be doing."

She took a deep breath to try to calm down her racing heart. "Don't tease me."

"But it's so much fun."

"It's sweet torture." She took an unsteady step backward, remembering where she was.

Damon had a confident smile on his face. He knew exactly what he had done to her.

A minute later, Francesca came out of the dressing room in her first outfit—the black cutout dress that Trihn had worn to the Chloe concert.

"Wow," Trihn breathed.

"This is fabulous," Francesca said, twirling.

"Isn't it great to see all your dreams realized?" Damon whispered.

"Is this what it feels like when you're recording?" she asked in awe.

"Long hours. Big payoff."

"That is definitely this feeling." She pointed to another room. "Francesca, you can head in there. The photographer should be here any minute."

Francesca winked and then headed into the other room.

Damon's hands ran down Trihn's sides. "I have to say it. That dress looked better laid out on the DJ booth while I fucked you."

She shivered all over at his touch and the memory that came with it. At this rate, they would have to find a place for a quickie.

Eric appeared at that moment and motioned for a man to walk over to them. "Trihn, photographer is here," he called.

"Thanks," she said, sidestepping out of Damon's arms.

"Trihnity," the man said with a smile. He pulled her in for a hug. "I've missed you."

Her eyes gleamed as she turned to Damon. "This is Gabriel. He came all the way from New York City for this."

Gabriel stuck his hand out, and Damon took it.

"Damon, nice to meet you. You must be Trihn's boyfriend."

"That's right," Damon said, shaking tightly.

"I hope you're treating my daughter right."

Damon sputtered and then looked between the two of them, noting the resemblance. "Yes, sir. You must be Trihn's father. It's an honor to meet you."

"You can drop the sir and call me Gabriel."

Trihn laughed when Damon turned to her with his mouth still open.

"You could have warned me," Damon said.

"But that wouldn't have been any fun." Trihn giggled. "My dad is a fashion photographer. He's photographed all the famous models and for all the best magazines."

"Wow. That's incredible. This should be great for your designs then."

Gabriel nodded. "I'll do my best to make the designs shine, but with the models she has, I think it will turn out all right." He looked into the room that had been set up for him to photograph in. "Haven't seen Francesca in almost two years."

"She's excited to work with you again," Trihn told him.

"I should go arrange the equipment to my liking, but first, what are you doing after school lets out?" he thoughtfully asked Trihn.

Trihn chewed on her lower lip. She had always been a daddy's girl. When the stuff with Preston had gone down, her father had been the one to let her leave and process and help her get set up at school. But she had a feeling that she knew where this was going.

"I'm not sure," she said.

"I'm not going to insist that you come to Lydia's wedding, like your mother, but I would appreciate it if you came home to see everyone. Your mother misses you, and maybe if you talked to everyone in person, we could get this cleared up." He sounded so hopeful.

"I don't know, Dad."

"I love you, baby girl. But just give an inch for me."

Trihn looked up into his eyes and realized it was as close to pleading as he would get. She had never really been able to deny him anything, and he was the same way with her.

"All right," she said finally.

"Damon, you're, of course, invited as well," Gabriel said automatically.

"Thank you, sir."

Gabriel laughed. "Just Gabriel."

"I would love to come and meet the rest of Trihn's family."

Gabriel glanced at Trihn and smiled. "I like him."

Trihn chuckled. "Me, too."

"All right. Back to work. Let's get started," he said.

Gabriel hurried into the next room, and they could hear the shrill squeal as Gabriel walked in on Francesca.

Damon raised his eyebrow and crossed his arms. "You bombarded me with your dad without warning."

Trihn cracked up. "Yep. You did good."

"One minute, I was talking about fucking you, and the next, I'm meeting your father." He shook his head. "At least I'll have a warning when I meet your mother and the infamous Lydia."

Trihn frowned and looked away. "Yeah, about that...you really don't have to come with me if you don't want to."

"What are you talking about? Of course I want to come with you." He grabbed her by her shoulders and looked her square in the eyes. "I have every intention of being there when you have to go through that situation. I know it's not going to be easy or comfortable, but I'm not here just for the good. I'm here for everything."

"I love you," she whispered.

"I love you, too," he said with a smile. "Now, go make your dreams come true."

Trihn spent the next couple of hours working with the models, fixing minor issues on the designs, and basically running around like a madwoman. Her father was a professional, and with so many of the models having real-life experience, it made the process go by so much faster.

"That's a wrap," her father said some hours later.

The entire group cheered and congratulated Trihn on the success of her first official photo shoot. It felt incredible. All the models had photographed beautifully in her clothes. And with this, she hoped that she would have a fighting chance as a sophomore design major in such professional competition. If anything, she had put her heart and soul into it, and that showed through every product.

Her eyes sought out the one person she wanted to share this accomplishment with. But she didn't see Damon.

"He's out back," Eric said, realizing who she was looking for.

"Oh. Okay. Thanks."

"Hey, Trihn?"

"Yeah?"

"I just wanted to say that I'm happy for you. I know not everything has been smooth sailing, but I think he's an infinitely better choice than Neal. He's a good guy."

She smiled. "I think so, too, but it means a lot to hear you say that."

"Good job on all of this. Wish I could have been more help, but it seems like you have it all taken care of. I'm going to head out."

"Thanks, E."

He tipped his head at her and then started to leave with the models who had changed out of her one-of-a-kind designs.

Trihn headed out the back door and into the darkness beyond. She saw a silhouette of Damon with his hands in his pockets. He was staring out at the campus that was softly illuminated by streetlamps.

"We just finished," she said.

He quickly turned around. "Hey. Sorry I wasn't in there for the finale."

She waved her hand and came to stand next to him. "Doesn't matter. You were there for basically everything else."

"Yeah." He took a deep breath of the dry, dusty Vegas air.

"What's up?" she asked, intuitively sensing a shift in him.

"I have some news."

"Oh?" She swallowed hard. The way he'd said it didn't make it sound good. "The stuff Chloe told you to keep your phone on for?"

"Yeah. Our song is going to be the opener for the new album."

"Oh my God!" Trihn cried. "The opener?"

"It should release internationally in a week or two. Damon Stone featuring Chloe Avana," he said wistfully.

"Your name is first?" she asked, confused.

"Yeah. The DJ's name comes first and then the singer. That's how it's normally done, and Chloe insisted we keep it the same—not that it changes anything, except for the order."

"Um…I think that changes a lot, Damon. You're going to be the first artist listed on an internationally bestselling song. This isn't just a couple of million YouTube views. This is *it*."

He nodded. "Yeah."

"So, when do I finally get to hear it?" she asked.

"As soon as I can play it for you, I will," he softly told her, still looking out into the abyss.

"I'm so excited for you. Why aren't you more excited?"

"They asked me to be in the music video for the song."

"That's incredible!" she said.

But he still looked sad.

"What is it?"

"Nothing," he said, shaking his head. "I guess I've just had such a great week with you that the thought of going back to LA is painful."

"Oh." She reached out for his hand, pulling it from his pocket. "But this is your dream. You want me to pursue my dream, and I want you to pursue yours."

"I might have to miss the fashion show," he said, wincing as he delivered the news.

Her stomach dropped, but she managed to hold it together. He had been there enough for her. She needed to be there for him.

"That's okay, Damon."

"It's not."

"Damon, look at me."

He did as instructed.

"You are going to be in a music video for the debut single on Chloe Avana's new album. You absolutely cannot be sad that you're missing one fashion show to do that. I promise you, I will have other shows."

He pulled her in close, holding her tight, and he rested his chin on top of her head. "I just want to be here for everything. I don't want to miss a moment with you."

"We're going to have so much more time than this."

"When all your dreams come true, you're supposed to live happily ever after." Damon kissed her forehead. "No one ever tells you what you have to sacrifice to get there or that your happily ever after comes with a world of different stresses you never imagined."

"That's the funny thing about dreams. They're always better when you're sleeping."

TWENTY-SEVEN

"SERIOUSLY, HOW DO YOU have so much shit?" Bryna complained, hoisting another bag into the trunk of Stacia's SUV.

Trihn shrugged. "It's an in-case-the-world-ends assortment of things."

Her hands were trembling, and she felt like a bug was coming on. Everything about today put her on edge and worried her. It was the big day.

"What if it sucks?" Trihn asked.

"You're Trihn Hamilton. It won't suck," Bryna said.

"Plus, we've worn the clothes. They're awesome," Stacia said. She dropped one last bag into the very full trunk. "I think that's it. Time to go."

Trihn hopped into the backseat, and Bryna took shotgun. While Stacia drove, they blasted the radio on the way to the Vegas Strip where the fashion show would be held in one of the many glamorous ballrooms at Caesars Palace.

The girls had done their hair and makeup beforehand, knowing that they would be swamped with work once they got there. Trihn had decked them out in her designs, and she had to admit that they looked like a certified squad—the bitch, the slut, and the badass.

The radio crackled as the announcer came on. "Welcome back! We have a special announcement. A world premiere that just released. You're hearing it here first. The first single off of Chloe Avana's new self-titled album."

"Turn it up!" Trihn cried.

Damon hadn't let her hear the song yet. He had said that he wasn't approved to do it, even while making the music video. He'd promised to let her hear it as soon as they were done. The song must have leaked before then.

Stacia flipped the switch, so the volume cranked to max.

"Debut artist DJ Damon Stone, featuring Chloe Avana. This is 'We Never Met.'"

Trihn rocked back into her seat with her mouth open. Her heart beat fiercely as the song started. When Chloe's vocals cued in, the girls all started dancing in the their seats.

"Oh my God," Trihn said.

She knew those lyrics. She had heard them only twice before—once in a recording and once when Damon had sung them to her, acoustic-style, in his bedroom. This was *her* song.

Even though it was Chloe singing her song, it was still pretty crazy that there was a song written about herself on the radio. Plus, Damon's backup vocals sounded amazing, and if she closed her eyes, she could remember him singing it to her.

When the song ended, Stacia turned the music down. "That was so good," she said.

"It's my song," Trihn said, slightly dazed.

"Your song?" Stacia asked in confusion.

"Yeah. He wrote it about me."

"And he let Chloe sing it?" Bryna asked, raising her eyebrows.

"Yeah, I guess. I mean, he didn't tell me what song he was recording. When I asked him when I could hear it, he said when he was cleared for it. I guess it got leaked early or something," she said.

"Suspicious," Bryna said.

Stacia smacked her on the arm. "No, it's not!"

"Sounds just like Chloe to me."

"I'm sure it's not like that," Stacia said.

"Guys, I'm sure he has a legitimate reason for not telling me about the song."

"Yeah, but what about this music video?" Bryna asked. "Aren't the lyrics basically about finding his dream girl in a club? What are the chances that they made Damon and Chloe find each other in the club for this music video?"

Trihn frowned. She hadn't thought about that. "I don't know, Bri. You know Hollywood."

"Stop freaking her out," Stacia said. "Damon is a good guy. No one should be suspicious. His song is on the fucking radio!"

"I'm not suspicious of Damon," Bryna said immediately. "Just Chloe."

Trihn nodded. "Yeah, well, it's his first single. I'm not going to worry about any of that until after the fashion show."

They pulled into the parking lot, and a few of the volunteers came out to get the rest of Trihn's equipment. Then, they sauntered into Caesars Palace as if they owned the place.

Backstage was full of senior design students who Trihn had been sharing studio space with for the four months she worked on this project. Models were running around half-naked with their hair and makeup in different stages of disarray. Designers were fluttering by, trying to fix issues and doing adjustments.

When Trihn made it to her models, Francesca had already organized the girls into groups. Hair and makeup was all but done. The girls just had to get into their clothes, and they would be all but ready to walk the runway.

"You're a goddess," Trihn said before kissing Francesca on both cheeks. "I could never thank you enough for doing this."

"What kind of friend would I be if I didn't help you in your time of need?" Francesca eyed the other designers' work and raised an eyebrow. "And it looks like many are in some desperate need."

"Okay, everyone," Trihn said, rounding up the troops. "Once you're finished in hair and makeup, please get into your outfit and line up in order. If you have any questions, please direct them to me, Bryna, or Stacia."

The volunteers had placed the last of her designs on a rack, and girls started rifling through the bags to collect their outfits. It was less organized than Trihn would have liked, but as long as they were all where they needed to be, then it was fine.

About half an hour before the show started, Trihn was fixing a zipper on a girl's skirt when Bryna snuck up behind her. "Hey, I have a surprise for you."

"Wha—" Trihn asked through a mouthful of pins.

"I need to steal you."

Trihn took the pins out of her mouth and finished the last stitch on the hem of the skirt. "I think that's good. Let me know if it doesn't hold up."

"Thanks, Trihn!"

She turned back to Bryna with raised eyebrows. "What's up?"

"I might have called in some favors."

"Oh, Lord, what did you do?"

Bryna grabbed her arm and dragged her up the stairs to the stage. From their viewpoint, they could see out to the crowd that had started filing into the ballroom. Only a few rows in the back left were still open.

Trihn felt the familiar sense of stage fright take over, and she put her hand on her chest. "That's a lot of people."

"Yeah, but look." Bryna pointed to the front row, and Trihn followed her line of vision.

When Trihn saw who Bryna was pointing at, Trihn gasped and smacked Bryna on the arm. "You invited Gates?"

"Ouch. Take it easy! Of course I invited Gates, but it's not just that. Look at his date."

"Fuck," Trihn whispered when she saw the tall leggy blonde with bright red lipstick in a two-piece white-skirt-and-crop combo seated next to Gates. "Is that—"

"Yep," Bryna said, popping the P.

"I thought she was dating Calvin Harris!"

"Oh, who can keep up? She's here with Gates, and that's all that matters. It looks like she's brought some friends, too."

"I can't."

"Yeah, I have a feeling this is going to be all over Page Six in the morning. I don't think they've been photographed together before." Bryna nudged Trihn and smiled. "You'd better win this thing, so you can get your name in the paper, too."

"You're unbelievable."

"I know," she said, flipping her long blonde hair over her shoulder.

"Everyone, gather around!"

Trihn looked over her shoulder and saw Teena Hart gesturing for all the students to get together to talk before the show started. Trihn hurried down the steps and shouldered into the lineup.

"Thank you all so much for the endless hours of hard work and dedication to your craft. It'll all culminate in tonight's performance. We have some exceptional guests in the front row of our audience tonight, so be prepared for more press than intended. We're working on controlling the situation, but we didn't exactly anticipate celebrities showing up to this round."

Trihn glanced over at Bryna, who snickered.

"In any case, that doesn't change anything for you. As you know, the winner of this show will go on to New York City to compete nationally. This year, for the grand prize in New York, the winner's line will be picked up by Bloomingdale's and be featured in *Glitz* magazine."

Trihn's mouth dropped open. Bloomingdale's was her dream store. Of course, she had a lot of hurdles she would have to jump before she got to that, but just the opportunity was unbelievable. And to get into *Glitz* magazine, where her mother was a senior executive for the company, *without* her mother's help would be so satisfying.

"But no matter what happens here today, you have all completed your assignments, and you are all winners in my eyes. We'll be starting in just five minutes. Please get your models ready. Thank you, and good luck."

Teena left to introduce the fashion show, and all the designers scattered to get their models into order and make final adjustments.

It felt like hours before it was finally Trihn's turn. Bryna and Stacia squeezed her hand before leaving to go watch her big moment.

Francesca was her first and last model, and before Trihn walked out onto the runway, Francesca enveloped her in a big hug. "Show the world what you're made of."

Trihn nervously smiled at her and then took the stairs to the stage. She catwalked the runway like she was born to be onstage. A microphone was waiting for her at the end, and she stepped up to it with her heart in her throat.

"Ladies and gentlemen, I'm Trihnity Hamilton, and this is my designer collection, Clothes by Trihn. The look I'm showcasing for you today is a street-to-runway look that you can wear anywhere. Whether walking the streets of New York City, dancing on a rooftop in Milan, or lining the red carpet in Hollywood, Trihn fashion can take you there because I've been there as a ballet dancer in New York City, a model in Milan, and now fashion designer here in Las Vegas. Welcome to my personal street style, Clothes by Trihn."

At her last line, Francesca walked out onto the runway in Trihn's signature black cutout dress. The crowd cheered as she and Francesca circled each other. Francesca winked, and then they passed one another.

When Trihn made it backstage once more, she put her hand to her chest and breathed in, feeling relieved. She had forgotten how nerve-wracking it was to be onstage. She worked with the rest of the girls before they went on at their allotted times.

Trihn hurried over to help Francesca into the final piece. She was the only model who was wearing two items, but Trihn wouldn't have it any other way.

The dress was everything on Francesca's tall frame. A floor-length gown hugged her hourglass figure. The bottom half was a see-through black-and-silver mesh that wisped and circled perfectly on her figure while half-concealing her tall black heels. It had a heart-shaped plunge neckline and sleeves that snaked loosely around her biceps. It was the only thing in the line that Trihn had never worn, and seeing it on Francesca made Trihn think that no one else should ever wear it.

Francesca walked out in that dress, and it was as if the world erupted. The audience roared its approval. Everyone was on their feet. Trihn stared with her mouth agape at what she was witnessing.

This, this right here, made all her hard work worth it. What she'd had to endure to get that sketchbook back from Neal for this design, the long hours at the studio, the sleepless nights, it was all for this moment.

Bryna and Stacia ran back to Trihn when it was over and practically tackled her.

"You were amazing!" Bryna said

"That dress!" Stacia cried. "I need one just to wear around the house."

"It really was stunning," someone said behind her.

Trihn whipped around with her eyes wide. "Chloe!"

"Hey!" she cried. "Surprise! I brought you a present."

Damon appeared from around the corner with a huge smile on his face. Trihn forgot everything else. She only saw her boyfriend standing there. He wasn't supposed to be here. He was supposed to be in LA, filming a music video. He'd been gone for a week already, and she'd missed him so much.

"Damon," she said, throwing herself into his arms.

"Hey, love." He kissed the top of her head and breathed her in.

"What are you doing here?" she asked, stepping back.

"You think I could have actually missed this?"

"But you're supposed to be filming," she insisted.

"We wrapped up early," Chloe told her. "We thought it'd be fun to surprise you. Plus, the song is releasing tomorrow, and Damon wanted to play it for you before it went up."

Bryna narrowed her eyes at Chloe. "Up to the same antics as ever, Chloe?"

"What are you talking about?" Chloe asked.

"We heard the song," Trihn said, meeting Damon's eyes. "A radio station leaked it early."

"Shit, I wanted to play it for you first," Damon said.

"Come on, girls. Everyone, get onstage, so I can announce the winner," Teena said, breaking the moment.

Damon looked like he wanted to say something more, but Trihn briefly kissed him on the lips.

"You can play it for me later," she said before walking away to the fate of her career.

TWENTY-EIGHT

"AFTER CAREFUL CONSIDERATION by the judges, we announce the winner of the eleventh annual Teena Hart Fashion Show…Trihnity Hamilton."

Trihn's hand went to her mouth, and she felt her legs turn to Jell-O. "Oh my God," she cried.

The crowd applauded, and her designs were paraded out onto the runway one more time to showcase the winning talent. Francesca took Trihn's hand in her own and raised it high overhead. Trihn laughed brightly and wrapped her friend in a big hug. Cameras went off all around them. The audience rose to their feet once more to celebrate, and then it was all over.

As Trihn stepped offstage, she truly realized what this moment meant. Her designs were going to be on a runway in New York City. She would be competing for a spot in Bloomingdale's. There was still a chance her dreams could all be realized. Despite leaving NYU's fashion school and walking away from this very possibility, it was within her reach all over again.

Backstage was a mess of a cleanup. Trihn was so busy that she didn't even have time to talk to Damon about the song issue. In fact, Damon and Chloe basically got bombarded by people who realized who they were. Chloe had to step out with her bodyguard, Mateo, to get some breathing room, which was perfectly fine with Trihn.

By the time she was finished and all the models had changed out of the clothes, Teena took ahold of her designs for safekeeping, and Trihn was free to go. Everyone was standing around, waiting for her, even Gates, his date, and her friends.

"All ready!" Chloe said, appearing out of nowhere. "Let's go!"

"Wait, what?" Trihn asked.

Damon sidled up next to her. "Well, this was supposed to be a surprise, but it seems the radio ruined part of it."

She looked up at him with wide eyes. "And here I thought *you* were the surprise."

Damon wrapped his arm around her waist and pulled her close. "Well, this whole night was supposed to be about you anyway. I'm so proud of you. You deserved to win everything and more."

They followed the group to a giant stretch limo that Chloe had waiting for them. It just barely fit their entire entourage as it whisked them down the Strip and to a private club where Chloe had reserved a booth with bottle service.

The place was a standard nightclub with high-tech lights and loud music. Girls were dancing on platforms scattered throughout the room, and scantily clad girls were taking drink orders and pouring drinks at tables. This place was exceptionally elite. Trihn could see a dozen other celebrities in the VIP area, and everyone seemed to be in their element.

Trihn took a seat next to Damon, and Chloe plopped down on the other side of him. Across from them in the booth, Bryna was talking rapidly with Gates. His date didn't even seem to mind. She and her friends were standing around and dancing with drinks in their hands. Stacia was eyeing Chloe's bodyguard, who was pretending not to notice the attention.

Chloe had a girl pour out tequila shots, and everyone took one. Chloe nudged Damon and winked. He laughed at her and just shook his head.

Chloe raised her glass high. "To Trihn and her amazing clothes!"

Trihn raised her glass with a smile. Her boyfriend was here. She had just won a major fashion show. She was on top of the world.

Yet when she looked between Damon and Chloe, Trihn couldn't shake the feeling that something was off.

She tipped the shot back without a second thought, ignoring the burn in her throat. She gestured for the girl to pour another round as Chloe leaned in and whispered something in Damon's ear. He smiled down at her and said something back that Trihn couldn't quite hear. Chloe laughed and nodded back.

"I think now is perfect," Chloe said with a coy smile.

Trihn's stomach plummeted, and she tried to remind herself that they were just friends. That was all.

Trihn quickly reached for her shot and stood, raising her own glass. "To Chloe and Damon's new single."

Everyone reached for their glasses and took the shot with her. Bryna kept glancing between Chloe and Trihn with concern on her face. It was bad when even Bryna was worried.

Trihn plopped back down in her seat and looked away from Damon and Chloe. She was about to get up and join Gates's date when she felt Damon touch her arm. "Trihn, you okay?"

"Yeah, I'm fine."

He laced their fingers together and kissed the top of her hand. "I'm sorry that you heard the new song on the radio first, but I thought you'd like to hear it again with me."

Trihn's eyes flickered to Chloe, who seemed preoccupied with staring at Bryna and Gates. Her eyes were wide with wonder and something else Trihn couldn't quite place. At least she wasn't staring at Damon.

"And with Chloe?" she asked.

He shrugged. "She requested it."

Just then, the DJ started speaking, "And with a special request put in, here's the new one by Damon Stone and Chloe Avana, 'We Never Met.'"

Damon started singing the song directly to Trihn. He only had eyes for her. It was as if they were sitting in his apartment again with him strumming along on his acoustic guitar as he poured out his heart and soul. She stared into the endless depths of his dark eyes and felt herself melting all over again. Just hearing him sing it to her changed everything.

Then, Chloe tugged on his arm, leaning into him with big puppy-dog eyes. "Damon, come on. Sing with me."

He shrugged Chloe off, never tearing his eyes from Trihn, as he continued singing. Trihn's eyes darted to Chloe behind him, and she just looked annoyed that she wasn't the center of attention. Her eyes kept shifting around the booth from Damon to Bryna and Gates, as if she wanted everyone to pay attention to her.

Chloe leaned into Damon and tried to pull him toward her again, but Damon simply ignored her.

He stood and held his hand out for Trihn. She placed her hand in his, ignoring Chloe's frustrated expression. When she stood, he twirled her in place, despite the intense backbeat and the dance music. He lightly held her in his arms, and their bodies moved together, as if they had been made to. Their movements had always been synchronized. They'd danced together long before they had fallen in love.

This felt right to Trihn, being in his arms like this with just his body pressed against hers, her hand in his, and him singing to her.

The song ended, and the people around them applauded Chloe and Damon's new song. Chloe smiled all around, happily taking the praise. Damon never broke eye contact with Trihn. There was so much in that unspoken communication.

"I'm so excited that Damon is going to be coming on tour with me!" Chloe announced casually.

Trihn tore her eyes away from Damon to look at Chloe. "What?"

"Christ, Chloe," Damon growled.

"What?" she asked, seemingly oblivious.

"You're going on tour?" Trihn asked.

"Yeah," he said with a sigh. "Let's go somewhere and talk." He glared at Chloe as he pulled Trihn from their booth.

Trihn could hear Bryna shrieking at Chloe before she and Damon were even out of VIP. Trihn would not want to be the one the other end of that conversation.

Damon pulled her out to the outdoor patio, which was mostly abandoned because of the heat. There was a bartender at a bar, and a few people were scattered around. Damon wasn't recognizable yet, like Chloe and Gates were, so they were fine to grab their own couch and fend off the staff who wanted to get them drinks.

Trihn sat in perfect silence while Damon seemed to scrutinize her face.

"Talk to me," he encouraged.

"What do you want me to say?"

"What you're feeling. That look on your face when Chloe said I was going on tour with her..." He sighed, clearly frustrated. "I never wanted to be the person to cause you to look like that."

"I just don't know why this is the first I'm hearing about all of this. The tour, the song, this big surprise with Chloe?" She shrugged. "Why didn't you tell me the song was 'We Never Met'? Or ever play it for me?" she asked.

"Honestly, I wanted to surprise you. I wanted to play it for you first, so I could look you in the eyes and sing *your* song to you."

She shook her head. "I appreciate that, but it just kind of sucks being the last to know."

"I wrote this for you. I thought you'd be happy."

"I am happy—for you! I'm so excited that my boyfriend has a song on the radio."

"You don't really seem happy."

Trihn sighed. "It's not about the song. It's about being the last to know. I mean, you did a music video to this song. Tell me that it's not in a nightclub and you and Chloe somehow find each other."

Damon didn't say anything for a minute. "It's what that song is about," he finally said.

Trihn rolled her eyes. "That's what I thought."

"I legitimately thought that you'd be happy about this."

"And that's why you hid it?"

"I didn't mean to hide it. I wanted to surprise you. I guess I should have told you," he said, flipping off his hat and fiddling with it. "You get kind of wrapped up in everything in LA once you're there. You don't stop to think that something could be a bad move."

"Wrapped up in things like Chloe?" Trihn couldn't stop the pang of jealousy that hit her.

"Yeah," he admitted. "Sometimes."

Her eyes snapped to him, filled with anger. "Seriously?"

"Not like that!" he amended quickly. "I just mean, with her enthusiasm for the music and the industry. She makes everything out to be an adventure, and you just get sucked into her Chloe vortex. She planned this whole thing for you, you know?"

"And you don't find it strange that she's planning surprises for your girlfriend so that she can announce to *everyone* that you're going on tour with her? Not to mention, her leaning into you and grabbing on you," she said in a rush. "Is that normal in this Chloe vortex, too?"

He sighed and pinched the bridge of his nose. "No. I don't know what's up with her tonight."

"Really? I think it's pretty obvious myself."

"She's not into me, if that's what you're insinuating."

"That's exactly what I'm insinuating. The first time I met her, she was this lonely girl who couldn't even get close to the guy she was on tour with because she was having panic attacks and worried about being seen in public with people. Now, suddenly, she's *everywhere* with you."

"It is *just* business," he told her.

"Does she know that?"

"Yes. She knows that because I am here with my girlfriend, who, for some reason, seems to be insanely jealous even though I've made it clear from day one that she is the only person I want," Damon said, his tone sharp.

"How could I not be jealous? You know I have trust issues, and now, she's with you all the time. She seems very comfortable with touching you. I think it's crazy to ask me not to be worried about that," she told him.

Damon stood and shook his head. "You have *nothing* to worry about. Can't you see that I'm standing here with you? That I want you? I sang the song to you. I came back to Vegas for your fashion show for you. Chloe doesn't even factor into my universe, outside of music."

"Well, the way she was acting tonight doesn't exactly give me a vote of confidence."

"I'm standing here, telling you that you're the one, that I love you, and that no other girls exist to me, and all you see is the bad."

"I don't just see the bad. I see reality."

"Your reality," he said, pointing his hat at her. "And your reality is skewed. You are so desperately terrified of me being Preston that you don't even realize that you're pushing me away."

"I'm not afraid of you becoming Preston! I just don't trust her," she said.

"Then, trust me!"

"I would if you were honest with me!"

Damon shook his head. "One song. One surprise. And I'm back at square one. I'm sorry. I just can't do this."

He turned to start walking away, but she grabbed his arm.

"What?" she asked in shock. "What are you saying?"

"I'm going to go back to LA tonight with Chloe."

Her mouth dropped open. "Are you...are you breaking up with me?"

He dropped his head and then kissed her forehead. "No." He sighed heavily. "I love you, Trihn. I do. But until you let go of the past, I don't know that you'll ever trust me. And what is love without trust?"

She opened her mouth to say something to stop him, but he just kissed her again.

"We have a lot of promotion to do for the album and the tour. This was always going to be a short trip, but I wish it had ended under better circumstances."

"Damon," she whispered, "I love you."

"I know." He kissed the top of her head again. "I love you, too."

And then he turned and walked away from her, taking her heart with him.

TWENTY-NINE

TRIHN STARED BLANKLY up at her ceiling.

She had been lying in bed all night, trying to figure out where everything had gone so horribly wrong. At some point, she must have drifted off from exhaustion, but when she awoke again, she continued staring and mostly stressing.

Damon was the best thing that had ever happened to her. That much, she was pretty certain of. He loved her for the person that she was, not the one who had crawled into a hole and buried her head after having her heart bruised and broken. He was there for her when she needed someone. He had fought for her from day one.

And she had run him off, too.

He'd said they weren't broken up, yet she felt numb, as if they had.

She had gotten so worked up about Chloe, and their argument had escalated so quickly that she hadn't even stopped to hear what he was saying. He didn't want Chloe. If he had, there would have been no reason for him to pretend to want Trihn. But she hadn't been able to see that last night.

Between Chloe grabbing on to him, them laughing together, and the thought of the music video and tour, Trihn's blood had boiled, frying any rational thought.

Chloe just seemed starved for attention from a real human being. She acted...*young*. That was the only word Trihn could use to describe her. Despite growing up while acting in Disney and then moving to Hollywood for music and film, she still seemed so...young.

And Trihn had just let the whole thing get to her instead of seeing how much Chloe probably just needed a friend, and Damon was a good guy.

He wouldn't cheat on Trihn. He knew what that would do to her, and he wasn't that guy. He wasn't Preston.

Maybe Damon was right. Maybe she had been comparing him to Preston, comparing everyone to Preston. And all that had done was drive her completely insane.

Preston was her first boyfriend, her first love. But it had been a charade. Maybe he had been into her. Maybe it had all been a game. She didn't even want to know at this point. But what she did know was that it hadn't been anything like falling in love with Damon.

When she had started dating Neal, she had been so afraid to let other people in. She'd never told Neal about what had happened with Preston. She'd never let Neal see her vulnerable like that. And in turn, she had let him emotionally abuse her. Their relationship was like trying to fit a round piece into a square hole.

But from day one, she and Damon had made perfect sense. It was her own fears and doubts that had created the wedge between them.

Letting go of her past wouldn't happen overnight. But if she didn't start today, then she could lose Damon, and that wasn't acceptable.

Resolved to make this better, Trihn reached for her phone, and it immediately started ringing in her hand. She startled, sitting up in bed and looking at the display.

A smile lit her face. *Always in sync.*

"Hey," she said into the phone.

"Trihn," Damon said with a breath. "I was up all night, thinking about you."

"Me, too."

"Shit, I am so sorry. I should never have left last night."

"No, you were right. I understand why you did it."

"You do? I still don't," he said quickly. "I should have stayed. I should have been there for you. I should have reminded you a thousand times that you were the one for me instead of blowing up on you. You can't help your fears, and all I did was make them worse."

"Stop," she said. "Please stop. You don't need to apologize. I should have trusted you instead of freaking out about Chloe."

"But I should have drawn a bigger line in the sand with her. There should have been no reason for you to ever doubt that something was going on. Ever."

"I know. I wish I hadn't freaked out. I don't like that the anxiety gets ahold of me like that. I've just never known anything besides cheating and heartbreak," she told him. "It's not fair to you for me to assume that you're going to be the same. I don't want to compare you, and I'm going to be better. I'm just trying to figure out this loving relationship thing."

"Well, I'm still going to be here. We'll figure it out together, okay?"

"Okay. I wish we'd figured it out last night, so you could be here in my bed right now instead of on the phone."

Damon laughed. "Yeah. There are a lot of better things we could be doing right now. I'm pretty sure none of them involve arguing or sleeping."

"Mmm…no, not at all."

"Fuck, I miss you. A couple of hours was not enough time with you."

"I know. I miss you, too. Next time, we should use our time much more wisely."

"I have every intention of doing just that," he said, his voice low and husky. "Stripping you naked and running my hands down your body."

Trihn slipped back under the covers of her bed and closed her eyes, imagining just that. "I like the sound of that."

"You moaning in my ear when I grab your hips and pull you toward me."

Trihn whimpered softly into the phone at his words.

"Just like that," he said. "I spread your legs apart to take a taste of you."

"Damon," she groaned, not sure if she was stopping him or telling him to continue.

"Are you touching yourself?" he asked. His voice was strained. "I want to imagine you fucking yourself while you're thinking about me."

Trihn slipped her hand under the hem of her tiny sleeping shorts. She ran her finger across the wetness pooling in her center from his words and started rubbing slow, gentle circles around her clit.

"Trihn?"

"Yes." She had forgotten that she hadn't said anything. "Yes, I am."

Damon grunted, as if the power of that confirmation turned him on even more. "I would give anything to see this right now."

"You lick and suck me until I orgasm," she ventured.

"No. I lick and suck on your clit with two fingers inside you, and you come on my fingers so hard that I can do nothing but bury my dick inside you."

"Oh God," she murmured, picking up the pace as her own orgasm hung just out of reach.

"Fuck," Damon said, his breathing erratic. "I'm just imagining you moving on top of me with your tits bouncing and your smile euphoric."

"You holding me in place and working my hips." Her body shuddered, and she felt her orgasm hit. "Oh. Oh God."

"Christ," he growled at her words. "You just came."

"Yeah," she breathed.

And then she heard Damon exhale heavily into the phone.

"Whoa," he murmured. "That was...fuck, I'm going to need a shower."

She laughed breathily. "That makes two of us."

"You're so sexy when you talk dirty."

"Me? You were the one talking dirty," she said.

"Yeah. Shit. I wouldn't take it back. Listening to you come on the phone is only second best to seeing your face when you release in person."

Trihn's cheeks heated at the comment, despite what they had just done. "When exactly do you think you'll get to see that again?"

"I wish I knew the answer to that. I want to go with you to New York when school is out, but I think our first tour date is around then."

"Right. I understand. Where are you opening the tour?"

"St. Louis, and then we'll be all over the country. I'll send you a schedule. Maybe I can try to get some time off right before our New York show and go with you then."

"I like that idea. I'll have to tell my parents we're pushing the date back. I don't really want to go without you if I don't have to."

"And I want to be there to meet the rest of your family."

"Okay. I'll call my mom when we get off the phone to tell her what's going on."

"Trihn," he said softly, "I'm sorry again about blowing up last night."

"I'm sorry, too. I want to trust you. I'm going to do better."

"I love you."

"I love you, too."

They ended the conversation, and Trihn hopped into the shower.

She knew that she needed to call her mom. She would want to know about the fashion show and when Trihn was coming to New York, but Trihn was dreading the call. It would be easier just to call her dad and push the date back, but she knew she'd hear from her mom about it again anyway.

Despite the fact that she knew that she needed to call, Trihn put it off. She had finals to study for, and since the fashion show had taken up all her time, she felt so far behind in her classes.

She spent the rest of the weekend studying and decided she would call after her classes were over. Tuesday was a reading period anyway, and then all of her finals were on back-to-back days.

As she was leaving her last class of the day, her design teacher held her back. "Trihn, can I speak with you?"

"Sure." She jogged over to the front of class. "What's up?"

"Well, first, I wanted to congratulate you on your win. I don't think we've ever had a first-place win by a sophomore student. That gives me high hopes for your future academic career in fashion here at LV State."

Trihn smiled bright. "Thank you. I'm really excited about everything that's going on."

"And, second, Teena wanted to talk to you in her office for a few minutes about what is happening, moving forward. She said she was free all afternoon."

"Oh, great! Thank you."

"Good luck."

Trihn hurried over to Teena's office, and as she was waiting for Teena to be free, she received a text message from Damon.

> *Wish you were here.*

> *Me too.*

> *No one tells you the part of music that is a job. And it's definitely not the music.*

Trihn laughed at his comment. She knew he was in promotion hell.

> *Maybe you'll learn to love the spotlight.*

> *Don't hold your breath.*

> *You're doing exactly what you want to be doing and the thing you love most in the world. Millions of people would kill to be in your shoes right now. Enjoy it!*

> *You're right. I love you.*

> *Love you too. Gotta go. Meeting with Teena.*

> *Knock 'em dead.*

Trihn stuffed her phone back into her purse and then entered Teena's office.

"Ah, Trihn. Good to see you. Congratulations again with the fashion show. I knew that you had it in you."

"Thank you. I can't believe this is real life."

Teena smiled. "It's a huge accomplishment at such a young age, but I don't think that is anything new to you."

Trihn shrugged. She'd had her fair share of adventures, but this, she felt she had truly earned.

"In any case, we need to get you out to New York as soon as possible."

"We do? I thought the fashion show wasn't until July."

"That's true, but you're going to need to be there sometime soon to make sure everything is set for your trip. I have a whole list of things that you'll have to accomplish out there, and once we settle on a date, I can book you a flight and hotel and then finalize your itinerary."

"Oh, okay," she said, deflating.

She was about to tell her family that she couldn't come home without Damon, and now, it sounded like she couldn't wait to do this stuff. There was no way she was going to be able to push this back to the start of July when Damon would be in town for the NYC show.

"Is that a problem?"

"No, not at all. I can make it work."

"I didn't think it would be an issue. You're from there, aren't you?"

"Yes."

"Wonderful. Will you still require a hotel in Manhattan then?"

Trihn nodded without hesitation. "Yes. I don't have anyone I can stay with in Manhattan."

Her parents lived in Brooklyn, and there was no way in hell she was going to stay with Lydia.

"Excellent. As soon as you pick a date, we'll get this all cleared away."

Trihn left Teena's office, feeling let down. She was excited—and nervous, stressed, overwhelmed—to do the work for the fashion show in New York. But she'd thought she could do all the work from here. She was not looking forward to being in New York and dealing with Lydia's upcoming nuptials.

Trihn raised her chin and reached for the confidence that Damon had instilled in her. She was not going to be a pawn in Lydia and Preston's game.

Trihn would go to New York for work, and that was it.

THIRTY

A FEW WEEKS LATER, Trihn stepped off the plane at JFK Airport in New York City. She twisted her neck and felt a pop, releasing the tension from the six-hour flight into the city. It wasn't a flight she relished taking and even less so knowing that Damon was so far away, playing a show in Orlando that night.

It was still crazy to think that he was out on the road, touring the country, when only a couple of months ago, he'd been fired from his job as a DJ and started working at Posse. Not to mention, "We Never Met" had debuted on the *Billboard* Hot 100 at number two, had been sitting at the number one spot for the last two weeks, and the music video—which she had finally watched and hadn't been as bad as she'd thought—had around seventy-five million views. The full album had skyrocketed straight to number one, and Trihn had no clue when it was ever going to move.

She hurried down the terminal, ready to be out of this airport. She always preferred LaGuardia, but the nonstop flights to JFK were better. And she hadn't had any control over her flight since the school provided it.

She wheeled her hardside spinner suitcase through the airport and then out to the baggage claim. Her dad was supposed to be here, so she wouldn't have to drop seventy-five dollars on a cab to the city. But when she scanned the line of people, she didn't see him.

She was just pulling her phone out to give him a call when she heard her name.

"Trihn, over here!"

Trihn followed the sound of the voice and sighed heavily when she saw who it was.

Lydia stood off to the side in wide-leg cotton pants and a crocheted bra top. Her blonde hair was parted down the middle and hung nearly to her waist. She had on a headband to complete her ensemble. She couldn't have looked more different from the rocker-grunge style that Trihn always sported.

Trihn wheeled her suitcase over and stopped in front of her sister. "I thought Dad was coming to pick me up."

"I volunteered when I found out you were coming into town." Lydia pulled her into a hug that Trihn reluctantly returned. "I've really missed you."

"I was home for New Year's."

"That was almost five months ago," Lydia said. "I used to see you every day."

Trihn wanted to say, *Whose fault is that?* But she held her tongue and just shrugged. "Yeah. We should go."

"Oh, right, sure. Do you have more luggage? Did you check a bag?"

"Nope. Just this one. It's a short trip."

Lydia's face fell, but she quickly recovered. "Oh. Well, we'll make the most of it then!"

Trihn saw Lydia glance down at her ring and waited for it to happen. Any minute now, Lydia was going to thrust that thing in Trihn's face and want her sister to be happy for her. But to her surprise, Lydia just took the suitcase out of Trihn's hand and started walking out to the parking lot.

They didn't say anything to one another as they crossed the street to a shiny black SUV. Lydia clicked the unlock button and popped the trunk. Trihn assessed the vehicle. She didn't think Lydia had a car. In fact, Lydia was potentially even a worse driver than Trihn had been when she lived here. Las Vegas had caught her up pretty quickly. She had to drive everywhere there, but Lydia hadn't had that advantage.

"Nice car. When did you get this?" Trihn asked.

Lydia looked up at Trihn after hoisting the bag into the trunk and shutting the hood. "It's Preston's."

"Oh." Trihn hurried around to the passenger side to hide her distaste.

Lydia got in the car, backed out of the parking spot, and drove them to the exit. Trihn was right. Lydia wasn't any better of a driver than Trihn remembered. It was almost painful.

"Do you want me to drive?" Trihn asked.

"What? Why?"

"Because I do it all the time, and it looks like you haven't driven in a long time."

"It's fine," Lydia said. "I wanted to drive you into the city. I really wish that you were staying with me."

Trihn froze. "I'm going to be super busy. I didn't want to inconvenience you." *Or be anywhere near Preston.*

Lydia read straight through her comment. "It wouldn't have been an inconvenience at all. It'd have been great to have you around."

"Well, I'm really just here for work. I have a full itinerary, and the university put me up in a hotel. So, I'm just going to stay there."

"Right," she said, deflating. "Dad mentioned that."

"Yeah." Trihn looked out the window to avoid the tension.

"I'm just really glad you're here. I thought you might actually not come home."

Trihn didn't have it in her to tell Lydia that she hadn't wanted to come home, and the thought of seeing her sister and Preston and having anyone bring up their wedding had nearly kept Trihn's ass firmly in Nevada. She figured her silence was clue enough. And they remained in silence the rest of the way into the city.

It was sad honestly. Trihn had been so close to Lydia before this. She had looked up to her sister, practically idolized her. And now, their relationship had been reduced to rubbish, all because of some stupid guy. If only Lydia could see it that way.

Lydia pulled up in front of the hotel where Trihn was staying in Midtown. It wasn't as pompous as some of the surrounding buildings, but she didn't intend on spending a lot of time inside either. Even though she'd left New York for good, that didn't mean she didn't miss her home. And she wanted to make the most of the time she had while here.

Trihn hopped out of the car and grabbed her bag from the trunk. Lydia awkwardly stood there, shifting from one foot to another.

"Okay. Thanks for picking me up," Trihn said.

"Of course. It was good to see you."

"Yeah."

"I hope we can spend some time together while you're here. Pencil me into your busy schedule."

"We'll see."

Lydia reached forward and pulled her into a quick hug before disappearing. Trihn was so surprised that she'd let her. With a shake of her head, Trihn went to check in at the hotel. She didn't know what was up with Lydia. *Is this an act to get back in my good graces? Or is she actually trying to be better?*

She deposited her bag in her room and changed into black jeans, a white V-neck, and flats. Even though she had her own style, it had been ingrained in her since her modeling days to show up neutral, like a canvas waiting to be painted.

She returned to the streets with her itinerary pulled up on her iPhone. She had to check in at an endless list of places to make sure she was approved and ready to go. She needed to see the venue. She needed to check the dressing rooms. She needed to consult security and shipping to figure out the best method to get her designs here in one piece. She needed to consult the makeup artists and hairstylists, so she could portray her vision. She needed to have a meeting with the board for the fashion show and with her own personal assistant, which was just insane, and another meeting with the camera crew. And the list went on and on.

By the time she had done only half of those things, Trihn felt exhausted. No wonder Teena had scheduled her to be here for three days to get through this stuff and why she hadn't come along to deal with the tedious details.

Trihn walked up to a vendor to get a bottle of water. She paid for it with cash, which she always liked to have on hand in the city, and then started skimming the magazines. This had been a habit while she was modeling. She'd liked to see if any of her friends had made it onto the covers, and when she'd had free time before dance, she would pick one up and flip through to see if she could find a familiar face.

Trihn jolted. "Whoa!" *Speaking of a familiar face.*

She snatched the tabloid magazine out of the stand and stared at the cover. In big letters, it read, *Chloe's Secret Love*, and it had a giant picture of Chloe and Damon on the cover. Trihn opened the tabloid and flipped to the page listed. There, in detail, was a series of pictures of Damon and Chloe together. In one, they both had their heads down as they moved through a crowd. A similar picture had Damon with his arm slung over Chloe as they walked into an arena. A few other pictures had them standing side by side at various venues.

Trihn started reading the article with shaking hands.

CHLOE AVANA'S ROMANCE WITH DJ DAMON STONE WAS STRICTLY OFF-LIMITS.

Add another guy to the increasingly long list of people Chloe Avana has been photographed with during the last couple of months. Even before their single "We Never Met" rocked the charts, the two had been spicing it up behind the scenes.

Relatively unknown Damon Stone supposedly rose to fame after playing a remixed version of Avana's hit single "Heartbreaker" at a Las Vegas nightclub. But an anonymous source close to the couple says that they'd known each other long before that moment, and no doubt, things had been hot offstage long before the couple came out as the sizzling new duo.

Trihn stopped reading after that. Her heart rate leveled out, and she very carefully replaced the magazine in the stand.

What rubbish!

These tabloids always made something out of nothing. Whoever this anonymous source close to the couple was clearly didn't actually know Chloe or Damon.

Trihn had been the one to introduce them in the first place. He'd never come close to meeting Chloe, and in fact, he'd been a *total* unknown, not relatively unknown, before that moment.

The one incriminating picture with his arm around Chloe was probably because she had been freaking the fuck out about the crowds. The press didn't know about her fear of crowds and the panic attacks she suffered from.

But Trihn and Damon both knew that happened, and he had likely just been protecting Chloe and trying to calm her down. All the other photographs looked as if they had been taken on tour or during promotions. It was probably a fact of life that if he was going to be around Chloe, then Damon was going to be photographed.

Trihn reached for her phone and sent a text to Damon.

I love you.

He responded almost instantly.

I love you too.

How is Orlando?

Don't know. I haven't seen anything other than the airport, hotel, and arena.

No Disney World then? Harry Potter world? Platform 9 ¾? Butterbeer?

Nope. Chloe said we'd have to get a backstage pass to the park to even go. No standing in lines. No wandering around and taking in the scenery.

That sounds awesome. Well, the lines part.

I'd rather go with you.

Maybe once you're off the tour we could go.

I'd like that. How's NYC?

The same.

Have you seen your family?

Lydia picked me up at the airport unannounced.

Sounds like her.

Yeah. She was fine I guess. Didn't wave her ring in my face or mention the wedding at all actually.

> *Well, I hope it stays like that. I have to get in for a sound check. I'll try to call you after the show. I love you.*

I love you too.

Trihn pocketed her phone, feeling better about the stupid tabloid that she'd read. She hadn't doubted Damon. She'd always figured that 99.9% of everything in those things was fake, but it was surreal to see her boyfriend in there and the ridiculous things it'd said about him and Chloe. *What's next? Chloe was going to be pregnant, but she wouldn't know who the father was? They'd both end up on cocaine and in rehab and have a secret wedding? Because…everyone had secret weddings.*

Trihn felt like she'd made so much progress since she and Damon had started dating. In the grand scheme of things, it hadn't been that much time, but she'd been feeling stronger and stronger in their relationship. A few months ago, she wouldn't have been able to take the sight of that tabloid, even knowing it was false. Now, she just shrugged it off, texted her boyfriend, and daydreamed about going to The Wizarding World of Harry Potter at Universal Studios with him.

THIRTY-ONE

TRIHN STOOD OUTSIDE of her parents' townhouse in Brooklyn, contemplating whether or not she wanted to walk inside. She had promised her dad that she would stop by for dinner one night while she was in town. And since she had finally completed everything she needed for the fashion show, as listed on her itinerary, and she would be flying back to Las Vegas tomorrow, she figured tonight was the night.

She was actually excited to see her dad. And while she wanted to see her mom, she wasn't looking forward to the inevitable wedding conversation.

So far, Trihn had avoided talking about it. She wouldn't mind avoiding it altogether—or at least waiting to have Damon's support.

But she pushed her shoulders back and entered the house anyway. "Mom! Dad!" she called, nudging the door closed behind her.

"Trihn!" her mother said. She rushed from the kitchen into the foyer and tightly hugged her daughter. "It's so good to see you. I have missed you so much." She held Trihn at arm's length and examined her. "Did you get taller? Skinnier? Are you eating?"

Trihn laughed. "Yes, Mom, I'm eating. And God forbid, I get any taller."

"It feels as if I haven't seen you in ages. I don't think I could go another six months. You have to come back before Christmas."

"Don't worry, Mom. I'll be back when Damon is in town for his show and for the fashion show."

"Maybe you should just stay here until the fashion show."

Trihn blanched. "I can't. I have a lot of work left to do for it."

"Of course you do." Her mother, Linh, walked them into the living room. "You're a Hamilton. We're all strong and independent. Now, tell me more about everything. Your boyfriend, Damon, is a musician, right? And the fashion show—well, I know all about that since *Glitz* is a sponsor this year. Let me get you a drink."

Trihn was about to tell her not to worry about it, but it seemed like she was excited to do things for her daughter. Instead, Trihn just took a seat in the living room and drank in the familiarity of it all. She'd missed this, being home. It felt right here, like this.

Linh returned a minute later with a glass of lemonade.

Trihn took it from her hand and sipped it before answering the deluge of questions, "Yes, Damon is a musician. He's on tour right now with Chloe Avana."

"Your father mentioned that. It must be hard."

"It is," she admitted. "He's in Orlando right now. He'll be in Atlanta tomorrow."

"And will you get to see him anytime while he's on this tour?"

"Well, when he's in New York City."

"Yes, but from the details Gabriel gave me, that's a month away."

"I don't know," she admitted. "It all happened so fast."

"We make time for the ones we love. I'm sure you'll figure it out."

Trihn couldn't decide if that was a backhanded comment about her not coming home enough or not. So, she just chose to ignore it.

"And you won the fashion show at school. You're up against some stiff competition. Your father showed me the images he had taken of your designs."

"He did?" Trihn asked, surprised. She hadn't really discussed this with her mother, but it made sense that she would keep up with her daughter's life even if she weren't as involved as she used to be.

"Yes."

"What did you think?" Suddenly, Trihn felt as if she were holding her breath.

After all, her mother, the fashion magazine senior executive, judged these things for a living. Normally, Trihn wouldn't have even asked for her opinion. Her mother was a critic. That was her job. But Trihn couldn't help herself this time.

"They remind me of you, but besides your final piece, they weren't expressly original," Linh said.

"Oh."

"They are excellent for a second-year student though, Trihn. You should be proud of your accomplishments. Just because I don't think your line is boutique wear doesn't mean that it wouldn't sell exceptionally well to the masses. There is a huge difference." Linh shrugged her dainty shoulders. "You'll find your place. Now, come on. Dinner is almost ready. We should go into the dining room."

"The dining room?" Trihn asked.

With only three of them, it always made more sense to eat in the breakfast nook for most of their meals.

"You're here for one night. I'm doing a bigger meal!"

Then, Linh traipsed into the kitchen, leaving Trihn feeling uneasy.

Trihn followed her mother and stopped dead in her tracks. *Of course.* She shouldn't have been surprised, yet she was.

Lydia and Preston were standing side by side in front of the stove. Preston had his hip leaned up against the oven, and his eyes were fixed on Lydia as she was stirring something in a large pot. Lydia was wearing a simple sundress that came to her knees and hippie hemp sandals. Her hair, hanging loose to her waist, was a soft blonde color with platinum highlights. Preston looked as if he had just come from work in a blue plaid button-up with his sleeves rolled up to his elbows and slim-fit charcoal slacks. He was well-groomed with short hair and just a five o'clock shadow gracing his chiseled jawline.

No matter how many times Trihn saw them together, she always felt like the air had been sucked out of the room. She just remembered the time at the Hamptons when everything had flipped on its head. Preston was Lydia's. They were engaged.

Trihn felt as if she were intruding on a private moment. But as soon as she started to inch back out of the kitchen, Preston turned his head and looked straight at her, freezing her in place. Bright blue eyes wrapped her in a spell and rooted her to the spot on the floor. A slow smirk stretched across his face. It was painful to witness.

"Hey, Trihn," he said casually.

When Lydia whipped around, there was no semblance of his dirty smirk.

"Trihn!"

"Uh, hey."

"So glad that you decided to have dinner with all of us."

"Yeah…"

"Mom made your favorite."

"I'm just going to go find Dad." Trihn slowly eased out of the kitchen, making sure not to look at Preston. She only saw Lydia's distraught face at her own apparent fear before she hurried from the room.

When she turned back to the living room, she found her dad striding into the room from upstairs.

Trihn walked right up to him with her arms crossed. "Thanks for the heads-up about the ambush."

Gabriel chuckled and pulled her in for a hug. "I've missed you."

"Yeah, but you said we were just going to have a small family dinner."

"We are. There are only five of us."

"I thought you meant just the three of us," she accused.

"I never specifically said that, and anyway, as soon as I told your mother that you were coming, she invited Lydia. There was no way around it. You should have known that."

Trihn sighed. "If I slip out the front door, maybe no one will notice."

Her dad gave her a stern look that told her even he wouldn't let that slide. He likely didn't want to hear the complaints from everyone at the table if she disappeared.

"Come on. You can sit by me." He put his arm around her shoulders, and they walked into the dining room.

Trihn took the seat next to her father while her mother fluttered back and forth between the kitchen and dining room, depositing dishes. With the number of plates out, it was practically Thanksgiving.

Lydia carried in one last dish and placed it at the center of the table. She took an empty seat, and Preston walked in a second later, sitting down directly across from Trihn.

Trihn sighed and looked toward her father. "Any interesting shoots lately?"

"Besides yours?" he asked with a smile.

"Oh!" Lydia said, jumping in, uninvited. "Tell me all about your fashion show. Can I come to the one in New York? I'll be a free photographer or whatever you need."

"I don't know, Ly. Details are kind of up in the air on whether I'm going to have anyone with me, aside from the models. The show is even providing an assistant."

"That's great, honey," her mom said, entering the room and taking a seat. "Though I know Lydia would love to work with you in her spare time while you're here."

"I really would."

Trihn nodded. "Yeah, but like I said, we'll have to see."

Everyone dug into the food, saving Trihn from having to say much more about it.

"So, are you really dating that guy who sings that new song with Chloe Avana?" Lydia asked.

Trihn squared her shoulders. "Yeah. Damon."

"Damon Stone. Is that his real name?" Lydia asked. "Don't they all have fake names?"

"Yeah, a lot of them do, but no, that's his real name. We went to a show for this guy named DJ Poet, but his real name is James Poe, and the studio thought that was boring."

"I've heard his stuff before," Preston said. "Poet, that is."

"But…I'm confused. What happened with Neal? He was so sweet," Lydia said.

Trihn clenched her jaw. "It just didn't work out. Damon is a much better choice."

"Do you get to see him much? Mom said he's touring."

"He just went out on the road. He's normally in Vegas. He was a DJ at a nightclub I frequent. That's how we met."

"Interesting. It must be hard to be away."

Trihn nodded. "Yeah, but we talk a lot. So, it's not the end of the world."

"That's good," Lydia said.

The conversation switched to other topics, and Trihn actually found herself relaxing. She'd been home a couple of times since the Preston fiasco, but usually, she had been so uncomfortable that she would have to leave the room to get away from the tension. Preston put her on edge, and she knew he liked to do it on purpose. It must have been Damon who changed all of that.

"Trihn?" Lydia said.

Trihn jerked her head up out of the pasta she had been eating. Her mother's food really was delicious. She hadn't realized that she had completely zoned out of the conversation.

"What?"

"We were just talking about going upstairs after this. I'd like to try on my wedding gown, so you could see it."

Trihn swallowed hard. "I didn't know you had already purchased one."

"Well, you don't return my calls," Lydia said softly.

"I, um…probably have to go right after this."

"Trihnity," Linh said. "You can stay for a bit to see her dress."

Trihn bit back a snide retort and looked at her meal. She didn't think she could stomach seeing Lydia in that dress. But maybe with the way things had been going, it wouldn't be that bad. Trihn could just disconnect the who and the why and only see the amazing craftsmanship because she was sure that their mother had had it custom-made.

"Sure," Trihn finally said. She looked back up.

Lydia lit up like a light bulb. It was like she had just come downstairs on Christmas morning. "Great. I'm excited."

Preston reached over and took Lydia's hand in his. "When do I get to see it?"

Trihn swallowed back the rising bile in her throat.

Lydia giggled. "Not until the wedding day, of course."

"That seems fair." He slowly drew her hand to his lips, and just as he placed a light kiss on the top, he turned and looked at Trihn.

She nearly choked and shoved her chair back. "Excuse me. I just have to...take my plate in."

"Don't be silly, Trihn. I'll clear the table," Linh said.

"No, it's fine. I want to do it." She scooped up her plate and left the table. *So much for being comfortable.*

Trihn tossed her plate into the sink with a sigh. Resting her hands on the counter, she leaned forward and tried to regain a sense of equilibrium.

"You made a quick departure," Preston said, appearing in the kitchen a minute later.

"What do you want?" she asked with venom in her voice.

"Just came to check on you."

"I'm fine. You can go now."

"So, another new boyfriend?" Preston said, ignoring her comment.

"Yep. Damon is amazing. He really loves me."

"I'm sure he does. What's not to love?"

Despite her best effort, she winced at that comment.

"I read a few interesting things about your boyfriend."

Trihn glared at him. "I really don't want to talk about this with you."

"Do you honestly think that he isn't sleeping with Chloe Avana?"

"You're an asshole. That shit isn't true."

"Is that what he's saying?" he asked, leaning against the counter and looking down at her.

She hadn't realized he had gotten so close. He was practically hovering over her. She took a steady step backward.

"That's what I'm saying."

"You can do better."

She scoffed. "You don't know anything."

"Come on, Trihn. You and I both know that some new guy could never compare to me."

Trihn snapped her eyes up to him. She couldn't believe he'd had the gall to say that to her.

He'd teased her about Neal when they were together, but she had always extracted herself from the situation as soon as possible. And then she'd blocked the memory from her mind. This was different though. This was about Damon, and Preston hadn't even fucking met him!

"You're right," she said finally.

Preston smiled wide.

"Damon doesn't compare to you. In fact, I'd never, ever want to put you two in the same category because Damon is twice the man you'll ever be."

Trihn pushed past Preston and went back into the dining room. "I'm leaving."

"What?" Linh said.

That was shortly followed by Lydia's, "You can't leave yet! My dress!"

"You can tell that to your fiancé." Trihn shook her head. "It was good to see you guys, but I have to go now."

After she grabbed her bag, her mother tried to stop her at the door. "Trihn, please don't go. What's wrong with you?"

"No one here would even believe me. So, why should I bother?"

"We'll listen. What is it?"

"Preston! God, can't anyone else here see what he's doing? He's a lying, manipulative slimeball. He just came on to me in the kitchen when no one else was around so that there would be no witnesses."

"Trihnity," her mother admonished.

"Don't even say it. Just don't." Trihn sighed. "I love you, Mom, but I'm not going to come back to New York again unless it's to introduce you to Damon or for work. I just can't handle this, and I don't need the stress in my life."

She hugged her mom and then hurried out of the house. It wasn't until she had made it back to her hotel that she felt the weight lift off her chest. She was miserable about how Preston had acted, but in some way, it just proved what she'd already known. Preston was an asshole, and she couldn't pretend otherwise for Lydia.

Trihn curled into bed and was falling asleep when her phone started ringing. She reached for it and saw Damon's name on the screen.

"Hey," she said with a sigh.

"Hey, love. Oh, how I have missed that voice."

She laughed softly. "I miss you. How was the show?"

"Orlando was incredible, and now, we're on our way to Atlanta. How was dinner with your parents?"

"Lydia and Preston showed up, and he was a total asshole."

Damon was silent for a full minute.

"Are you still there?" she asked.

"Yeah, just reining in my anger."

"Join the club."

"Well, I have a long drive ahead of me," he said into the phone.

She imagined him lying back on a bunk in a van driving them up the interstate toward Atlanta.

"Are you about to go to bed?" he asked.

She nodded. "Mmhmm."

"Early flight, right?"

"Yeah."

"All right. Just close your eyes, love, and forget all about what happened at your dinner. Just pretend I'm sitting in front of you, strumming on my acoustic guitar."

And then he started singing. The words were slow and soft, almost like a lullaby. Before she knew it, she drifted off to the sound of his voice, which proved to be a much better ending to a tiring day.

THIRTY-TWO

"SHIT. FUCK. FUCK. FUCKING HELL!" Trihn jolted out of bed and started running around the hotel room like a maniac.

While falling asleep to Damon singing had been the most epic night, not setting her alarm and subsequently sleeping through her flight had not been as awesome.

She quickly stuffed everything back into her bag and was on her way to JFK within ten minutes. She was so late. There was absolutely no way she could make it now, but hopefully, the airline would take pity on her and let her board a later flight.

She jotted out a text to Damon while sitting impatiently in the backseat of a cab.

Missed my flight. Fuck.

That sucks. Are they going to let you switch flights?

I don't know. I'll have to see when I get there.

Come here instead.

To Atlanta?

> *Yeah. The show isn't until later, and we don't leave for Charlotte right away. You could stay the night. I'd pay for you to fly back to Vegas.*

Trihn stared down at her phone in shock. *Is this for real?* That sounded like a much better option than returning to Las Vegas.

> *That would be amazing! I'll see if the airline will go for it.*

> *Let me know. I'd love to see you. It's been too long!*

The rest of the ride to JFK was a lesson in self-restraint. Now that she had a better destination, she was so anxious to get to the airport that she couldn't stop the jitters.

Once she finally paid the cab and wheeled her suitcase up to the airline counter, she was practically bouncing with excitement. A ten-minute conversation with the airline proved even better than expected, and soon, she was clutching a one-way ticket to Atlanta.

A couple of hours later, Trihn was standing outside of Damon's hotel in Atlanta. She couldn't believe she had just flown there instead of going home.

She'd texted him that she had gotten a flight to Atlanta, and he'd sent over the hotel information. He'd said they had a morning rehearsal, and then he was just going to be chilling in his room. When she landed, she was supposed to text him, but she'd thought she'd surprise him at the door.

Trihn knocked twice. When no one answered, she knocked again.

"Fuck, I'm coming, Chloe. Give me a minute. Jesus."

The door swung open and revealed Damon without a shirt and in a pair of dark jeans that were unbuttoned at the waist. His hair was perfectly messy, and stubble had grown in across his jawline. He looked like a sexy fucking mess.

"I hope you don't always answer the door for Chloe like this," Trihn said, arching an eyebrow.

"Bloody hell," he breathed. "You're the best fucking sight of my life."

Trihn laughed right before he crushed his mouth down onto hers. He grabbed her bag and dragged her into his hotel room. Before the door was even closed all the way, Damon was peeling the layers of her clothes off her body. She was actually quite happy at the state of his undress because it made it easier just to slide those pesky jeans and boxers off his legs.

He hoisted her legs up around her waist and carried her over to the king-size bed.

"I missed everything about you," he murmured, crawling onto the bed and rocking forward on top of her. "Your beautiful body." His hands ran down her sides. "Your amazing lips. That voice. Say my name."

"Damon," she purred into his ear.

"Fuck, that makes me hard." He roughly kissed her. His hands tangled up into her hair. "This hair. I've dreamed about pulling this hair."

He knotted it in his hand and yanked until she arched her body, giving him access to her neck. His kisses traveled along the hollow of her neck to her collarbone, rubbing his chin across her skin and leaving wonderful fucking scratches.

His dick rubbed against her, and all thoughts of the orgasm she had given herself at the sound of his voice disappeared. There was nothing like the real thing. And she could give herself a pretty amazing orgasm without his help. She opened her legs wider for him, begging for him to be inside her.

And they bucked together at the same time. Their bodies joined, and Trihn released a low moan. It had been so long. Their thrusts were measured and in sync. Each of them was desperately hungry for the other. All those days apart had just fed the ache between them.

She let loose, clutching on to his back and digging her nails into his skin. He pumped three more fierce thrusts into her and then emptied himself with a cry.

Her fingers slowly relaxed, and she pulled him closer to her, leaving several light kisses across his shoulders.

"I love you," she whispered.

"I love you, too," he said into her shoulder. He pulled back from her embrace and kissed her on the mouth. "I am so glad that I suggested you come to Atlanta. I will always remember that Atlanta is a good place."

"Best idea you've ever had."

"Working up the nerve to talk to you was the best idea I ever had."

"Then, you wouldn't have had any of this—the single, the record, the tour."

"You. Just you."

The pair quickly showered off the smell of sex and then headed out, hand in hand, to explore and find some food.

Damon donned his characteristic flat-brim hat and pulled it lower over his eyes than he normally wore it.

Trihn laughed. "Afraid you're going to get mobbed?"

He made a face. "It happens on occasion. Chloe draws a crowd."

"I saw that."

"What do you mean?"

"The tabloids," she said. He frowned, but she pushed forward, "They were all over New York at every magazine stand. Kind of hard to miss."

"Yeah. Paparazzi hound her. It's crazy." He scratched the back of his head. "None of that stuff is true though."

"I know," she said automatically. "Unless you and Chloe had somehow met before I introduced you, I think it's safe to assume that you didn't have a secret love affair before you went public."

Damon looked so shocked by what she had just said that all she could do was laugh.

"People are fucking saying that?" he asked.

"You rose out of obscurity. There must be a reason."

"Or I just got lucky."

"No. You're talented. Talent recognizes talent."

The pair entered Piedmont Park and started walking on one of the trails. Cyclists and runners flew by them as they leisurely strolled around, taking in the blisteringly hot and humid Atlanta summer.

They were almost to the other side of the park where Damon had gotten a recommendation for a place to eat when a group of girls who had to be in high school ran up to them. One girl in particular seemed to be the ringleader.

"Are you Damon Stone?" she asked in a rush.

His eyebrows shot up, and he apologetically glanced over at Trihn. "Yeah, I am."

"Oh my God! Oh my God! I can't believe you're here. Is Chloe here with you?"

He shook his head. "No, I don't know where she is."

"But you two are together."

"I—"

"Who is *this* girl?" the girl asked, eyeing Trihn up and down. "If you're cheating on Chloe, you'll have the Avanaddicts after you."

Trihn stared at this girl in disbelief. Clearly, she was not the only one who had seen the tabloids, and apparently, everyone else believed them.

Damon looked at the girl. "We're not together."

"Good. You'd better not be with someone else," the girl said rather vehemently.

Damon had been talking about himself and Chloe, but the girl thought he'd meant himself and Trihn.

He opened his mouth to correct the girl, but she just kept talking, "Now, can you take a picture with me and my friends?"

He shrugged, slightly exasperated, and shot Trihn a sheepish look. "Sure. Why not?"

The girl thrust her phone into Trihn's hand a bit begrudgingly. Trihn thought, at any minute, they might have a mini riot caused by a group of fifteen-year-olds on their hands. But after she took their picture, the girls disappeared, all whispering to themselves.

Damon shook his head. "I'm so sorry. I had no idea that was going to happen. I don't go anywhere without Chloe or an escort. I didn't think fans would even recognize me without her." He anxiously glanced around. Some of Chloe's fears about crowds had gotten to him. "We should probably get moving." He took Trihn's elbow and gestured for them to exit the park. "Last thing we want is for our location to be noted on Instagram and for the paparazzi to show up. I don't want to drag you into the papers."

"It's okay, Damon. Slow down. It'll be fine."

He slowly eased up, and his shoulders dropped back to normal. "You're right. I didn't realize how psycho Chloe's fans were. Did that girl call herself an…what was it?"

"Avanaddict," Trihn filled him in. "It's her fan club."

"Yeah. I think I've heard Chloe mention them, but that was something else. I'm sorry again."

"Don't apologize. You can't change how random people are going to react. As long as nothing is going on between you and Chloe, then it doesn't matter," Trihn honestly told him.

"And nothing is going on."

He laced their fingers back together and pulled her into a diner. They ordered burgers, fries, and a salted caramel chocolate milkshake to split. Then, they chatted over their meal.

It was so nice to just *be* with Damon. Sure, there was madness all around them from the tour and Chloe and her Avanaddicts, but when it was just the two of them, it felt totally natural.

They spent the rest of the afternoon touring the more accessible parts of the city. If they'd had more time, Damon promised he would have taken her to the aquarium, but with the concert coming up, they only had enough time to wander around Centennial Olympic Park and the CNN Center, and then they rode the Ferris wheel.

They talked about the various tour stops so far, and Trihn filled him in on everything that had happened in New York. Damon looked like he was going to punch a hole through the Ferris wheel window when she told him what Preston had said in the kitchen.

Overall, it had been a totally relaxing day. It was just what she needed.

But when they made it back to the hotel, that all changed.

THIRTY-THREE

"WHY HAVEN'T YOU been answering your phone?"
Chloe practically shrieked the minute she saw Damon.

"Hey, Chloe. Meltdown much?" he joked.

"We have to be at sound check in half an hour. No
one knew where you were!"

"I was with Trihn."

"Hey, Trihn," she said before rounding on Damon
again. "Why the hell weren't you answering your phone?"

"Because I was with my girlfriend and didn't need to
be hounded by your incessant text messages. I see you
every day. I don't see her enough. I wanted to be present.
So, get over your hissy fit. You could have gone on
without me. I'm really only desperately important for two
songs."

Chloe narrowed her eyes and then stormed off.

"Diva moment," Damon growled.

"Is she normally like this?"

"No," he admitted. "She's normally cool."

They started to follow Chloe when she turned to face them again. "What did you two do this afternoon?"

"We walked around the city. Why?" Damon asked.

She thrust her phone into his face. "You met an Avanaddict, and I wasn't even there for the picture. But more importantly, Trihn is now on everyone's radar."

"So?" Damon asked.

"Not that I care that everyone knows you're dating someone, but I have a feeling the paps are going to get crazier after this."

Damon took the phone from her and read the Instagram picture Chloe had just been tagged in.

> @avanaddict1234 with @damonstone in #piedmontpark missing our queen @chloeavana! Don't worry Chloe! We yelled at him for being with another girl. #chloeavana #queen #addict #dontmesswithourgirl #squee #OMG #didthatjusthappen #toorealforlife #nofilter #totallyafilter #ATLlife

"God, that is hard to read," Damon complained.

Trihn peered over his shoulder, reading the message. "Who cares about one girl?"

"The paparazzi who stalk me and now Damon. Everyone is going to be wondering who said girl was," Chloe said. She swept her gaze over to Damon.

"But I don't care if they know who Trihn is," Damon said.

"Yeah, well, you might if the tabloids start calling you cheating scum because they have pictures of you two together. This is why we have a publicist. I'm going to message her now, so she knows what we're dealing with."

"It's only an Instagram picture," Trihn noted.

"Welcome to my life," Chloe said. She sighed and took her phone back. "Sorry, I'm in ultra-crazy mode. I haven't been sleeping, and this shit is just getting under my skin. It is good to see you, Trihn."

"Maybe we should just go to sound check and not worry about one picture," Damon suggested.

"You're right. I hope it all just blows over," Chloe said.

But the look on her face said she didn't think it would.

Backstage was a chaotic mess.

Trihn was hanging out in Damon's dressing room in Philips Arena. It was a sold-out show at a major venue, and everyone was running around like crazy, getting things ready. The opener was onstage right now, which meant they only had another half an hour before Chloe would go on.

Damon was alternating between tuning his already in-tune guitar and messing around on the piano. He would sing occasionally, but it was more to fight the nerves than to warm up.

She was excited to see him perform again. It felt like forever since she had been backstage with him and Chloe. Trihn and Damon had come a long way since they first started dating.

"What are you thinking?" Damon asked.

"Nothing. Why?"

"You're smiling."

"Am I?" she asked, unable to mask her grin.

"You are."

She shrugged. "I'm just happy for you. Excited to see the show."

"It'll be good to have you here again. I'm more involved musically with the whole production. I only sing on the two tracks, but since I play so many instruments, production let me switch instruments songs. It's more interesting, I think—or at least more fun," he said with a smile.

"Good. You're too talented to play backup."

He chuckled. "'We Never Met' is sitting at number one on the charts under my name. I don't think I'm playing backup."

"True."

Damon stood from where he had been seated at the piano and walked over to Trihn. He held his hand out for her, and she took it. He hauled her to her feet. She stepped easily into his arms. Then, he started moving. Slowly, their hips swayed back and forth, their bodies were pressed tightly together, and he was drawing her hand up to twirl her in place.

She laughed. "What are you doing?"

"Dancing."

"You're about to go onstage in front of thousands of people, and you're back here, dancing with me?"

"Mmhmm," he said, pulling her back in and nuzzling her neck.

She sighed into his embrace and couldn't deny how amazing this was.

Their bodies moved together in a seductive dance that they were all too good at. She dropped his hand, wrapping her arms around his neck. He gripped her hips. Her fingers threaded through his hair, and suddenly, he claimed her lips.

They were still dancing, despite the fact that there was no music. If they had been back at the hotel, this would have been leading straight to that king-size bed again. But now, it was just hot and sensual and making her completely weak in the knees.

Then, the door swung inward.

"Damon, I just wanted to go over—" Chloe abruptly cut off.

Damon didn't jolt away from Trihn, like she'd expected.

He kissed her on the lips and smiled at her before turning to Chloe. "What's up?"

Chloe was beet-red. She cleared her throat. "Sorry to interrupt. I just wanted to go over that one part in 'Heartbreaker.' It's hell on my vocal cords."

"Sure. Let me get you in key."

Damon kissed Trihn's cheek one more time, and then he and Chloe sat at the piano and worked on the song she had sang a hundred times before.

Chloe had real talent. It was clear why she was successful. But her insecurities about her success were also blatant in the way she always looked for reassurance from others around her. Trihn would never have seen it before, but she recognized things about Chloe the Girl that she would never have seen in Chloe the Mega Superstar.

By the time they finished up, an assistant came by to collect them, and then Trihn was deposited backstage, so she could watch the show.

It was different this time, seeing Chloe and Damon onstage together.

That first night, Damon had been a nobody. He had played one song, and Trihn had felt so proud of him.

Now, when Damon walked on that stage, there were as many cheers for him as there were for Chloe. The fans adored him. He wasn't here by chance or luck. He was here because he was meant to be here.

All the hours recording and doing promotional tours, all the endless tour dates away from home, all the time he'd had to be away from her had coalesced into this one moment. Damon Stone had been made to be on that stage.

He hadn't been joking when he said that he played a bunch of instruments. He went from guitar to bass to drums and back to guitar. He played three songs on the piano, and then, he ended up with a trumpet that he recorded live and then fed into the feed for the crowd.

His talent and complete adoration for the music mesmerized Trihn. Somehow, he had taken Chloe's tour and made it about both of them.

By the time "Heartbreaker" and "We Never Met" were played as the grand finale, the crowd was in an uproar. Philips Arena was on its feet, and Trihn couldn't blame them. Damon and Chloe made a rocking duo.

Damon came offstage with a wide grin and sweat dripping down his face. He took off his baseball cap and wiped his forehead with his soaked shirt. Chloe followed behind him, living off the energy from the concert.

Chloe catapulted into Damon's arms. He laughed and swung her around before placing her back down on her feet.

"That's the best it's ever been!" she said, jumping up and down.

"It really was," Damon agreed. "God, that crowd. It's like a life force."

"It so is. One more bow!" Chloe grabbed his hand and pulled him back toward the stage.

He apologetically looked at Trihn, but she didn't say anything as he and Chloe ran back out together.

"Ladies and gentlemen, thank you so much for bringing down the house tonight here in the ATL. I'm Chloe Avana, and this is Damon Stone. And we love you!"

Chloe blew a kiss at the crowd, then at Damon, and then back at the crowd. She hoisted his hand in the air, and the room erupted all over again.

This time, when he ran back offstage, Damon scooped Trihn right off the ground, pulling her against his chest. Trihn tightly held on to him. She slid down his body, and he planted a kiss on her lips.

"I want you at every show."

She laughed. "I wish."

"Let's make it happen."

"Damon…"

"We can try."

"I have the fashion show," she reminded him.

"It's better when you're here."

"I think so, too, but I have work."

"You're right," he said, leaning toward her. "I'm just on a high from the show, and I want you here for everything."

"Mr. Stone, we should move this to the dressing room," Mateo said. "People will be backstage any minute."

"Sure," Damon said. He pulled Trihn forward and back into the dressing room.

He stripped out of his shirt and toweled off before changing into a new shirt.

"Chloe was pretty…affectionate after the show ended," Trihn said. Then, she quickly added, "Not that I think anything is going on."

"Well, good. There are just a lot of endorphins and so much excitement by the end. It's hard not to want to celebrate when you come offstage. Plus, she's not normally this high-stress, so it's easier to *want* to celebrate with her."

She thought Chloe was a little touchy, but it was innocent, so it really didn't matter. Trihn didn't want to stress about it when it was clear that Damon was into her and only her. He had told her that time and time again.

"I believe you."

Damon leaned down and kissed her on the lips. "I'm going to go meet some fans, and then we can go back to the hotel and repeat this afternoon."

Trihn laughed and pulled him in for another kiss. "Deal."

THIRTY-FOUR

THE NEXT DAY, Trihn had to forcibly remove herself from the hotel premises.

She and Damon had spent all night in his room, and to say that she didn't want to leave would be the understatement of the century.

The idea that he'd had after the show kept ringing through her mind the entire plane ride home.

She wanted to stay. She wanted to join him on tour. She wanted to be with him for every concert and every different city. She didn't want to miss a moment of it.

But reality crashed back in, and she knew it wasn't possible. If she didn't have the fashion show to worry about, she might have made it work for a little while. *But what would happen when school starts?* She couldn't leave school. That would never be an option.

By the time Trihn landed back in Las Vegas, she felt more confident about her departure.

But when she switched her phone off Airplane Mode, the slew of messages didn't help anything.

The first few were from Bryna.

> *Are you with Damon?*

> *Bitch, answer your phone.*

> *Your face is showing up online. Tabloids are kind of going crazy. When you get this, don't check the news.*

Trihn frowned and kept reading. The next message was from Stacia.

> *Hey! Answer your phone! We've all been calling you! Bri is flipping her shit, and now I'm worried.*

Then, there was one from Damon.

> *I know you're on the plane, love, but Chloe was right. Paps took pictures of us together in ATL. The story is that you're a homewrecker. Working on the details of what our statement is going to be to the press or if we should just let it blow over. Call me, so I know you're okay. I hate not being with you during all of this.*

Trihn took a deep breath. They'd been expecting this, begrudgingly accepting that Chloe was right about the paparazzi. It must have been pretty widespread for it to have completely freaked out everyone she knew in the time it had taken her to get to Las Vegas.

As soon as she was off the plane, she called Damon back. She was glad that she only had a carry-on and could hurry out of the airport and into a cab.

"Hey, love," Damon said.

"Hey. So…I'm a homewrecker. That's a new one. It's usually the other way around."

"Yeah, sorry. I guess I was completely unprepared for this sort of thing. I thought we could hang out anywhere we wanted, unmolested."

"Guess not anymore. Am I free to walk around without people following me?" Trihn asked, only half-joking.

"Yeah. I mean…I don't think anyone is going to bother you if I'm not with you, but if they do, just say, *No comment*, and walk away. Hey, hold on."

Through the muffled phone, Trihn could hear him yelling something to Chloe.

"Miss Paranoid over here says you'll be fine but to be on alert until it dies down," he said.

"This feels absurd, Damon."

He laughed. "It really does. I don't think it's a big deal. No one actually believes tabloid bullshit."

Trihn didn't think that was true, but as long as no one in her real life thought what the press had been spinning was true, then it wouldn't matter to her.

"Thank you for being so awesome about this. I can't wait until New York when I can hold you in my arms again."

"I can't wait either. But I should probably give Bri and Stacia a call. I guess they saw the tabloids and are freaking out."

"Oh, Jesus. Okay, yeah. Tell them I said hi."

"I will. Love you."

"Love you, too."

Trihn immediately texted Bryna back to let her know that she had just left the airport and would be at the apartment soon. Her return text was classic Bryna.

> *Hurry up and get your ass over here. I need answers, woman!*

Trihn arrived at her apartment a half hour later and was surprised to find her home holding way more people than she had anticipated.

Bryna was talking on the phone and pacing a circle in the carpet. Eric was standing next to an African American guy from the football team who she had met before with Maya.

Dray or Drayton?

Trihn wasn't sure if he and Maya were officially dating or not, but him being in her house with his arm around her beautiful friend made her think that was the case.

The most surprising thing, however, was the fact that Stacia was currently sitting on a tall blond football player's lap who was not her boyfriend...or sort of boyfriend—whatever Marshall was. Instead, Stacia was laid out on Pace's lap, as if they hadn't spent the last six months at each other's throat—and not in a good way.

Trihn immediately saw why Bryna had been so short in her text messages. The history between she and her stepbrother, Pace, was poor at best. Despite the fact that Bryna had been moving forward and getting along with her family since the birth of her half-sister, Zoe, Bryna still didn't much like or trust Pace. And that was obvious in the glares she kept shooting his way.

"Our local celebrity," Eric said when Trihn finally edged through the door.

"Hey, E."

Bryna's eyes snapped up to her. "I have to go," she said into the phone before abruptly hanging up. "There you are!"

"Hey, everyone. Didn't realize I was walking into a party."

"Yeah, well, you were supposed to be back yesterday," Bryna said.

"Went to see Damon in Atlanta instead. He flew me back this morning while they went on to Charlotte."

"I think everyone knows that already," Pace said with a chuckle.

Stacia smacked his chest. "Have you read any gossip lately?" she asked Trihn.

"No, but Damon told me what the press was saying about me. It's not a big deal. It's all a lie anyway," Trihn said with a shrug. "Damon and Chloe aren't together, and I'm obviously not a homewrecker."

"I told you she wouldn't be worried," Maya said. She was pouring drinks in the kitchen, working even when she wasn't at her job.

Bryna smiled. "I'm glad. It seems Damon has been good for you. I thought we would have a mess on our hands after this shit."

"Such confidence in me, Bri," Trihn said. She rolled her eyes and started walking back to her bedroom.

Bryna followed her and grabbed her arm just before she could disappear. "You're sure you're okay?"

"Totally," Trihn said automatically. "Chloe flipped when she found out that Damon and I had been out in Atlanta. Some girl took a picture with him and Instagrammed it to Chloe, putting it on the press's radar. It's literally the dumbest thing I've ever had to deal with. If I thought for one minute that any of this was a threat, that Chloe was a legit threat, then maybe I'd be worried. But I have *no* reason to think that. None."

Bryna pursed her lips and looked down. Her eyes fluttered back to Trihn's, but they didn't exactly meet hers when she said, "You're right. None."

The entire thing did not blow over like Trihn had wanted.

She was stuck in Vegas, working on her fashion line and getting ready for the big show in New York, which meant there were no more pictures of her and Damon out in public together. But there were enough photos of the two of them on their social media accounts, and those were now crawling all over the Internet. Trihn had to make all her accounts private to keep people from commenting on her shit. It was annoying for all of a couple of hours before she shut it all down and went back to work.

Chloe and Damon were both asked questions about their love lives, but their answers were usually, "No comment," or "It's personal."

Trihn was fine with that. She didn't exactly want to be out in the spotlight or have paparazzi to deal with while she still had so much on her plate. But part of her also kind of wished that she could just come out and say that she and Damon were together. Trihn knew it was business, but it seemed stupid to just ignore it.

She had just finished up another day locked away in the studio and was on her way to meet her friends at Posse when her phone chimed.

I'll call you when I can. It's not true.

Trihn had been so out of the loop while working that she didn't even know what the hell Damon was talking about.

She pulled up Facebook to see a slew of posts about an anonymous hacker posting nude photos of celebrities stolen from their phones.

Trihn groaned. "Disgusting."

Don't these creeps know that celebrities are people, too?

No one should have access to personal information, let alone to very personal images meant for a significant other. Trihn clicked through the list of hacked celebrities' phones, and she froze. It was a relatively long list, but two names popped out at her.

Chloe Avana.

Damon Stone.

Shit! She didn't know what that meant, but she had a feeling it wasn't good.

Trihn pulled into Posse's parking lot and searched for their names, as related to the scandal. About a hundred different sites appeared at once.

She clicked on the first one.

CHLOE AVANA NUDE!

Anonymous hacker group strikes at celebrities once more. This time, Chloe Avana, former Disney star and platinum-recording artist, is revealed in a series of naked photographs. These photographs were allegedly extracted from her phone as well as from the phone of her current fling, DJ Damon Stone, whom she recently recorded with on her latest number one hit, "We Never Met."

These photographs come on the wave of another breach of security for celebrities and bring up a call for increased…

Trihn stopped reading as she tried to process what the article was saying. It was obvious, of course. She knew what they were saying. But…she couldn't comprehend the other part.

Why would Damon have those photographs on his phone?

She knew he had immediately texted her to let her know that it wasn't true. So…it must not be true. That didn't seem like Damon at all. It didn't make sense.

She leaned her head against the steering wheel and tried to make all of the puzzle pieces fit together. The hacking group had no reason to lie about where the images had come from—or at least she didn't think so. She really knew nothing about them.

But if Damon didn't even ask for nude pictures from me, why would he want them from Chloe?

The only way it could be possible, in her mind, was if Chloe had sent them to Damon, unprompted.

Or Damon was a liar.

Trihn squeezed her eyes shut and shook her head at the ludicrous thoughts. It was a mistake. It wasn't true. The press was manipulating her, and she needed to wait to hear from Damon before freaking out about this. She needed to trust him and believe in him, as he had done for her all those times. They were a team. That was all that mattered.

Taking a calming deep breath, she exited her car and entered Posse.

Her friends were hanging out at the bar. Maya was pouring drinks and laughing with Drayton and Pace. Eric planted a kiss on Bryna's forehead while Stacia was dancing around in a too-short skirt. When they saw her, their faces fell, and they all looked stricken.

Great.

"Hey," Trihn said. "We have to quit meeting like this."

"Have you not heard?" Bryna asked.

"I saw. But it's not true. Damon said it wasn't true."

Trihn realized how ridiculous she'd sounded when a bunch of them winced. *Have I become that girl again? Am I making excuses for Damon when he could be doing whatever he wants behind my back?*

God, insecurities on red alert.

She needed to pull herself back together. Damon was not cheating on her. He would never have flown her to Atlanta or texted her reassurances or totally fallen in love with her if he wanted someone else. She would not let this stress her out. There was an explanation for it all.

"Can I talk to you?" Bryna asked.

She looked nervous. That was not a good sign.

"Sure," Trihn said hesitantly.

Trihn glanced over at Eric, and he looked worried. She didn't know if it was about the stuff that had come out in the press or if it was about what Bryna was going to say. Either way, it was not good.

The girls walked across Posse and then went outside to the patio. They sank down onto a bench next to the empty pool. For the summer, the university had emptied out, aside from the football players. During the day, it would be busier out here, but right now, they basically had the place to themselves.

Bryna looked directly in Trihn's eyes. "I've never told *anyone* this story before. I swore that I wouldn't let it get out to the press, so I've held my tongue. And it's been hard. I've wanted to say something for a long time, but it didn't feel like my place or the right time."

"You're freaking me out."

"I just need you to promise that you won't say anything about this to anyone…even to Damon."

Trihn chewed on her lip. "Does this have to do with Damon?"

"Not directly."

"Okay…I won't say anything."

"When I was dating Gates our senior year, he was on the set of *Broken Road* with Chloe in Atlanta. I met Jude one night at a club and decided I wanted to sleep with him. So, I called Gates in the middle of the night and broke up with him."

Trihn laughed. "You're serious?"

"Yeah. Gates laughed at me and said we'd talk about it later, but to me, we were over. When he got back to LA, he acted as if we weren't over. Jude was a one-night stand that Gates knew about, and I decided he was kind of right. You can't break up with a guy like Gates on the phone."

"Okay…"

"Well, the reason Gates was okay with Jude was because he told me that, on the same night, he'd slept with someone else, too. And since we'd both done it with nobodies who we'd never talk to again, it didn't matter," Bryna said.

Trihn's stomach knotted. She had a horrible feeling that she knew where this was going. "But it did matter?"

"Yeah, I found out later that the girl had been interested in him the whole time, and that night was just a culmination of all their flirtations. And that girl was Chloe Avana."

Trihn sat very still, processing Bryna's story. "So, *that's* why you hate her."

"Yes."

"So, what you're saying is, she's biding her time until Damon and I are on the rocks to…what? Swoop in?"

"I'm not saying that history will repeat itself," Bryna amended. "We were younger and dumber. I think that's why Chloe was acting like a jealous maniac that night at the club after your fashion show. She and Gates have had a rocky relationship since then. I don't really know what's up with them. My guess is, she's still pining for her first love in some way, despite her cool, confident girl exterior that she portrays to the press. But that's neither here nor there with Damon."

"This explains…a lot," Trihn admitted. It made her feel a little better and a little worse.

She hadn't thought she had anything to worry about because Chloe wasn't the type of girl to do something like that, but now, Bryna was saying that Chloe was absolutely that girl.

"I'm sorry I didn't tell you sooner. But with these photos coming out…I didn't want you to go in completely blind."

"You don't think that they were on Damon's phone, do you?"

Bryna cringed. "I want to say no because Damon seems like a good guy. But I've seen good guys corrupted before, so just be cautious."

"Thank you for telling me, but I don't think this changes much. Either he did or didn't have these pictures. Either there's an explanation for it or not. But Damon loves me, and I love him. He's not into Chloe."

Bryna looked at her with pitying eyes, and Trihn just wanted to scream. She wasn't crazy for thinking like this. She would show everyone the truth.

"His LA show is tomorrow," Trihn told her. "Let's drive to the show and surprise him. You'll see it for yourself."

They all would.

THIRTY-FIVE

CONVINCING HER FRIENDS to go to Chloe and Damon's show in LA wasn't as hard as Trihn had thought it would be. Eric and Maya both had to work, which also ruled out Drayton, but Bryna and Stacia were all in. And though Bryna had tried to argue for Pace not to join them, he was seated in the driver's seat with Stacia in the passenger seat and Trihn and Bryna in the back of Stacia's SUV as they headed south on I-15 toward Los Angeles.

Somehow, Bryna had managed to work her magic and get them killer seats in the second row. She had complained that it wasn't first row or center, but Trihn thought second row on the left side of the stage was a lucky grab on the night before the show. But that was Bryna.

Trihn was excited to see Damon perform again. The girls had no idea what they were in for. It was nothing like him deejaying at Posse, and they hadn't been to a show of him performing with Chloe yet. Trihn really thought that videos didn't do it justice either.

"So, did you talk to Damon about this?" Stacia swiveled around in the passenger seat to look at Trihn and Bryna.

"About the show? No, it's a surprise," Trihn said. "I thought we were all in on that."

"I mean, the pictures…of Chloe."

"They weren't from his phone."

"You said that already," Pace chimed in.

"I talked to him last night once he'd gotten into LA."

Damon had called as soon as he could, but he hadn't had that much free time before this show.

"Is there any reason those pictures could have been on his phone?" Stacia asked.

Pace chuckled. "Oh, there's a reason."

Stacia smacked his arm. "Not helping."

"Damon isn't like that. He's in love with me. Why would he have suddenly changed his tune?"

"Because Chloe is hot?" Pace asked.

"She's gorgeous," Trihn said. "But Damon doesn't see her like that. And if he did, then he wouldn't be fighting for us to work out. I'm pretty sure he could have already had her if he wanted." Trihn glanced over at Bryna. "You're being awfully quiet about this."

"I don't like to be wrong, so I'm not chiming in."

"Comforting."

"If you believe him, then I'm sure it's nothing," Bryna said after a moment.

"Look, when I talked to him, he said that those photos were real. They weren't Photoshopped."

"Sweet," Pace said.

Trihn shook her head. "Chloe agreed that they had been on her phone at some point, but she never sent them to Damon. Damon said that he'd never seen them before. They both think it's spin from the press, saying it's from his phone, since they're in the public eye right now."

"Okay, but why would an anonymous hacker group lie about where the photos came from?" Stacia asked intuitively.

"I asked the same thing. That was the part that worried me," Trihn admitted with a frown.

She hated doubting Damon at all, but the evidence was damning. When she had picked up the magazine in New York, she had known how Damon and Chloe met, so it was laughable. When the press had started saying that Trihn was a homewrecker breaking Damon and Chloe up, she had been there to see what was going on. But these pictures...they'd just come out of nowhere.

"And what did he say?" Pace asked. "This should be good."

"If you're not going to be supportive, you can shut the fuck up," Stacia warned him.

He smirked at her before facing forward and remaining silent.

"Damon didn't know why the hacker had lied about that, but since this anonymous group could be anyone. We don't know their motives."

"Convenient," Pace snapped.

Stacia glared at him. "That's it. You're not getting fucked tonight."

His eyes widened. "Like hell I'm not."

"You're being a dick."

"Last I checked, you liked that."

"Will both of you shut up before I vomit in Stacia's car?" Bryna spat.

"Anyway," Trihn said, "I just...choose to believe him. If I didn't, where would I be? Back in the same black hole of, *Woe is me! My boyfriend is cheating on me.* I just can't think that's Damon. So, unless I see something to the contrary, I'm not believing it."

With that declaration, the rest of the car fell silent. Stacia flipped the stereo on, and "We Never Met" blasted through the speakers. Trihn couldn't even be surprised at this point. The song was *still* at number one, and it seemed that all the press, negative or otherwise, was only helping their fame. Guess it was true. There was no such thing as bad press.

By the time they reached the venue, the opener for the show had already gone on, and everyone was milling around, anxiously waiting for Chloe to perform. Trihn noticed a group of girls wearing Avanaddicts shirts and holding up signs, and she quickly veered away from them. No need for a repeat run-in with some crazy fans. She just hoped that she wouldn't be recognized.

Trihn took the seat at the end of the aisle next to Bryna and tried to relax.

Bryna was on her phone, likely annoyed that she had to sit through another one of Chloe's concerts. Trihn thought she liked Chloe's music, but the stuff with Gates must have really hit home. Bryna held a grudge like no other. Even though she was happy with Eric and Gates was ancient history, Bryna still didn't trust Chloe. Trihn really wanted to prove her wrong.

She grabbed her phone out of her bag so that she could text Damon. But when she looked at the screen, there was already a message from Damon waiting for her.

Chloe is in one of her moods tonight.

Are you pulling your hair out?

I'm going to rip hers out if she doesn't chill. Panic attacks on top of panic attacks.

Then, another message dinged immediately after that.

Shit! Maybe I shouldn't have put that in a text message. What if our phones get hacked again?

Both Chloe and Damon had gotten new phones after the hacking incident. And Trihn knew that he probably didn't want anyone to read his personal information or get that personal information about Chloe, but the word *again* made her cringe. It was as if the last time had revealed something from his phone.

> *Sorry, love. I have to go onstage in a minute. Wish you were here.*

Trihn smiled at that. She was here. He just didn't know it.

> *Good luck.*

Just then, the lights flickered, and a cheer rose up from the audience. Everyone got to their feet just as Chloe appeared onstage in a cloud of smoke, singing the opening song to her self-titled album. She was wearing a two-piece black sequin outfit and killer heeled booties. Her dark hair was parted down the middle, and she looked fierce. No one would guess that she had been having panic attacks all day. The stage was her playground, and nothing could touch her there.

The crowd was enthralled. Trihn even had to admit that it was hard to tear her eyes away from the show to search out Damon in the back. He was playing guitar without any spotlight on him. He was just jamming away back there, as if he were a part of the band.

It wasn't until he switched to the piano and a spotlight hit his head that the crowd even realized he'd been hiding in the back. Her Damon was perfectly happy out of the limelight, just playing his heart out in peace.

Halfway through the next song, Chloe strode over to the piano. The crowd roared when she neared Damon. Tabloids had done their job. Chloe sang into Damon's ear and then propped herself up on his piano. He looked up at her while he played. He had a dreamy smile on his face, like he was having the time of his life. But to the crowd,

Trihn was sure it looked like he was adoring Chloe and not the music.

It was the same set that they'd played in Atlanta while Trihn had been there a couple of weeks ago. Trihn recognized when they switched from the up-tempo songs into the power ballads. One of Chloe's quick changes had her out of her skimpy attire and into a long flowy white dress that glittered and sparkled for all eyes to see.

When Chloe started in on "Homesick," a major hit off of her debut album, she entranced the crowd. The song was about a girl holding out for her first love and how being without him made her homesick.

As Chloe carried it into the second verse, Trihn gasped. She looked over at Bryna. "This song…"

Bryna nodded. "Yeah."

"It's about Gates?" Trihn whispered, leaning toward her.

"It was so blatantly obvious when it came out. I was shocked that not even the conniving press figured it out."

"I just…wow. I never would have known."

Trihn looked back up at Chloe, feeling a little sorry for her. Not that what she had done to Bryna and Gates was right, but she must have felt something real for Gates to have written such a moving song about him.

Then, Trihn noticed that something wasn't quite right. Chloe was still singing, but tears, real tears, were streaming down her face. The audience was totally silent now, watching her cry through the song.

As if a flood had finally broken inside her, the words to "Homesick" were broken in her mouth, and she couldn't seem to quell the tears. The microphone was on a stand before her, and her hands holding it were shaking. Then, one of them bunched up into her perfect hair, and the other followed, as if she were trying to hold herself together but failing.

Then, she broke off her singing entirely.

She just stared forward at her captivated audience.

Crying. Shaking. And emotionally spent.

Her body collapsed into a puddle on the floor. Tears wracked her body, and great hiccuping sobs could be heard to those nearest to the stage.

Bryna and Trihn exchanged worried glances.

What the hell is happening to Chloe?

They watched as Damon rushed to her side, sliding to a halt before her. Everyone else was paralyzed, unable to put together the breakdown with the mega superstar they all knew and loved.

Damon was softly speaking to her, trying to coax her to her feet, but she wasn't budging. Without a second thought, he hoisted her into his arms and started to walk offstage. The audience applauded quietly. Trihn had only ever heard of such a thing happening when a football player had gone down with an injury, and they'd finally carted his body off the field.

As soon as Chloe was removed from the stage, everyone broke out into whispers.

Trihn didn't have any answers.

Bryna nudged her. "Hey, you can still kind of see them," she said.

Trihn looked to where Bryna was pointing, and sure enough, Damon had carried Chloe to the side of the stage. It was only visible to people who were seated at an angle, but they could just make out the outline of two bodies.

Chloe was on her feet, and Damon had his hands on her face. Trihn couldn't tell much more than that from where she was standing. She assumed he was trying to get Chloe to calm down and snap out of whatever episode she had just dissolved into. He'd said that she was stressed and in a mood that day. This must be the result of all that stress, but Trihn couldn't believe Chloe had actually broken down onstage in front of everyone.

Trihn had her eyes glued to the pair. And just when she was going to grab her phone and find out what the hell was happening, her world shifted as Damon's and Chloe's lips met.

THIRTY-SIX

DAMON AND CHLOE WERE KISSING.

Trihn reeled at the sight before her. Tearing her eyes away from them, she heavily sat down in her seat. She took healing deep breaths and tried to keep her stomach from lodging itself in her throat.

This couldn't be happening again. Not another time.

She had come here for her proof, and there it was, right before her eyes. Clearly, everyone had seen the truth but her. She hadn't wanted to believe it. No, she *hadn't* believed any of it. Damon loved her. He wasn't supposed to hurt her. He was supposed to be different.

Fuck! It hurt. She had known it would hurt. She had told him from the beginning that she couldn't handle it a third time. She couldn't be cheated on and come out okay with it. She'd barely survived last time. Her heart was breaking all over again.

She should have read the signs for what they were instead of brushing them aside. Now, here she was, barely breathing, as her boyfriend was kissing another girl. It didn't even seem possible.

Her Damon couldn't hurt her this way.

"Trihn," Bryna whispered, putting a hand on her shoulder, "we should get out of here."

"I'm not leaving without talking to him," she said with conviction in her voice.

"He did stop her," Stacia said.

"Awesome," Trihn said sarcastically.

"I just mean…maybe it was unwanted?"

"Are you defending him?" Trihn asked.

"No," Stacia peeped.

"Yes," Bryna corrected. "Yes, she is. Let's talk to him first."

Trihn stood and threw her hands wide. "Yes, let's defend him, even when we see with our own two eyes what he did."

"If I could interrupt," Pace said, holding his hand up.

"You can't," Bryna snapped.

"You're causing a scene," Pace growled low.

Trihn and Bryna both stopped what they were doing. Looking around their area of the arena, they saw it was true. Eyes were drawn toward them. Several girls had taken pictures of them. Some of them even seemed to have recognized who Trihn was.

"Shit," Trihn whispered. "We should go backstage."

Her friends nodded without a word. They veered out of their aisle and headed toward the nearest exit. Trihn heard her name as she passed by the Avanaddicts. She ducked her head and hurried out of the room. The last thing anyone needed after Chloe's breakdown was to draw attention to Trihn.

Bryna had been to the arena before and lapped them around the room to the backstage entrance. A crowd had formed by the door, and a bouncer was standing there, directing people to return to their seats.

"What's going on?" Bryna asked the nearest girl.

"They won't let backstage-pass holders in to see Chloe even though we paid for them."

"Once again," the bouncer's voice boomed, "if you are not on the approved list to be backstage, then you should all return to your seats. No backstage passes will be granted at this time. I don't have official word yet on a refund. Please return to your seats."

No one moved.

"Are you on that list?" Bryna asked Trihn.

"Damon doesn't know I'm here."

"Then, maybe you should get ahold of him."

Trihn nodded. "Yeah. Right. Okay."

She grabbed her forgotten phone to text Damon, but she already had a message there. That was fast, considering what he'd just been doing.

I love you.

Trihn wanted to melt at those words, but it just infuriated her. He'd just been kissing Chloe, and now, he wanted to tell her he loved her. *Did he think that the word would get out, and he wanted to protect himself before she could find out?* Because she had seen it firsthand and wasn't going to roll over.

Then, you should let me backstage.

What?

Surprise…I'm at the show.

In Los Angeles?

Yep.

Fuck…I'll be there in a minute.

Trihn showed the messages to Bryna. "Clearly, he knows something is up."

Bryna and Stacia frowned but didn't say anything. They all waited impatiently for Damon.

A few minutes passed before a bouncer called over the crowd, "Trihnity Hamilton!"

Trihn's head whipped around, and she raised her hand.

"You're all cleared."

A bunch of girls glared at her. Bryna and Stacia both squeezed her and wished her good luck.

"I'll see you guys later."

"You'll do great," Stacia said.

Bryna just smiled forlornly. Trihn took a deep breath and then elbowed her way through the crowd and past the bouncer.

Damon was standing on the other side of the door, looking as ruggedly handsome as she had ever seen him. At the moment, it was actually unfair for him to be that attractive. He still had on the dark jeans and dark blue T-shirt he'd had on while onstage. His baseball cap was missing, and he looked like he wanted to be fiddling with it to give his hands something to do.

"Hey," he said. His face brightened when he saw her, and he pulled her against him.

Trihn was stiff in his embrace, and he quickly pulled back. He looked concerned at her lack of enthusiasm. And she figured he had every right to be afraid after what had just happened.

"Um...let's get out of here. We'll go to my dressing room."

She followed behind him as he hurried away from the crowded backstage area. Trihn wondered if it was to tell the crowd that the show was over. Chloe hadn't looked like she would be ready to go back out there anytime soon.

But who knew? Maybe Damon's kiss had reenergized her.

Trihn frowned at her own negative thoughts as she followed him into the dressing room with his name on it.

By the time she walked inside, she was seething. All she wanted to do was blow up and demand answers, but she also wanted to give Damon a chance to tell her the truth.

"Not the best concert for you to show up to," Damon said, closing the door behind her.

"Why is that?" she asked. *Because you kissed someone else?*

"Chloe just had a breakdown onstage. The staff took her to the hospital. We don't know what the fuck is going to happen to her. It sounded like they were already talking about checking her into some rehab facility for emotional and stress-related issues."

"Oh."

That was not the right answer.

She crossed her arms and waited for more, for him to tell her what had happened between him and Chloe.

"Panic attacks and everything finally got to her," Damon said. He reached for his hat and plopped it back down on his head. Then, he immediately removed it and started rolling it between his fingers. He looked up and met her eyes. "I guess she just cracked."

"And that's the reason I shouldn't have been at this show?"

He narrowed his eyes in confusion. "You're upset."

"Yes."

"Because of Chloe?"

Trihn gritted her teeth. "Are you going to act like you don't know?"

Damon opened his mouth to respond and then shut it. He shook his head to reorient himself and sighed heavily. His head dipped back for a fraction of a second as realization seemed to dawn on him as to what she was getting at.

"You saw her kiss me."

The truth was like someone branding her skin—fiery hot and impossible to remove.

"I saw you two kiss—along with hundreds of other people, I'm sure."

"It wasn't like that," he said immediately.

"Oh, really?" she asked. "Do you want to tell me what it *was* like, Damon? Because I was standing there and saw what happened with my own two eyes. My friends were worried about me because all this shit was showing up in the tabloids. I defended you, even laughed it off, because you love me. You would never do something like that. I brought them here to the show to prove to them that their worries were unfounded. Then...*that*." She gestured to the stage where she saw them kiss. "Do you have any idea what the fuck that felt like?"

"No. Fuck...I couldn't imagine how I'd feel if I saw someone else kiss you. I'd want to murder them."

"Basically. So, who do I kill first? You or Chloe?"

"Please understand—"

"I understand! Chloe is into you and saw her chance."

"She kissed me. I didn't kiss her back," Damon told her. "It really didn't even happen. You know I have no interest in her."

He took her hands in his, but she pulled away. She had seen it happen. She so desperately wanted to believe him, but he couldn't just blow it off.

"Do I? Clearly, she has interest in you!"

"She's emotionally unstable! I don't care how she fucking feels about me," Damon said. He drew her toward him. His dark eyes stared down at her with passion and worry and hope and despair. "All I care about is how you feel. That's all it."

"Well, I'm pissed!"

"I can see that, but there's no reason to be. It wasn't a real kiss. I didn't even want it. I shoved her away from me once I got over the shock of what the hell was happening."

She sighed. "I just want to know if it's happened before. Tell me the truth, please. I can handle it."

"No! Jesus Christ, Trihn! She had a mental breakdown and kissed me. I stopped her, and they carted her away to the hospital. I am sorry that she did that. I am sorry that you had to see it. I am sorry that you feel hurt and betrayed. You're looking at me like I ruined your world, but please, please see the truth."

"I want to. I want to believe you," she said, a tear leaking out of her eye. She hastily wiped it away. "I want to trust you."

"Then, trust me. I love you with all my heart. I want to marry you one day…if you'd have me." Damon kissed the tips of her fingers. "You're it for me. You have been since day one, love. That's not going to change—not now, not ever."

Real tears hit her anew—but not from the pain of what she had witnessed. It was from the shock and realization of what he was saying.

"You want to…marry me?" she gasped.

"Absolutely."

"I don't know what to say."

"Just say you're mine. Say you have no reason to doubt me because I would never, ever do anything to hurt you."

"Really? Nothing happened?" she asked, hope filling her up.

"I swear, nothing happened. There's no room in my heart for anything, except for you. You're the person I want to share every moment with."

"Even that kiss with Chloe?"

"I would have much rather it been you," he said.

Damon set her hands on his shoulders and started moving their bodies together. This was how it had all started. Dancing, the music, the movement—it was so effortless with them.

"I'll say it as much as you need to hear it, but I would never cheat on you," he told her. "I want you. Just you. Only you. Forever you."

Trihn looked up into his face, absorbing everything he'd said. A million emotions ran through her in that moment. She had no way of knowing whether or not his story was true. But when she looked into his eyes, she saw only sincerity.

Damon was exactly the guy she'd thought he was. She had just gotten so wrapped up in what she had seen that she hadn't put it into context. *If Damon feels something, anything, for Chloe, wouldn't he be at the hospital with her?* Instead, he was here, trying to convince Trihn how much he loved her.

"Would you have told me about the kiss?" she asked cautiously.

He took a deep breath and nodded. "As much as it would have hurt me, I would have told you. That's why I messaged you, telling you that I love you, like you did in New York when you were stressed. That was where my head was, and I needed you to know it right away."

Damon leaned forward and pressed his lips to her forehead. He sighed when she didn't pull away.

"It is so good to see you. I just wish that every time we were together, something horrible didn't happen. I'm over it all. The next time the press asks me a question about my relationship status, I'm telling them I have a girlfriend and that Chloe and I were never together. I'm tired of not commenting and letting them say whatever they want. I'll fix this, okay?"

"Do you think it'll change anything?"

"It will change how I feel, and I hope it will change how you feel about what's out there. I don't want to be idle about it. I'm not ashamed of you. Even if the media lies and twists it, at least the truth will be out there."

Trihn bit her lip and nodded. "I'd like that."

He sighed and looked down. "There's something else."

Fear ate at her stomach. "What?"

"I was going to tell you in person in New York City when I went to meet your family because it won't be officially announced until then anyway, but since you're here…"

"What is it?"

A smile spread across Damon's face. "'We Never Met' was just certified platinum."

Trihn's mouth dropped open. "Oh my God! Platinum! You guys have sold a million copies?"

"Yeah. And it's all because of you. None of this would have happened without you. You're the reason for it all. You're my platinum girl, and I wouldn't have it any other way."

THIRTY-SEVEN

AFTER THE CONCERT ENDED, Damon insisted Trihn stay with him in LA.

No one was permitted to visit Chloe in the hospital, other than family, and keeping the press away was nearly impossible. It was worthy of Britney Spears's meltdown in 2007. Luckily, Chloe hadn't shaved off her beautiful hair.

But due to the emotional stress on the tour, Chloe was flown directly into a rehab facility, and the rest of the summer tour was canceled. She assured her fans that she would be sure to make up all of the missed shows in her next international fall tour but that she needed to take care of herself first.

She and Damon drove back to Las Vegas together with the promise from his manager and agent that they would find something else for him to do until Chloe was back to herself. Trihn could see how upset they were at the loss of profit from the tour. But since "We Never Met" was still at number one and sales had apparently increased since Chloe's breakdown, Trihn didn't think anyone was actually hurting for money.

The best part of the whole thing was that Trihn got Damon all to herself again. She would be lying if she said that they didn't need this time together. To have him around, in her bed and out with her friends, was pure bliss. When they went out, they would have to stay only in VIP areas because his face was so well-known that he would get mobbed. But she didn't care. She knew things would cool down with time. And she was enjoying the make-up sex in the meantime.

Trihn couldn't believe that the day had finally come when she and Damon were going to New York. Her designs were as good as they could get, and she was traveling with the clothes the week before the show. She'd promised her parents that she'd have a few days free, so the rest of her family could meet Damon. She was excited and nervous about that.

"Are you ready?" Damon asked as they stepped off the plane at JFK Airport.

"Ready as I'll ever be."

He pushed their luggage, including the giant chest of clothes she had brought with her for the show, on a cart. He had his signature cap low over his eyes as they moved through the busy airport. Someone had recognized him on the flight, but since he'd flown them first class, it hadn't been as big of a deal as Trihn had thought it would be.

A black town car was waiting for them when they walked outside, and a large African American guy in a black suit opened the door and then took ahold of their luggage. They both hopped into the back seat. Damon flipped his hat off his head and leaned over to kiss Trihn.

She took the hat out of his hand and plopped it on her head. "There. Now, no one will know who I am either."

He narrowed his eyes at her and popped it off her head. "If that stupid clip would just go away, then maybe people would leave me alone."

"Doubtful," she said. At least she had stopped cringing about the video that was spreading of him and Chloe kissing at the show. "Not when your track is still at the top of the charts. Biggest hit of the summer. Everyone is tired of hearing it on the radio already."

"I'm not."

"Of course you're not. It's your song, silly."

"And about my girl," he said, pulling her closer, as the car started moving through the New York traffic.

They arrived at her parents' townhouse a solid hour later. Both of them were desperately tired of traveling and ready to do a whole lot of nothing. The driver helped them unload their bags just as Trihn's parents walked out of the front door.

Trihn went to the door and hugged them both. "Mom, this is Damon."

Damon stuck his hand out, and they shook. "So nice to meet you, ma'am."

"Please, call me Linh. It's so nice to finally meet you. I've heard only good things about you."

Damon smiled brightly. "That's good to hear. It's glad to be in the city. I've never been to New York—well, not officially. My mum and I traveled through on our way from London, but I was young, and we just had a layover."

"You didn't tell me that," Trihn accused. "I'll have to show you around, and we can do touristy things."

"Are you from London?" her mother asked, pulling Damon inside and continuing to chat.

Trihn and her dad brought in the last bag.

She dropped her suitcase in the foyer and hugged her dad. "It's good to see you."

"You, too, kiddo. Glad you could get your boyfriend here. Your mother has been bugging me nonstop about him."

"He was a little busy up until this point."

"You know how she is."

Trihn nodded and walked into the living room when she heard her name. "What?"

"Since you're here for a little while and don't have to run off to a concert like originally planned, maybe we could drive out to the Hamptons."

Trihn narrowed her eyes. "You had this all planned."

Linh raised her hands. "It's just a suggestion."

Damon met Trihn's eyes and shrugged. "Up to you. It is quieter than the city."

Trihn took a deep breath. *Why am I even surprised by this?*

Her mother had been trying to get her to talk about the wedding and everything that was going into planning it since the engagement had happened. Trihn had stopped answering her calls. Of course, on her one trip home, her mom would take her back to the Hamptons where it had all gone down and where Lydia was going to get married.

But this time, she wasn't as upset. She had Damon at her side. Her past was just that—the past. She had moved on from what had happened. All she needed to do was face it and prove it to herself.

"All right," Trihn said finally, taking the seat next to Damon. "If Damon is going, then I'll go."

"Great!" Linh said. She clapped her hands and looked up at her husband with raised eyebrows, as if she had just won a victory.

Damon kissed Trihn's cheek and whispered softly in her ear, "I love you."

Trihn and Damon stepped out of her parents' SUV and breathed in the salty sea air. Trihn hadn't realized how much she had missed it here. She hadn't been back since Lydia and Preston had gotten together.

"This is our home away from home," Trihn told Damon.

It was a massive white beach house that they rented from a friend of her mother's at the magazine. Usually, it was just for a week in the summer, but since the wedding was going to be here, the owners were pretty lenient about their time.

He raised his eyebrows. "And here I thought you came from humble beginnings."

Trihn laughed. "I did…kind of. It's not like Bri."

"No, it's not, but *humble* is not the word I'd use," he said.

"And what are you now, rock star?" Trihn grabbed her bag out of the back and slung it over her shoulder.

Damon dropped her suitcase onto the driveway and laughed. "Not a rock star. Still a DJ, love."

"I wouldn't say you're exactly humble anymore."

"Humble beginnings."

Trihn was walking backward, teasing Damon, as they neared the side door to the house when she heard voices behind her. Damon had stopped moving and was staring at the door. Trihn whirled around and saw what he was staring at.

Déjà vu hit her fresh. Lydia and Preston were standing in the doorway. It was here where she had found out that they were together. It was here where her world had shattered into a million pieces.

Damon came and put a protective arm around her waist.

"Hey," Trihn said finally. "Mom failed to mention that you guys were already here."

Lydia brightened and traipsed down the stairs. Her long blonde hair was up in a high ponytail, and she was wearing a bright yellow sundress. "We wouldn't have missed it," she said, stuffing her hands in the pockets of her dress.

Trihn noticed she was barefoot.

"Oh my God, are you Damon?" Lydia asked.

"That's me. You must be Lydia," Damon said, his accent thick.

Lydia looked like she wanted to rush over and hug him, but she somehow managed to control herself. "It is amazing to finally meet you. I love your music. Both of us do." She waved for Preston to come down the steps. "This is my fiancé, Preston."

Damon released Trihn to step forward and offer his hand to Preston.

"Oh, I've heard a lot about you," Damon said, his voice low.

They were nearly eye-level with one another, and Trihn could see that their handshake was more of a squeeze. They warily eyed each other, sizing the other one up.

"That right?" Preston asked.

Damon laughed at Preston seemingly rising to the occasion and then released his hand. "Yeah. You two are getting married, right?"

"Yes," Lydia beamed. "I hope you will join us."

Damon caught Trihn's eye, ignoring Lydia's apparent charm. "We'll see. Come on, love."

Damon offered Trihn his arm, and they strolled into the house with their luggage without a backward look. Trihn showed him where the room was, and they stashed their bags.

She collapsed back onto the bed with a laugh. "That was hilarious. Did you see the look on his face?" she asked.

"I was preoccupied with yours." He sank down on the bed and looked over at her. "You're not still thinking about him, are you?" His words were hesitant, as if he hadn't wanted to ask.

Trihn quickly sat up and looked deep into his eyes. "No. I didn't mean it to come out like that. Don't get me wrong. I don't want them to get married, but it's not about me. It's about Lydia. I wish I could prove to her that he's not a good guy. But it has nothing to do with how I feel about Preston at all."

"Okay. I just wanted to make sure that, when you saw him, it didn't change anything."

"Are you that worried about our love?" she asked.

"First love is hard to overcome. He was the guy you compared everyone else to. You've spent two years obsessing over a few days spent here at this beach house. I just want to make sure you're okay, that we're okay," he told her.

"I am. We are," she told him. "I've realized there are more good memories here than bad ones. I wish I'd seen it earlier. I was worried that being in this room would remind me of the time he and Lydia had had sex loud enough that I could hear it, driving me from the Hamptons entirely," she said quietly.

"You never told me that."

"It's a dark memory. I don't like to think about it. But being here with you is just right. It's about new memories." Trihn smiled. "You're my future. I don't want to live in the past."

"Well, good," Damon said before kissing down her neck, "because I like the idea of us having a future together."

"Mmm…me, too." She leaned her head back, getting lost in his kisses and forgetting everything else.

THIRTY-EIGHT

"WHAT ARE YOU TWO DOING HERE?" Trihn screeched.

She and Damon had managed to survive an awkward dinner exchange with Preston and Lydia the night before. And to avoid another such encounter, Trihn and Damon had to decided to spend the day on the beach. But she definitely had not expected to see her two best friends from home strolling toward her.

Trihn tackled Renée in a hug. She was a petite African American girl with black hair, and she was the most amazing ballet dancer Trihn had ever seen. It had been crazy to be separated from her, but when they were back together, it was as if no time had passed.

"Hey, hooker," Renée said with a laugh.

Trihn turned her sights to her other best friend, Ian. She released Renée and pulled Ian into a hug. The two couldn't have been more different. Renée had grown up in the Bronx with a single mother and was constantly helping to provide for her younger siblings. But Ian was from old money, and his parents owned the beach house next to Trihn's. He preferred cardigans and computers and was embarrassed by Renée's crude humor. But they somehow worked.

"I've missed you both."

Ian smiled. "It's good to see you, too."

"This is Damon."

"Damon Stone," Renée said, eyeing him up and down.

Shirtless, he was just wearing blue swim trunks, and Trihn knew he looked amazing.

"Well, I have to say this is a massive improvement," Renée added.

Trihn laughed and looked at Renée in exasperation. Ian and Damon shook hands and immediately started talking as if they were old friends.

It felt...amazing. Trihn couldn't believe how great it was to just be out in the sun in her all black bikini, lying in the sand with her boyfriend and best friends, with no worries. No Preston and Lydia. No Chloe. No paparazzi. It was just a relaxing day.

Except it wouldn't last.

After they'd been out for an hour, two figures started traipsing toward them on the beach.

"Oh no," Renée said.

"What?" Trihn asked. She put her sunglasses back on and squinted in their direction. "Oh."

"Are they really coming over here?"

"Looks like it."

Damon frowned. "Lydia really wants you to be at that wedding."

"No fucking way!" Renée cried.

"I have to agree. It would be disastrous," Ian said.

"And I don't want to go, so she can shove it," Trihn added.

The group fell silent as Lydia and Preston drew near.

"Mind if we crash this party?" Lydia asked. "We brought some more beer."

Preston dropped a cooler into the sand before anyone could decline, and he started handing out beers. Trihn reluctantly took one, hoping that the alcohol would soothe their bad company.

Lydia laid down another blanket in the sand and spread it out. Preston stripped out of his own shirt and tossed it into a bag before joining her.

Damon's gaze rested back on Trihn, and she smiled confidently. She was not going to let this ruin their afternoon.

Trihn leaned in and planted a kiss on Damon's lips. "This is much better than tour buses and hotel rooms, isn't it?" she asked playfully.

"Definitely."

"What was that like?" Lydia asked. "Touring, that is."

Damon leaned back on his elbows. "Busy and wonderful. Always going, going, going with no time to do much else. Going a lot of places but seeing nothing. Have to say though, performing in front of tens of thousands of people never gets old."

"That sounds incredible. I wish I could have gone to one of your shows." Lydia smiled sweetly. "I would have made the New York one if...well, you know...it was still happening."

"Yeah," Damon said.

"And what about Chloe Avana?" Preston said.

"What about her?" Damon asked.

Trihn bit her lip and looked between the two of them. Preston had brought Chloe up on purpose.

"Is she really in rehab?"

"Yeah, she is. She had a mental breakdown. I'm pretty sure everyone in the country saw proof of that," Damon said.

Despite the fact that Chloe had briefly come between him and Trihn, he still sharply defended Chloe. She was a friend and a coworker, and he hated hearing people who didn't know her talk about her. He would give Bryna a pass for her dislike of Chloe. Though, after Chloe's breakdown, Bryna's dislike had somehow lessened.

"I don't think that's the only proof the world saw," Preston said before tipping his beer back.

"You mean the kiss video?" Trihn asked boldly.

Preston shrugged. "We all saw it."

"And somehow you think that makes it your business?"

"Trihn," Damon said softly, "it's fine. I haven't been able to go more than a few hours without hearing about that video. I have a feeling it's going to follow me everywhere."

"And you're still together?" Preston asked. He stared at Trihn, waiting for her answer.

"Obviously." Damon leaned forward and kissed Trihn on the mouth.

Trihn smiled and sighed before turning back to Preston. "Are you done with your interrogation?"

Lydia smacked Preston's arm. "Don't be such a downer. I'm sure it's fake. Trihn picked a real keeper—a famous musician on tour with Chloe Avana and with a number one hit at that."

"That just went platinum," Renée chimed in. She shrugged when Trihn looked at her. "I've been following his career, too."

Damon laughed. "I'm glad you all approve of my career. It's a crazy life, but I wouldn't have any of it without Trihn."

Lydia giggled, and Trihn was pretty sure even Renée swooned. Trihn felt herself relaxing again. Preston didn't have any ammunition against Damon. And the more he acted like a dick, the more even Lydia seemed to get annoyed with him.

"Come on, Trihn, Renée," Lydia said, grabbing her arm. "Let's leave the boys alone and go take a dip in the water."

"All right," Trihn said. She stood and reached for Renée, who hopped up to join them.

The girls all ran, *Baywatch*-style, into the water, laughing and splashing each other, until they were waist-deep in the blue ocean. Renée immediately tied her hair up into a ballet bun to keep it from getting wet. Trihn didn't even care at this point.

If someone had told her that she'd be back in the Hamptons, enjoying her time with her sister again, she would have laughed in their face. But the truth was, it was nice to be here with Lydia—Preston, not so much. This seemed more like the sister she had grown up with than the sister he had turned against her.

"God, it's so good to have you here," Lydia said. "Both of you. It's been forever since I've seen you, too, Renée."

Renée nodded. "Yeah, well…we're all busy, I guess." She looked at Trihn with raised eyebrows. Clearly, that was the nicest thing she could have said.

"And you and Ian? I would never have guessed. For the longest time, I thought he had a crush on Trihn, but I'm so happy for you."

"He did," Renée said. "It was fucking weird, but it somehow works between us."

"Not somehow," Trihn said. "It makes perfect sense."

"And Damon seems pretty incredible," Lydia said.

"He is," Trihn agreed.

"I just…I know this isn't a popular topic, but I really would like for you all to come to the wedding," Lydia said. Her eyes were fearful as she waited for the backlash.

"No," Renée said before Trihn could respond, "Sorry but no."

"I really didn't expect it to go this way," Lydia said softly.

"What way *did* you expect it to go, Lydia?" Trihn asked.

Lydia took a step back and looked out across the water. "I don't know. I thought…I guess I didn't think it was as big of a deal as you made it out to be. I thought, with you gone, you'd come to see that I love Preston even though we all had a falling-out."

"Lydia, it's not a falling-out. It was you choosing him over me, betraying your sister for a guy. That's not something reparable by just hoping it will go away."

"I guess I just never realized that. I've had a lot of time to think since the engagement, and I wish I could change some things, like have you know that I didn't mean for it to be a choice between you and him. I think I was just emotional and irrational at the time. I thought you would come around, and we'd all figure it out. But…well, I'm sorry, Trihn," Lydia said. She wiped a stray tear from her eye.

Trihn sighed. "It's okay. I have Damon now, and I'm doing better emotionally. Plus, it would be nice to have a sister again…but I still can't come to that wedding."

"On principle," Renée agreed.

"Okay," Lydia said meekly. "I wish the wedding were tomorrow though, so I could just get it over with."

"What? Why?" Trihn asked. That didn't sound like Lydia.

"I did something really dumb. I told Preston that I didn't want to have sex until we got married."

Trihn's mouth dropped open.

"Isn't it a little late for that?" Renée asked.

"Have you ever gone that long?" Trihn added.

"No," Lydia admitted. "I mean, it's just for the month up to the wedding. But, damn, it's awful."

Trihn laughed. No wonder Preston was in such a bitch mood. He was probably dying for some action. He wasn't the type to wait.

"Well, good luck with that," Trihn said, unable to conceal her laughter. "I'm having none of those issues."

"Me either," Renée said.

"Yeah. I just thought it would be good for us."

Trihn shook her head. "You're a nutjob."

She turned back to face the beach and realized that Ian was standing between Preston and Damon. Preston looked to be fuming, and if Trihn was seeing correctly, Damon looked like he was…laughing.

"Oh, Jesus," Trihn whispered.

She was running through the water as fast as she could and hurtled up onto the beach. She could hear splashing behind her and knew the girls were following.

"What the hell is going on?" Trihn asked the guys.

Damon was, in fact, laughing in Preston's face. "Nothing, love. Just having a much-needed conversation with your sister's fiancé."

Preston looked pissed off. Trihn could practically see the steam coming out of his ears.

"Fuck you," Preston said to Damon.

"I'll really pass," Damon said.

"Well, I've already fucked her, so have fun with my sloppy seconds."

Trihn gasped.

Just then, Lydia ran up beside them. "What's going on?"

Damon's eyes turned stone-cold, and he shoved forward until he was right up in Preston's face. Trihn thought he was going to start swinging at any second.

"I'm going to let that slide, but if you call my girlfriend a name again, I will beat the shit out of you," he said, his voice like ice. "It's actually pretty entertaining to see how pathetic you really are."

"What the hell did you say?" Lydia asked, turning her eyes on Preston.

"Nothing, babe."

"Don't *nothing, babe,* me, Preston." She turned to Damon. "What the hell did he say?"

Damon stepped back and shrugged. "You'll have to ask your fiancé." Then, he looped his arm with Trihn's and started walking with her, away from the beach.

"What the hell just happened?" Trihn asked when they were out of earshot.

"He was trying to press my buttons. It just turns out that he's the total douche bag I envisioned him to be."

"Yeah. God, I'm sorry. What did he say anyway?"

Damon glanced over at her. "Do you really want to know?"

"Yeah, I do."

"He accused me of sleeping with Chloe."

"What?" Trihn asked. "How the hell did she even come up?"

"He feigned interest in her health."

"Of course he did."

"Then, he tried to tell me that he and I were the same. And that was the wrong fucking thing to say. He got pissed when I told him I could never be as much of an asshole as him, and then I started laughing at him because we couldn't be more different, and I told him as much. Ian tried to defuse the tension, but by then, Preston was pretty pissed."

Trihn tilted her head back in frustration. "Jesus, I'm sorry. You shouldn't have to deal with his shit. I shouldn't have left you alone."

"Love, I can handle myself. And to be honest, it was good to see him get pissed off," Damon said with a laugh. "I've been worried about meeting this guy for months, and now that I've met him, I've realized there was never any reason to worry."

"I love you."

He smiled. "I love you, too."

"Do you want to hear something funny though?" Trihn asked.

"Sure."

"Lydia told me that they're not having sex until they get married."

Damon burst out laughing. "Of course they're not. I'm not even surprised." He dragged her body against his as they made it back up to the house. "That does give me an idea though."

"Oh?"

"It's dirty."

"You have my attention."

"Totally wrong in every way."

"I'm loving the sound of this."

Later that night, Trihn and Damon were lying on her queen-size bed. It was still early for Damon to be tired, considering the night owl that he was, but he held her in his arms. They'd had dinner with Ian and Renée instead of braving another awkward Preston experience.

Overall, the trip had been a resounding success. Trihn had gotten to spend some much-needed time with her friends, had talked some sense into Lydia, and had shown Preston that she was better off with Damon. All around, she had just been having an amazing time. She and Damon would have to leave the next afternoon to make it back to the city to prep for the fashion show, and she was surprised to find that she was going to miss the Hamptons.

Damon kissed her temple and threaded his fingers out through her long hair. She sighed and closed her eyes.

"Are you going to tell me about this devious plan of yours? I've been dying to know about it all day."

"In a minute," he said.

She lay there in silence with only the sound of his heartbeat in his chest and the feel of his fingers through her hair.

Then, they heard a door slam in the room next to them. Trihn could hear Lydia's and Preston's soft voices as they moved around. They had gone out to meet some of Lydia's friends.

Damon shifted under Trihn, sliding his fingers under her chin and tilting her face up to meet his lips. He kissed her, slow and tender. She moaned into his mouth as his hands slipped down her sides. He tugged at her camisole and pulled it over her head.

Realization dawned on her. "What are you doing?"

Damon gave her a devious smile. "I'm about to make love to you, if that's okay with you."

He raised an eyebrow, and she just laughed.

"You're doing this on purpose."

He rolled over on top of her and kissed his way down to the waistband of her boy shorts. "Oh, yes, I'm doing this on purpose."

She squeaked when he yanked the boy shorts off her hips and then kissed her clit.

"You know what I mean," she gasped when he started licking her.

"Shh, love. If you're going to talk, I want to hear you crying out from coming on my face."

Trihn's head dropped back down on the pillow, and she complied. With every bite, lick, and suck, he drew her closer to the brink of orgasm until she couldn't hold back any longer. She banged her hand against the headboard, which rattled against the wall, and then she started giggling.

"Fuck," she groaned, tugging on him to come back up to her. "Fuck me."

"I thought you'd never ask," he joked with a smile.

Then, he entered her body, moving back and forth with such intensity that she wasn't sure she was going to be able to hold it together for a second time. He leaned forward onto her, holding most of his weight on his elbows. All she could do was stare up into his big brown eyes. Her breathing was coming out short.

Damon kissed her lips and pressed into her harder. "I love you," he groaned.

"I love you, too." She grabbed him for another kiss. "God, you feel amazing."

"I just want you to let go for me. Come with me, love."

She tilted her head back and let go, just like he'd asked. "Fuck, fuck, fuck. Yes. Oh my God," she cried.

Her body shook, and she disintegrated into a million little pieces at his insistence. He was right there with her, doubled over her as he released.

Trihn sighed as she finally came back to herself. "Oh God, you're right," she whispered.

"What?"

"It was dirty and totally wrong in almost every way."

He raised his eyebrows. "I have no idea what you mean."

"I think you do, considering we were loud enough to be heard throughout the whole house," she said.

"It felt good though, right?"

She smiled and nodded. It had felt good—the orgasms and the small dose of payback.

THIRTY-NINE

TRIHN STARED OUT AT THE OCEAN visible in the distance from where she was standing at the edge of the pool on the back deck. She and Damon would be heading back to the city with Ian and Renée that afternoon. Ian was unsurprisingly taking summer classes, and Renée had no intention of sticking around with just his parents, no matter how much they liked her. Trihn's parents would follow later that week, so they could get back in time for the fashion show.

Damon was finishing packing upstairs and promised to bring everything out to the car, so she could enjoy some last-minute sand and surf. He'd gotten a phone call from his agent as she was walking out the door and figured he would be a while.

The silence and peace was just what she needed before she returned to the insanity of high-end fashion. She had put in countless hours making her clothes runway-worthy.

She really wanted to prove her mother wrong and show that the designs could be designer and not mass-marketed. So, she'd added some flare to the runway performance. The models would all be flying in tomorrow morning, and she was just about ready to get back to work again.

"What a vacation, huh?" Preston said from behind her.

Trihn whipped around. There was no one else there. She and Preston were alone again.

"What do you want?" she asked.

"So defensive. Can't I just come out here to chat with my future sister-in-law?"

Trihn nearly gagged at that word. "I'd rather leave here on a high, so I think I'm going to bow out of this conversation."

She tried to move past him, but he reached out and grabbed her arm. "Not so fast."

"Let me go."

"Trihn, come on. Just stay and talk to me for a minute," he said, his voice soft and encouraging. It had lost all the bite, and for a split second, he'd sounded like the man she had fallen in love with.

"Don't think I don't know what you're trying to do, using that voice with me," she spat, wrenching her arm out of his grasp. She crossed her arms over her chest, conscious of the fact that she was wearing nothing more than a black bandeau bathing suit top and tiny black cutoffs.

"I'm not doing anything," he said, the edge coming back. "I just want to talk to you."

"Okay, fine. What do you have to say to me that is so important?"

"I think you're making a horrible mistake," Preston said.

She raised her eyebrows. "Me, too. I'm still talking to you."

"Damon is not the right guy for you."

"And you think this, why? Because you met him and realized that he was better than you in every possible way? Because you saw everyone swooning over him?" Trihn shook her head and started walking away.

"He's sleeping with Chloe Avana. You know that, don't you?" he yelled, running ahead of her to face her.

She stopped in her tracks and glared at him. "You disgust me. I don't have to defend Damon to you because I know the kind of man he is. He has proven himself to me time and time again. And this is really rich, coming from you, considering you cheated on me the *entire* time we were together!" she yelled into his face. "You were sleeping with my fucking sister. Then, you had the audacity to lie and turn her against me."

"We were together, but we were never exclusive, Trihn," he said, his own voice rising.

He was clearly pissed about Damon and trying to rile her up. She hated that it was working, but she was also glad that she was having this conversation because this sure as fuck was the last time it was ever going to happen.

Trihn saw a figure coming down the stairs, as if brought forth from the screaming match. It was Damon. He looked like he wanted to rush out to save her, but when Lydia and her mother joined him, he held them back, as if telling them to just watch.

"We saw each other every day. You took me out on dates. You chased me and pursued me. You assured me that we'd be together come the fall term. You begged me to stay the night at your apartment. How the hell was that not exclusive?"

"Fine. All of those things are true, but you know I had to choose Lydia. I had no other choice. Your mother already knew me as her boyfriend."

Trihn narrowed her eyes, disgusted. There it was, laid out before her. She had always suspected what it was, but to have him actually admit it…

"So, this was always about the magazine then? Just a stepping-stone in your career? You hurt me, and you're only with Lydia because it'll help you climb the corporate ladder. Do you even *love* her?"

"It doesn't matter whether or not I love Lydia. That's not the point of the conversation."

"Then, what is the point of the conversation?"

"What do you even know about this Damon guy?" Preston asked, changing the subject.

Trihn rolled her eyes. "Why don't you just admit it? You don't like that I'm dating someone else. You don't like that you can't push me around and flirt with me behind everyone's backs. You don't like that you aren't in control."

Preston took a step forward and pressed his hand onto her hip. He brushed a loose wisp of hair from her face and leaned forward. To anyone watching, it looked as if he was going to kiss her. She even froze for a moment, horrified that he would even consider it. They were out in the open. He didn't know that others were watching behind his back, but just the thought should have scared him off of it. He was losing his edge.

Out of the corner of her eye, Trihn saw that Damon and Lydia were both moving forward, as if to stop what was going to happen.

"That was quite the performance you put on last night," Preston said.

"Is *that* what this is about?" she snarled.

"I don't like other men playing with my things," Preston growled.

"I'm not your thing anymore," Trihn said, slapping his hand away. "You had me for too long, as it was. I pined over you, broke over you, nearly destroyed a perfectly good relationship over you, but I'm done letting someone as pathetic as you control me." She took a step back and squared her shoulders. "I am not a puppet, and you no longer control me. I pull my own strings now."

Trihn brushed past him, rocking into his shoulder, and walked away. Lydia's mouth was hanging open, and there were unshed tears in her eyes.

"He's all yours," Trihn said.

"Wait," Lydia said. "Wait for me."

Damon pulled Trihn into his arms and kissed the top of her head. "Are you okay?"

Trihn released a deep breath. "Yes. I'm glad that happened."

"I wanted to say something, but I thought…everyone else should see."

A slap rang out across the deck, and Trihn turned to witness Preston with his head turned to the side and Lydia shaking out her hand.

"How fucking dare you!" Lydia cried.

"Lydia, babe—"

"Don't even try it. You lied to me. This entire relationship is a lie. You made me turn against my own sister when she was right all along, wasn't she?" Lydia shook her head. "After two years, you still consider her your plaything, and all the while, you've been using me to get ahead."

"And me," their mother said, stepping out onto the patio.

"Lydia, you know it wasn't like that," Preston all but pleaded, losing his composure. "Mrs. Hamilton, of course I would never use you or your daughter."

"The wedding is off," Lydia told him. She was wiggling out of her engagement ring.

"What?" Preston gasped.

Trihn found herself gasping, too. After all this time, Lydia was finally seeing the man that she had chosen. She was seeing the person who Trihn had left behind all those years ago. Trihn was starting to wonder if maybe getting away had been the better deal.

"It's over!" Lydia cried, pushing the ring into his hand. She hit his chest a couple of times, and when he reached for her, she shoved him away. "Get away from me. Don't fucking touch me. I want all of your shit out of my apartment."

"Lydia, you can't do this."

"You'll find that I'm perfectly capable of making my own decisions without your input." Tears started falling out of her eyes. "Now, leave."

"Lydia—"

"Go!"

Preston opened his mouth to say something more, but he just slunk away like the rat that he was.

"And Mr. Whitehall," Linh said, getting formal, "I'll need to see you and your supervisor in my office on Monday morning. We have some...rearranging we'll need to do in the marketing department."

Preston's mouth hung open, but he just mumbled something incoherent and stumbled away.

For a solid minute, everyone just stood outside in shock with only the sound of Lydia crying breaking up the silence.

Trihn finally moved out of Damon's arms and walked over to Lydia. "Hey," she said, pulling her sister into her arms.

Lydia kept crying hopelessly for a few more minutes before her tears began to wane, and she was just left with a pitiful hiccup. "I'm sorry," she said, wiping at her eyes.

"You just dumped your fiancé. I don't think you should be saying sorry to anyone," Trihn said.

"No. I'm sorry for not believing you. I have never seen that man before. Not once. He was never that way with me. I just...I can't believe the things he said to you and the way he acted," Lydia whispered. "Do you think he cheated on me...besides with you?"

"I really don't know," Trihn said. She figured he had. It was in his nature. But she wasn't about to say that to her sister when she was hurting.

"Yeah. He probably did," Lydia whispered. "If he's so nonchalant about you…then probably." She covered her eyes and took a few deep breaths. "God, I am an idiot."

"You just fell for it. We both did," Trihn said.

"And the way I treated you…" Lydia shuddered. "I'm so sorry, Trihn. You're my baby sister. I should have been there for you instead of assuming that you were lying to me. We were both so young and stupid, but it's not an excuse. I was wrong. I just didn't know it. How could you ever forgive me for all of that?"

"I already have," Trihn admitted.

She hadn't really known it until that moment, but it was true. She had forgiven Lydia for her callousness and bitchiness when everything had gone down. Trihn had been on the wrong end of Preston before, and Lydia had been blinded by it. Her sister was sincere, and Trihn had moved on. And since Lydia had now cut the cancerous man out of her life, there was no obstacle between them any longer.

"You're too good to me."

"No. I've just had two years to think about what would happen if this moment ever came about, and now, we're here. I love you, Ly. You're my older sister. I hate seeing you unhappy."

"I was going to be married in a month. What will I do with the dress and the decorations and all the vendors?" Lydia asked in a ramble, seeing all the hard work she had spent the last six months doing unravel before her eyes.

"Don't worry about it, dear," Linh said. "I'll handle everything. If we can't return it, I'm sure there is a perfectly good girl in need who would want a one-of-a-kind wedding dress."

Lydia hiccuped both a laugh and a groan. "You're right. It should go to someone else's big day." Then, she burst into tears all over again.

Preston left in his SUV without so much as a word, and it was another hour before Lydia was consolable. Ian and Renée showed up at the tail end of it. Both hesitantly looked around, as if they were entering a war zone.

"What's going on, everybody?" Renée said.

"Hello, Mrs. Hamilton," Ian said, always polite, even under the circumstances.

"Hello, Ian, Renée."

Lydia looked up at Ian and Renée through her puffy red eyes. "I broke off the engagement."

Ian's mouth dropped open, and Renée's eyes were as wide as saucers.

"Wow, Lydia," Renée said. "I'm sorry."

"Don't be. No one else is."

"Well, I'm sorry you're upset."

"She's going to be okay," Trihn said, rubbing Lydia's back. "Still in shock."

"Yeah. Shock that I wasted two years of my life!"

Renée's eyebrows rose. "Okay. Well then…we were just seeing if you guys were ready to go, but if you're not—"

"Can I go with you?" Lydia asked. "No offense, Mom, but I don't feel like sitting around here, thinking about him."

"Of course, honey," Linh said comfortingly.

"Is there room? Am I intruding?" Lydia asked, sinking back in on herself.

"There's plenty of room," Ian informed her.

"And you're more than welcome," Trihn added.

"Okay," Lydia said with renewed energy at the thought of having something to do. "Thank you, guys. I appreciate it. I'll just…go pack my things."

"That was…unexpected," Renée said once Lydia was out of the room.

"Yeah." Trihn nodded. "But also…*finally*."

"WELCOME TO MY PERSONAL STREET STYLE—Clothes by Trihn," Trihn said, spreading her arms wide for the crowd.

She was standing at the center of the runway with a million lights on her and hundreds of people watching and waiting for her designs to grace the runway. It was exhilarating and terrifying.

She kept the smile wide on her face as she turned and walked off the runway, as if she had been made for it.

Francesca passed by her with a wink just as "We Never Met" started to play.

Trihn stepped off the runway and rushed over to the assistant who had been assigned for the show. The girl was a godsend. She knew her stuff, and Trihn was certain she couldn't have put on such a big production without her.

It was incredible to stand backstage, even more so than last time. The thought that she would have her designs on a New York City runway for a fashion show had only crossed her mind in her dreams. Even if nothing came from it, the experience and realization of a dream made her hard work totally worth it. This moment was worth it all.

They rushed Francesca into the last outfit, and then she walked back down the runway. It was mesmerizing, and that dress always seemed to make the right impression. When Francesca made it back to the staging area, Trihn rearranged the girls so that they could all go and stand onstage one more time, and then it was all over. All of that work was for a whole three-minute song.

When Trihn was finished, Teena Hart was waiting for her backstage. She looked gorgeous in a sleek black dress with her hair stick straight and parted down the middle, falling to her shoulders.

She hugged Trihn. "You were marvelous."

"Thank you!" Trihn said, beaming.

"Far exceeded expectations."

"I appreciate everything you've done to help me get to this moment."

"You put in the work. You're here because you have talent. And even if you don't win today, we'll spend the next two years honing that talent."

Trihn smiled even wider. "I look forward to it."

Teena nodded and then walked away to speak to someone else. Trihn rounded the corner to a section of the dressing room and stopped dead in her tracks. All of her models were clustered together, and a bunch of the other models were all in a mob-like mess. She didn't know if models were hurt, in a fight, or had completely lost their minds.

"What the hell is going on?" Trihn asked.

"Damon Stone is here!" one girl gasped.

"I wonder if that means Chloe Avana is here!" another girl said.

Trihn laughed and started pushing her way through the girls. "That's enough. Go mob someone else."

And then there he was, looking as sexy as ever. He was missing his signature baseball cap, and Trihn was shocked to see that he was in a goddamn sexy three-piece suit. She walked right up to him and kissed him square on the mouth.

"Is this designer?" she murmured when they broke apart.

The girls who had been surrounding them disappeared when they realized Trihn and Damon were together.

Damon laughed. "Straight to the point. I was told I had to dress up for this sort of thing, and I thought I'd surprise you."

"Not sure if I've ever seen you out of jeans."

He raised an eyebrow. "Now, we both know that's not true."

Trihn giggled. "All right. What are you doing backstage already? I thought you were out there with my parents and Lydia and the girls."

"I brought you something."

"Oh?"

Damon reached into his pocket and pulled out a Hershey's Kiss.

Trihn dipped her head back and laughed. "You and your Kisses."

"I said I would earn your kisses."

"And you did," she agreed. She took it out of his hand and popped it into her mouth.

"Well, I guess that was the warm-up. Let's see if I do this right." This time, he pulled out a medium-sized blue box. It was not just any blue. It was Tiffany blue.

Her stomach dropped.

He turned the box toward her and opened the top. Inside was a slender silver chain holding a crystal-clear diamond haloed in another circle of diamonds.

Trihn gasped and put her hand to her mouth. "Oh my God...Damon," she breathed.

"I saw the first deposit for my earnings from 'We Never Met,' and I couldn't resist. It's platinum. That was my only requirement. You're my platinum girl after all. Rare and beautiful. You should be wearing it."

Trihn laughed softly. Her eyes were wet. She couldn't believe this.

"Allow me?"

She nodded and turned around. He removed the necklace from the box while she lifted her hair. He gently placed the diamonds around her neck where it rested against the center of her chest. Once he clicked the clasps together, he kissed her neck.

"Perfect. Just like you."

"You're incredible," she said, moving into his arms. "Thank you. It's too much."

"Nah. It'll never be enough for you."

Trihn shook her head. *How did I get so lucky?*

"There's one more thing I wanted to tell you before the madness happens back here."

"Something else?" she asked, trailing her fingers over the new necklace.

"I got a call from my agent. They've been working to figure out what's next for me while Chloe...heals."

"That's good. What's the next big step for Damon Stone?"

"He thinks I should get a DJ contract in Las Vegas."

"What does that mean?" Trihn asked. "Working clubs again?"

"Sort of. But instead of sporadically, I'd get a contract for a certain amount of time, and I'd be required to DJ there for so many shows a year. They think I could get a big club at one of the massive Vegas Strip hotels," he told her. "More importantly, I'd be there with you and not away on tour unless I wanted to be."

"That sounds incredible! When will you know if you'll get a contract?"

Damon smirked. "Just got off the phone. It's a done deal. I just have to sign the paperwork."

"Oh my God!" Trihn shrieked. She jumped into his arms, and he held her there. "I'm so happy for you."

"Well, I didn't mean to make this day about me. I was just too excited that I would be back in Vegas with you that I couldn't wait."

"No, I'm so glad that you told me. It's unbelievable."

"It really is. And I can still write, record, and tour whenever I want as long as I meet the contractual agreements," he said.

She kissed him and smiled. "The world is at your feet."

"Just you. You're what matters."

"Attention, all designers, please report back to the stage," a man said, walking around the room.

"That's me," Trihn told Damon.

"Knock 'em dead, love."

Trihn got into line with the other designers and tried not to let the nerves get to her. She knew that most of the other students here had a lot more experience than her. But that didn't mean she didn't want to win. She could only hope for the best at this point.

She walked onstage with the other girls and waited as the judges announced the winner. Her eyes were fixed on the crowd bathed in soft light.

"And the winner of the thirty-seventh annual National Fashion Show and the grand prize of a spotlight feature in *Glitz* magazine along with a contract with Bloomingdale's goes to…Tiffany Ryu."

A short Asian girl two people down from Trihn collapsed into tears as her name was called. Trihn felt a pang of disappointment and jealousy as the girl walked forward to collect her prize, but she let it pass. She had more time to get there.

The other girls were ushered offstage, and Trihn walked right into Damon's arms.

"Sorry, love."

"It's okay," she said, brushing it off. "You win some. You lose some. There's always next year."

Trihn left Damon's arms to help her assistant finished cleaning up her space. The girl just pushed Trihn away and told her to go see her family while she finished up. Trihn hugged the girl one more time for her work.

When Trihn walked back out into the audience with Damon on her arm, everyone was there—her family, her New York friends, her Las Vegas friends, and even their boyfriends.

"Oh, honey, I'm so sorry," her mother said, pulling her in for a hug.

Then, her dad hugged her next.

"It's okay. I didn't expect to win. It was worth the experience."

Lydia hugged her next. "You did great. I have a million pictures to show you later." She hoisted her massive camera.

"I can't wait to see them. I'm glad you all could make it."

Renée and Ian both congratulated her on being in the fashion show.

"I want that black dress though," Renée said. "I'll send you my measurements."

Trihn laughed. "Done. I'll start taking orders."

"Speaking of orders," Maya said, coming up behind her, "I still need that skirt."

"And holy shit, what is that?" Bryna said. She snatched up the diamond necklace around Trihn's neck and was staring at it. "Tiffany's?"

Trihn nodded. "Yeah. Damon got it for me."

Bryna whistled low. "Diamonds and platinum. Good choice." Her eyes turned to Eric. "I'm in need of some glitter, Cowboy. Make this happen."

"You have enough diamond jewelry in your closet to buy a small island in the South Pacific," Eric said.

"And?"

"And you're ridiculous. Congratulate your best friend."

"Congratulations on choosing a real winner, Trihn. You're practically on my gold-digger level at this point," Bryna said with a wink.

"You're a real bitch, you know that, right?" Trihn asked with a laugh.

"I know it." Bryna hugged her tight. "Congrats, babe."

"Ah, congratulations from me, too!" Stacia said, wrapping her arms around both of them.

"You two are too much," Trihn said.

Stacia stepped back into Pace's arms, and Bryna returned to Eric. Even Maya had Drayton with her. It made Trihn's hearth happy. Everyone who mattered in her life was here. So, it didn't even matter that she'd lost because she seemed to have won so much more.

"Trihnity Hamilton?"

Trihn turned to face a tall, skinny woman with blonde hair in a black designer dress and Jimmy Choos. "Yes. Can I help you?"

"It's nice to meet you. I am Patricia Young, and I represent a New York–based client. May I have a word with you?"

Trihn's mouth nearly dropped open before she remembered herself. "Of course."

Trihn was glad that she had opted for her favorite Louboutins that day as she followed the woman to a more private location.

"I'd like to get straight to the point, Miss Hamilton. I'm a buyer for a New York–based boutique, and I believe you have exactly what we've been looking for, a fresh new style that captures a new vogue in fashion."

Trihn's eyebrows rose. "Wow. Thank you."

"Do you have interest in selling the line?"

"I…" Trihn murmured, speechless. "Yes. Yes, I do."

"Wonderful. We're interested in purchasing it, and we'd like to speak with you further about it. How much longer are you going to be in New York?"

"My family is from here. I can stay as long as needed," she said. Her heart was pounding, and she was trying not to show her utter disbelief.

"Perfect. Let's schedule a time to meet. Here's my card." Patricia pulled a crisp card out of her wallet and handed it to Trihn.

They talked for a few more minutes and agreed to meet and go over the rest of the details. Trihn was overflowing with excitement by the end of the conversation.

"It was a pleasure to meet you, Trihn. I think this will be an excellent match."

"Thank you so much."

They shook hands, and then Trihn walked on air with her head floating in the clouds back to her friends.

"What was that about?" her mother asked first.

"I just got an offer for a New York boutique to buy my clothing line," she gasped.

The noise of everyone screaming and congratulating her all at once nearly knocked her off her feet.

She laughed and reeled back. "I have a meeting with the company next week to discuss everything."

"We must go out to celebrate," Linh said.

"I have to agree with that," Bryna said.

"Drinks are on me," Damon agreed, wrapping an arm around Trihn and kissing her temple.

The entire group stood around, congratulating Trihn, until they finally left the ballroom to find a restaurant and bar for drinks. Trihn and Damon lagged at the back of the group. He had his arm casually looped around her waist, and she leaned her head against his shoulder.

"So, another week in New York?" Damon asked.

"Mmm, yes, it seems like it. I guess you'll actually get the real tour you deserve."

"I want to see everything with you. Where will you take me?" he asked.

"Everywhere," she breathed.

"The world is at your feet," he said with a smirk.

Trihn deeply kissed him, not caring that they were trailing so far behind the rest of the group.

"Just you," she breathed, repeating his words. "You're what matters."

And they walked, hand in hand, down the New York City street with their entire lives spread before them, secure in the knowledge that, at the end of the day, at least they had one another.

Eight Months Later

THE LIMO HALTED directly in front of the red carpet. The tinted windows obscured the celebrities hiding within the posh climate-controlled vehicle bursting with champagne and Hershey's Kisses. The press was waiting on the outside, anxious to get the first glimpse of the stars before they made their long walk down the red carpet and into the Staples Center in Los Angeles where the Fifty-Eighth Annual Grammy Awards would commence.

Trihn leaned against Damon in the backseat and fiddled with the diamond bracelet on her wrist. "I cannot believe this is actually happening," she said.

"Me either. The Grammys...that's huge," he said with a shake of his head.

His hair was perfectly in place, and it was strange not to see it messy from being under a baseball cap all day. Someone had cleaned him up all nice, but he still looked like her man—utterly delicious.

He pressed a soft kiss to her cherry-red lips. "You look gorgeous."

"You don't look too bad yourself."

"Are you ready?" he asked.

She nodded.

Damon knocked on the window twice, and then the door opened from the outside. He stepped out first to an outrageously loud cheer. He turned around to help Trihn out next and kissed her hand once she was steady on her four-inch Louboutin high heels. They both smiled for the cameras, knowing that this was going to be how much of the next hour of their lives would go.

Once they were through the first group of people, it only marginally calmed down. The crowd would go crazy every time Damon walked by, and Trihn couldn't blame them. He and Chloe had been nominated for six awards combined, including the hotly contested Record of the Year and Album of the Year.

When the nominations had come out, they had all been floored.

Chloe had flown in from Los Angeles to party with them. Her stint in rehab had been more than good for her. She'd returned a new person. Her panic attacks had subsided for the most part, and she had taken time to focus on closer personal relationships. Her next three songs on her self-titled album had come out in the past couple of months, and it felt as if they were the only things on the radio.

But her increased fame also rose Damon's. His club in Las Vegas was packed for every show, and he had started working with other artists on an album that was set to release later that year. It was hugely anticipated, and the preorder numbers were through the roof.

"Damon Stone, can we do a quick interview?" a man said for E! Entertainment.

"Absolutely." Damon smiled and walked with Trihn over to the red-carpet hosts.

He shook hands with Ryan Seacrest, who plastered on a smile.

"Hello, everybody watching at home. I'm here right now with Damon Stone, the celebrity DJ who took the world by storm with his hit single, 'We Never Met,' with superstar Chloe Avana."

"Yes. Hello, Ryan. Hello there at home," Damon said in his sexy British accent.

"And who are you accompanied by tonight?"

Damon put his hand on Trihn's back. "This is my girlfriend, Trihnity Hamilton."

"Excellent. I've recently heard a lot about your girlfriend in the magazines," Giuliana Rancic said. "You're a fashion designer with Clothes by Trihn. Are you wearing your own design tonight?"

She looked at Trihn's floor-length emerald-green dress. It had a sweetheart neck before sweeping into her tiny waist and then dropping down to the floor with a small train. There were sleek cutouts to the dress from the back of her ribs, down across the sides of her waist, and over her pelvic bone, making her appear taller and slimmer. Her hair had been blown out and styled into supermodel waves that hung down her back. She was obsessed with the look and was certain only a hairstylist could perfect it.

Trihn smiled. "Yes. This is a one-of-a-kind Trihn."

"Just Trihn," Damon corrected. He gestured to his black tuxedo. "This is a Trihn design as well."

"A well-worn suit to women is like lingerie for men," Giuliana said with a wink.

"Damon, you're up for four awards tonight for your hit with Chloe Avana. What did you do when you found out that you'd been nominated for so many?" Giuliana asked.

Damon laughed. "I was on my way to pick up Trihn when I got the call about it, and we both just sat in my car. Honestly, we were in shock. I called Chloe next, and she screamed in enough excitement for the both of us."

"Speaking of Chloe for a minute, she helped skyrocket you to this fame, but it was your song and your lyrics that truly shone. We're all excited for some more of that," Ryan said.

"Absolutely. I can't wait for you all to hear the new album. The first single with Ed Sheeran should be releasing in the next week. He, I might add, is just the most amazing and talented person to work with," Damon said.

"Ed is a great guy all-around," Giuliana agreed.

"One last question before you have to go," Ryan said. "How does it feel to be up for Best New Artist?"

"Incredible. It's an absolute pleasure to even be nominated alongside such other talented artists. Everyone's work truly speaks for itself. I can't wait to get in there and see how it all pans out."

"Thank you so much for your time," Ryan said, shaking Damon's hand.

"We're all ready to see how it pans out, too. Best of luck," Giuliana said.

Damon and Trihn both smiled and then walked out of the way as another couple came to take their places.

"I told you," Damon whispered in her ear as he threaded them through the crowd.

"What?"

"That, one day, I'd be on the red carpet, and when someone asked what I was wearing, I'd tell them just Trihn."

"You're ridiculous, but I love you."

"I love you, too," he said before kissing her hair.

They weaved their way down the red carpet and finally made it out on the other side. They both took a breath, and Damon took her phone out of his suit pocket and handed it to her.

"It's been going off like mad."

Trihn checked it and saw texts from all her friends. All the girls were at home, glued to the TV, hoping to see her at the Grammys red carpet preshow. They'd all caught the plug for Clothes by Trihn on *E! Live from the Red Carpet*, and they were freaking out. She knew that it was killing Bryna not to be here, but tonight was really for Damon.

Trihn texted back to her friends to let them know that she wouldn't be able to respond much after this.

Bryna's response was instantaneous.

> *Have a great time, you lucky bitch, and tell Gates I said hi!*

Trihn laughed.

Gates was apparently seeing someone new right now, and Bryna didn't approve. But she and Eric were doing amazing, all things considered, so she couldn't meddle—or at least she couldn't openly meddle. Eric was trying to convince her to move in with him, and she claimed she needed her independence. Trihn had a feeling that she and Stacia would lose her to him next year, but it would be all right. Bryna was a better person with Eric.

Unlike everything going on in Stacia's life.

Stacia had spent half of the football season torn between Marshall and Pace, and that was probably because the team had spent half of the year deciding which quarterback to use as their star. When Marshall was selected halfway through the season, Stacia had made her pick. She and Marshall were…something else. He was almost too nice for her. Bryna liked to see Pace pissed off, so she didn't say anything about Stacia's relationship with Marshall. When Pace started sleeping with Stacia's friend from home who was a freshman cheerleader at LV State, even Trihn had let it go.

The football season had gone all right after that, but they hadn't made it to the playoffs, leading to another year of disappointment. Marshall had elected to go to the NFL draft, ignoring the advice from the coaching staff. When even Eric had yelled at him, Trihn had known it was a dumb idea. Eric only yelled when it was directed at Bryna or when he was as pissed off as psychotic drunk Bryna. But the draft wasn't for another couple of months, and Stacia was over the moon that she'd get to go with him to the draft in Chicago.

Luckily, Maya had gotten accepted to graduate school to get her masters in creative writing, so she and Drayton could continue dating without a long-distance relationship.

Trihn's friends had diverse lives, but she loved being there for them through it every bit as much as they loved texting her while she was at the Grammys.

Damon and Trihn were escorted to their seats at the front of the room. They weren't seated long before Chloe bounded over to them with her current man, some backup dancer she'd met on her last tour, who would also be in her performance tonight.

"Trihn!" Chloe said, pulling her in for a tight hug. "You look incredible."

"Thank you."

"And this dress! I'm jealous that I didn't get that one-of-a-kind," she said with a smile.

Trihn had designed Chloe's dress, too. It was a fire engine–red lace creation that hugged her Latina body in all the right places. Trihn knew she had three other costume changes for the night for when she was announcing awards and performing, not to mention the after-party and the after-after-party. But Trihn was grateful to have created Chloe's red carpet dress. It would help her blooming design career.

Her designs were consistently in New York boutiques right now, playing nice with the rich and trendy—something her mother had thought would never happen. Trihn's third year of school in the fashion design major had been almost entirely upper-level seminars with Teena as they worked together to make her dreams of becoming a famous designer a reality. Teena wanted Trihn to open her own boutique in New York or Las Vegas, but Trihn wanted to establish herself more before sinking her investment into a store. Between her fashion line and trying to finish school, she was already incredibly busy. She didn't think she could run her own boutique yet, too.

Chloe stuck around and chatted for a while and then took the seat next to them for the show.

Trihn glanced around at the packed room. She couldn't believe how many famous people were all in one place. It was disorienting, knowing everyone in the vicinity and listening to their music and having them somehow know her, too. At this rate, she would be designing only for celebrities. She thought that would be an okay gig.

The lights dimmed, and the host came out to begin the show. Act after act went onstage, taking the crowd by storm, and doling out gold record players.

Chloe performed in a scandalously sheer number for her new song, "Naked." And then she came back out onstage a half hour later in a conservative floor-length white dress that sparkled like the sun with none other than Gates Hartman in a tuxedo.

Trihn hadn't seen Gates before this moment and was surprised that he was announcing with Chloe. As far as Trihn knew, they still didn't talk to each other. Maybe things had improved since her rehab stint.

"Ladies and gentlemen, this year, we have the opportunity to announce the nominees for the Best Compilation Soundtrack for Visual Media," Chloe said.

"As you know, Chloe and I have worked in film together and always applaud the amazing vocal melodies that bring our films to life," Gates said. He turned to face Chloe with that dazzling smile.

She stared at him a heartbeat too long before realizing she'd missed her cue. "And we're pleased to announce that we will be working on a new movie of our own and hope that, in the following years, we'll see our own soundtrack back up for nomination."

"And now, the nominees," Gates said.

Trihn raised her eyebrows. *Gates and Chloe are working on another movie together. Well, that is not going to be good for their relationships.*

"That should be interesting," Damon whispered.

"Very."

"She's going to need to watch out with him."

"What do you mean?" Trihn asked. She glanced over at him. Per Bryna's request, she had never told Damon what had actually happened with Gates and Chloe.

"You know." He nodded his head at them.

"Do *you* know?" she asked.

"I mean…Chloe told me…if it's what you think it is."

"You know!" she gasped.

"I just couldn't say anything."

"Does she still like him?" Trihn hissed.

He shrugged. "Who knows? Guess they'll figure that out."

Trihn laughed softly and then turned her attention back to the stage.

As the award night wore on, it seemed to take longer and longer to get to the awards that they really wanted to see.

Finally, the time came.

"And the winner for Best New Artist goes to…"

The anticipation was killer.

Damon squeezed her hand as they waited, her stomach in knots.

"Damon Stone!"

The crowd cheered.

They both stood, and he pulled Trihn in for a hug. "I love you."

"I love you, too," she said, tears shining in her eyes.

Damon accepted his Grammy. "Wow. Thank you so much. You have no idea what this means to me. A year ago, I was deejaying in clubs in Las Vegas, and now…a Grammy. I want to thank everyone who helped get me here—Jason Carlo, Freddie Hope, Carson Cameron, the team at Sony Music, Tiffany Holly, Chester Ambrose, Sage McHugh, and Courtney Lord. Also, Chloe Avana, for discovering me. My mum, Melanie, for always believing in me. And my wonderful girlfriend, Trihn. Without her, none of this would have been possible. Thank you." Damon hefted the award overhead and then followed the announcers offstage.

Trihn applauded with the crowd. Her heart was in her throat. All those hard times were for this. It was worth it.

Damon reappeared a few minutes later, and she hugged him so hard until the awards started again, and the cameras came back on.

Chloe won Best Pop Solo Performance and Best Pop Vocal Album, but she lost out for Song of the Year and Album of the Year.

The last category came up for Record of the Year.

"'We Never Met' by Damon Stone, featuring Chloe Avana!"

The crowd went crazy. Damon and Chloe went up to accept the award together. Watching them onstage was the most unbelievable experience.

They both gave acceptance speeches that Trihn heard through a blur.

By the time the show was over, Trihn hurried backstage to see Damon taking a picture with his two awards. He grabbed her around the middle and swung her around.

"I'm so proud of you," she told him.

"I'm just doing what I love."

"And you're incredible at it. We're never going to be able to go anywhere anymore."

He laughed. "Why?"

"Not with your recognizable face!"

"We'll go wherever you want. Travel the world. You and me."

"How about Las Vegas? I've gotten kind of fond of the city…and having you close."

"Well then, how about you move in with me?" he said, dragging her body against his.

"What?" she asked in disbelief.

"Bri is going to move in with Eric. Stacia is going to drop out of school to be an NFL quarterback's wife. The apartment will be empty. I want you close. I want you with me. I want you to be mine, so we can start building that future we've been talking about."

"I think we're already doing that," she whispered.

"Well, what do you say?"

Trihn didn't even have to think about it. "Yes."

"Yes?"

"I'll move in with you."

A smile split his face. "And here I thought I was going to have to convince you."

"Well, it won't be until my lease ends."

"I can live with that. That's only a couple of months away."

"You know…I really hope Stacia doesn't drop out of school."

Damon laughed hard and kissed her cheek. "Out of all those things, that's what you latched on to."

She giggled. "Mostly that I'm moving in with you in a couple of months."

"I like the sound of that."

"A Grammy award winning music artist," she said, raising her eyebrows.

"Fuck, that sounds good." He smiled. "But mostly that you'll be moving in with me."

"You've changed me for the better, Damon Stone. I'd go to the ends of the earth with you."

"And I intend on taking you there."

The End

**STAYED TUNED FOR STACIA'S STORY
IN THE NEXT BOOK IN THE
ALL THAT GLITTERS SERIES:**

SILVER

COMING FALL 2016!

ACKNOWLEDGMENTS

NO BOOK IS WRITTEN IN A VACUUM. So many people helped me get to this point, and thank you to each and every one of you who was there for me while writing this novel. It's one of my favorites!

Here's a special thank you to people who were there along the way—Rebecca Kimmerling, Katie Miller, Diana Peterfreund, Polly Matthews, Lori Francis, Katie Ross, Christy Peckham, NANO Wrimo, Corinne Michaels, all the girls of FYW, Jovana Shirley of Unforeseen Editing, and Sarah Hansen of Okay Creations.

Most of all, YOU! Thank you for picking up this book and giving it a chance. I hope you read and enjoy all of my Glitter Girls! Stacia's book is up next in Silver coming Fall 2016!

ABOUT THE AUTHOR

K.A. LINDE is the *USA Today* bestselling author of the
Avoiding series and the All That Glitters series as well as
seven additional novels. She grew up as a military brat,

traveling the United States and even landing for a brief stint in Australia. She has a master's degree in political science from the University of Georgia and is the current head coach of the Duke University dance team. An avid traveler, reader, and bargain hunter, K.A. currently lives in Chapel Hill, North Carolina, with her husband and two super adorable puppies.

K.A. Linde loves to hear from her readers!

You can contact her at kalinde45@gmail.com or visit her online at one of the following sites:

www.kalinde.com

www.facebook.com/authorkalinde

@authorkalinde

CPSIA information can be obtained
at www.ICGtesting.com
Printed in the USA
BVOW08s1657150217
476305BV00001B/115/P